P9-BZV-914

THE GIFT OF LOVE

Patrick took Camille's left leg and ran his hands down her slim calf, removed her soft hide boot and slowly placed the glowing amber bracelet around her ankle and fastened the clasp. It had belonged to his father, and his grandfather before him.

He held her for a long moment. "I'm giving you this because it is the most precious thing I own. They are my past. You are my future."

Camille wrapped her arms around his neck, felt the bristle of his beard against her cheek and the way the gold of the bracelet circling her ankle still held the warmth of his body. "I have nothing to give to you in return."

"You are giving me yourself."

"Yes."

"That is everything I want."

Camille shifted restlessly and looked up to the painted nighttime sky, where stars flickered, winked, and shone steadily. "I can scarcely believe how you feel for me. It is a dream too beautiful, a reality difficult to accept."

Patrick searched her features in the moonlight. "You have never felt truly loved the whole of your life."

"I have not."

"Can you feel it now?"

"Yes. With more than words and past your touch on my skin. I feel it in my soul."

BOOK YOUR PLACE ON OUR WEBSITE AND MAKE THE READING CONNECTION!

We've created a customized website just for our very special readers, where you can get the inside scoop on everything that's going on with Zebra, Pinnacle and Kensington books.

When you come online, you'll have the exciting opportunity to:

- View covers of upcoming books

- Read sample chapters

- Learn about our future publishing schedule (listed by publication month *and author*)

- Find out when your favorite authors will be visiting a city near you

- Search for and order backlist books from our online catalog

- Check out author bios and background information

- Send e-mail to your favorite authors

- Meet the Kensington staff online

- Join us in weekly chats with authors, readers and other guests

- Get writing guidelines

- AND MUCH MORE!

Visit our website at
http://www.kensingtonbooks.com

VEILED PROMISES

TRACY MACNISH

ZEBRA BOOKS
Kensington Publishing Corp.
www.kensingtonbooks.com

ZEBRA BOOKS are published by

Kensington Publishing Corp.
850 Third Avenue
New York, NY 10022

Copyright © 2005 by Tracy MacNish

All rights reserved. No part of this book may be reproduced
in any form or by any means without the prior written consent
of the Publisher, excepting brief quotes used in reviews.

If you purchased this book without a cover you should be aware
that this book is stolen property. It was reported as "unsold and
destroyed" to the Publisher and neither the Author nor the Publisher has received any payment for this "stripped book."

All Kensington titles, imprints, and distributed lines are available at special quantity discounts for bulk purchases for sales
promotion, premiums, fund-raising, educational, or institutional
use.

Special book excerpts or customized printings can also be created to fit specific needs. For details, write or phone the
office of the Kensington Special Sales Manager: Attn. Special
Sales Department. Kensington Publishing Corp., 850 Third
Avenue, New York, NY 10022. Phone: 1-800-221-2647.

Zebra and the Z logo Reg. U.S. Pat. & TM Off.

ISBN 0-8217-7952-4

First Printing: October 2005
10 9 8 7 6 5 4 3 2 1

Printed in the United States of America

In loving memory of my poppops,
Charles Harry Nish,
whose stories are often told,
and always with a smile.

Is Rioghal mo Dhream.

ACKNOWLEDGMENTS

The author's sincerest thanks and best wishes to:

Brent Monahan, fellow writer, generous mentor, and good friend, who was the first person to believe in my writing, who gave unselfishly of his extensive knowledge and limited time, pushed me when I needed it, and received nothing in return but my abiding gratitude. My agent, Mary Sue Seymour, and my editor, Audrey LaFehr, both of whom were unafraid to take a risk on my novel. My sister Aislinn, who knows how to have fun better than anyone I know, and often drags me along, willing or not. My mother, Trish, who read the manuscript eight times and counting. My two very best friends, Katrina and JoanMarie, two ladies who lead by example, who always listen, and whom I lean on more than they know (special nod to JMB, for the help with the title). My in-laws, Pat and Hank, for producing my favorite German and all-around world-class guy.

Best for last, my son, Ethan, for teaching me lessons in love every single day.

And to my husband, Randy, for all the support, all the belief, and all the nights. It's all because of you.

*Three grand essentials to happiness in this life are
something to do, something to love,
and something to hope for.*

—Joseph Addison

CHAPTER 1

Beauport, 1743

Did the devil dwell inside her? The whispers had returned in spite of her efforts in self-discipline. The longings she had been told were pure evil seethed in her veins and through her mind, until they became her past and her future, her present and her every thought. The compulsion from within that couldn't be beaten out, that wouldn't be punished away.

Perhaps her mother did know the truth of the matter.

And it frightened Camille. She didn't want to contemplate her own depraved longings. She didn't want to feel the hatred that spawned the thing that whispered words of survival. Words of escape.

So she thought of something else, something to distract her. While her eyes stayed fixed in a look of practiced attention, her mind roved the property that had served her as home since the day of her birth.

Spring had finally come. The once-naked trees around Beauport now wore a frosting of tiny leaves, promising summer's dense, verdant foliage. The morning sun glistened on the springy new grass and, with warm persuasion, seduced the tightly furled shoots of wildflowers and bulbs alike to expose their inner beauty and wantonly flaunt their heady scents. Behind her the brick mansion stood like a proud English soldier, just as clipped in mannerism and overdressed. Its columns glared stark white in the sunlight, contrasting the lush greenery surrounding it as nature rejoiced, celebrating the rebirth from winter's killing grip.

But the voices filtered back into her mind. The voice of her yearnings competed with the stern tones of her mother, who sat in the shady confines of the carriage, rapping out orders and issuing warnings. Her mother, Amelia Mary Bradburn, ninth Duchess of Eton and mistress of Beauport, paused in her sentence and peered at her daughter. With pale blue eyes as watchful as those of any predator, she assessed Camille's expression.

"Were you listening, child?"

"I was. I am."

"What did I say?"

"I am to manage the staff in your absence. I am to practice the clavichord daily. I am to see to the final fittings on my new gowns. I am not permitted more than an hour to ride each day, chaperoned. I am not permitted to leave the grounds or to go into town, unless accompanied by Father or Eric."

"Excellent," Amelia said softly, "but you forgot one thing."

Camille resisted the urge to fidget or look away. As she answered, the breath broke in her throat. "I will be watched."

"Yes." Amelia's lips narrowed into a thin red line. "I do not deny I am hesitant to leave you without a maid to oversee your every moment. However, I hope that at twenty years of age you will exhibit the self-control of a young woman who no longer requires constant supervision."

The driver of the carriage approached, slapping his thighs with his gloves and whistling a tune Camille didn't recognize. He hoisted his large frame onto the narrow driver's bench and tugged on his gloves. The carriage bounced and then settled as it took his weight. The matched team of horses pricked their ears in collective excitement, feeling the slight ripple through the reins as they were lifted and held. A gelding stamped his feet and snorted, startling a flock of starlings from a tree. Camille watched as they darted first to the east before abruptly changing direction, heading to the west with flapping wings and loud cries.

Momentarily mesmerized, Camille watched them fly away until they were nothing more than flecks of pepper winging freely over the tangle of trees that began the woods. The woods that beckoned Camille to come and relax in its gentle green light, beneath the knotty limbs that stretched above her head like knuckled fingers.

She dragged her eyes back to her mother's, knowing that if her gaze rested too long on what lay outside her boundaries, she would be punished for her flagitious longings.

"I will obey."

"Honor thy father and mother, child. It is the Lord's word. Not mine."

"Yes, Mother."

"One day you will appreciate me. One day, when your husband speaks of his wife with pride, and your children bear the prestige and privilege of their birth, you will thank me for the attention I paid to your upbringing."

Camille bowed her head, unable to force out any more words of obedience.

"When I return, I will expect a good report." Amelia reached up and rapped on the roof of the carriage, signaling her readiness to depart. Before the footman could close the door, she issued her final warning. "Remember, child, one will reap what one has sown. Obedience will bring the rewards of future privileges. Disobedience will bear the harshest of consequences."

The door was shut, and Camille stepped back a few

paces, out of the way of the dust kicked up by the convoy of carriages bearing her mother and her retinue of maids, men, and guards as they rumbled down the winding drive of crushed stone. She watched until they disappeared from sight, and only then did relief begin to seep through her body, warm and relaxing like a few sips of wine.

Then she recalled what her mother had said. She looked around, wondering who watched her. Wondering if they were watching her now.

Camille turned on her heel and headed into the shade of the manor, up the wide marble steps and through the heavy, carved front doorways. Her mother made two trips to London each year, one in spring and one in fall, to visit the house she had had built when Camille was a small girl. Amelia preferred London to the country home, never ceasing in her resentment at not being permitted by her husband to reside there yearlong. She held the time she spent there in the utmost importance, claiming that only through her personal holidays there could she endure her familial tribulations. Those absences Amelia insisted on had been some of the happiest times in Camille's life, shadowed only with the knowledge that her mother would return.

Was it wrong to hope for the demise of one's own mother? To fantasize that what would begin as a simple heist on the roadside would turn into something more than just a robbery for jewels and coin. To picture in great detail the greed and madness in the corrupt light of the gunman's eyes. To envision her mother spread out in a pool of silk skirts and flowing blood, silenced forever.

With some effort Camille pushed those thoughts from her mind, knowing them to be evil and that enjoying them so greatly showed evidence of wickedness.

The house still held the cool of the night. Everywhere one looked the eye rested on something of beauty, whether it be the curving, ornate stairway or the intricate marble foyer, where the family crest had been inlaid in fifteen colors of shiny stone. Camille turned left and headed into the parlor, where the clavichord she despised stood awaiting her practice session with its black-and-white toothy grin.

Her father started at the sound of her footsteps, pulling away from the young servant girl and dismissing her with the flick of his finely boned wrist. She scampered from the room at a near run without looking at Camille, closing the French doors behind her round bottom. Kenley sighed and sank into a plump wing chair.

Camille felt the heat rise in her neck and creep into her cheeks. "I can come back later, Father."

"No, no need. I was merely instructing Molly as to how I like the starch in my shirts."

"Molly is kitchen help, Father." Camille felt some satisfaction as the deepening color on Kenley's face matched her own.

"Don't you have studies today?"

"I concluded the last of my studies seven months ago."

"Ah, yes, of course. Right. Well, then."

"I am to practice my music." Camille gave him the way out, wanting the end to the uncomfortable situation as much as he did. But Kenley glanced to the French doors longingly, and Camille had a better idea.

"I am permitted to ride for an hour. Perhaps I'll do that now and practice my music later."

"Fine idea. A beautiful morning. Perhaps you'll see Eric. I believe I left him in the stables less than an hour ago."

"I thought my brother said he had business today? Something about him selling the house and land Grandfather left to him?"

A frown of disapproval flitted across Kenley's distinguished features. "Listening in while men are speaking of financial matters is not appropriate for a woman. Repeating what you heard later is even less so."

"Eric discussed his intentions with me, Father. He went so far as to ask my opinion."

Kenley arched a brow. "I shall not mention this to your mother. 'Twould only upset her."

Camille understood perfectly. The entire exchange had never happened, including her walking in on her father with his hands in the bodice of the kitchen help. "If you will excuse me, I'll take my ride now."

Kenley bid farewell with a slight inclination of his head. "And if you happen to pass her, please send Molly back in. I have a matter that requires her expertise."

Camille kept her expression neutral and left the room, heading through the mansion toward the back, where the rich scents of bread mingled with the musty smells of jarred vegetables and fragrant boughs of dried herbs. She entered the interior kitchen where food was prepared prior to and after being cooked in the out-kitchen. A smile curved her lips as she felt the familiar surge of happiness upon seeing Flanna, who had been on the staff even before her father had been born.

Flanna worked industriously, her every movement an economy of motion. She hadn't changed much in all the years Camille had been coming to the kitchens to visit her. The gray hair streaked with reddish strands remained in the same neat bun. Her eyes, blue as a robin's egg, still held the sparkle of a young woman, and could see more than what a person showed. Camille sometimes thought those Irish eyes could see into her very soul.

When Camille had been a young girl, she used to wish that Flanna had been her mother. She would lie in her bed and wonder what it would be like to have those kind hands smooth her hair from her forehead, or to have those sweet lips press a kiss on the tip of her nose. She would create lifetimes with Flanna, a history of shared feelings and understanding, of tea and toasted bread when she felt ill, and encouraging pats on her arm when she recited a history lesson perfectly.

But she was not a child anymore. Her parentage remained as unchangeable as the rise and set of the sun and the moon. She knew that. She accepted that. And she hated it.

"Good mornin', dearie. I hear your mother's off to the city?"

"She is," Camille confirmed, looking over her shoulder out of habit before she stole a small piece of cheese from the chopping block where Flanna toiled.

"An' what will you be doin' to occupy your time, Miss? I also hear you're to be goin' about your days unfettered, what with you bein' fully grown."

Camille grinned a little, a small smile full of wicked longing that was just enough to communicate to Flanna exactly what Camille wanted to do with her free time.

Flanna rolled her eyes. "Ah, dearie, will you never learn?"

"'Tis a necessary evil."

"I hate seein' you hurt. Canna you content yourself? Canna you find a way to be happy wi'out it all?"

Camille didn't reply, because she didn't have the answer.

Flanna lay down her knife and leaned forward, looking directly into the vivid green beauty of Camille's eyes. "If you go, somehow she'll know. Is what you're doin' worth it?"

Camille considered her questions. She had thought about all of it many times, especially after she had been caught and punished. She had never been asked to explain it, though. Speak out loud so her ears would have to hear her mouth voice feelings and compulsion.

"I pretend I am free," she began softly, remembering clearly how it had felt in the past to sneak away and savor her stolen moments of liberty. "My station is not so different from yours. 'Tis just as predestined, and I am prisoner as much to my family as to my gender. But for a space of time I am bound to no one. I am not lectured for my obstinacy or punished for my truculence. I am free, Flanna. Not in reality, I know. But in my own mind, to pursue who I am and not who I am ordered to be. It is beyond price, that freedom. However false it may be, it is worth the cost."

Flanna saw the light in the verdant eyes of her young

mistress, somehow savage and innocent at the same time. Even after all her years of servitude, she realized her own desires for that very same freedom had not completely diminished. The borrowed light illuminated Flanna's dark, forsaken desires, until both women felt overwhelmed with the need and the ache for it.

"Aye," Flanna whispered, "I know of what you speak."

Camille took Flanna's hand in her own, squeezing the chapped skin and feeling the strength there. The quiet strength of a woman who had served others all her life, but had still not lost herself. And the found understanding with another woman filled a space in her. She gave Flanna's hand another squeeze. "I need to know who watches me, Flanna. Can you find that out for me?"

Flanna didn't hesitate. "I've already been askin' about."

"Thank you."

"Aye, you go, dearie. I have work I must do if anyone will be eatin' lunch."

Camille glanced to the window at the beckoning spring day. "I will walk to the stables and ask Dyson to saddle my mount. 'Tis too glorious a day to send someone after my bidding."

The two women exchanged a smile and Camille waved goodbye as she stepped outside into the bright sunlight. Just then she remembered she had forgotten to find Molly and send her back into the parlor. She shrugged away the order, deciding to let her father pursue his lust without her help.

The stables stood in the distance, a mammoth brick building that housed nearly a hundred horses. Like his father before him, Kenley loved to breed horseflesh and had taken it to an art form. He sold and showed some of the finest steeds in all of England. Camille had always been interested, wanting to learn about breeding. But that had been deemed a male pursuit, and denied her. Camille had listened, though, and absorbed as much as she could. She had even somewhat impressed her brothers and her father with a few quiet comments.

One day a foal had been born that her father had considered a mistake, with eyes too small and wide set, and markings he described as ugly. He had ordered it put down and Camille had thrown a fit, going so far as to hurl herself between the baby and the pistol. She had cried and begged and bargained, and Kenley had relented and allowed the foal to live. It had been the one concession Camille could ever remember that either of her parents had made for her.

Kenley had also commented the foal was living proof Camille had no stomach for breeding.

Nevertheless, Camille loved her horse. She had hand-fed her grains and watched her grow from filly to mare. She wandered through the stables with her skirts held up to keep them from getting soiled, heading to the stall where her mare was kept.

As she approached, she heard the familiar deep voice of her brother. A smile curved her lips at the pride in his tone. She could hear him telling the story of the huge stallion he had just purchased, the purity of his lineage, the elegant length of his legs, the mare he would breed him with in the summer.

Camille cleared her throat lightly as she drew near, and two men swung around at the unmistakable sound of a lady's approach. Camille stopped and dropped her handfuls of satin, forgetting everything from the hay that would cling to the bottom of her skirts to the dust on the wide, rough planks of the stable floor.

"This is my sister, Camille," Eric said, his voice still rich with that same note of pride. "Camille, this is Patrick Mullen."

Patrick took her fingers, his thumb a quick caress that felt too brief as he let go. "My pleasure, my lady."

But Camille scarcely heard him. She must have said something appropriate, because both men smiled. It then occurred to her they might be laughing at the color in her cheeks or the fact that her eyes had not left his face. And yet, she didn't quite care.

He was fascinating. In the dim light of the stables, where the masculine scents of leather and horses mingled with fresh hay and dry grain, he looked perfectly at ease. Tall and ruggedly built, he had a face out of a Celtic fable, with eyes the color of the ocean during a storm. When he smiled his teeth flashed in the dusky light, a wild grin that had her heart thumping.

He had said something, and she had missed it. "I'm sorry?"

"I asked if you like horses, my lady."

And a voice as mellow as brandy.

"Indeed, I do. I love riding."

"Your brother has been giving me a tour of your family's stables. It's been quite impressive and informative."

Camille didn't know what to say. She smiled.

Patrick grinned at her again, knowing she was uncomfortable, but not ready for the conversation to be over. "Do you have a horse of your own?"

"I do."

Patrick offered his arm. "Introduce me, would you?"

Camille hesitated, hearing Amelia's voice in her head warring with her own desires. *Lead us not into temptation, but deliver us from evil.* Camille placed her hand tentatively on Patrick's arm, feeling his warmth, his strength under her fingers. "Certainly."

Eric watched them wander away, looking at each other instead of where they were going and completely forgetting his presence.

Camille swallowed hard, and then again. Her mouth felt too dry and her hands shook. But he didn't seem to notice, as he chatted with her about nothing in particular. Camille stopped at a narrow stall.

"This is my mare."

He could hear the fondness in her voice. "What's her name?"

"Indue."

"Indue?" Patrick mentally searched his extensive knowledge of language and couldn't find a meaning. "I've never heard that name before."

Camille's lips curved upward in a shy smile. "Indue. Indue time she'll be a pretty horse."

Patrick laughed. He rubbed his hand over the velvet nose of the mare, who searched for a carrot in his outstretched palm. "She's very sweet."

"I love her," Camille said simply.

"Lucky horse."

Camille blushed again, hating the flood of heat that gave away her nervousness. Patrick didn't seem to notice. He murmured to Indue, chuckling as she nuzzled his palm again and snorted. "She's hungry?"

"She's always hungry."

"Like Tate," he said, more to himself.

"Tate?"

"My boy."

"Oh," Camille whispered. "I didn't realize you were married."

Patrick didn't laugh at her artlessly blurted comment. "I'm not. My cabin boy. Tate is sort of my adopted son. He lives on my ship with me."

"Oh," Camille said again. "You live on a ship?"

"Most of the year, aye."

"A home on a ship," Camille said aloud, thinking of what that must be like. "This is your profession?"

"Aye. I am a merchant, like my father." He spoke quietly, watching her mind turn over what he said. Her face hadn't turned aside with snobbery at the revelation of his common birth, but instead she seemed to be mulling over his words behind those amazing eyes.

"It must grow lonely."

Sad eyes, he thought. She said "lonely" as if she understood the concept well. "It can, if you let it get to you. I keep busy, twelve-hour shifts and I read on my off hours, when Tate isn't pestering for a game of chess."

"You have seen the world, then."

"I have seen most of the ports the world has to offer. Incredibly little of the actual world, though."

"Do you care for what you do?"

He gave her question careful consideration. "I do, though probably not how you mean. I care for the way it pleases my da."

Camille said nothing, but Patrick didn't miss the ironic smirk that crossed her face for the briefest second. "Perhaps you think that is a less than admirable reason to choose one's means of life?"

Camille's eyes flew up to his. For a reason completely unknown to her, she felt compelled to tell the exact truth of what she had been thinking. "I only wondered what it must be like to please one's father."

His eyes searched hers thoroughly. He said nothing, only reached out to lightly tug on a stray curl that had fallen to rest on her shoulder. He grinned down at her and she felt her insides tighten. Indue nickered and nuzzled Patrick's arm.

Camille laughed. "She is quite demanding of affection. It appears she has deemed you friend, not foe."

"She is too sweet to have foes." Patrick resumed his stroking as he spoke.

"Temperament aside, she is not my father's favorite."

"Do you ride her often?"

"I am permitted an hour a day."

"Permitted?"

"Yes."

The way she answered definitively, he understood. "Well, perhaps one day you'll reserve that hour for me, and you can teach me how to ride."

Her brows shot up. "You can't ride a horse?"

"I've never tried."

"You're teasing me."

"No."

"Truly?"

"Truly."

Camille thought about that for a moment. "And you'd have me teach you?"

"Why not?"

She couldn't believe he'd ask such a plain question. Surely he was teasing her. But he looked at her patiently, waiting for her reply, without a trace of irony. "I am a woman."

"Indeed."

The word was like a warm caress, a benediction. It ran through her, heating places in her body that made her suddenly aware of her innocence. Many men had called upon her; never had any single one of them made her feel this way.

"I would love to show you."

"Excellent. Tomorrow?"

Camille's face fell. She tried to hide it, but he was watching closely.

"No?"

"I doubt I could get permission for such a thing. It would be highly inappropriate."

"I see."

Patrick was still rubbing Indue's nose, along her long face, around her pricked ears. His touch looked soft, gentle, methodical. Indue stood perfectly still, as if hypnotized by the stroking. Camille watched his large hand move over her, tracing her markings, sweeping around her eyes. Camille's skin tingled as if he were touching her, responding to just the suggestion of his caress.

"You didn't say she is ugly," Camille said, her voice sounding small and soft.

"Who is ugly?"

"Indue."

"Is that what you think?"

"No, I think she is beautiful. But most—rather, no one else—seems able to see beyond her physical attributes."

"But you do?"

"I always have."

"Do people see beyond your physical attributes?"

Camille looked up at him once again to see if he were teasing. "Pardon me?"

"You're beautiful. Do most people see past that?"

Camille realized he was serious. His hand had stopped its stroking, and his eyes were fixed on hers, the most incredible color she had ever seen. She felt a little dizzy, a touch queasy. Had he just said he thought she was beautiful? "Most people don't see me at all, and when they do, I doubt they see past my facade."

"Good."

"You think that's good?"

"No, I think it's good that you realize it."

Camille just looked at him. Looked into those eyes while her heart fell at his feet. And she wondered if he knew it. She forced some normalcy into her demeanor, relying on years of training and etiquette to save her from making a complete fool of herself. "Are you going to stay for the evening? If so, I will let the staff know to set an extra place."

"First invite me to lunch."

"Lunch?"

"Aye, it's scarcely noon."

"Right. Lunch. Would you like to stay for lunch?"

"I'd love to," Patrick said softly. "Now invite me to go for a ride with you. We'll ask your brother to chaperone. I'll probably kill myself, but I'll die happy."

He let his hand run down her arm as he said it, ending at her hand with the word "happy." He held on, his fingers entwining with hers, sending frissons of heat running through her, like tiny bolts of lightning in her blood. She wondered if he felt it.

"I never would have guessed I'd be so glad I accepted your brother's invitation to come see the stables."

Camille knew exactly what he meant. "I was supposed to be practicing the clavichord. I don't usually come to the stables this time of day."

"Fortuitous."

"Yes," she whispered, nearly undone by the feel of his hand on hers.

"The ride?"

Camille glanced down at her gown of pink satin, its simple lines, square neckline, and seed pearls completely inappropriate for riding. "I will need to change."

"Fine. May I walk with you to the house?"

Again, Camille laid her hand on his arm and let him lead her through the dim and narrow labyrinth of the stables, and then finally out into the beaming sunlight of late morning. Eric stood in the narrow strip of shade just outside the wide doors, leaning against the brick and smirking the way only an older brother can.

"What did you think of my sister's mount? A real beauty, isn't she?"

"She is." Patrick hadn't taken his eyes from Camille, though. "But it seems there is more to her than that."

Eric straightened and began to meander toward the manor. "True enough, I suppose."

Camille tore her eyes away from Patrick and spoke nervously to her brother. "Will you come riding with Mister Mullen and me? Perhaps he has informed you he has yet to sit a horse."

Eric shrugged carelessly under his tailored jacket, his demeanor as suddenly distant as his mind. "A ride sounds fine."

Camille let out a breath she hadn't realized she held. She cast a sidelong glance up at Patrick, seeing the crinkles of a smile around his eyes as he flashed a grin at her. He leaned down, his lips brushing against her ear as he whispered, his breath a warm tingle she felt to her toes. "Call me Patrick."

"Patrick," she said softly, the only word she could summon to her lips as her breath caught.

"Aye, I like that much better."

The walk to the mansion seemed too short, and before

Camille knew it she was flying into her rooms, frantically calling for Brigid to help her change. She yanked a riding gown out of her armoire, struggling to pluck open the laces on the back of her gown while kicking off her silk slippers. Brigid scudded into her rooms as she always did, moving at her own pace, her dour expression firmly entrenched in the deep grooves around her eyes and lips. Without a word she helped her mistress change into her riding habit of ecru linen, lacing her tightly. A few passes with the brush over Camille's black hair restored it to a neat twist. A straw hat with a wide brim was placed on top to shield her skin from the sun. Camille slipped into her riding boots and gave herself a final appraising glimpse in the mirror. She saw a girl whose color ran high in her cheeks, an unfamiliar sparkle in her green eyes.

Her fingers reached out to touch the girl in the looking glass, whose silvery reflection looked so different from the image she usually saw. Gone was the shadowed, serious expression. Instead her face bloomed with the colors of spring itself, shades of pinks and creams and green.

Male laughter drifted up to her rooms, an unfamiliar sound in the Bradburn home. Camille knew it could be only Patrick who brought levity into those rooms where austerity usually reigned. The glass felt cool under her fingertips as she rested them on the reflection of her cheek.

He had changed so much, already.

CHAPTER 2

As Camille descended the stairs and approached the parlor, she saw Patrick, his back to her, unaware of her presence as he stood facing the painting that Camille loved best. He stood tall and broad shouldered, with the lean strength that came from daily hard work. Dark auburn hair hung in waves away from his sun-burnished skin, and Camille noticed with interest that he shunned the English fashions and wore his hair unbound and unpowdered. It added to his rugged appearance, she thought, as did his finely tailored clothes that weren't fussy, but had been cut for fit and function.

Patrick looked away from his study of the portrait hanging above the mantel as Camille entered. He gestured to the likeness of the blond woman in the picture. "Your mother?"

"My grandmother, Elizabeth. She was my father's mother."

Patrick looked from Camille to the painting, and then back. "You favor her, somewhat. Not in coloring or feature, but there is a resemblance just the same."

"Then the painter was indeed talented. He must have captured what my mother says is in our nature."

"What's that, then?"

"Rebellion." Camille said the word on a sigh, as if she tired of hearing it even from her own lips.

He thought about that for a moment, looking again to the portrait before looking back to Camille, his expression appraising and curious. "Is that what you think? You are rebellious?"

Camille stared at him levelly, wondering if he realized that in the space of an hour he had asked for her thoughts and opinions more times than she had been asked in the whole of her life.

"I suppose I struggle with it."

"What is it you don't have that you think you want?"

He didn't ask her snidely or with disdain, as some might, given the obvious wealth surrounding her and the prestige of her family name. Instead, he looked as though he understood something she didn't need to tell him. Which made her want to tell him all the more.

"Freedom," she said in a near whisper.

He nodded briefly, his eyes still connected with hers. Vivid green meeting stormy dark blue across a room, carrying a current they both felt. Footsteps sounded in the hall and Patrick turned to a table of gleaming mahogany where a chessboard of green and white marble sat, its pewter figures set up for a new game. He glanced at Camille as Eric strode in wearing his riding clothes.

"Do you play chess, my lady?"

"On occasion."

Eric looked at the clock on the mantel. "We should ride now, or else miss lunch."

Patrick rolled his eyes. "To my death, then."

Camille laughed and placed her arm on Patrick's, leading him through the foyer and out into the brilliant sunshine. "Surely not as fatal as that. I'll see to it you live long enough for me to trounce you in a game of chess."

"Would you care to wager on that? I'll warn you, I've spent many hours hunched over that checkered board."

Camille glanced back and saw that her brother followed

behind but not too closely, shielding his eyes with the back of his hand. As usual he wore the faraway expression that meant the thoughts in his mind consumed his attention and he was scarcely aware of his surroundings.

"What shall we wager, Mister Mullen?"

"Coin?"

"I have no coin of my own to wager."

"None?"

Camille shook her head. "Nothing."

"Then if you beat me, you shall win a hundred pounds."

Camille's eyes widened at the sum. "And if I lose?"

Patrick leaned down to her ear, his breath a warm caress. "A kiss."

Camille turned her head to look at him in surprise, so that their faces were now only inches apart, those lips of his close to hers as if he meant to collect payment now for a game not yet lost. And Camille suddenly had the thought she would let him win. Just once, to see what it was like to feel a man's lips on hers. Not just any man, but this one.

"A kiss matched to a hundred pounds," she said shakily. "Deal."

Patrick straightened, pulling away from her reluctantly. "What would you buy with a hundred pounds?"

Camille thought only for a second. "I'd save it."

"For what?"

Camille envisioned herself hopping into a hired livery, fleeing the church where her mother would one day soon force her to wed a man she didn't love. She forced a laugh for Patrick's benefit, dismissing the absurd thought of running away with only a hundred pounds to her name. "I don't know."

"I think you do know, my lady."

But she wouldn't tell him. "Where are you from originally?"

"From no one place, really. I lived in Ireland for a time when I was a boy."

"I hear the Irish in your accent."

"Most of our crew is from Ireland, as well as my da and grandda. I suppose that is why the accent lingers."

"Did you like it there?"

Patrick remembered a home full of laughter, rolling green hills, and his mother's music. The scents of baking brown bread and stories at bedtime. "Aye. I was very happy there."

"Why did you leave?"

"My mother died. When she was gone, my da took to his ships and never looked back. He had given up sailing for her and tried to set down the roots she had wanted, to make the home she had needed. But farming wasn't for him, nor was anything else. The sea is in him, like blood. There's no denying who you are."

"But now?"

"Now he wants something more." Patrick didn't say it was respectability his father craved. Lands and titles and wanting what he hadn't been born to have. Conlan had sent his only son to England to buy him more than a house, but a piece of a heritage he didn't possess. And as much as Patrick didn't need or want that, he did as his father had asked, hoping that the demons that had driven them across the seas were finally tired, and that his father could have the rest he deserved. But Patrick had found more than land in England, he thought as he cast a side-long glance to Camille. Much, much more.

They reached the stables and found that the stable hand had saddled up their mounts. The gelding that had been chosen for Patrick pleased Camille, for she knew him to be a sweet-tempered, docile steed. Eric swung up into his saddle and sat back lost in his thoughts, content to allow his sister to entertain the man who he hoped would relieve him of the property he didn't want, and provide him with enough coin to have all the things for which he lusted. Camille showed Patrick the basics of the saddle and reins, giving him a brief but thorough description of their purpose and use. Patrick nodded when he thought he understood and asked questions when he didn't. Finally, Camille gestured to the stirrups.

"Time to start, Mister Mullen."

"Patrick."

"Patrick. Time to start."

Blowing out a breath, he grabbed the pommel, slid a booted foot into the stirrup, and vaulted himself up and into the saddle. Camille smiled up at him, her eyes sparkling.

"You tell lies, Patrick. You have done this before."

"I would never lie to you, my lady."

"Camille." She glanced over to her brother, who gazed off vacantly. "But only when no one is listening."

"Camille," Patrick said softly.

She shivered at the sound of her name on his breath. Patrick saw the pulse in her neck throb and saw the tremble take her pink, parted lips. He felt the thunder of his own heartbeat, the curl of desire in his belly.

She broke the spell by pulling her eyes away from his and backing away, her hand pressed to her chest.

"We must go."

Distracted, Camille clumsily seated herself in the sidesaddle she detested and hooked her knee around the pommel. She arranged her skirts until they fanned over Indue's flanks like a medieval banner, and then looked up to Patrick. "Ready?"

Patrick gripped the reins, thrilled by the feel of the steed beneath him. "Aye. Where shall we go?"

"To the ocean, or have you had enough of it?"

He grinned at the challenge in her voice, the glint of teasing in her eyes. And then, as he stared into those eyes, as green as the Irish hills he had run free on as a boy, he said something he didn't even know he remembered. "'My bounty is as boundless as the sea, my love as deep.'"

And when he saw those eyes go soft and her pink lips part again with that sensual tremble, he knew why he had said it.

Camille closed her eyes for a second, then spoke. "'The more I give to thee the more I have, for both are infinite.'"

Eric grunted and smirked. "If you two are going to sit on your horses and quote Shakespeare to each other, I'll be returning to the house. My head aches, and I've a need to lie down before I eat."

"If you consumed more food with your evening meals than you did gin, perhaps your head wouldn't ache."

Patrick looked at Camille quickly, to see if her expression matched her prim tone. But she was smiling at her older brother, a narrow black brow elegantly arched.

Eric whirled his horse around toward the stables. "Either way, I'm not riding. I need to lie down."

Camille found herself at a loss, torn between wanting to ride with Patrick and see the ocean and the fear that if she were at this moment being watched, the unchaperoned outing would be reported when her mother returned. The evil had come back, whispering for her to do her heart's desire, to ride with Patrick alone, to talk with him for a while longer, and to bask in the dizzy thrill she felt simply by being near him. However, she knew that going off alone with a strange man would be enough to ruin her reputation permanently, if anyone saw or found out. But even worse than any damage to her reputation would be the repercussions dealt by her mother for such flagrant disobedience. A ride with her brother and a business associate would appear innocent; a ride alone with Patrick while Eric went to the house would be as detrimental to her as if she had removed her clothing and offered Patrick her virginity. Indecision reigned supreme, nearly causing her to panic at the thought of having to choose, knowing that each path held a hell of its own.

Patrick saw the confusion on her face and sensed her unhappiness. "We don't need to go riding today. I'd be happy to join you another time."

"No," Camille said with finality. "I want to go."

Eric shifted in his saddle to look directly at his sister,

disbelief on his face. "Camille, be rational. You cannot go off unchaperoned again."

"I want to go," she repeated.

"Is a ride worth it?"

She felt the blush ride up her face at her brother's question, afraid Patrick would divine the meaning. "Please, Eric. Come riding?"

Eric sighed heavily, then pinched his brow where his headache throbbed mercilessly. "Go ahead, Camille. I won't speak of it."

And he turned and rode the short distance to the stable doors, swung down, and handed the reins to Dyson before heading back to the house without a backward glance.

Patrick watched Camille's face carefully, noting the odd expression of relief and anxiousness. "Truly, my lady, we can schedule a ride another time when we are suitably chaperoned. I have no desire to place your reputation in jeopardy, to be sure."

Camille fiddled with her reins rather than meeting his eyes. "Do not concern yourself, Patrick. I wish to ride with you."

"Can you send for someone else to accompany us, then? A maid, perhaps?"

Finally, she brought her eyes up to meet his, and regardless of her trembling hands or the color in her face, she spoke the truth to him once again. "I would like it very much if we could ride together now."

Patrick raised a brow, but held the reins more firmly. "As my lady wishes," he said with a smile, and then gestured in the general direction that Eric had taken. "He's interesting, your brother."

"He has much on his mind of late."

"The selling of the land?"

"Not just that, but that is the means to an end. He wants away from all of this." Camille gestured in a wide sweep.

"He can't run from who he is."

Those eyes turned sad again, and Patrick regretted the words as they left his mouth.

"I know. Who of us can?" she asked softly.

Patrick wasn't close enough to touch her, to smooth back her black hair, or to kiss the sadness from her lips. Even if he had been, he had no right to. So he forced himself to smile again for her benefit. "Could you guess at my favorite thing?"

Camille held his gaze for a second and thought about it. "No. I couldn't guess."

"Try. You don't know me very well, so I'll give you a hint." He leaned forward, speaking confidentially. "It isn't English cooking."

Camille giggled a bit, allowing herself to be caught by his good humor. "Very well, I'll hazard a guess. I'm going to say reading."

"Not quite, but you're very close. Fact is, my favorite thing is a story."

Camille clucked to Indue and they began to move along the grounds, through the manicured lawns of Beauport, heading to the trail that led through the wind-gnarled trees until soil became sand. "A story? Written or spoken?"

"It doesn't matter, though I prefer spoken. Then, the tone of the storyteller tells as much as the words themselves, rising and falling, pausing and proceeding. There isn't an Irishman or Irishwoman I know of who doesn't stop and listen when a story is being told, and I'm no different."

"Look at you, Patrick. You're riding well."

Patrick glanced down. "I've had the best of teachers."

Camille tossed a look behind them and saw no one. Still, she wondered how severe a penalty she risked for this indulgence. But as her attention fell once again on Patrick, all thoughts of punishments faded. Whatever it was, she would feel it had been worth it.

"Tell me a story then, Patrick."

"About a warrior who lost his love?"

"His lady love or his ability to love?"

"Ah, Camille, you torture me with your insight. He lost both, you see, in one battle. But 'twas not a battle for land or honor or even glory, but a battle in himself. And as we know, 'tis the most brutal of them all, isn't it? Our warrior had much in the way of what a man wants, strength, vigor, valor. But he was vain, and it clouded all he saw. Not vain of his appearance, mind you, for he found little pride in his flowing hair or his battle scars, or anything physical. But he was haughty of his worth.

"After a battle in a faraway village, he came upon a beautiful young peasant girl, barely a woman, but with wise eyes and an astounding capacity for understanding. She saw into him, you see, past his fleshly scars and viewed the ones on his soul. The scars of battle and bloodshed that time could never heal. And she loved him despite it, loved him for it. She held her warrior and poured her love into him, washing him with her tears until his soul was clean, and she cried for the wounds he couldn't weep for himself."

Patrick paused then, moving in time with his mount as it picked its way along the path under the trees. He took a deep breath and then began again.

"And for a while, he let himself be swept away by her comeliness and her love. He allowed it to touch where no one else had cared to, and he nearly was overcome with the simple beauty of it. Of them. But his arrogance grew apace with his newfound love. For a gift is as much about accepting as it is giving, isn't it? And he couldn't accept the gift of a peasant, nor could he find acceptance in his heart for all that love. And so he left her there, his pretty peasant girl, to cry for him for eternity. And they say the silver river that flows through that village is made of her tears, pure as her heart and crystal clear."

Camille stayed quiet, thinking of the tale she had been told and of the man who had told it. Her throat had grown tight at the thought of all that feeling wasted, of the family they could have been. If only the warrior had trusted himself enough to accept it, and trusted his peasant girl enough to continue to extend it.

"'Tis a beautiful story, Patrick."

"Aye."

"And sad, too."

"Aye, as all good stories should be."

"No happy endings? No eternal, abiding loves? Can't it ever work?"

He heard her forlorn tone and ached for her. "Aye, Camille. I believe if two people want it badly enough, it is destined to work. Love, real love, mind, not the fancy of stories, is too strong to be broken when shared equally."

And in that instant, Camille decided to throw the rest of her caution to the wayside. She would trust, as the warrior hadn't. She would give, as the peasant girl had. "You've seen enough of the ocean, haven't you?"

"For a lifetime."

"Then I will take you somewhere else. A secret place where I have taken no one."

He cocked an eyebrow. "I won't say no, but I'll ask if you're certain you wish to share such a place."

Camille felt a fist squeezing her heart at his question, knowing that the simple thing he asked implied he would understand the very thing she was giving him. She nodded her assent, unable to speak. She clucked to Indue and led the way. They veered from the path and into the thicket, slowing the pace as the horses had to pick their feet over dense underbrush and rotting logs.

The light filtered through the trees, tinted green and gilded with gold by the combination of new leaves and spring sunshine. She breathed deeply, inhaling the scents of lichen and ferns, wildflowers and damp, mossy soil. Birds darted from trees to the ground and back to the trees again, contributing to the hushed music of the woods with the flap of their wings. Insects hummed and squirrels darted out of their paths, all the while surrounded by silent, timeless rock and creaking, age-old trees.

"'Tis a magical place," Camille sighed.

"Aye."

"I come here whenever I can."

"How often is that?"

"When my mother is not at Beauport."

"But your father allows it?"

"My father sees what he wants to see, and that usually is confined to the skirts of any woman who isn't my mother."

"Ah." Patrick chose not to say more, knowing that those who speak ill of their family are often defensive when anyone else follows suit.

"I've been coming here since I was a girl. Sneaking out to the woods where I could be alone with my thoughts. I found my special place a few years ago and have been coming back to it ever since."

Since she was a girl, he thought. She could scarcely be beyond that, now.

"How old are you, Camille?"

"Twenty. And you?"

"More than twenty, to be sure. Just barely over thirty, I am."

"And you've never married?"

"I've never been in love."

She laughed out loud, setting birds to flight and adding to the music of the forest around them. He watched her quizzically, thinking about what he had said in relation to her mirth. When the peals of laughter subsided a bit and Camille calmed, she looked at him, wiping her eyes. Then she saw he was serious.

"Oh," she said, a bit embarrassed.

"This amuses you."

"Amuses? No, Patrick, it absolutely entertains. To think of the fancy and ideal of it. Just the pure foolish romance of it."

"And what will you marry for, if not love?"

"Land, title, birthright, duty, heirs." She listed them off in a litany too familiar. This time it was her turn to lean forward and speak confidentially. "Not necessarily in that order, mind you."

Patrick shook his head. "I'd give you my pity, but you'd no doubt resent that."

Camille shrugged, a delicate motion that did anything but communicate lack of caring. "I am powerless to change who I am or what I was born to be. Just like you. Just like everyone."

"But it does not stop you from wanting something different."

For a moment she turned and stared at him, their eyes meeting with that same intensity as in the parlor, as if their feelings and thoughts could be conveyed through just looking into each other's eyes. "No. It does not stop the longing. Nothing ever has."

And when he looked at her and told her he understood, she believed he did and it comforted her. Even though she didn't understand why.

The thicket grew more crowded, as tangles of brambly bushes and snarled undergrowth grasped and snagged at the hooves of their mounts. The horses lifted their feet higher, pressing forward, until the trees suddenly thinned into a tiny meadow. A small stone cottage rose up from the ground, its thatched roof and sturdy oak door still intact. Wavy glass sparkled and sunlight glinted off the mica in the stones, making the place look as though it had been created by sprites and fairies who wanted to cast a lure. But if time had forgotten the place, the forest had not. Everywhere vines grew around it, as if the woods were trying to swallow the cottage whole with its relentless growth of ivy and roses.

"Every year the roses bloom in spring," Camille said, wondering what Patrick would think of her place. "Tudor roses, pink as a seashell and just as beautiful. I thought about trimming them once, but I like the way they grow, wild and unchecked."

Patrick turned to her, grinning like a boy who'd been

given a new toy. "Magic," he said softly, and slid down from his horse.

Camille dismounted and gathered both of the horses' reins, leading them into the meadow while Patrick explored. He jogged lightly around the cottage, seeing it possessed only one door and four windows. A small, crumbling well deteriorated in the rear, and he paused to watch Camille draw up fresh water for the horses. She had removed her hat and pushed up her sleeves. It struck him how willingly she did the chore, struggling to turn the rusty crank and lift the heavy bucket. He approached her, his tread silent on the carpet of new grass. She sensed his proximity, turning slightly to look at him.

Patrick saw a mixture of apprehension and fear in her eyes, her lips parted again in that trembling way that made him want to cover them with his own. He reached over and grabbed the handle to the bucket, lifting it easily from the hook and setting it in front of the horses.

"It looked heavy."

"It is heavy. Thank you."

She stood so close, in that enchanting place. Her hair smelled of lavender. She looked up at him, still with that look in her eyes, as if she was half afraid he'd kiss her, half afraid he wouldn't. And her lips. They were making him insane with their pink, parted invitation.

"I want to kiss you, Camille."

"We haven't played chess yet."

He laughed softly. "Consider this an advance payment. I wasn't going to let you win."

Because she didn't say no, he dipped his head to hers. That first brush of lips touched them both, magical, soft. His sweetest, her first. She moved her lips under his, doing what he did, obeying her body, obeying nature. His arms slipped around her waist and her arms looped around his neck, his hair brushing against her fingers. He pulled her closer, until her breasts were against his chest and she could feel the pounding in his heart; she wondered if he could feel the wild thumping of her own.

And it was like remembering, Camille thought. Meant to be and so right. As if every dream she had ever had had come true, here in his arms with his lips on hers. And then the kiss deepened, and she stopped thinking, stopped having any thoughts outside the rushing in her ears and the feelings in her belly, in her legs, and in her heart. Soft as velvet and potent as brandy, his kiss made her head spin as his tongue touched hers in a rhythm as old as love. She reveled in the hard length of his body against hers, the spicy clean scent of him, the heat that gathered in her center. She melted against him like sun-warmed honey, pouring herself into the kiss, giving herself over to all of it.

Patrick held himself on the brink of propriety all the while she returned his kiss. He even stayed in control when she went soft and yielding against him, so he could feel all the curves of her body. But when she made the sound deep in her throat, that purring, throttled moan, he lost restraint. His hands traveled up the elegant length of her back and held the back of her head, his fingers slipping into her black hair, dropping pins to the ground and drawing another of those mind-numbing sounds from her throat, long and deep.

He stopped. Before things progressed any further, he forced himself to stop kissing her. He pushed her away gently, keeping his hands on her shoulders deliberately, lest they wander.

"Stop. It shouldn't have gone that far."

Camille tried to regulate her breathing while holding herself back from leaning back against him and begging him to put his lips on hers again, transporting her back to that wonderful place of holding and caring, tasting and feeling. She stood on shaking legs, eyes closed, feeling the hot melt of her insides.

Patrick traced her collarbone with his thumbs, the

softness of her skin like silk, so delicate. "I hope I didn't scare you," he said softly.

She leaned into his touch. "'Tis as if I have known you before. I do not fear you."

"And you brought me to your special place."

She looked up to him, her eyes connecting with his. "Yes."

He smiled and let his hands wander to the nape of her neck, his fingers stroking upward until they were entwined in her hair. He felt her shiver at his touch, and his smile deepened, growing darker and very male. "I want to kiss you again, but I won't. Not now."

She let out her breath, only then aware she had been holding it. He slid his hands back to her shoulders, down her arms, and took her fingers. The image of Indue in the stables popped into her mind, of her mare standing hypnotized under Patrick's touch, just as Camille now stood, completely entranced. Enthralled.

"Take me inside, Camille, and show me your cottage. I want to see the place you love."

She kept hold of his hands and led him to the door.

CHAPTER 3

The cottage never seemed to change, she thought with a contented sigh. It looked perfect to her with its rustic furniture, its cavernous stone fireplace, and wide-planked floor. But most of all, absolute quiet reigned in that tiny space. She relished its silence most of all, sacred and still, as if the place held air from a more ancient time.

Camille watched as Patrick moved about in her special place, happy to have him see what meant so much to her. He ran a finger along the stone mantel, lightly touching the arrangement she had made of seashells and last year's dried roses.

"You put these here?" he asked.

"I did."

"Just like you, they are. Timelessly beautiful. A simple pleasure."

She felt the rising heat again in her cheeks, the rush of blood, and the pain in her breast, like condensed emotion.

"Whose place was this?" Patrick asked, glancing out the back window and spying the weather-beaten well.

"I don't know. When I first came here, it looked as though someone had left and thought they'd be back the same day. There was even dried food in bowls. I came back months later, and still nothing had changed. That was years ago. Whoever lived here obviously isn't returning."

Patrick glanced to the small pallet in the corner, narrow and unlikely to support more than a single person. The place had been set up for the comfort of one, he noticed, as there was only one chair with a cushion, and only a solitary lamp. A tiny table, rough hewn and scarred, sat in a corner, with a rickety chair at its side. Papers and stacked books covered the surface, an inkwell and quill at the ready. He wandered over to the papers and began to read the one on top, finding a poem about loss and rejection, nature and survival.

He looked up to Camille, finding her flushed. "Your writing?"

She nodded and turned away from him, facing the cold fireplace. "I am not much of a poet, and even less of a writer. But sometimes it seems to help."

"What does it help?"

"I can feel as though I haven't lost something of myself. As if I'm a part of something bigger. Shakespeare wrote, as did Milton and Fielding. They are men, and my paltry words do not compare to their talent, but the want is the same. To make something different. A different world, a different feeling, maybe a different person of yourself or of the reader. There is power in the written word, and I have loved it all my life."

Patrick stared at her narrow back and the tumble of black hair he had released from its moorings when he had buried his hands in its soft depth. He watched as her shoulders lifted in a sigh he felt more than heard, and as she tilted her head down he looked longingly at the curve of her neck and the delicate shape of her jaw. His chest grew tight, and he could barely breathe. And he knew right then that this was important. More than a flirtation or a passing dream, but something that would stay with him always. Change him forever.

Camille turned to face him, with sad eyes and a wistful smile. "Will you tell me another story?"

"I'd rather make our own."

"Our story wouldn't likely have a happy ending."

"It would be a tale of great love."

Camille felt the pressure in her chest grow stronger, a storm gathering. "Great love followed by great loss?"

"The outcome would be uncertain, but it would be a pain I think I'd endure for a taste."

She looked at him directly, letting her eyes meet his across the cottage. Never had simply looking at a person communicated so much, she thought. How could it be? "Do you suppose a free man could love such a girl, who has nothing of this world to give him?"

"She could give him of herself."

"That could consist of only words and sentiment."

"And a memory he would take to his grave."

"Yes," she whispered. "Already I know I will never forget you."

He shifted his weight, cleared his throat. "You do not see me as a commoner."

"I can't help seeing you through my clouded perception. No one can see what is real in a person. We all see what we want to see, what we decide to see. Perhaps what we need to see."

"What do you see when you look at me?"

"Life," she said without hesitation. "I see everything that defines life itself. Freedom, vitality, honesty."

"I see those things in you, also."

"No. I am the exact opposite of that. I am not free, I am unimportant, and I am rarely honest."

"But why are you different with me?"

Camille turned to the windows and watched through wavy glass at the horses placidly grazing in the intermittent patches of sunshine. "You are unlike anyone I have ever met."

"Yet that does not frighten you. You brought me here,

to your special place. You share yourself with me without reserve. All of that is honest. Can't you see that?"

"It is not without fear, Patrick. It is without regard. Surely you see that difference? I will be punished for this indulgence, if I am caught."

"Punished? How so?"

Camille averted her face, humiliated. "'Tis inconsequential. The sun is high overhead, and Flanna has no doubt prepared a splendid meal. If we are not back to dine, my absence will certainly be noticed."

Patrick didn't press her for details, seeing her discomfort. Instead he opened the door and held her lower back as she exited, pleased by the simple delight of touching her. Camille paused by the well and picked her pins from the grass, tidied her hair, and settled her hat back in place. They mounted their horses in silence, Camille with the satisfaction of seeing Patrick swing into the saddle without a hitch.

"You'll be pleased to know that Flanna is also Irish, and her cooking is not the usual English fare." Camille cast a sidelong glance to Patrick as she spoke.

He looked at her, straight into her eyes where she couldn't hide from him. "Will you be injured because of this ride, Camille?"

She hesitated, then answered. She couldn't bring herself to be dishonest with him. "If I am caught."

"Who will hurt you?"

Camille felt the burn in her back where the lash had been laid against her with enough force to tear skin. "My mother, though she doesn't do the deed herself." She shifted in the saddle and cleared her aching throat. "Patrick, please do not ask anything more. I cannot bear it."

"You have been bearing it too long, and alone. But I will say nothing more of it, unless you tell me yourself."

"'Tis the English way. I am not different."

"You are different, and you are also wrong," Patrick said succinctly, his voice rising with the emotion of imagining her beaten. "Will you defend to me the ones who hurt you?"

"I am never sorry I have sinned, only that I have been caught. Would you defend the thief who steals or the magistrate who sentences him? I take risks. I let the evil sway my thoughts. I do not obey. I sin."

"You are not evil, Camille. You are human."

"We are born in sin."

"And God loves us, despite it."

Camille fell silent, pondering his words. She watched as if an outsider as she headed back to her family's mansion, almost able to see the expression of contemplation and dread on her face. The tangle of woods opened again, and this time they flowed into the manicured lawns and formal gardens surrounding Beauport. As they ambled in the direction of the stables, Camille felt her heart begin to race, cold sweat gathering on her skin. The shiny black carriage was as unmistakable as the ducal crest emblazoned on the sides in gold.

Amelia had returned.

Hot tears sprang to Camille's eyes while cold dread churned in her belly. Camille knew she would be caught. She knew she would pay. Without thinking, her fingers went to her lips where Patrick had kissed her.

Patrick saw her face freeze, a mask of fear and a struggle for control. "Are you well?"

She didn't answer him. Camille scarcely heard him as she saw her mother on the front steps of the great house. Waiting. Watching.

Camille dismounted and ascended the steps, careful not to look back at Patrick and not to look directly at her mother. She kept her eyes downcast, her hands folded neatly in front of her skirts.

Amelia swept her gaze from Patrick to her daughter. She raised her hand and gestured to the house, and Camille obeyed, entering silently. Amelia brought her attention back to Patrick, and lifted her skirts, descending the steps to approach him. Patrick slid from the horse and handed the reins to a stable hand who took them and hastily headed in the direction of the stables.

"You have business with my son?"

"I do."

"Can you tell the difference between a grown man and his younger sister?"

"Indeed."

"Are you unaware of the impropriety of a man and a woman going off alone together?"

Patrick looked Camille's mother over from head to heels, taking note of the high powdered wig, the heavy makeup, pale eyes, and the curvaceous, petite figure that defied the amount of clothing she wore. Amelia Bradburn looked nothing like her daughter.

"I am aware, Your Grace, that nothing improper passed between your daughter and myself. She simply agreed to take a ride with me when Eric declined."

"Lord Bradburn to you, heathen," Amelia hissed. She drew back, composing herself. "My son is in the parlor. Join him and conclude your business."

"And your daughter?"

"She is not your concern," Amelia stated flatly.

"I requested she accompany me. She merely granted my wish."

"With what other requests did she comply?"

Patrick smiled, slow and confident. "Do you see me as a temptation, Your Grace?"

"I see you for what you are. Common and droll, seeking to purchase what you have no rights to."

"Land is for sale. My father's coin is adequate." Patrick took a few steps closer to Amelia. "Do you not want my kind so close? Will I serve as a reminder that everything in this life bears a price, even land your family called their own?"

Amelia's voice came hard and cold. "That land is my son's to sell. It is of no consequence to me."

Patrick turned in the direction of the house, satisfied he had gotten her to explain herself. "I will see your son now. Please excuse me, Your Grace."

Without waiting for her dismissal, he headed into the mansion. He glanced up the curving marble staircase, where Camille had likely retreated. Patrick wondered if the punishment she spoke of would be administered for the short ride they had taken, and if so, what exactly the duchess would have done to her.

"Are you hungry?" Eric approached Patrick from the parlor, a glass of gin dangling from his long fingers.

"Not really." Patrick turned and faced him, looking directly into green eyes nearly as vivid as Camille's. "Will your sister be hurt?"

Eric hesitated, then answered, "That is not your concern. 'Tis family business."

"You are her family. 'Tis your business, then."

"A daughter is her mother's worry."

Patrick turned aside, frustrated beyond all measure. "How can you not help her?"

"Why not ask me to solve disputes between the Tories and the Whigs? You could even ask that I whip a feckless king into action. But instead, you think to change what is inevitable. Camille controls her fate by her actions. The choices she makes decide her destiny, to a great extent." Eric raised his glass and drained it. "If she would only accept that."

Eric turned and headed into the dining room, stopping at the sideboard to refill his glass. Patrick stood in the grand foyer surrounded by glittering crystal and gleaming dark woods, paintings by masters and the work of great craftsmen. In contrast, the poverty of ideals staggered his senses.

The door closed behind him, and Amelia entered with a swirl of fresh air. Her features grew hard as she found the Irishman still looking at her with an odd expression of distaste and curiosity.

"The promise of a free meal isn't enough to lighten your mood?" Amelia asked.

"I've lost my appetite."

"Shall I offer you a brandy?"

"I'd like that, Duchess."

Amelia felt her own prick of intrigue. This man didn't apologize for his lack of birth, any more than he seemed impressed by the privilege of hers. But he had bearing just the same. A certain arrogance tempered with humor. And his face. She couldn't stop looking at his face. Annoyance returned as a tingle ran through her body. "Follow me, then."

Patrick fell into step behind the rustle of her skirts. "Will your daughter be joining us?"

Amelia poured a generous splash of brandy into a snifter and pressed it into Patrick's hand. "I suppose you think I should feed the child to reward her disobedience?"

Patrick remembered Camille's slim curves and the way her soft skin stretched over her collarbones. He clamped a tight lid on his simmering temper and sipped the brandy. "Everyone needs to eat, Duchess."

"What we all need is salvation," Amelia replied piously, as she poured herself a sherry. "Perhaps through hunger she will learn obedience."

Amelia seated herself at her place in the center of the table and spread a linen napkin across her lap. Servants took the cue and began to enter the large dining room, their trays burdened with steaming silver bowls of food. Patrick took a seat next to Eric and watched as roasted pork, pungent vegetable soup, warm rolls, and pudding were set down noiselessly. Patrick found his plate heaped with the fare as he took notice of the empty chairs with places set for Camille's father and his daughter.

"Your father is also not dining?" Patrick asked Eric.

Amelia spoke before Eric could respond. "My husband says my presence sours his stomach," she announced without shame. "Had one of our carriages not suffered a broken wheel, I would be on my way to London, and Kenley would be having his meal in peace. Of course, Camille would be gallivanting unsupervised, for neither Kenley nor Eric seems inclined to chaperone the child or to send a maid in his stead."

Eric shook his head slightly with disgust and drank, picking at his food while he stared through the heavily draped French doors to the fine day he felt too dismal to enjoy.

"Did the broken wheel cause any injuries?" Patrick asked.

Amelia raised a brow. "'Twas the carriage bearing my trunks."

"I hadn't noticed it when I rode up to the house."

"We left it in town for repairs," Amelia said evenly.

Patrick buttered a roll and took a bite, considering her answer. "You'll be delayed, then?"

"I will stay for as long as I choose, Mister Mullen."

"And your other sons?" Patrick asked, avoiding her assertion. "Eric said he had brothers."

"They are at university." Amelia sipped hot broth from a spoon and cocked an eye to Patrick. "You are inquisitive."

"I am."

"Curious of the lives of your betters, are you?"

"Curious in general, Duchess."

Amelia took a small bite of the pork and chewed it thoughtfully. "Eve was curious. It led to the destruction of everything that was good."

"Perhaps God was curious, which led to the creation of everything in the beginning."

She tilted her head, her pale eyes glinting with amused interest. "You know your Bible?"

"I do," Patrick affirmed. And then he leaned forward and dropped his voice so his point would hit home. "Not just the parts that suit my needs."

Amelia held her breath for a second before she laughed. But the sound was forced. "The entirety suits only One's needs. To forget that is to forget the higher purpose."

Patrick took a spoonful of soup and found it excellent. "We are in agreement, Duchess."

"So you lust for my daughter, do you?"

Patrick's head snapped up and he saw the dare in her eyes. The challenge to confirm or deny. "I find your daughter to be a beautiful, interesting young woman."

"'Tis not an unusual thing, is it? This wanting what you cannot have. A desire for what is forbidden. The scriptures are rife with examples of ones who overstepped their bounds. Those who allowed their desires to rule their sensibilities."

Patrick regarded Amelia, saw her trap, and sidestepped it. "I am here only to buy land for my father."

Amelia gestured to her son with the sharp end of her fork. "And well you should, for he will never do anything with the land other than bemoan its weight on his shoulders, and his own lack of real wealth. Why, dare I wonder aloud if Eric pines for the day when his father and I drop over dead so he can squander his fortune in peace?"

Eric glared briefly at his mother, sipped his gin, and remained silent and sullen.

"Not a word in rebuttal and 'tis no surprise. Eric resembles his father in dark looks and also in dark moods."

"Is it any wonder Father chooses to dine alone?" Eric asked Patrick.

Patrick kept his expression neutral and neglected to answer, bringing his napkin to his lips. He let his eyes wander around the huge dining room, noticing two servants silently flanking either side of a set of doors. They stared straight ahead, expressionless and immune. Patrick wondered if any of the staff dared to bring Camille food when her mother denied her. He wondered if Camille dared ask for their help.

And then he remembered Camille struggling to bring up a heavy bucket of water from a crumbling well. She had looked as though she had relied on herself for everything she had ever needed for so long, it didn't occur to her to ask for assistance. He promised himself she'd get it anyway.

"The meal was excellent, and I thank you for your hospitality," Patrick said. "I have matters in town that require my attention, so if you'll excuse me, I'll be on my way."

"I'll ride with you, Patrick. I've a need to clear my head." Eric pushed away from the table and stood, his tall frame close to Patrick's in height.

Amelia looked up to Patrick and smiled tightly. "You are staying in town, then?"

"For a while, yes. I checked into the Goodrow Inn."

"Shabby place. Frequented by whores and adulterers."

"And how is it you know the place so well, Duchess?"

"It behooves me to know the goings-on of my town."

Patrick leaned his hip against the table and lifted a brow. "Any time you need to check, I'd welcome a visit from you."

Amelia opened her mouth as if to speak, and then closed it again as she thought better of it. Under her thick coating of pale cosmetics, her face grew warm. Finally, she gathered her wits. "I'm not one of your common wenches, and I won't be spoken to in such a manner."

But her tone gave her away, thick and rich.

"Aye, Duchess," Patrick agreed with her confidently. "You are not common, but I am."

Amelia regained herself and stood in a rush as Eric watched in amazement. He saw his unflappable mother turn a darker shade of pink. He would have sworn he saw her wring her hands. But the moment was gone in an instant, and Amelia rebounded.

"Good day," she said flatly and turned, leaving the room in a flurry of silk and linen, trailing a light scent of lemon and vanilla.

Patrick chuckled and laid his napkin on the table, beside his plate still laden with food.

"Now, before I leave, will you tell me which room belongs to your sister?"

"So you can get her in more trouble?"

Patrick lifted his plate. "Of course not. So I can bring her some lunch."

"If my mother found out, Camille would pay dearly." Eric remembered the time Camille had been caught with a risqué novel that their brother Niles had let her read. Camille had scarcely been able to walk after her punishment for wantonness and desires of the flesh.

"Only if she gets caught," Patrick corrected. "That is why you will go and distract your mother."

"I have nothing to say to my mother that would hold her interest for more than a minute."

Patrick grinned again, a wild smile that caught Eric with its spirit. "You will confess."

"Confess?"

"Aye. You will tell her of a woman in town who has caught your eye. A married woman, just the sight of whom inflames you with carnal passion. A common woman, no less, but one of uncommon beauty. You will confess your desire to kill the woman's husband, so you can have her for yourself."

"She will not believe me."

"The story isn't a new one. 'Twill resonate with her; I promise you that." Patrick picked up the plate of food and dropped an extra two rolls on top before covering it with a clean napkin. "I'll need twenty minutes. Be creative."

A look of decadent amusement stole onto Eric's face. "No matter how this turns out, 'twill provide more excitement than this mausoleum has seen in months. Camille's is the balcony over the rose gardens, to the back, facing west."

Patrick slipped out the French doors and headed around toward the back of the mansion. Eric shrugged his shoulders with resignation at the lie he would tell, knowing that lust for a woman was the opposite of his problem, and that his real predicament could never be discussed or confessed. Especially to his parents, who counted on him for heirs. He swallowed his trepidation and hurried into the parlor to divert Amelia.

Patrick skirted the manor, keeping close to the shade. He saw rose gardens in the distance and picked up his pace until he approached them. Orderly rows of manicured bushes grew against short, white fences. All around him tightly furled buds held the secrets of intoxicating scents enclosed in velvet petals amidst thorny, jagged stems, like princesses guarded by dragons. The balcony jutted over the garden, stretching out to the west just as Eric had said. The French doors yawned open, and the spring breeze caught the heavy drapes and swayed them as if music had convinced them to dance. Patrick saw a pruning stool kept close to the house, where thick, dirt-stained gloves and pruning instruments gave testament to the efforts involved in keeping the trailing, climbing vines in check.

He cleared the stool, set the dish on its seat, and carried it over beneath the balcony. He then picked up the plate and stood on the seat, bracing himself on the bottom of the balustrade. He set the dish of warm food on the floor of the platform and looked through the open doors, spotting Camille seated at her dressing table.

She sat with her hair unbound, as if she had combed it and intended on pinning it back up, but had gotten distracted. She held a book in her lap, reading, while she wound a lock of hair around a slender finger. As if transfixed, her eyes were soft and her face dreamy, while she allowed the words of the author to take her to a different place.

"What are you reading?" Patrick whispered.

Camille jumped to her feet at the sound of his voice, the book falling forgotten to the floor. "You cannot be here."

"'Tis too late, Camille. I am here."

"But my mother," Camille whispered desperately, casting a glance to her closed door. "She will come soon."

"I will leave sooner," Patrick promised, enjoying the way

her hair hung around her shoulders, streaming to her waist in absolute disarray. "Come and eat."

Camille saw the plate on the floor of her balcony and her belly growled. "You brought me food?"

"'Tis only fair. You wouldn't have had to do without lunch if you hadn't taken me riding."

"That was my decision. I wanted to go."

He liked the resolute set of her jaw, delicate and firm. "Come and eat, Camille. This stool isn't like to support my weight much longer."

Camille's stomach clenched like a fist, and she gave in. She sat on the balcony, her skirts folded all around her, and she plucked the napkin from the plate. Roasted pork and pudding supported rolls, and Camille let out a little sigh of delight. She picked up a morsel of pork and popped it into her mouth while she scooped up some pudding with a roll.

She started to say something, but he shushed her. "Just eat. We have only a few minutes."

Camille looked at him gratefully and continued to feast on the unexpected meal. She ate it all, even though she had been full before it was gone because she knew she would be denied food that evening. When the plate was clear, she sat back and exhaled with the pleasure of a hunger fully sated.

"What were you reading?"

"Shakespeare."

"Which one?"

"Would you believe *Romeo and Juliet*? And then here you are, under my balcony?"

"I'd believe anything you said. Why *Romeo and Juliet*?"

She lowered her eyes and her heart drummed, sending a thrum of blood under her skin. "Because of what you quoted."

"Did you see me?"

"In every word," she whispered. She looked back to him, able to see only from his chin up as he watched her with those fascinating eyes that seemed to miss nothing. "But again, 'tis a story that ends sadly."

"We could take ours from fairy tales instead of literature. They usually end well."

Camille's lips lifted at the corners in a mischievous smile. "I am even endowed with a wicked mother."

Patrick grinned and then glanced behind himself and then behind Camille. "I should go. I don't want to make things worse for you."

Camille shrugged, lightly dismissing his worry. "Thank you for the food."

"Will I see you again?"

"Under my balcony on a starry night?" The words came on a sigh, images of a young Romeo risking everything for his lady Juliet a fanciful dream in her mind.

"If you're inviting me, Camille, I will return."

And with that, she was back in reality. "Surely, you know the consequences of such a thing, Patrick." She spoke the words softly, but with all the feeling in her heart, hoping that he would want to come just as she hoped he would not. That perhaps just the wanting he had to see her again would last her a lifetime.

"I know the consequences of not coming back, and that means not seeing you again. Does that sit well with you, my lady?"

It was all she could do to imagine him in her rooms, to wonder what that would be like, a few stolen hours of talking with another person who seemed to understand her in a way that she hadn't known she'd always craved. But the risk of such a thing—if he pressed her physically. "You would come into my rooms? Alone?"

"Alone is the nature of such a rendezvous, Camille. You would need to trust me as a gentleman." He grinned, then, recklessly. "Of course, one cry from you would bring all of England down around me, and don't think I don't know it."

Camille bit her bottom lip, thinking of the pleasure of

it. Knowing the danger of it, as well. If he were caught, there would be floggings for certain, both hers and Patrick's, devastation to her reputation if anyone found out, and imprisonment for Patrick; that is, if her father didn't see fit to shoot him for trespassing. But then again, if she did not invite him to come again, she would never see him again. And for some reason, a reason she didn't think she could have ever explained with words, seeing Patrick felt more important than anything else.

The evil slipped into her mind, threading its way around her intentions, until all she could think of was how to see Patrick again, and to the devil with the risk. "If you come tomorrow night, I will hang a ribbon from the rail if all is well."

"On the morrow, then."

Patrick lifted the empty plate and climbed down, replacing the stool and gardening tools where he had found them. He lifted his fingers to his lips and then waved. He turned and crossed the property at a silent jog until finally turning the corner and slipping out of her sight.

Camille's lips still burned with the memory of his kissing her, the way her blood had warmed and her skin had melted. She ran her fingers through her hair, touching her scalp where his fingers had massaged, and all at once she couldn't breathe with the thought of his touch again, his kiss, his words, and his eyes, looking at her and seeing into her. Seeing things no one had ever looked for, and finding pieces of her she hadn't known she still had.

She got to her feet and turned around, looking into the room where she would soon be receiving her punishment, but knowing it would be different this time. Before the moon set a second time, she would see him again. And it didn't feel evil or wanton to crave it, she noticed. Instead, it felt real and important, as if her whole life depended on knowing him, and seeing him again.

CHAPTER 4

Camille leaned forward against the balustrade, her hands clutching at the railing with force enough to whiten her knuckles.

Under her balcony the cultivated rose gardens slumbered in the twilight after a day spent in the sun. A season of vibrant color and heavily scented summer nights lay in wait, held up by spindly fingers studded with razor-sharp spines.

And like the roses, Camille awaited the promise of another day.

A strong breeze scented with spring molded her dressing gown to the contours of her slim body and swept her hair away from her face. Camille leaned into the rush of air and inhaled deeply, as if she could draw the very freedom of the wind inside her.

Behind her, her bedroom door opened and then closed with a soft click of the latch. Camille shut her eyes at the sound, struggling to breathe through strangling dread. Amelia's muffled tread on the thick carpet grew closer, until she heard her mother's voice behind her.

"Foolish child."

Camille turned and faced Amelia. "I am sorry, Mother. I thought my actions would help Eric with his sale."

"Liars will not inherit God's kingdom," Amelia said flatly. "I see that man with a woman's eyes. Your lies will not convince me of honorable motive."

Amelia came out onto the balcony and looked out over the tended gardens and then up to the dusky sky, where stars were just beginning to make their appearance. The crescent moon rose up over the line of trees in the distance, illuminating the treetops and casting long dark shadows.

"You certainly didn't waste time, did you? I had not been gone more than a few hours, and already you had disobeyed me."

Camille looked down to her slippered toes.

Amelia still looked over the property, her voice as soft as the air. "All of your life I have striven to ready you for your future. I have taught you what I know, and what I did not know, I had tutors teach you. I have been firm, yes. Perhaps even unyielding at times. But I have sought only to remove this rebellion from you. To prepare you for life with a husband and children of your own." Amelia turned and faced her daughter in the dim light. "What will all your longings bring you, but misery? What place have your flights into nature when your future lies indoors?

"Your days will be long and unbearable if you do not resign yourself, child. Your father's mother was just the same, and only hardships greeted her at every turn. Will you be like Elizabeth? Will you spend a lifetime wanting what you cannot have?"

"Grandmother wanted only a bit of happiness."

A flash of anger lit Amelia's eyes. "Elizabeth wanted everything. No woman ever gets all of what Elizabeth wanted. And when life denied Elizabeth what she yearned for, she took it anyway."

Camille remembered how her grandmother had turned sad and quiet whenever Camille had asked about the days of Elizabeth's youth. Camille never knew what had broken her grandmother's heart. She had known only that it had never healed. "What did she take?"

"What she had no rights to," Amelia countered, unwilling to reveal family shame and secrets to her daughter. If no one else would protect the family, Amelia would. "And I will not have my only daughter behaving the same way, with disregard for her station in life."

"I know my duties, Mother. You have taught them to me well."

"Not so well. You rode off with that Irishman the instant the opportunity presented." Amelia reentered the bedchamber, and Camille, knowing without being told what was expected, followed her. "And so, once again, you have forced my hand. Perhaps your hunger will teach you that I can take away what I give, and remind you that you exist because I allow it."

Amelia opened the door to the hallway and gestured for Edward to enter. "And I shall not shirk my God-given duties as a parent, that I should spare the rod and spoil the child."

Dismay washed down Camille's spine and churned her belly, and she wondered how bad it would be this time. Edward stood as he always did, impassive and emotionless, a thin black riding crop in his huge fist. He had been hired as a footman, but his blind obedience and silent nature had endeared him to Amelia for other tasks. Camille never saw him set himself to any duty, except for when Amelia called him to do her bidding. Camille hesitated, sick with dread. She wondered if she asked Amelia about a scripture or begged for a moment to pray, she could put off the suffering. But the waiting seemed worse, that sickening delay between knowing your punishment is coming and the actual whip on flesh. "Where would you have me?"

Amelia gestured to the bed. "The same as last time."

Camille removed her robe and laid it on the covers before wrapping her arms around one of the thick, carved posts of the large bed. The thin gown she wore would provide no protection, she thought, holding to the column. She forced herself to breathe and held to the feelings she had had earlier in the day, when riding with Patrick and taking him to the cottage had seemed worth risking this very thing. She felt her lips on his, the stubble of his beard against her chin. She felt that warm rise of heat in her blood, and the tingle that ran through her body at just the hope of his touch.

Nothing broke the hushed quiet save the measured ticking of the timepiece on her mantel, marking each passing second with its insensate serenity.

Finally, Amelia broke the silence. "Only in the middle, Edward. I do not want wounds showing above the cut of her gowns."

She signaled for him to begin.

The thin whip sliced through the air and cut through the thin cotton of her gown and into Camille's skin with a sickening sound. Edward's aim held true, and an old wound nearly healed instantly turned fresh with blood. Camille squeezed her eyes shut and clenched her teeth against the cry of pain that demanded release. Again the quirt fell against her back, this time with more force, so that Camille swallowed back a hot rush of bile. She would not cry out; she would not vomit. If only one triumph would be had, it would be that Amelia would not know the extent of her pain.

Camille held on and endured eight more lashes, each as violent, each leaving welts, bruises, and blood in its wake. But no sound came from her and no tears slid from her tightly closed eyes. She would weep later. For now, she inhaled her breath as the quirt was raised and released it as it struck her, silent and enduring lest Amelia think she had broken her.

Amelia raised her hand to stay the whip.

Edward stopped and wiped the blood from the quirt, his face as expressionless as when he had entered. Ten lashes or one hundred, it mattered not to him, as long as his mistress was pleased.

Amelia crossed and opened the door to the sitting

room, gesturing entrance to the small woman in the hall and dismissing Edward in one fluid motion. Brigid came well prepared for the duty at hand. She stood behind Camille and inspected the damage done to the ravaged skin of her narrow back.

"Lie on yer bed and we'll get ye cleaned up," she instructed.

Camille obeyed, moving slowly and carefully. Warm, sticky blood ran down to her legs, and blistering pain seared her back into one large, burning agony for which there would be no relief for days. This she already knew.

Clean rags soaked in witch hazel were laid in strips across the wounds by the efficient hands of Brigid, the maid who had taken care of her for as long as Camille could re-member. But not once could she recall kindness or a sem-blance of caring from the woman. Brigid simply completed her tasks as they were required, and she did so today, ad-ministering to Camille's needs as she was duty bound. Brigid washed Camille's skin, alternately sponging away blood and wiping on a balm of chamomile and oil.

Amelia surveyed Brigid's handiwork. She shook her head at the mess of old scars, fresh wounds, and bruises in varying stages from recent to healing that comprised her daughter's skin. "What needless stupidity. Bandage her and put her to bed."

After Amelia swept from the room, Camille buried her face in her pillow and allowed a whimper of pain to escape. But it didn't stem the tide. Instead, it opened the gates and Camille wept, pouring out her pain with hot, fast tears while her maid methodically blotted away her blood.

Camille slept fitfully, tormented by dreams of death. In her visions she fell from great heights or she was chased a great distance, always hunted, never safe.

When morning finally arrived, Camille felt grateful to be able to rise. She had been confined to lie only on her belly through the night, while the muslin bandages stuck to her wounds despite the oily salve. She groaned as she pushed herself from the bed, stiff from her inability to change position, shaking from the pain. Her back throbbed and her head ached, and a glimpse in the mirror confirmed her pale skin and red-rimmed, bloodshot eyes.

Even so, she had no regret.

Through the night when she had awoken, sweating from her nightmares and queasy from the pain, she thought about Patrick and the time she had spent with him. Camille had spent years trying to avoid being beaten and punished. But no amount of obedience had ever been enough. She remembered being tied to the leg of the dining room table, while her stomach clenched and hurt from lack of food while she had to endure the smells and sounds of her family eating. That had been because she had lacked submission. Countless times she had been laced into a backboard so tightly her arms had lost feeling, because her posture had been lacking. And the lashings. They were for the more serious offenses, and Amelia always found justification for her causes.

The excuse would always be found. Punishment would be delivered no matter how diligently she tried to obey. For that very reason, Camille did what she wanted without regard.

On legs that trembled, she made her way to her armoire. She reached into a basket and pulled out a long, red velvet ribbon.

The door opened. Camille quickly set the ribbon back in the basket. Brigid entered, scuffling into the room.

"Yer mum says yer to go into town, an' ye need to get dressed an' 'ave yer meal first."

Camille nodded wordlessly and selected a gown of ivory lawn, sprinkled with a print of tiny, budding pink roses. The gown had a high back and a generous cut through the waist, but even so, Camille dreaded the idea of laces. Brigid filled a bowl of water and Camille took her cloth, lathered it with lavender soap, and began to wash.

After she patted dry, Brigid changed her bandage dressing and helped her into her undergarments, mercifully lacing her loosely and then finally into her dress. Camille sat at her dressing table and held still while Brigid combed her hair and swept it into a simple twist, bound with pink ribbon and a carved, gold comb. She pushed aside the silent offer of cosmetics to hide the redness around her eyes. She'd sooner look haggard than wear the stark mask of Amelia.

She shrugged away her maid's hands and rose, making her way out of her rooms and down the long staircase and into the dining room. With difficulty she sat and ate creamed fruit and hot oats. She sipped chocolate though she preferred tea, knowing that Amelia thought chocolate to be the more fashionable choice. When Amelia swept into the room and raised a brow, Camille stood and smiled politely.

"Are you ready, child? The carriage awaits."

"I am."

Amelia turned, and Camille followed her outdoors. As the day before it, the sun beamed in a nearly cloudless sky. Camille turned her face to the sun briefly and felt its warmth before climbing into the shady confines of the conveyance after her mother. The carriage rumbled down the path and inside Camille clenched her teeth against the pain screaming in her back, as the jostling coach caused her stays to push and press against her fresh wounds.

She forced her mind away from the pain. Camille sat on Indue's back in the quiet spring sunlight. *My bounty is as boundless as the sea, my love as deep.* She could hear his voice, deep and confident. *It would be a tale of great love.* And she could see his eyes, just above the floor of her balcony as he watched her eat the food he had thought to bring her. *If you're inviting me, Camille, I will return.* He was kissing her, his hands in her hair and his body against her own. His tongue touched hers, lightly at first, until he had tilted her head back and taken what she gave. Camille felt the memory in her entire body, even in her toes. She shook with the anticipation of seeing him again, her belly turning over at the idea of kissing him again.

Amelia fanned herself and watched her daughter, who sat on the bench seat across from her, eyes closed with a dreamy smile. The duchess narrowed her eyes in speculation.

They approached the town of Southampton in good time. Dogs ran in front and behind the carriage before scurrying away after the shouts of the driver and footman. Outlying buildings stood in different stages of repair, most neatly whitewashed with pretty gardens. Shops selling dry goods, cured and fresh meats and fish, fabrics and textiles were flanked by vendors with carts full of produce and breads. Children ran freely, their mothers busy haggling for a better price while supporting babies on hips gone wide from childbearing. The playful shrieks of the children mingled with the shouts of storekeepers and the harried voices of wives on a tight budget. Flowers spilled from window boxes and lined the stores and houses in neat rows. Inns and alehouses abounded, the windows tightly closed and curtained as harlots practiced their trade. Sailors and merchants mingled with the crowd, easily distinguished by their dress and their rolling walk, fresh from the docks and in search of food and women.

Camille peeked out the window of the carriage, excited to be in town. "Will I be allowed to visit the bookstore?"

Amelia sighed, annoyed at the same question Camille asked every time they ventured into town together. "If you are obedient, I will give you a coin and allow you to purchase a book or two before we venture home."

Camille smiled. "Thank you."

Amelia nodded and began to gather her reticule and papers. "I have an appointment at the parish this afternoon. 'Tis a private matter, and so you may browse the bookstore while I attend to it."

Real excitement brewed in Camille at the thought of paging through books unattended.

"First I shall see the seamstress." Amelia alighted from the carriage and shook out her skirts, frowning at a small boy who ran by so closely he kicked dust on her hem. Camille smiled at the child, liking his brown eyes as round as moons and his pointed chin. He ran so freely, she thought with envy. Just ran and giggled, with dirty hands and wild hair. Camille sighed and fell into step behind her mother once again, following her into the shop run by Madame Colette.

The Frenchwoman moved at a fast pace, tiny hands flying while she shouted orders. Her hair was nearly as dark as Camille's, threaded with silver and cut straight across the bottom so it swung at her shoulders. Madame Colette had worn her hair in that style since Camille could remember, yet it always fascinated her. She liked the short, thick fringe that brushed just the tops of Colette's eyebrows and the way her hair flipped as she spoke, framing her animated face. Like many French women, Colette was more sensual than beautiful, possessing that certain quality that made it difficult to stop watching her.

But all activity in the shop ceased as the Duchess of Eton entered.

"Your Grace, I did not expect you today," Colette stammered in perfect English. The Duchess's disdain for people who lived in England yet could not speak the King's English was legendary. None dared speak to her in a foreign language.

"My trip to London was delayed, and so I have decided to see to a few details. I am in need of lingerie, some dressing gowns, and also some shifts. My daughter will also need the same."

Madame Colette nodded and began to pull out bolts of fabric, silks and sheer, soft cottons. Amelia chose from them decisively, adding lace and ribbons, ordering embroidery and beading. She rapped out her orders as Colette wrote them down.

"Our sizes are the same as our last fitting. I need them by the month's end."

Colette didn't argue or protest that the length of time was inadequate. She knew from experience the duchess would pay handsomely enough that all other orders could be placed on hold. She observed with sharp eyes as the daughter of the duchess fell back into step as they left the shop, and mused for just a moment about the sad eyes of the girl, and how she always watched her with such interest, so different from her own daughter. Then she clapped her tiny hands together and began to shout again, delivering a stream of French that commanded her staff to drop what they were doing.

Amelia paraded down the street once again, stopping at several more stores along the way. They shopped for footwear and made a stop in a coffeehouse, where Amelia sat and drank chocolate while they watched the townspeople milling outside the windows. Camille followed her silently into the Goodrow Inn and stood by the doors as she had been told, while her mother had a whispered conversation with the proprietor. Amelia pressed a gold coin into the innkeeper's hand, and then they left once again, back into the throng of people on the street. They walked and Camille followed, keeping her eyes on her mother's skirts and ignoring the people who stared at her. She heard the whispers, but didn't appear to hear what had been said, that the duchess's daughter had fine clothing and pretty hair, but that her disposition was sour. Camille could never have explained to them that she had not been permitted to look at or speak to the people whose station in life was beneath hers. Even though she envied their simplicity.

Finally Amelia stopped in front of the bookstore. "You may browse in here while I visit the parish. Do not leave this store. I will return very shortly." Amelia pressed her hand on Camille's back to get her full attention. "Do not do anything foolish."

Camille accepted a coin from her mother and entered the store with a smile. A bell rang as the door opened, and then rang again as the door closed. A shopkeeper came to the front, carrying a stack of books. He recognized Camille immediately. "My lady, welcome. Please look at whatever you wish."

Camille nodded her thanks and went to the back of the store, where volumes of Homer gathered dust beside the works of Shakespeare. She ran a hand across the leather, picked up a book, and opened it to a random page, seizing the moment to inhale the musty scent of paper and ink. She began to read, lost in the magic of words on a page. So lost, she didn't hear the bell ring or the footsteps behind her.

"Now what are you reading?"

Camille dropped the book again, spun around to the familiar voice. "You cannot be here."

He grinned, slow and sure. "I am here. Haven't we done this before?" Patrick bent and picked up the book, closed it and looked at the title. "Shakespeare again?"

Camille grabbed his hand and led him further back into the store, where stacks of books blocked them from the view of the window to the street. Patrick ran a finger over her frown. "I saw your mother leave. I waited until she was gone from sight before I followed you in."

"You've been following me?"

"I have."

"Since when?"

"Since you left the dressmaker's."

"But how did you know I was in town?"

He reached out and took her hand, playing with her fingers for a minute before kissing the tips. "The carriage."

"Oh," she whispered, unable to say anything else as his tiny kisses sent warm waves of delight through her blood.

"You don't look around."

"What?"

"When you walk behind your mother. You don't look at what's around you."

"'Tis easier that way. Then I don't have to see everyone glaring at me."

"Perhaps they stare because you're beautiful."

"No. I hear what they say."

"That you are lofty and snobbish, an ice princess, and that you are enthralled with your own beauty?"

Camille's cheeks turned pink and she looked at the floor. "You've been listening under the eaves of those who despise me."

"I've been asking around town about you."

Camille shrugged a little and then wiped her dry cheek, as if at the memory of tears shed for that very reason. "I am not well liked."

"That is only what some of them say," he said quietly, still holding her fingers. "Others say you are quiet and bright. Still others say you are gentle and kind, and all agree living with your mother would be hell come to earth."

Camille looked up to him, looking in his eyes and seeing sympathy and understanding. And that alone was enough to make her lips start to tremble, her heart start the pounding that made her fingers shake. "Has your curiosity been satisfied?"

"Not even close. I want to know everything about you."

She could scarcely breathe. "Just ask. I will tell you anything."

"What is your favorite color?"

"Pink. Palest pink, like the roses at my cottage." Camille glanced around and hoped the storekeeper would not overhear, but saw he was in the front of the shop and busy unpacking a carton of new books. "My turn for a question. How old were you when you first kissed a woman?"

"Fifteen. My turn. How old were you when you first kissed a man?"

"Yesterday. What is your favorite food?"

"Biscuits and gravy. When were you born?"

"Twenty-fifth, April. You?"

"Twenty-ninth, October. Did you like my kisses?"

"Very much. How old were you when your mother passed away?"

"Eight. What is the most precious thing you own?"

"A letter my grandmother wrote me before she died. Same question to you."

"This bracelet." Patrick held up his wrist and showed her a bracelet of finely wrought gold set with glowing amber gems. "It was my grandda's. My da gave it to me after my grandda died. If you could go anywhere in the world, where would you go?"

"I don't know enough of the world to answer that, except to say I would go where I would be free. As free as a woman can be. Did you like my kisses?"

"More than biscuits and gravy. More than calm seas and clear skies. More than anything I can think of." He brushed his thumb over her inner wrist where her pulse throbbed. "Aside from riding Indue, being in your cottage or reading, what is your favorite thing to do?"

"Walking on the beach and watching the waves roll in. I imagine the rest of the world out beyond the water, living lives, loving, fighting, having babies, and dying. What are you most afraid of?"

Patrick bent down so his forehead rested on hers, his breath soft and warm on her mouth. "Never seeing you again."

Then he kissed her, gently. Nothing more than his lips brushing hers, but enough to drench her body with heavy, hot sensation. Just as quickly he stopped and straightened. "I'll come to your balcony tonight and hope to see a ribbon."

And he walked away, leaving her there to stare after him as he thanked the shopkeeper and left with the jangle of the bell.

* * *

Camille had completely composed herself and picked out two new books by the time Amelia arrived back to fetch her.

"Did all go well at the parish?"

"Indeed. I will be sending old clothing later this week, so see to it your wardrobe is cleaned out of anything unfashionable or worn."

"I will."

Amelia turned and left the shop. Camille fell into step behind her once again, this time looking around at the faces of the people around her. To her surprise she saw that some did smile shyly and nod in a friendly way. Camille smiled in return.

The spring air touched Camille's skin and wove its way inside her, around her heart and through her body like a melody. A secret smile played across her lips, a memory of a kiss, brief but sweet and lingering. Her fingers shook again and she tightened her hold of her books as she walked, looking up to the clear sky that seemed as limitless as her future plans to see Patrick again, and the intoxicating knowledge that he wanted to see her just as much.

Their footman saw the approach of his mistresses and leaped to open the door of the carriage. Before Amelia and Camille could board, a saucy voice halted them.

"Clement day, isn't it?"

Camille turned to look into the pretty face of Veronica, the daughter of Madame Colette. Her warm brown eyes were flecked with amber lights and her lush red mouth always looked like it had just been kissed. She wore her hair the way her mother did, unusual and striking with a fringe of dark brown above her eyes and the cropped flip brushing her shoulders.

"'Tis a beautiful afternoon, Veronica. How pleasant to see you again." Camille now stood alone as Amelia climbed into the carriage and waited, flicking her fan impatiently. But Camille lingered, wanting to get to know this enigmatic young woman whose age was the same as hers, the way she had always longed for a friend her age. Yet it seemed so unlikely that any commonality could be found with the daughter of a seamstress, who walked the streets freely and seemed so confident and at ease. And such a friendship would not be tolerated by her mother, Camille knew for certain.

Veronica's exquisite mouth curved upward. "You look well, my lady, as always."

"And you are as lovely as ever, also."

Veronica smoothed her tiny hands over a gown of crimson satin, cut in the latest French fashion. "My mother is a magician with needle and thread."

"It suits you in color and style." And it did, hugging Veronica's curvy shape and accentuating her petite charm.

Veronica lifted her shoulder in an appealing French shrug, for a second looking just like her mother. "I am hopelessly enamoured, my lady. I dress to dazzle a very handsome man."

"Are there to be vows and church bells in the future?"

"If only I can catch his heart, my lady."

Amelia tapped the roof of the carriage with her fan and made no effort to hide the rude tone in her voice. "Camille, bid farewell."

"I must say adieu, Veronica. I hope to see you again."

Veronica laughed and gestured to the Goodrow Inn. "You will know where to find me, my lady."

Camille glanced that way and saw the stone inn in the distance. "Your man stays there?"

"Camille," Amelia said again, the warning thick in her tone.

Camille didn't hesitate. She boarded the carriage and raised her hand to wave to Veronica, who returned the wave and walked away, her red skirt twitching and her short, dark hair swinging.

As they rode home Camille ignored the pain in her back, which seemed to worsen as she sat still. Visions of a friendship with Veronica flashed through her mind, as she pictured drinking tea with her while they giggled about the men they fancied and the kisses they stole. They would talk about everything and anything, while Madame Colette rolled her eyes at the way the girls could talk for hours. Veronica would tell her about her man from the inn, while Camille would tell her about Patrick, and they would confide their feelings and their deepest fears and dreams. Such companionship, Camille mused, like a sister. She sighed deeply, letting the image soften the ragged agony that comprised her real life.

When she arrived home Camille practiced the clavichord while her mother listened and then ate some food while her mother complained about the lack of any real entertainment in town. Then she recited scripture to her mother while Amelia did needlepoint, until she finally was excused to lie down in her rooms.

But Camille didn't lie down. She sat on her bed and held the long velvet ribbon, as crimson as Veronica's gown. Twisting and smoothing it, she waited while the clock on the mantel ticked away the seconds as they bled into minutes and then hours, while the sun traced its path across the sky.

CHAPTER 5

Patrick stood in the woods that flanked the back of the mansion, scarcely able to make out Camille's balcony in the darkness. He wore simple black breeches, a black shirt, and black leather boots that hugged his calves, ending just below his knees. He had waited there under the trees, the night air sighing around him in the hushed dimness, while waiting for the manor to fall asleep. Life and death waged subtle warfare in the copse, the air thick with the moist, ponderous scents of decay and new growth. Clouds had rolled in toward dusk, obscuring the moon and promising rain. With a seafarer's skill, Patrick lifted his head and sniffed the air. No rain yet, he thought. Not for hours.

He saw the light in Camille's room grow brighter, as if she approached the windows with a candle. And then she appeared, through the parted drapes and out into the night, stooping low to hang a ribbon from the balustrade. He bent down, picked up a black canvas satchel, and began to move, silently, treading over the fragrant moss, damp with evening's dew, and through the snarled undergrowth that spread from bushes to vines to rotting logs. Once out of the thicket, he prowled through the manicured lawns. He moved quickly, keeping quiet and reaching Camille's balcony in less than a minute. The orderly roses slumbered around him: some bloomed now, betraying their presence with heavy, redolent scents. Patrick leaped and grasped the base of the balcony, pulling himself up until he could reach his leg out and get a foothold. He held to the balustrade and inched his way up, until he could swing his body over the rail. Silent footsteps took him to the open French doors and through the sundered drapes.

Camille sat on her bed, waiting for him, that now-familiar tremble taking her lips. "You look like a pirate," she whispered.

"You look like an angel," he said quietly, setting down his bag. He looked around the opulent, candlelit room. Tapestries and a plush Persian rug warmed the space, and tall, carved wood furniture, dark and gleaming, spoke of tradition and heritage. He went to the bed and ran a finger over the soft silk of her buttery yellow coverlet. "Very nice."

She shrugged. "My mother chose it."

Her hair hung unbound to her waist again, smooth and wavy from a recent combing. He reached out and fingered a loose curl. "You have beautiful hair."

She smiled uncertainly, suddenly extremely aware that she sat on her bed while he stood over her, a man in her rooms while her family slept. The impact of the many dangers dawned on her all at once. She shifted her legs over the side of the bed and rose, instantly sorry she had remained in her dressing gown and robe as Brigid had left her after her bath and toilette. Her back began to burn again, itching and throbbing.

Patrick held his breath at the sight of her. Without stays and layers of clothing, she looked even longer and thinner, more delicate. But more than that, the sight of her in her nightclothes, with the fragrant scents of her bath heavy in her room and on her skin, was so intimate, so very trusting. It touched him deeply. "I brought you something."

She turned around, green eyes wide and curious. "You did?"

He nodded, pleased with her excitement. He reached

into his bag and pulled out a long rectangular wooden box. It was heavily carved, hinged on one side, clasped on the other. "Here, open it." He held the box out to her.

Camille accepted it and took it to her small table, opened it, and gasped with delight. "A chessboard."

"I bought it years ago in the Caribbean. 'Tis made of sandalwood, which gives it that scent, and the pieces are of carved marble, though they have been rubbing against each other in the bag for so many years, much of their detail is lost." Patrick opened a velvet sack and spilled out black and white marble chessmen.

Camille seated herself at the table and began setting up the board. "Where is the Caribbean?"

"South of the New World. 'Tis beautiful there, like paradise. White sand and clear, turquoise water. Dolphins chase my ship and the birds are bright, the people generous and relaxed, and there are trees, branchless but for a crown of leafy palms on their tops."

Camille tried to envision such a place, so foreign and exotic. "Do they speak English?"

"Most do, aye. In fact, 'tis likely where I'll settle when my father no longer needs me."

"Why there, when you could go anywhere in the world?"

Patrick moved his pawn. "'Tis the only place I never want to leave when I'm docked there. And aside from that, there is much need for commerce. I could finally settle down but still ply my trade."

Camille mirrored his move, sliding her pawn into place. "You want to settle, then?"

Patrick slid his pawn up a space. "Of course. I want a home and a family."

"You will not stay in England with your father?"

"My father has determined he wants land in England. That doesn't mean he'll stay here. I have the idea that once he sees he cannot buy what he's looking for, he'll move on."

"What is he trying to buy?"

Patrick moved his knight. "What you have."

"I have nothing."

"Titles, land, credibility."

"Nonsense." Camille said flatly, moving her bishop. "All of that is meaningless."

"Not to those who have never had it. He has tried all his life to live up to everything his own father wasn't. My grandfather, Rogan, was a pirate of the worst kind. He raped and murdered his way across the ocean, and my father hated him for the life he was forced to live. When my father finally could, he took a ship and some gold and swore he'd never steal again. He's now so scrupulously honest, he's called the Merchant Prince in every port, though many have taken to calling him the Merchant Priest."

A dimple flirted with the corner of Camille's mouth as she grinned up to him, moving her bishop while she commented, "As you are the son of the Merchant Prince, I shall have to remember to bow and scrape in your presence. Your title far outweighs my own."

Patrick laughed. "Oh? And as the daughter of a duke, what does that exactly make you?"

Amusement faded from Camille's eyes as her back ached with the truth of exactly what she was. "Chattel."

Patrick let go of his knight and looked at her, her face alternately shaded and burnished by candlelight. Stared into those extraordinary eyes that communicated wordlessly to him in a way he couldn't understand.

Camille blinked back useless tears and gestured to the board. "Your move."

"Maybe I don't want to play anymore." He never broke the hold of her eyes.

"Then what?"

"Tell me."

"I cannot."

"You will. Not because I tell you to, but because you need to."

Camille pulled her gaze away from his, staring at the chessboard at pieces that showed she was bound to lose the game. "There is much you do not know about me, and just as much I do not know about you. That makes us . . ." her voice dwindled off as she searched for the words that evaded her.

"Fascinating."

"No, Patrick. Strangers."

"Wrong." His voice was gentle but firm. "You would never invite a strange man to your rooms at night."

"You do not want to know."

"Don't decide for me."

Her head snapped up, and her voice grew hard. "Don't pity me."

His eyes flashed, his temper beginning to simmer. "I pity only the weak."

And her defenses crumbled as quickly as they had arisen. "Very well."

She stood and unbelted her robe, letting it fall to the floor. She turned her back to him and unlaced the front of her gown to her belly, lifting the bottom of the neckline up until it was under her chin, so the wide-open neck hung down her back. She lifted her hair to expose her skin, wincing with humiliation at the sound of rushing breath hissing through his teeth.

Patrick stood slowly on unsteady legs, astonished at the criss-cross of silver scars, raised and puckered. Fresh wounds sliced through the old, bright red welts and dark red scabs. Bruises mottled her skin, too, purple, green, and yellow, surrounding the weeping cuts of a recent lashing. His stomach churned and he reached out, touching her shoulder so lightly she scarcely felt it, turning her to face him.

Tears as silver as her scars slid down her cheeks. Patrick cupped her face in his hands, tilting it up to his. He bent and kissed away the salty drops, wishing that kisses were enough to take her pain. His mouth moved to hers and he touched it lightly, brushing against the trembling lips that haunted his mind since he had first seen them. And even before that, though he knew not how.

Camille wrapped her arms around his neck, not caring that her gown hung open or that he had seen her greatest shame. It seemed he saw inside her, past her shell and into her heart, where nothing external mattered. Even scars. So she opened to him completely, without reserve, giving him her mouth and her body to do as he wished, believing she wanted what he desired, and that her trust would be honored.

He pulled away from the kiss, still holding her close, his voice tight with emotion. "You don't deserve that treatment."

And because she didn't know what to say in response, because she really did deserve a punishment if she had known the consequence when she committed the crime, she said nothing.

Patrick felt her stiffen against his words and he figured she didn't believe him. "Parents are supposed to protect their children."

"If beating me prevents me from sinning, that is a form of protection, no?"

"Twisted logic." His voice sounded flat and unequivocal. "Real obedience stems from respect, not fear."

"Do you respect God for His ability to take your life, or fear Him that He will judge you and do so?"

"Amelia is not God. Her ways are self-serving and vermiculated."

Camille yawned and closed her eyes, soothed by his warmth. "But in this house, she is god. She rules my life, watches me, owns me. She can destroy me."

"You have not let her, thus far."

"She will take as much as I allow. I keep some things for myself."

"Your reading and your cottage?"

"And now you." She sighed and leaned her head against the curve of his shoulder, pleased by the warm closeness of his body, the feel of his strength, the clean scent of him. She couldn't find it within herself to care that she sinned by having him there, that the feelings he provoked in her were lustful and wrong. "I find peace with you, Patrick."

He didn't respond to that, afraid he would say too much, things that it was too soon to say. "You are tired."

"I didn't sleep well last night."

"Then I will leave so you can rest."

"No. I would rather deny sleep than have you leave."

"Then I will stay, and you will rest anyway."

Patrick extinguished the candles and led her to the bed. He sat on the side of the bed, holding the covers for her to slip under. She did so, and then he slid down and he held her close, careful not to touch her back. "Sleep and I will leave before dawn."

"Kiss me goodbye now, then, in case I don't wake when you leave."

Desire curled in his belly again, tight and hot, as her warm body pressed against his own. Curves against angles and hard pressed against soft. She smelled like a garden of lavender and she felt like silk. "I can't kiss you in this bed, else it will become a marriage bed."

"I can imagine worse fates."

"Than marriage to me or what follows?"

"Either, though I spoke of intercourse."

Patrick raised his brows, taken aback by her frank manner. "How is it you know of what passes between a man and a woman, and that you speak of it so bluntly?"

"Does that offend you?"

"No. But 'tis unusual, to say the least."

"I live on a horse farm, Patrick. I understand how foals are made. I assume it is not so different for human animals."

He chuckled under his breath. "'Tis different enough, but the idea is the same. I'm surprised you're not afraid, after seeing animals mate. It can be violent to watch."

"I'm more afraid of endless childbearing than of sex itself."

"Well, that can be prevented."

Camille raised herself up on her elbows to look at him. "Truly?"

"Truly. There are things that can be done."

"What things?"

Patrick could hardly believe he felt himself blushing. "Things that would be most inappropriate for a maiden to hear."

Camille snorted, a most unladylike sound. "Nonsense. 'Tis my body. Who else has more of a right to hear of it?"

He laughed again and pulled her back into the crook of his arm. "Just as the man completes the act, there is an emission. If the emission doesn't happen inside the woman's body, 'tis much less likely she would conceive."

"Oh." Camille mulled over this information, too intrigued over the sudden feeling of control for her future to be bothered with embarrassment. Then a thought dawned on her. "But the man would have to be willing."

"Aye."

"Does that mean less pleasure for the man?"

"Aye, though there are also things that can be done."

"What things?"

He blushed again, but grinned despite himself. "Things I am not discussing, no matter how persuasive your argument."

Camille settled against him and yawned. His body was hard and warm, and she thought it the most comfortable sensation in the world, to be held by him in her bed. All else seemed a great journey away, beatings and control and the danger she risked in having him with her, all countless miles from her. She did not want him to go. "You will not sleep past dawn?"

"I often take the night shifts, so keeping awake isn't a trouble for me. I can sleep in the morning at the inn. Your mother won't check on you, will she? I don't want to put you in danger."

"I'm always the safest after a lashing. She thinks it will make me more obedient for a time."

"Do they?"

"They used to, when I was small. But since it is inescapable, I began to do as I wished."

"So sad, Camille."

"I am not sad. Not with you."

He kissed the top of her head and rubbed his cheek against her hair. "I want to see you again."

"I will hang the ribbon again tomorrow night, if you wish."

"I wish."

She yawned again. "I wish, too."

"What do you wish for?"

"I wish this night would last longer than the hours left."

"We will have another night, tomorrow."

"But eventually the nights will run out. You will complete your business and leave and I will marry a man of my mother's choosing. I will never see you again."

Patrick didn't tell her he had already decided against the land Eric wanted to sell him, and that the only reason he remained in Southampton was for her. "For once, Camille, you do not know what the future holds."

Camille sighed and didn't argue. She knew the future as she knew her past. Inevitable and inexorable. She felt even more exhausted. "Good night, Patrick."

"Sleep well, Camille."

He held his cheek against her hair, inhaling her scented warmth until he felt her body relax and her breathing grow soft and regular. He smoothed the hair back from her face and studied her delicate features in the dimness. He pressed another kiss to her forehead, thinking of the pain she had suffered and endured.

Camille would not know he had never lain with a woman like this, holding her tenderly. Patrick had found relief with women but nothing more. His interludes usually left him with a feeling of melancholy that made him question his need for the release in the first place.

But not so with Camille. Patrick found satisfaction in her

presence alone. The simple act of holding her filled a place in him he didn't know he had. He understood that she needed him, but he hadn't realized that he needed her, too.

Amelia swept into Camille's rooms and pulled back the window drapes so the light of late morning assaulted the bed. Camille sat up in a rush, looking to her side and then to the table where she had played chess before Patrick had climbed into her bed and held her while she slept.

But he was gone, and her mother stood over her, looking at her expectantly. "I slept poorly. Whilst I lay in my bed, I decided to plan a dinner party. We shall invite a few of our closest peers, and I will include Bret Kimball, the son of the tenth duke of Somerset."

Camille rubbed her eyes and glanced again around her room, looking for any signs that would tell of her nightly visitor. But Patrick had been thorough and careful. No traces of his visit remained. "A dinner party sounds lovely, Mother."

"You will wear your new gown, the one with silver embroidery. I will see you look your most splendid."

"I will attempt to please you."

"'Tis not myself I seek to please, but your future husband." Amelia let the last word hang like some new and frivolous adornment to the room, while she gauged Camille's reaction. "Lord Kimball is most anxious to set eyes on you, as I have spoken of your beauty to him on numerous occasions."

When Camille said nothing while she stared at her with those eyes so like Kenley's, Amelia felt annoyance grow apace with her desire to spark a lively response. She egged her daughter further, throwing open the doors to the armoire and pulling out a gown, knowing how Camille hated it when she chose her clothes. "I have need to visit London as well. I cannot languish here in the country for too long, else the lazy days and endless nights wear away

at my mind. As a matter of course, given your recent rebellion, you will be accompanying me to the city."

Still Camille remained silent, rising from her bed and
washing before obediently dressing in the gown of her
mother's choosing. Amelia felt her oppressive discontent
increase further, fed by boredom and the remembrance
of the sounds emitted from Kenley's rooms late in the
night, quiet moans and muted giggles. "You do not ignore
me, child."

Camille recognized the manic note in her mother's tone
and sought to soften it with meekness. "I will do as you
wish. I shall have Brigid pack my trunks."

But Amelia felt no satisfaction for her vitriolic mood in
her daughter's bland submission. It hid sedition and truculence, just like Elizabeth's defiant nature. A pretty face
and guileless eyes shrouding mutinous thoughts and dev-
ilish, devious plans to disobey. Like the Pharisees Jesus
spoke about, she thought, whitewashed tombs concealing
rotting decay. "Finish dressing and come to eat. You will help
me plan the dinner party and then you will practice the clavichord. I will have you play for our visitors, that your betrothed can see his future wife is graceful and musical.
You will then read a sonnet for our guests, that Lord Kimball can see you are literate. There will be dancing, and you
will show all the steps you know. You will be gracious and
humble, and I demand you keep your own thoughts to yourself. I enjoin you from speaking unless you are spoken to."

But if Amelia's demands to prance her in front of their
guests like a marionette on strings pricked Camille's
pride, no response came to give reason for a punishment
or stern reprimand. She only lowered her head in what
looked like proper yielding.

"As you wish, Mother."

The whispered compliance drove Amelia to the end of
her patience and she stormed from the rooms, slamming
the door behind her.

Camille paced for a while around her rooms, wavering

in her own feelings. One moment she felt elated with the tender memory of being held and understood. Her skin tingled, hot and curious, when she thought of him on her bed stretched out beside her, his voice tight and husky when he said he couldn't kiss her. Then like a cloud, bleak despondency returned to shroud over her happiness with the latest information her mother had dispensed. Finally she stopped pacing and stood in front of her open armoire. Camille pulled her long red ribbon from the basket and held it to her heart, wondering how it was possible to feel simultaneously liberated and imprisoned.

CHAPTER 6

Spring passed into summer like the wind through the trees. Camille spent her days in Amelia's company, planning for a dinner party where she would meet her future husband. She penned invitations and sent them by courier. She discussed menu selections with Amelia, made lists, and spoke about them with Flanna. She saw to fittings on her newest gown and decided on a hairstyle. The clavichord rang out with her ministrations as she bent to the keys with a dedication for which Amelia commended her. The ballroom was aired and cleaned under Camille's direction, as were the guest rooms. Hundreds of candles were ordered so the evening would be festively lit, and champagne was delivered for the betrothal announcement. Amelia had decided to declare the news to their closest friends for the first time in Beauport, and then they would do so again for new guests in London. So Camille endured Brigid's unwanted assistance, as her skin was massaged with oils so that her future husband would enjoy the touch of her. Her hair was brushed and washed and then brushed again, so the sheen would be pleasing to him. And Camille did all of this under Amelia's nose, demonstrating again and again that she had been adequately taught how to run a household and was prepared to be a bride.

But she spent her nights wrapped in Patrick's arms, whispering with him about everything that mattered and much that didn't. Hopes, dreams, and idle musings. Patrick came to her nightly, a routine that felt as natural to them as breathing. She began to know him, his every detail, from the smoky tone in his voice when he wanted to kiss her to the steady thud of his heart when conversation dropped off and she lay with her head on his chest. They played chess and they discussed books and philosophy. They sat out on the balcony and looked at the stars under the crescent of the moon while Patrick showed her the constellations and explained how he could find his way around the world by what was in the sky. Always, when Camille would grow sleepy, Patrick would lead her to the bed and kiss her until they grew hot, and then hold her and tell her a story while he waited for their blood to cool, until finally she drifted to her dreams.

It was a night like this when Patrick smoothed her hair away from her face and pressed tiny, nibbling kisses on her mouth. Midnight had slipped by, and somewhere in the lost hours of morning the kisses turned deeper, urgent, more persuasive. He pressed his body against hers in the bed and Camille could feel his need, the hot, hard pressure of him against her.

And she yielded to him and to his craving, opening like a flower to anything he wanted to take. And she wanted to give to him, too, so she ran her hands over him, through his hair, pulling him even closer to him, wanting him to feel the strength of her own desires building under her skin.

"Will you show me?" she asked against his mouth, breathless.

He knew exactly what she meant, could feel it in the way she moved against him. "I won't take your virginity."

"I want you to."

"No. It would be wrong."

"I want to know what it feels like with someone who cares for me. I want you to show me what it is when it means something, besides mating for heirs and the release of a husband who wants variety from his mistresses."

"Camille . . ." his voice trailed off as she pressed kisses against his neck and up around his ear, the way he had done to her. His whole body throbbed with pounding desire and when her tongue flicked over his skin, he nearly gave in to her request. "Stop."

Her breath felt hot against his ear. "Please."

"I can't."

"Please don't reject me."

He rolled on top of her, kissing her long slim neck where throaty moans vibrated against his lips. He let his hands travel over her, skimming her curves and then finally cupping her face where he held her still so he could look at her in the dim light of the single candle. "I love you."

Soft, velvet warmth slid through her, as much from the quietly pledged words as the way he spoke them, sincerely and openly as if he had shown her his heart. "I love you, Patrick."

"Then marry me."

She tried to pull back. "You know I cannot."

"Run away with me, Camille. I will take you anywhere in the world."

"You would hate me after a time."

"I could never. 'Tis an impossibility."

She was trying to disentangle herself, but he wouldn't let go of her. "I would become the pathetic girl whose parents didn't love her, whom you saved due to some outdated chivalry. What would become of us after you tired of the rescue and had to live with my reality?"

He kissed her hard on the mouth, cutting off her words, tongue on tongue in a kiss as ancient as the passions that drove it. When Patrick pulled back, he looked at her. "Your reality is with me. I don't want to save you; I want to marry you. I want to make love with you on rainy afternoons. I want to grow old with you and have a granddaughter with your eyes and hair. But most of all, I want to spend the rest of my life helping you believe that you are worth all of it, and more. That you deserve better than I can give you, even when I give you my best."

Camille let out her breath and closed her eyes. "I am at a loss."

"Say yes."

"How can this be real?"

"'Tis a gift, you see."

She opened her eyes and stared at him, saw the smile that played at the corners of his lips, like a challenge. "Like the peasant girl."

"Aye. Remember, a gift is as much about the accepting as the giving. How much will you risk for me, Camille?"

Camille remembered the story, exactly as it had been told and the way she had felt after the hearing, of the loss of a family that could never be. She pictured herself as Patrick's wife, the mother to children born because they were wanted, not because of titles and bloodlines. She saw a home filled with simple things and abundance of everything that mattered, love and nurturing, trust and respect. She could see it all, down to the grin on Patrick's face while their son chased the ocean waves. She could smell the scent of a fine meal and hear the laughter, like music. It was so real, almost like a memory of a day gone by and savored. She took the first and most frightening step toward it all, a running leap into the unknowable.

"I will marry you."

That wild grin looked like the one in her mental picture, slow and untamed in the flickering candlelight. "Tell me a story, Camille."

"I know only the stories you tell me, Patrick."

"Tell me a story from your heart. A secret story you can tell no one but me."

She smiled into his eyes. "A woman's heart has many secrets. Which shall I reveal to you?"

"Tell me of a woman whose family betrayed her with their lack of love, and how she found it anyway with an unsuitable man, a commoner. Tell me how they ran away together and made their own life."

And so Camille settled in the crook of his arm and told him the story of the Irishman. He was a thief, really, who stole the heart of the sad English girl, and then stole her from her family before they could wed her into a loveless marriage. Her voice caught in her throat as she described the girl as sad no longer. She paused after they agreed to marry. "They have no clergy, Patrick."

"They marry each other in the sight of God, under the moon and in front of the ocean."

"You are a desperate romantic."

"I am an Irish sailor, Camille."

She acknowledged that as adequate explanation with a smile and a nod. "Very well. So they run off and marry in front of the ocean, pledging themselves to each other for eternity. They steal away to her cottage, where he makes her his wife in truth. And then?"

"He sends for his ship and they sail away. To a new land, where she runs freely."

"Freely," Camille repeated, taken with the thought of it.

"Does the story please you, Camille?"

"It does," she said softly, still dreaming. "But for one thing."

"Hmm?" He ran a hand over her shoulder and down her arm, playing with her fingers and picturing the ring he would have made for her.

"She wants to have his child."

"So soon?"

"Yes. She wants a baby with his eyes, like the color of the ocean before a storm."

"So she shall have it. He has always wanted babies."

Camille cocked an eyebrow. "She said baby. Not babies."

He laughed and pulled her closer. "One to start, and they will have no more than she desires. Lord willing."

"When will the story come true?"

"I will send for my ship tomorrow, but it will likely take

a fortnight to arrive. I will also send word to my father and tell him of my plans."

She hesitated, and her voice grew small and quiet. "Will he approve of me, do you think?"

"Aye, my insecure bride. He will adore you as I do, and will without a doubt approve of your eagerness to provide him with a grandchild."

"Will you marry me tomorrow, then?"

"Aye, love. I will marry you tomorrow. Now sleep and I will go."

Camille held on to Patrick's arm. "My mother says she is taking me to London after the dinner announcement and our guests depart. The dinner party is only a week away. What if the ship doesn't arrive before then?"

"How long do your guests linger?"

"Sometimes only a day or two, but often four to six days."

"It will be close, but we will figure something out. I will not let you slip away from me, Camille."

"What if I am taken from you?"

"I would find you."

"You say that so assuredly."

"I am certain of only a few things in this life, but I know you are mine in a way that is essential. I would always return to you, like the tide to the shore."

She kissed him with all her feeling, melting away her vulnerability with the heat of his mouth. Hearts exposed and feelings laid bare, they pressed their bodies to each other, anxious to be joined. And when he broke the kiss and whispered his love in her ear, Camille closed her eyes against the ecstasy of being cherished and wanted. He climbed from her bed and left her room without a sound, pausing only for a second in the doorway before disappearing behind her drapes to leave her alone in the dark with only promises, hopes, and dreams to sustain her through the next day.

* * *

Patrick awoke with a start, aware that someone had entered his rooms in the inn. He rolled to his side and grabbed a dagger, sitting up and listening, his ears tuned to the intruding presence. A creak underfoot, the methodical fall of footsteps, and the distinct sound of rustling skirts had Patrick lowering his dagger, covering his nudity.

Veronica pushed open the bedchamber door and stood in the archway, looking striking in a gown of sapphire silk. The cut flattered her narrow waist and hugged her high, full breasts. She stood and stared at him in his bed, her face poised but her eyes roving the length of him, from bare chest to covered loins. "You do not leave your rooms in the daytime."

Patrick set his dagger back on the small bedside table. "You have been monitoring my comings and goings, have you?"

"Where do you go every night?"

His question answered, he ran a hand through his hair and sighed. "I visit a friend."

"A woman?"

He recognized the feline pitch and saw the glitter of jealousy. "Veronica, I am not beholden to you."

"Are you this calloused to all the women you take to your bed?"

"That was weeks ago, and you said you understood the nature of our entanglement."

Veronica moved closer to the bed, her dark eyes edged with amber lights of anger and interest. "Do you think so little of me?"

"You were not a virgin in my bed, Veronica."

"I am not a whore, either. I am selective and thought you a different kind of man."

Patrick recalled the lust that had hammered in his body, demanding release the night he had arrived in Southampton. He had been at sea for months, returning from a particularly rough voyage where the Atlantic had battered his ship and his endurance. The inn had been comfortable, the ale cool, Veronica so pretty. And willing. "I made you no promises."

"No?" Veronica began to pace the length of floor in front of his bed, pausing every so often to toss her hair back with the flick of her tiny hand. "You smile at me, talk to me for hours. You take me to your bed and say such elegant words, breathe in my ears while you touch my body. And I gave you everything, didn't I? Held nothing back, but you withdrew. You withdrew your body and your attentions."

Regret and guilt mingled, but Patrick could undo nothing that had been done. "I didn't intend to hurt you."

She stopped and looked at him, her eyes glossy and magnified by tears. "I am beyond hurt. I am humiliated."

"No. You were wonderful and sweet."

"Was I? Yet you could not see me leave quickly enough. You meet with the son of the duke and then I never see you again, but for an impassive hello on the street. Like I am no one to you! Like I am nothing more than a wench who once served you ale!" Her voice dropped, became almost pleading. "I have never felt for a man what I felt for you. I never touched a man the way I touched you."

He shifted uncomfortably in the bed where he had taken her with passion and need. She had been generous with her body, knowing how to tease a man to the brink before bringing him release. But there had been no real connection. A meeting of bodies, but not of minds. "What can I do or say? What we did is irreversible. Can I apologize? Will that be enough?"

But no apologies would soften the stab to her pride, that he had either found another woman, or worse, found her lacking. So Veronica whirled on her heel and left the room, slamming the door.

Camille awoke and dressed with Brigid's help. Amelia entered as Brigid finished securing her laces. She looked up to the mistress and then scurried to put away the toiletries and leave the rooms.

"You look well, child." She did, glowing skin and a dreamy light in her green eyes, a small smile playing about her full pink lips. Suspicion coiled in Amelia like a cobra. "Your duties these past weeks must agree with you. Perhaps a more diligent roster of activity is what you have been lacking all these years."

"I have enjoyed the additional challenge." Camille smoothed her skirts and glanced in the looking glass to give a final pat to her hair.

"Put on the jewelry that accompanies that gown. You will be receiving company."

Camille obliged and fastened a narrow gold chain around her neck. It suspended a pendant of diamonds surrounding a large opal in intricate gold, and matched earrings and a ring. Her gown of iridescent pink flattered her skin and contrasted her hair, while making her eyes appear even more vivid. Amelia watched her daughter with a measured gaze, as if looking at a painting and examining it for flaws. She appraised her from head to heels and then nodded briskly. "You are ready for him."

"Lord Kimball is here?"

"Yes," Amelia smiled. "He arrived early, that the two of you could spend time getting acquainted."

"How kind."

"Indeed." Amelia led the way out of her rooms and Camille followed. "I have praised your beauty to him. I'm certain he will not be disappointed. You are stunning."

A frown creased Camille's brows, for Amelia did not usually proffer a compliment unless to follow it with a reprimand. "Thank you."

"See to it you show him attention. The habit you have of dismissing a person with your disinterest is off-putting and offensive."

"Yes, Mother."

Amelia entered the parlor and stepped aside. "My daughter, Camille."

Bret rose and approached her, taking her hand and pressing a kiss to her skin, lingering for just a second too long. "My pleasure."

"I am pleased to meet you, Lord Kimball."

Bret stood and looked her over, as if she were one of her father's mares. But Camille didn't mind, for she assessed him in just the same manner. Blond hair, fair and shining, pulled back in a bagwig, framed a face of fierce bone structure, like a Greek god. His lips were the only slash of softness, and his eyes flamed bright blue. He smiled at her finally, breaking the intense scrutiny. "She is as lovely as you claimed, Your Grace. Perhaps even lovelier. I don't think words alone could have prepared me for the extraordinary color of her eyes, nor the exceptional shape of her face."

"She is our jewel."

"She is radiant. I am very pleased, Your Grace."

"As promised." Amelia sat and watched the two, her satisfaction evident.

"Lady Camille, may I pour you some chocolate?"

"That would be lovely, thank you."

And Camille sat next to her mother and smiled vacuously while she sipped chocolate and remarked on the weather, the terrible roads between Southampton and London, the dangers of traveling, and the lack of entertainment of a lofty nature in town. She kept silent unless directly addressed, and avoided any of the incendiary remarks that perched on her tongue, and instead said things that flattered and appeased. They went into the dining room and ate pastry and creamed fruit, and Camille glimpsed sunlight streaming through the window and fought the urge to slip away into a dream in her mind.

Eric strode into the room and stopped short, unaware a guest had arrived. "Kimball."

Bret stood and extended his hand. "'Tis nice to see you again, Eric."

"The last time I believe I took you for a sturdy purse over cards in White's Club."

Bret reddened slightly and cleared his throat. "The purse was yours and all the gin as well, if I recall correctly."

"A gentleman's comfort."

"And a son's downfall," Amelia interjected.

Eric ignored his mother. "I heard you lost a pair of fine horses to Bateman."

"A man loses, a man wins," Bret shrugged. "Sunderland tells me you got yourself pissed and tossed out of Almack's."

"A man drinks, a man gets tossed," Eric grinned. "I've a new stallion, if you've a care to ride later." Eric's smile broadened. "You likely have no horses of your own left to ride."

"Sounds pleasant enough. Shall I pack a bottle or two for you, or will you bring your own?"

"Bring two and we'll wager on who winds up with both."

Camille hid her laughter with a cough and took a sip of her chocolate, hiding her smile behind her cup. Amelia glared a silent warning to her, eyes narrowed, lips pursed.

Bret seated himself beside Camille once again and draped his arm over the back of her chair. "I will be occupied the rest of the morning. Perhaps even the afternoon. The ride will have to wait until much later."

"You and my sister?" Eric glanced to Amelia, who nodded slightly, an almost imperceptible inclination of her head.

"An announcement will be made at the dinner party," Bret said evenly.

Eric looked from Bret back to Amelia, and then finally at Camille, who returned his gaze, devoid of the expected distress. "This is acceptable?" He still looked at Camille, knowing she would not be free to answer, but unable to stop himself from asking.

Camille felt all eyes on her, suddenly pressured to find

the right thing to say. She struggled for a moment, then finally spoke, almost asphyxiating on the words. "Mother has chosen carefully on my behalf, and I am honored Lord Kimball finds me acceptable."

"Eric, I am fairly certain your father requires your assistance in the stables. Perhaps he needs you to geld something?"

"Father is in town, but I will leave you to your machinations." Eric wheeled on his heel and left the room.

Amelia arched a brow and sipped her chocolate. "So much like his father," she murmured.

"Do any of your children please you?" Camille asked the question before she could stop it. And once it had left her mouth, she winced, quite certain a punishment would follow.

But Amelia seemed to give the question consideration. "Niles and Jeffery are scarcely a bother to me, always at university. They are hardly a pleasure, however, since Jeffery is dull and Niles forever ill or trying his hand at medicine to cure illness. Eric is a burden. He has been a problem since his birth. Always grasping, it seemed; for what, I never could understand. He will be a duke in his own right, a man of power. But like Kenley, he wastes himself on liquor and horseflesh." Amelia sipped her chocolate again and leveled her eyes on Camille. "You have pleased me on occasion, child. At twenty you are a woman of grace and intelligence. You have learned scripture and music, and you have proven you can run an efficient household. Yes, you have pleased me in many ways."

Camille stared at her mother as if she had just sprouted wings and flown around the room. Amelia saw the look of obvious disbelief and laughed out loud. "You cannot fathom me, can you, child? You cannot grasp that all I do for you is done with your own benefit in mind." She shook her head, pityingly. "Always a foolish child, Camille. You must learn to accept that discipline is a part of life. Why, my own mother taught me the value of obedience. Not the way I have taught you, with explanations and leniency, but with strict and unfailing control. Dare I lift an errant brow in question, I would have been severely punished. But it taught me control. It taught me restraint."

Camille said nothing, lowering her head to stare at her plate. She didn't dare to press her fortune with any more untoward remarks. Amelia's charitable mood could be stretched only so far, she knew.

"Your Grace, your mother sounds like a formidable woman, much like my own mother." Bret leaned back in his chair and let his fingers brush the nape of Camille's neck where her hair curled in wisps.

"My mother was tyrannical." Amelia said the words flatly and with all the finality of a shattered glass.

"Well then, right," Bret mumbled, turning his attentions to the stroking of Camille's neck with more interest. "Your skin is so soft, like a petal."

Camille endured his touch, forcing her lips to curve in a smile. "My lord's hands are strong."

"Is my touch gentle enough for you?"

"Gentle, yes, but overwhelming."

Bret chuckled softly and ceased his stroking. "In time you will grow accustomed to my caresses. Perhaps one day you will even crave them."

Camille fluttered her lashes over her eyes in a show of chaste embarrassment. This brought more chuckles from Bret, and he looked to Amelia, pleasure written on his angular features. "She is a perfect rose, Your Grace."

"Do not think to pluck her too soon, dear boy. Wedding vows will be spoken before you press your favors. Of course, I am not opposed to your bundling with her. Let her know the feel of a man so the wedding night will not be a shock."

Camille knew bundling meant Bret would be permitted to lie in bed with her and stroke her body. In fact, as far as Camille had heard, bundling allowed nearly every-thing outside of intercourse to take place. A shiver ran though her body, of revulsion of doing such with Bret and memory of doing precisely that with Patrick combined.

She wanted Patrick's hands on her body, his skin pressed to her skin, his breath in her mouth. She wanted to pull him inside her, feed that burning ache in her body. And even as the thought whispered through her blood, curled her toes, melted her insides, Camille knew tonight she would receive all the answers to the mysteries of his body and hers. After she pledged her soul, she would offer her body.

But now was a waiting game. A playing of parts, and hers was one of submissive daughter and docile bride.

Amelia stood and waved away Bret's rising to his feet. "I need to go to town for a while. Camille, you will entertain Lord Kimball in any way he chooses."

Camille inclined her head obediently and waited until her mother swept from the room.

"May I show you the rose gardens, my lord?"

Bret smiled with satisfaction and stood, offering his arm to Camille. "Please, my lady. I relish the idea of those blooms paling in the face of your beauty."

"My lord offers compliments freely. Perhaps he will be shocked to find thorns on the stems and bugs in the blossoms."

"Beauty isn't about perfection, my lady, but about appeal."

Camille led the way through the mansion and around the back slowly. "Perhaps such attraction is a curse the flower must endure, that its loveliness entices all sorts of unsavory insects to crawl over and attempt to feed on it."

"What of the bugs, then? Are they not entitled to happiness?"

Camille forced an airy laugh, doing her best to imitate the vapid women she had met in London. "All this talk of insects makes my skin itch."

But she immediately saw her mistake as Bret tightened his hold on her hand, lowering his voice. "You speak of your skin while I can think of naught else. 'Tis but an hour's time I have known you, and already I am anxious to call you wife. I will speak to your mother that our engagement is too long. I do not wish to wait a year."

"Courtship is a fleeting time, not to be denied a young woman." Camille simpered up to him, hoping he would see her flushed cheeks as virginal nervousness rather than disgust, the fire in her eyes as curiosity rather than annoyance.

Bret grew serious. He turned to her and looked down into her face, striking her again with the vivid color of his eyes, the sharpness of his features, the lean strength of his form. He seemed like a god of ancient lore, powerful but tempered with human weakness. "I vow you will be happy as my wife, my lady. I know we are only strangers now, but I am confident you will find satisfaction with me."

"I am not troubled, my lord."

"Nor are you eager."

Camille felt her temper begin to crack like ice in water. "Shall I feign eagerness as well as stupidity? Would that please my lord?"

Bret's features tightened. A muscle in his jaw began to twitch. "You cannot seem to mask your disdain."

"I will work more assiduously."

"Do not bother. It is insulting to see the contempt in your eyes, but at least it is honest."

"Is it truth you look for, my lord?"

"A sort of truth, I suppose. Would it be troublesome for you to allow me a chance to dissatisfy you prior to your deciding to reject me?"

Camille let go of the last of her restraint, as curiosity and ire mingled. "My mother's interests lie in marrying me for advancement of her own plans. Not for my happiness. I expect the man whom my mother chooses for me to be owned by her in some fashion. This is my truth, my feeling, and my suspicion. Tell me your truth, my lord. What part of your soul have you sold to my mother, and at what price?"

Bret ran his hand over his face, blew out a short breath.

"I would rather not complicate the issue of our betrothal with the terms of your mother's and my agreement."

"But it is the essence of our reality. My mother already owns me. Are you certain you wish for her to control you, as well?"

Bret bent and sniffed a red rose, but his face showed no relaxed pleasure. He straightened and met her gaze once again. "It is unseemly to have you demand such information on our first meeting. You are to be wed, and if not to me, it would be to another man. Find contentment in the fact that I find you attractive, and that your waspish tongue does not deter me overmuch."

Camille lifted her shoulders and tried a little smile of truce. Tonight she would give herself to Patrick; shortly she would leave England with him. If all Bret needed from her was politeness, she could manage that. "Very well, then."

Bret gestured to the sky. "Pretty day, isn't it?"

CHAPTER 7

Amelia strode into the Goodrow Inn. She passed the astonished innkeeper and goodwife without a word. Up the steps and through the hall she walked with purpose, until finally she stopped and hesitated in front of Patrick's room. She held her fist up to knock and then dropped it to her side. Then she did it again.

Finally she knocked, a timid sound of hesitant flesh against stalwart oak. She waited as footsteps approached the door, forcing her face into composed lines. She looked down at her gown, patted her wig, and reassured herself she was still a fine, handsome-looking woman.

Patrick opened the door wearing only breeches, his sun-streaked hair mussed from sleep, and stubble shadowing his jaw. Surprise showed in his eyes and he lifted a brow as if amused by her presence. "Your Grace, you have not traveled into town to scold me for sleeping past the noon hour, have you?"

"'Tis hardly my concern if you choose to squander your days in such a manner. But it does cause me to wonder at what keeps you awake at night that you take your rest during the day."

"I am still acclimated to the night shift I take on my ship."

"Yes, I cannot forget you work for your keep." Amelia

ran a look over his unclothed torso, unable to keep her eyes from taking in the view of tanned skin and hard muscles.

"Duchess, is there some way in which I may serve you?" He tried not to sound impatient.

"I came to town to attend to business."

"Does this involve me in a way I am unaware?"

"Perhaps." Amelia gestured into Patrick's rooms. "May I sit a moment?"

"Of course. Please." Patrick led the way into his small sitting room and sat, eyeing her all the while and seeing her nervousness. "I would offer you a drink, but I have nothing in the room at this time. If you'd care for it, I could call for the innkeeper to bring up some tea."

"No need, thank you," Amelia said primly. "I shan't stay long."

Patrick sat back and got comfortable. "Does this visit have to do with Eric and the land?"

"No. I am unconcerned with my son's dealings. It has more to do with my daughter and myself."

"How so?"

"You said once you found her attractive."

"Aye. I admired her for the pretty woman she is, Your Grace."

"She is to be married."

"Sure she is, and I would imagine that is your custom to wed your daughter when she reaches a suitable age."

"Yes, as was I. But I now know the many truths of marriage. I am not innocent as my daughter is."

Patrick didn't like the look in Amelia's eyes, nor the spurt of uneasiness in his own body. "What truths are those?"

"I know the nature of men. I accept their character flaws as inherent weakness, and I have learned to use that frailty to my own advantage." Amelia tapped her fingers on her knees, wrung her hands, then looked at Patrick straight on. She didn't even try to quell the lick of excitement. "But I am a woman, and I have desires for men."

He hesitated, uneasy but curious. "Are you confessing or propositioning?"

"Both, I suppose." Amelia laughed a little, a quick giggle that sounded insecure and girlish. "Would you trouble yourself to view me as a woman and not as a duchess? Would you perhaps see some of the attraction you had for my daughter in me? After all, I am a woman full grown and ripe. I know how to please a man and please myself. And I am not so much older than you; I was barely Camille's age when she was born."

Patrick stared at her, unsure of how to respond.

Amelia saw his uncertainty and sought to alleviate his concerns and fill the uncomfortable silence. "I would expect nothing of you, of course, except your discretion. And if you were in need of monies, I would provide you with coin. I am not indiscriminate in my choosing; in fact, I have been celibate for many years now." Amelia didn't tell him she had never been with a man since Kenley. "But the day I saw you I felt a need, and the need has grown. My husband takes his comfort in many women and he has no interest in my bed, so you need not worry for his jealousy or any sort of recrimination." Amelia dropped her eyes to her lap as she felt the flush of humiliation creep over her skin. "I should not have come here. I take risks with my reputation and my eternal life. Fornication and adultery, yet I am nearly unable to think of anything else."

"Duchess, I . . ." Patrick stopped as Amelia flew to her feet.

"Say no more," she said briskly, outstretching her hand in a way that was a warning and yet still an invitation. "I can see by your reaction you are not interested. If you mention this meeting to another soul, I will deny it and swear you are a blackguard and a knave."

Amelia fled the room and Patrick sat for a long while, staring at the seat she had occupied and almost feeling compassion for her.

Amelia ran from the room, not seeing the hallway or the stairs but traversing them as if the dogs of hell licked at her heels. She rushed past the patrons in the shady main hall and out into the sunlight, barreling into her carriage without assistance. She pounded on the roof and shrieked to be on the way back to Beauport. And as they traveled down the bumpy road, Amelia wept for the first time in more years than she could remember.

The trip from Southampton to Beauport didn't take long enough for her tears of mortification to dry or her anger to abate. Instead, the anger grew, replacing any sort of sexual desire she had felt. She chastised herself for her weakness, jeered at herself for the way she had primped and bathed for the commoner, like some virgin bride on her wedding night. She mocked her lusty dreams and the way they had made her toss in sweaty sheets, scoffed at the lingerie she wore beneath her gown. With derision she recalled every detail of her meeting with him, from his raised brows and the shock on his face, to the way her eyes had trailed the thin line of hair from his belly to his breeches, making her want to unfasten them and explore his body.

By the time the carriage pulled up in front of the manor, Amelia's rage had grown to epic proportions, as unsatisfied longings mingled with a shame so great she demanded penance. She stormed inside, poured a stiff drink of sherry, and belted it down, fueling the flame of her anger with the burn of the booze. She poured another, drank deeply, and headed to her rooms to repair her makeup and her pride. But a giggle stopped her in her tracks and she peered into the parlor where Camille sat across from Bret, holding a handful of cards.

It was Camille, she thought nastily. Always Camille. Her daughter and her bane. Youth, beauty, and artless naiveté. The mariner would have relished a chance to take a toss with her, no doubt.

And in that moment, suspicions and memories became one, from her daughter's dreamy expressions to the way she looked around her rooms when unexpectedly awakened.

Amelia knew. She knew with the certainty of a mother, and the absolute sureness of a woman disdained.

She turned and ascended the steps slowly, thoughtfully turning over her options.

After the evening meal, Bret delighted Camille with tales of London gaming houses. "There is a club called Man's near Scotland Yard on the river, where men will not smoke. In fact, smoking is frowned upon. But they engage in the perfumed snuff, which brings on terrible fits of sneezing. So while my friend and I sat and tried to play cards, the fellows were blowing great winds of snuff all around us as we played, punctuated with loud sneezes and teary eyes. Needless to say, we took the hand."

"Not the hand with the handkerchief, I hope."

Bret laughed out loud. "No. Not that hand."

Camille giggled and looked over to Amelia, who still stared at her with bleary eyes and a sullen expression. "More sherry, Mother?"

"No more. I am past my limit." Amelia staggered to her feet and leaned heavily on the table. "Fetch Rachel for me, child. I need help to my room."

"Of course." Camille rose and hurried to the door, whispered to a servant, and then rushed back to Amelia's side. "May I help you to the door?"

"Do not touch me. You prance about enough as it is, and I will not have you lend me aid as if I were some elderly woman too feeble to walk about. So I am in my cups. Will you treat me as if I am infirm?"

Camille recognized the dangerous voice of an angry drunk, deliberate, surly, and hostile. She kept her tone light in response. "Very well. We will wait for Rachel."

"You look like him and you act like her. All my life I was groomed to live a certain way, be a certain person, and for what? So I could waste it all on your father's brats and a lifetime of disappointments." Amelia walked unsteadily to the end of the table, holding on to the backs of the chairs as she made her way. "Rachel!" She turned back to Camille and sneered. "I should have married you off to a man who would deprave you. I wish I had found the most disgusting old pervert in London, who would have spent the rest of his life twisting your mind and filling your belly with his unwanted seed."

Camille looked to Bret and then back to Amelia, remaining silent as her face grew hot with embarrassment.

"I found a young man for you, didn't I? One who would likely be entertaining in your bed, and I am sure he'll take to pleasing you, too. Do not all men lust for you, child? Do not all men simply fall to your pretty feet?" Amelia leaned forward, her wig askew and her eyes unfocused. "Wait until he sees your scars. Won't he want to know why you deserve them?"

Rachel entered the dining room and saw the situation immediately. She placed an arm around her mistress's waist and began to shush her with soothing promises of foot rubs and hot tea.

"Rachel," Amelia said with a sob in her throat, almost childlike. "Take me away from her. I do not want to see her anymore."

Rachel nodded to Camille and led Amelia upstairs, holding her skirts for her as they ascended.

Camille looked at Bret and sighed heavily. "I will retire also, if you don't mind."

"Of course not. I will see you in the afternoon tomorrow. I promised your brother an early ride."

Camille waited as Bret kissed her good night, full on the lips but with little heat. His lips felt dry and his tongue hesitant. Or was it simply that she felt no passion for him? she wondered. If she had wanted him the way she wanted Patrick, would his kisses feel differently? The kiss ended and she stopped speculating, ceased caring as she turned and climbed the staircase.

Once in her rooms, she called Brigid for a bath. While

the servants carried in large buckets full of steaming water, Camille waited by her dressing table just outside her bathing alcove. As Brigid unlaced her, she dreamed of the night to come. She dismissed them all after they filled the tub, even Brigid.

She wanted solitude while she prepared to be a bride.

She drizzled lavender-scented oil into the bathwater, slipped out of her clothes, and stepped into the huge copper tub. A sigh of contentment and release exhaled through her parted lips. Camille loved bathing, soaking in the warm water up to her neck and feeling the melt of her muscles. When the water began to cool, she lathered a cloth and washed her face and her body with the care of a woman who knows it will be touched and kissed. After she toweled dry, she began to dress, a simple shift of gossamer silk and silver embroidery. Her finest and intended for her wedding night. Over that she pulled on old fawn-colored breeches that had belonged to Niles and a shirt of white cotton. The clothes were simple and clean, pilfered from her brother's room. She wouldn't be able to climb up and down her balcony in a gown. Finally she turned her attention to her hair, remembering how Patrick had said he thought her hair to be beautiful. And so with that in mind, she brushed it until it shone with the luster of silk and then pulled back only the front and secured it with a ribbon, leaving the rest to hang in waves to her waist, unbound and maidenly.

Quiet sounds caught her attention and she turned around. Patrick stood between the parted drapes. His eyes traveled the length of her and he grinned, slow, sure, sensual. A smile that clustered her nerves into tight, tingling knots. He wore all black, as he'd done the nights he'd come to see her. Like a pirate, she thought, with a face from a fable and eyes like the sea.

"I am ready," Camille said.

"For all that follows, as well?"

Camille knew he didn't speak of wedding nights and

virginal shyness. She realized he meant leaving excessive wealth and embracing a simpler life. "For all of it."

"Let's go, then. The weather is with us. No clouds, a sky full of stars, and a moon that is so full it looks to bursting."

Camille closed and locked her bedroom door, pushed pillows under the covers to make it look as though she slumbered there, and extinguished the candles. With no light but moonlight to guide her and the rich scents of beeswax and smoke in the air, she followed him out onto the balcony.

He held her hands and lowered her to the ground and then followed her, dropping to the earth beside her. Patrick took her hand and led her into the shadows of the woods, until the leafy branches finally hid them.

Neither saw the man who stirred under the darkness of her balcony.

The woods sighed with night air and nocturnal sounds. Patrick held Camille's hand tighter, helping her when she stumbled in the underbrush. Somewhere an owl hooted and leaves rustled with tiny creatures taking cover, a hunter and its prey. Vines draped down from high branches like a fisherman's lines, snagging Camille's hair. She pushed them away and looked over to Patrick in the dimness, struggling to see his expression. He glanced over at her, a sidelong look where she caught the flash of his teeth, the carelessness of his grin.

"Are you frightened, Camille?"

"I've never been in the woods at night before."

"Neither had I, before I met you."

She stopped walking. Needed to confess. "I cannot cook. I am handy with a needle, but cannot promise to be able to make clothes. I have never tended a garden or cleaned or laundered. I have no real skills, Patrick."

Patrick's smile broadened. "Is that what worries you, then?"

"I have been trained as a wife who has servants. I don't want to disappoint you."

"I am not a poor man. You will have comforts."

"But will love be enough? What if you tire of me and long for a woman whose talents lie in more than day-dreams and conversation?"

"As long as you share your dreams with me, we'll be fine. You worry too much of 'what if' when our future will only begin with 'when.'"

"I love you, Patrick. More than life and beyond death. I will love you forever."

"Forever is a promise, to be sure. It's a gift you're giving me, you see." His hands held hers in the darkness, twined around her fingers like the brambles at their feet.

"A promise I willingly make to you this night. I would take my life rather than hurt you."

Patrick reached out and touched her face, pale in the moonlight. He brushed his thumb over her lips, watching as her lips parted and shook in response to his touch. "Come to the ocean, Camille. I want to marry you."

Camille felt some of the weight slide off her shoulders. "The ocean. I haven't seen it in so long."

She took his hand again, listening to the sounds of the woods and the rhythm of her own breathing. In that copse of trees things lived and died each day, she thought. Each thing dependent on another for every breath, every triumph.

There was no path to the ocean, but the trees began to thin and the soil grew sandy. In the distance they could hear the din of the waves, falling and receding. They at last stood on the beach and looked out over the dark waters, where moonlight turned the waves to silver and stars shone above it in diamond clusters. Camille held her breath. "The ocean is so different at night."

Patrick sat on the sand and stretched out his legs. "Different from this side of the sea, certainly."

"Are you glad to be on land?"

"Aye. I am anxious to be free of that way of life. I want a home."

Camille seated herself next to him, feeling the cold of

the sand seep through and chill her skin for the first time in her life. She ran her fingers through it, gritty and damp. "'Tis a night for firsts."

Patrick pulled her onto his lap, and she rested her head in the curve of his shoulder, comfortable and warm. "Do you marry me, Camille? Do you vow to be my wife until death parts us? Here in the sight of God, do you promise to love me forever?"

It seemed to Camille as if the entire world held its breath, waiting to hear her reply. "I do."

"I make the same vow to you. I will love you forever, and cherish you always. I swear it now, with God as my witness."

Camille pressed her lips to his neck, where his pulse throbbed.

"May I tell you a story?" he asked.

"Please." Camille settled her head back against the strength of him, listened to the rise and fall of his breath, the steady beat of his heart.

"I told you once of my grandda," Patrick began. "A pirate, he was, feared and fierce. He marauded his way across the sea with no conscience. He took what he wanted and he killed for sport, you see. Many years after my da left him, Rogan made his way back to my father to make amends. The years had mellowed him, and he had grown old and tired. He had learned that family was all a man really had, and he spent the last years of his life being the parent my own da had always longed for.

"Rogan taught me much, you see. He told me not only of the times when he won battles, but also of when he lost. He taught me to fight with cunning as well as restraint, so that I would win with my mind as well as my brawn. He told me of crimes he had committed, and taught me that not all people are only good or bad, but a blending of both. He had been as vicious and cruel as a man could be. His experiences had taken him around the world, but in the end he learned that what really mattered was love. Love of your family, and above all, love of yourself. He made peace with me and with my father, but I don't think he ever forgave himself of his sins."

Patrick pulled up his sleeve and unfastened the bracelet that circled his wrist. The amber stones gleamed their warmth even in the cool moonlight. "When my grandda died, my da gave me this. He told me that my grandda had worn it most of his life, and he placed it around my wrist in reminder of him. He said, 'Never forget that Rogan lives in me and in you, and that we all have the capacity for evil and good. You always have a choice between the two.'

"All my adult life, I have carried that with me. I have worn this and remembered. To me, it has represented everything I am, from my pirate grandda to my da, who despite it all is an honest merchant and a good man. They have made me who I am."

Patrick took Camille's left leg and ran his hands down her slim calf, removed her soft hide boot, and slowly placed the glowing bracelet around her ankle and fastened the clasp.

He held her for a long moment. "I'm giving you this because it is the most precious thing I own. They are my past. You are my future."

Camille wrapped her arms around his neck and felt the bristle of his beard against her cheek and the way the gold of the bracelet circling her ankle still held the warmth of his body. "I have nothing to give to you in return."

"You are giving me yourself."

"Yes."

"That is everything I want."

Camille shifted restlessly and looked up to the painted nighttime sky, where stars flickered, winked, and shone steadily. "I can scarcely believe how you feel for me. It is a dream too beautiful, a reality difficult to accept."

Patrick searched her features in the moonlight. "You have never felt truly loved the whole of your life."

"I have not."

"Can you feel it now?"

"Yes. With more than words and past your touch on my skin. I feel it in my soul."

Patrick looked out to the ocean where the waves swelled and crested. "You are like the sea. I could drown in your depths."

"I would rather take my life than see yours ended."

Patrick traced her face, his fingers lightly touching each curve. "'Tis the second time tonight you spoke of ending your life."

"Without you, there is no life for me."

"You are now my wife. There need be no life without me."

"I want you to make me your wife in truth."

"One day we will exchange vows with clergy, if that is what you wish."

"No. I mean, I want you to take me to the cottage and make me your wife. I want you, Patrick."

"I am yours to have."

Patrick lowered his head to Camille's and pressed a soft kiss against her willing lips. "With this kiss, I thee wed," he whispered against her mouth, and then the kiss deepened, grew warm. Tongue on tongue and breath mingling. His hands wandered her body, touching what only a husband had right to.

Sighs gave way to trembling, and Camille pulled her lips from his.

"Are you cold, Camille?"

"I am afraid."

"Of me?" Patrick ran his hand over her body. "Of this?"

"No. Only that this is a dream that has come to me in the night and will fade with the dawn. I fear that the very things that draw you to me will be what bring your contempt after you see me more clearly."

"I could not see you more clearly than I do."

"You are like no one I have ever known, Patrick. What you have inside you humbles me. You are the essence of what makes a man valorous. Too strong to prove your strength, too kind to watch someone suffer, too generous to cheat, too brave to lie. How can I think someone like you could love me?"

"You are wrapped up in my hopes and dreams. Without you, there is no future for me, Camille. When I told you our love is a gift, I meant from each other, not from me to you or you to me. Don't you see? We found something precious, like a diamond in the sand. But if you cannot believe you hold that gem, 'tis worthless. A rock amongst so many others."

The night suddenly felt too exposed, the sea too vast and inscrutable. Camille looked around, seeing nothing but ocean, sand, and long, dark shadows. But the wash of fear went through her, as if Amelia were somehow near. "Will you take me to our cottage?"

"I will. And when the *Nuala* arrives, I will take you anywhere in the world you wish to go."

"The *Nuala*? This is your ship?"

"Aye. My da named it for my mother. He said the ship was like her, tall, unassuming, and graceful."

"I wish I could have known her."

"Aye. She was a fine woman." Patrick sat with Camille in his arms and remembered the mother who had sung and laughed often, a blurry vision of long red hair and gentle hands. "'Tis fine we should think of her on our wedding night. The stories she told me always ended with marriage and happily ever after."

Camille sighed and rubbed her cheek against his shoulder, pleased just by the warmth and feel of him.

"Are you tired?" he asked.

"No, just peaceful."

"We should be on our way. I have a surprise for you."

She turned her head to look at him. "You do? What is it?"

He loved the way she got excited so easily. "You will have to come with me and see."

Camille jumped to her feet, smiling. She twirled once on the cold sand. "I love surprises."

"Then you'll love being married to me. Surprises are my specialty."

They walked to the cottage hand in hand, but not leisurely. They rushed with the impatience of lovers who knew their time had come. Again they traversed the brushwood and the moss, the ferns and the vines. They tripped over snarled bushes and cracked dry, dead branches under their steps. The woods enveloped them in its gnarled, darkened peace, and Camille felt the solitude of nature without feeling lonely. As it always was with Patrick, the way it had never been with anyone else. Heavy, perfumed scents of roses replaced the salty twang in the air as they grew closer, combining with the rich, rotting smell, the decay of logs, lichen, and leaves on moist earth. The woods opened to the little meadow where moonlight bathed the small cottage, the mica in the granite stones winking silver in the dimness.

The roses bloomed deliriously in wild, wanton clumps of sterling velvet petals and leaves that looked glossy and black in the dark of night. They sweetened the air, creeping over the cottage with chaotic impetuousness, entangled like embracing lovers against the walls. The night seemed quieter there, as if the place were held apart from the woods that surrounded it.

"'Tis always special here," Camille whispered.

"Aye. I feel it, too." Patrick pulled her toward the door. "Come inside."

He pushed open the door and bade Camille stand in the doorway with her eyes closed. "Hold there, while I light a candle."

She heard the strike of flint and the spark of flame, the muffled tread of his footsteps. "You may look."

Camille opened her eyes and saw he had made a nest of quilts and pillows in front of the fireplace. A bowl of fruit and a bunch of wildflowers and roses lay on the hearth. Candles lit the space, warm and inviting. "'Tis beautiful."

"Like you."

"Like us. The way we are together is magic."

"Aye. I'll drink to that." Patrick produced a bottle of brandy and two glasses. He poured for both of them and handed her a glass.

Camille sipped the amber liquid, feeling the burn slide through her body. "You make my head spin more than brandy ever could, Patrick."

"Perhaps you should lie down, then."

"Lie with me. I want to be your wife in every way."

Camille set down her glass and slipped off her boots. She unlaced the breeches and let them fall to the floor. With steady fingers she unfastened her brother's shirt and pushed it from her shoulders, letting it drift to the floor to rest in a puddle. She stood before Patrick, unclothed but for her shift and unashamed.

He went to her, let his fingertip run down her bare arm, felt her shiver of response. "Your skin is soft."

She felt her body grow hot, heavy, saturated. She felt suddenly foolish. "I do not know how to do this. What to do."

"I will show you." Patrick took off his shirt and took another step closer, so her breasts brushed his chest when she inhaled. She was so sweet, so innocent. She looked up to him with those green eyes full of trust. His chest ached from the sight. He felt his own nervousness, wanting her experience to be perfect. "You are in control of this, Camille. We stop when you say, and I won't do anything you don't want."

She nodded a little, tried to smile through lips that shook. He kissed her then, slow and soft. Let his lips brush over hers, tasting and feeling her melt. His hands gripped her waist lightly, skimming and stroking. He let his hands wander over the small of her back and then upward, under her hair.

He stopped dead. Under his fingertips he felt the raised stripes that reminded him that Camille came to him innocent in the ways of lovemaking, but well versed in the ways of violence. Slowly, he turned her so he could see her scars.

Camille resisted. "Do not look again. 'Tis ugly."

He insisted silently, turning her. Even in the dim light he saw puckered scars that would never fade. He lowered his head and brushed tiny, light kisses over the scars and scabs, wanting to heal her, needing to ease her. Wishing beyond all else that he could take her pain.

A tear escaped Camille's tightly squeezed eyes. A single, scalding drop that slid over her cheek and landed on her breast. Patrick turned her back to face him, pressing kisses on her shoulders, her neck, dipping lower to catch the tear from her breast with the tip of his tongue, stealing her suffering piece by piece.

Camille shook beneath his touch, lost in pleasure and sensation. His fingers touched her, his tongue teased her, his breath warmed her. She felt like a coveted sculpture, beautiful, cherished, valuable. She felt nothing but sensation, her nervousness burned away by the heat of his kisses. His hand cupped her face, the tips of his fingers touching her cheekbones while his mouth turned her body to hot liquid. She ran her hands over his back and felt his muscles shake with her touch and his self-control. She grew bolder, more curious, and ran her hands lower over his hips, feeling a warm burst of pleasure in her belly as he groaned and grinned against her mouth, darkly and fully male.

He dropped to his knees on the quilts, running his hands up and down her legs. Her knees grew weak and she knelt unsteadily before him.

"Lie down, Camille."

And she did, on her back while the candlelight sent shadows swaying around her face. He still knelt above her, his clever fingers unlacing her shift while his eyes held hers in thrall. He pushed the last of the filmy fabric from her skin, exposing the slender length of her. He looked at her for a long moment, his eyes running down her body.

"Beauty is a pale word to describe you. You are beyond lovely, past perfect."

"I want to please you."

"You do, love. And you will." He lowered his head to her body, a quick flick of tongue over her nipple, then lower to her belly and back. She arched, gasped, and then arched into the sensation again. His fingers skimmed her skin, touching her thighs, then her waist, the inner sides of her arms, and then her thighs again.

She ached, burned, moved her hips by instinct and distantly heard her own sighs and soft moans. Heat condensed under her skin, fluid, running to the center of her. She felt drugged and unable to move, but alive, as if every nerve prickled with attention.

Her soft sounds clawed at Patrick and fed the fire in his blood. He clung to her virginity like a buoy in choppy waters, letting the weight of her innocence force him into slow movements and gentle caresses. He felt her movements grow more insistent, and he knew what she craved even though she didn't. And so he began kissing her again, breathing her breath while his hand slid down her belly.

Camille was suffocating. His tongue traced her lips while his fingers parted and explored the core of the throbbing heat. Her muscles jerked, her throat moaned, her breath stopped. Nothing existed outside the moment and the flicking, circling sensation that made her dizzy, on fire. It built, grew, expanded until she felt an urgency like nothing else. She could hear his breathing coming in short gasps; she felt the heat radiating from his skin, feeding her burn. "Please." She didn't know what she asked for, but knew she needed something.

And he gave it to her. He lowered his head and touched his tongue where his fingers had been. Her whole body shook and a cry came from deep inside her. He laved and nibbled, lightly sucked and then licked while his fingers continued to explore, entering her. He flexed his fingers, stretching while she whimpered and trembled under the loving of his tongue.

He was coming undone with a throbbing need unlike any he had ever felt. She was ready; he could feel it, so hot and wet and ready. He lifted his head and resumed touching her, waiting until she was at the edge, and then began to gently ease into her, so tight, so sinfully hot. He groaned like a man being flayed, fighting for control. He pressed further into the soft, snug depth, felt the barrier of her innocence break, and forced himself to stop and wait for her pain to recede.

But Camille never felt pain. Only the delicious feeling of being stretched and filled and wanting more. She shifted her hips and pulled him deeper, smiling like Eve at the surge of power she suddenly felt as he moaned with pleasure. Pleasure she gave. And so she ran her fingers down his back and grabbed his hips. She pulled him inside her until her sounds matched his. He breathed words in her ear, blistering words telling her of the heat and feel of her, of his need and want of her. Like an animal that thrived only on instinct, she wrapped around him and moved into the sensations, a thing of nature and out of her control. Her climax drenched her and she cried out while he thrust into her again and again, taking her to a place where her only thought was yes.

He held himself from his own release, clinging to the ecstasy of his own control, suspended in the moment of her orgasm, the feel of her writhing beneath him. He held on until he could take the fire no more, until he could not endure another second of her untamed response and her throaty moans. Her body was like the sea, deep, wet, and visceral. He let go of the last of his restraint and let himself drown.

Camille lay still, feeling the weight of him on top of her, the feel of him still inside her. Her body pulsed, the memory of her own actions fresh enough to stain her cheeks with color and curve her lips. He lifted his head and looked at her, the candlelight glinting from his eyes.

"Did I hurt you?"

"I felt nothing but bliss."

He pulled from her, rolled to his side, and held her in the crook of his arm. "I love you, Camille."

She sighed and rubbed her hand over his chest, across his belly, and down lower, where he was still slick with their sex. "I want you to show me how to please you."

"You pleasured me more than you could possibly know."

"But not as other women have?"

Patrick raised a brow and half grinned as he looked at her. "That isn't a fair question. There is no good answer."

"I don't want good answers. I want truth. You have had sex with many women, no?"

A vision of Veronica naked and bent over him flashed through his mind, and then of Amelia, offering herself. He thought of exotic women in far-off ports, and island women with the sun in their skin. But the women he had taken to bed had been different from Camille. Not only because they had been experienced and many times calculating, but because Patrick had not wanted to know them. He had lusted, certainly. He had given them pleasure and received his own, enjoying their womanly charms as any man would. And then he had wanted to leave. There had been no looking at the clock and wishing for time to stand still, as he did with Camille. Instead, he had held them for as long as he had to without seeming cruel, and then he had left them without a thought, except for the melancholy feeling that made him promise himself it would be different the next time. But it had never changed.

Until now, he thought. "I have had sex before, aye. There have been other women, but none I have loved. I have never made love to any woman before you."

Camille narrowed her eyes. "Twisted reasoning."

He laughed. "A bit." He cuddled her closer to chest, his large hands spread across her narrow back. "My jealous bride, 'tis the past and I cannot change it. But I swear, I will be faithful to our wedding vows."

"As will I."

"You had better," Patrick murmured as he kissed her neck. "I would kill any man who touched you as I just have."

Camille leaned her head back, loving the way his kisses on her neck made her whole body tingle down to her curled toes. "I would never want another man."

He breathed against her ear, licked, and then bit her lobe. "I have never felt anything like what I feel with you. You are enchanting."

The fire was back, and with it, the heat. Camille stretched against him, running her hands over his body. "Show me how to please you."

Patrick groaned, just with the feel of her slender hands exploring him. "I shouldn't, for then you will own my body as well as my soul."

She pushed him onto his back and hovered over him. Her hair draped around them like a curtain as black as midnight and she leaned over him, resting her breasts on his chest. "I shall have to experiment, then, and do to you as you did to me."

And as Camille tortured Patrick relentlessly with hands, mouth, teeth, and tongue, Patrick surrendered.

In the early morning he took her back to the manor, while the diffused light of dawn struggled to chase away the darkness. The woods had come to life, it seemed, and Camille thought to herself that so had she. A maiden no longer, but a wife in deed as well as truth. And it was her truth, she thought defiantly. A vow as consecrated as any spoken in front of a priest. A vow as sanctified as any given with parental blessing.

She looked over at him, catching his eyes. Her cheeks flushed with color. "I may not be able to look at you without blushing ever again."

"A blushing vixen. I am truly a lucky man."

"You are wicked." She caught his grin and smiled in return, poking him in the ribs.

"As are you. And delicious, sensual, wonderful, and arousing. Shall I go on?"

"Please," Camille replied primly. "You may continue to compliment me profusely."

"I'd rather make love to you lavishly while I tell you of your charms, whispered in your ears while I am inside you."

She blushed furiously, neck, face, and ears burning. But her grin grew wider, secretive. "You may do so tonight."

"I will come to your rooms. I don't want you to risk sneaking out again."

"I will hang the ribbon, as always."

They reached the balcony, and Patrick lifted Camille up until she could grab the base of the balustrade, and then he gave her a boost over the rail. She turned and looked down at him, her husband, her lover. She felt suddenly alone again, as she faced returning to her family that day, dealing with Amelia and Bret. It was so easy to get lost in her future with Patrick and forget the present, her reality. All at once unsure of her ability to continue to endure it, she nearly wept. "Cannot we leave today? Must we wait?"

He saw the desolation in her eyes, felt his heart break at having to leave her there. "Where would we go, Camille? Your family would come looking for you, and without my ship I cannot get you out of their reach. The ship will be here in a fortnight, perhaps less. We must bide our time."

"I feel I have bided my time all of my life. I am tired."

"Go lie down and rest, love." But he knew physical fatigue wasn't what she spoke of.

"I am so afraid, Patrick. It seems the fears return to me when I am back in this house. I fear for all of it: the escape, the journey—even your love for me."

"The escape and the journey will not be easy, I'll grant you. But they will be worth your freedom." He cleared his throat and half shrugged, uncertain about how he could reassure her any more of the love he felt so deeply. He couldn't do any more than say words. "I can only promise you will one day be able to accept my love, Camille. What more can we do but let that happen?"

She pushed her hair back, wiping the back of her hand across abruptly tired eyes. "Even after the years pass and I am slowly stripped of my beauty, you will love me still?"

He pushed back his hair in an impatient gesture. His accent deepened with his frustration. "Is that what you're thinkin', then? That it's only your face I'm seein', an' not more? I ask you this, how am I to know you're not seein' me as anythin' more than a way out of this house?"

Camille felt her cheeks flush, partly with embarrassment and partly with anger. "I would never use you so callously."

"And yet you'll believe I'd do it to you, though?" He lifted his hands and spread them wide. "I see a future with you. You think I don't know that beauty fades? I will love you more after the years pass, Camille. *More.* The years will bring with them memories, happiness, and children. Our love is a living thing. We will tend to it, and it will grow stronger."

She looked down at him, and again saw a future of possibility, full of hope and love. He looked so earnest, so truthful, and in the secret place of her heart she realized that she did worry that she would never be good enough for him. "I only pray I do not disappoint you, Patrick."

"You haven't yet," he said, and he grinned in a way that had her blushing again.

Camille looked around and behind herself as the feeling of imminence she had experienced on the beach returned, accompanied by a prickling of fear plucking her spine. Just the thought of what Amelia would have done to Patrick and herself if they were caught made her nauseated. "Go. Go now, and I will see you on the morrow."

"I love you, Camille," Patrick said softly, once again, just for the pleasure of saying it.

Before Camille could respond, he turned and left the property at a soundless jog.

CHAPTER 8

The days dragged as if the sun's core had turned to lead. Camille sat at her dinner party surrounded by guests, Bret at her side and Amelia curiously absent. Glimpses of the still-blue sky peeked through the closed drapes. She sat watching in amazement as time stood still, silently cursing the sun and praying for the appearance of the moon.

Patrick came to her in the night.

Camille sometimes feared it was all a dream, while she waited for him. But then he would appear through her parted drapes, smiling in that ungoverned way of his that conjured images of pirates, exotic islands, and ancient tales. He kissed away her fears, stroked away her doubts, filled her body with his breath and his strength, and made her feel invincible. They made love in the dark. He knew her body as if he possessed a map, finding her secret places while she buried her head in a pillow to muffle her noise. He would come to her again, tonight, as he had done all week long since the night they had exchanged their wedding vows. With dreamy eyes and heated blood she thought about the night before, when he had used his mouth and his hands, making her plead, until she had climaxed uncontrollably, laughing, crying, shaking, and thrashing. And he had looked up at her when it was over, grinned, and began again.

A sensual shiver took her, irrepressible and hot at the center.

"Are you chilled, my lady?" A concerned frown knit Bret's brow as he leaned over to her, whispering in her ear. "'Tis quite warm today. I find no reason for you to grow cold. Are you well?"

"I am very well, my lord."

"Well then, right."

Bret sat up straight and took a small bite of the savory pastries Flanna had prepared as a first course. They had been lingering over the food for nearly an hour while waiting for Amelia to return from town. Eric had left to look for her, on the pretense of making sure all was well, when in fact only embarrassment prompted his concern. Kenley sucked his gin through the space between his teeth and leaned into the company of the comely lady beside him, well into his cups and an extended seduction. Camille recognized his advances, as he progressed from quiet chuckles to engrossed conversation, his head bent as he offered his ear to her lips for whispered confessions.

Candlelight glanced off the crystal and sent rainbows splashing across the dining room walls. Fresh flowers filled the air with fragrance. The guests had arrived and been entertained for the day with riding for the gentlemen, and gossip, tea, and biscuits for the women. The parlor had hummed with muted conversation and the continuous sibilant sounds of waving fans. The dinner hour had arrived. The guests had dressed and arranged themselves in the dining room, acting like well-behaved children at their first high tea. They had finally taken their seats and had begun to drink and eat, though the duchess remained conspicuously absent.

The curiosity that hung in the room like a cloud became agitated when Amelia arrived, her mood dark and her disposition sullen. For her part, Camille began to truly worry.

She watched as her mother entered and tossed off a curt excuse for her lateness, something about a broken wheel and an incompetent repairman. Then she left the room to change for dinner, and only her daughter noticed the slight weave in her step.

Camille signaled for the dishes to be cleared and the table prepared for the second course.

"Your mother is a mystery," Bret whispered in Camille's ear.

"Perhaps she is unwell."

"More like unhinged, methinks."

She arched her brow. "Why do you do business with her, then?"

Bret laughed quietly. "Business is such a mercenary word for your mother's and my arrangement. I have needs for things she possesses; she has needs for me as well. 'Twas symbiotic."

Camille eyed him, aware they were watched as they spoke softly to each other, careful to keep her face neutral. "Yet something hangs in your voice, my lord, like an unresolved conflict."

He brushed his hand over the back of her neck as he draped his arm on the back of her chair. "Perchance it is a desire unsatisfied you hear, my lady."

She resisted the urge to push his hand from her skin. "Your desires are not my concern as of yet."

"Soon, my lady. Soon."

Camille looked up as Amelia returned to the room. The men seemed to compete with each other in rushing to their feet. Amelia pressed her hands on her skirts to stop them from swaying, then ran hands that trembled over the icy blue fabric, her gown as pale as her eyes. Diamonds winked and glittered, a hard fire at her ears and around her throat. Even the fresh coating of cosmetics could not conceal the fact that the duchess had wept. At least, this was apparent to Camille. She doubted their guests would take note. The haughty hostess took her seat and the men sat. An immediate, nervous silence hung over the table.

The duchess took in her guests with a panoramic glance, fidgeted with her napkin in her lap for a second, and then caught her composure, her face drawing into well-worn lines. "Were it in my power, I would petition the king to have that incompetent thug of a wheeler put down like an ancient mule."

"What of the incompetent king, Your Grace?" quipped the Earl of Birmingham.

The nervousness dissipated as the laughter swept around the table. Servants carried in the second course, summer greens with stuffed fowl, and set the trays down with a flourish. The guests suffered their hosts, politely ignoring the silence of the duchess, the dissolute advances of the duke, the cautious wariness of their daughter. The meal ended finally, a great relief to all when Amelia suggested they retire to the parlor for music and drinks. The ladies and gentlemen arranged themselves on settees and chairs, and Camille took her place at the clavichord. Accurate yet hesitant, her fingers flew across the keys, making music sing through the instrument that had never sung through her heart. When she concluded, the polite applause sounded much the same, flat and without real emotion. Camille rose at the same time as did Amelia, taking her place beside Bret as Amelia stood beside Kenley. Just at that moment, Camille realized how odd it was that Bret's parents hadn't come for the occasion. Just as quickly, she dismissed the thought with the apathy of one who knows her time in a situation is limited, and the confidence that freedom drew closer with every second that passed.

Candles blazed and the setting sun's diffused light filtered through the drapes. People shifted, coughed, and sipped their drinks, bored with the obvious secret behind the gathering. Kenley rested his hand on Bret's shoulder and cleared his throat. "I am delighted you could all be in attendance today, for this is no ordinary day. This evening, I give my daughter in betrothal to Lord Kimball."

Polite applause sounded again, and Camille found her

mind wandering up the stairs and into her room, picturing the pink and gold light of the sunset casting a dreamlike quality onto the bed where she envisioned Patrick waiting. His hair, streaked with sun and burnished with red, spread over her pillow while he rested there, anticipating her return. She would strip off her clothes as she approached him, lie down beside him, and slip into his arms, her lips on his and then tongue sliding over tongue. Their breath would mingle and he would pull back, looking into her eyes. It would be all she would need, that simple, visceral connection that made words unnecessary.

Bret took her hand and slipped a ring onto her finger. She glanced down at it as if it shone against another's skin, set with a large emerald surrounded by diamonds. Camille labored out the appropriate response, along with a demure smile and a chaste kiss.

The party droned on until Amelia finally orchestrated a conclusion to the party as midnight approached, saw the guests' needs met for the night, and ushered Camille to her rooms. While Camille stood and endured Brigid's ministrations for bed, Amelia sat on a small chair and watched, her manner silent and still, her mood inscrutable. As the maid completed her tasks and left the rooms, Amelia followed her to the door, but did not exit. Instead she stood back as Bret entered.

Bret wore a blue dressing gown over nightclothes, his fair hair hanging to his shoulders. His lips smiled; lust shone in his eyes as he approached her. "My lady, I admit I have been looking forward to this night since your mother and I reached our agreement."

Camille looked at Amelia, disgust written on her features and heavy in her voice. "You will make a whore of your own daughter?"

"Not a whore, a wife. Bundling is a routine and much-needed part of courtship. You must learn the feel of a man, learn his body, and allow him time with yours."

"I will be gentle with you, my lady." Bret smiled again, and her body tingled with fear and revulsion.

"I do not love you. I do not want you to touch me."

"You will come to like it."

"And if you do not like it," Amelia said flatly, "you will learn to tolerate it. Such is a wife's duty."

Bret walked to the bed and sat on the corner, running his hands over the delicate coverlet. Camille watched as his hands, as white and soft as her own, touched Patrick's and her wedding bed. He fouled it with his masculine perfume, his unwanted presence, his arrogant assumptions that he could please her body when he did not even attempt to find her heart. She felt rage quiver inside her with the invasion of it all, and the sure awareness that he would molest her with his hands while her own mother would allow him to do so. Helpless fury blazed from her eyes and her every pore, but her mother only smiled at her.

"I will leave you to your lord's tender mercies."

Amelia turned to leave, but Camille's voice stopped her, a sound as hard and cold as the gems Bret had placed on her finger. "No chaperone?"

Her mother faced her, painted brow arched, mouth twisted in an ironic smirk. "Can I not trust you, child?"

"You worry for the trust of me? What of this man whom you barely know? I am but a lamb in the wolf's care should he decide to press his advantage and rape is his intention."

"Lord Kimball knows that to make a whore of his intended bride is not the course of wisdom."

"You trust him."

"I do not explain myself to children."

"If I am but a child, why do you leave me alone in bed with a man?"

"You are *my* child, and I will do as I see fit with you."

"As it has always been," Camille said bitterly.

"And as it will always be," Amelia countered. She turned and left the room, closing the door quietly. Camille could not help wondering if her mother did not turn the lock to taunt her with the plain truth that a prison need not have locks to hold a person inside. They need only no way out.

Bret approached her and tugged at her hand, leading her back to the bed. He didn't seem to notice or care that she pulled back unwillingly or that tears slid from the corners of her eyes. He pushed her onto the bed, turned, and lifted her legs and stretched them out as he lay beside her. With his head buried in her hair, he breathed into her ear, "You smell as heaven must."

"You will never make that comparison, I would wager."

"Do not be sulky with me, my lady. I only long to bring you pleasure." He ran his hands over her body, touching her belly and her thighs.

Camille's stomach churned in slick waves of nausea. She took a deep breath and closed her eyes, willing her mind to another place. She was in her cottage, watching as Patrick's long fingers touched her arrangement of seashells, wildflowers, and roses. *Just like you, they are. Timelessly beautiful. A simple pleasure.* She was on the cold sand, and he pulled her into his lap. *Here in the sight of God, do you promise to love me forever?* She had vowed, and he had placed a string of gold and amber around her ankle, where it now circled her skin, a glowing, burning reminder.

Tears slid silently down her cheeks as Bret brushed his hands over her body, touching her breasts, while Camille felt pieces of her vows break. Bret's breathing grew heavier, his caresses rougher. He pressed against her side and she felt his hot erection through her thin clothing. He was whispering in her ear again, telling her of his lust, urging her to touch him. Panting and sweating, he rubbed against her. Camille lay completely unmoving, tears welling through her closed eyes. He moved his pelvis up and down on her hip, teasing himself with the feel of her while she lay beside him, inert and unresponsive to any of his pleas for her hands to explore his body.

A tiny sound, the slightest movement of the drapes shrouding her balcony made Camille turn her head and open her eyes. Patrick stood outside the French doors, looking in as candles illuminated his wife in bed with another man.

Sobs racked her body, tore from her throat. Her hand reached out across the bed, and with her palm up she bade him stay away, lest he be killed as the intruder her family would see him to be. She endured Bret's thrusting, grinding efforts against her body to relieve himself. She ignored his hands as they clutched at her breasts and squeezed her nipples. She scarcely noticed his wet kisses on her neck and the heavy, panting breathing as he confessed his erotic desires.

She saw only the shadow of Patrick through the gap between her drapes, wept harsh, useless tears as she spoke to him with her eyes and the whole of her heart. She begged him to wait, pleaded with him to remain safely on the balcony.

He did wait. He waited, and he watched until the man shuddered his release. He watched with sick fury as the man rose away from his wife and self-consciously wiped at the wet mess in his nightclothes. He fought with the killing urge to rush into the room and tear away at the man with bare hands, ripping and destroying the blond beast who touched his wife and ignored her tears. But he would not sacrifice their future for the momentary satisfaction. Years at sea had taught him control. Rogan's and his father's tutelage had taught him discipline.

And then the man bade good night and left, and Patrick waited while Camille climbed from the bed on legs that shook. He watched as she struggled out of her soiled nightdress and washed violently at the skin on her hip, until Patrick could take the waiting no longer. He flung open the drapes, strode into the room, and held her while she sobbed, her body shaking with tears of humiliation and wrath. He smoothed her hair and kissed her face, her tears. She tried to pull away but he held on tighter, whispering fiercely into her ears all the words he needed to say and she needed to hear. "You are my wife. Mine. You are my wife. You are mine."

Naked, mortified, Camille turned and wrapped her arms around him, burying her face in his strong neck. He picked her up and carried her back to the bed, clinging to her as she clung to him. Patrick covered her, smoothing her hair and whispering more gently, "It has come, my ship. It comes off a long voyage and is in need of fresh men and repairs. I wanted to gather a crew and stock provisions, but I see there is no time for that. I will keep on only my best mates and gather what our basic comforts demand; we will leave tomorrow night and sail to Calais. The journey is short enough and we will find all we need there. I will not suffer to see you abide another night in this house."

Camille calmed and tried to take a deep breath, but it caught in her throat. Exhausted, she felt herself start to soften in his arms. "I want to leave now. I can scarcely face tomorrow and what it might bring."

"It will bring freedom in the night. But I need the morrow to prepare. The minute you set foot on my ship we need to sail, for your family will tear England apart to look for you. If they suspect 'tis I who has taken you, they will without a doubt search every port from here to the Americas. We will need a full night's lead and a careful plan to be sure."

She shuddered, rubbed over her body as if she could push away the feel of Bret against her and the disgust of her own passive compliance. She started to rise. "I need a bath. I stink of him as this bed now stinks of him."

Patrick bade her stay in bed and left her side. He poured water in the washbasin, lathered lavender soap on a small cloth, and began to wash her, starting with her neck where Bret had kissed and slowly working his way down, cleansing her skin. He wrung out the cloth and wiped away the soap while Camille watched him. He met her eyes, stormy blue against emerald green, lit by flickering candles and the steady silver moonlight.

"You are mine," he repeated.

"I am yours."

"He touched only your body." Patrick leaned and pressed his lips lightly to hers. "He did not savor your breath mingled with his." He kissed her neck where her pulse throbbed. "He did not feel the drumming of your heart against his mouth and know it beats only for me." He kissed the valley of skin between her breasts and felt her shiver. "He did not know your soul as I do and give you his as I have." Patrick's hand slid down her thigh, brushed over her knee, and traveled her calf until his fingers rested on the amber bracelet he had placed there a week before. "Our wedding vows are sacred, though they are unsanctified. You are my wife, and no man can claim otherwise."

Camille cupped his face, brushing over his lips with her thumb. "I have given you everything I have, yet it seems not enough. I wish I could give you my life somehow, all of what is inside me. Would you take it, I wonder? Or would you only give it all back to me, improved for the short time it lived in you? You have given me more than you have ever taken, and I feel my gifts are paltry to yours, my words insignificant to express my feelings, my body insufficient to house this love."

He lay on top of her, supporting himself on his elbows and pressing light kisses over her brows, her nose, her eyes, her lips. "If this is a night for wishes, then I shall have mine. I wish you could know the you I know. I wish you could see the woman I see and love her as I do."

She opened to him, ran her hands over his back, welcoming his weight and the feel of him sliding inside her. She caught the reflections of her face in his eyes. Her words came on a whisper of breath, a soft moan. "I see her, Patrick. I see myself in you."

"You are beautiful inside." His hands worked magic on her body and he filled her until she could take no more.

Camille shifted beneath him, her blood pulsing with his

touch. "Only in your eyes. That person exists only in your heart."

He pressed deep inside and then pulled away, returning and then receding again, a rhythm as old as the tides and just as full of the power of life. Camille felt the fullness in her heart and in her body, riches beyond her imagination. He whispered his love for her in her ear and shook beneath her curious hands. Her climax gathered like a tempest, stealing her breath as it broke loose, dragging her into its center and then setting her free. He pressed his mouth against hers, drowning her cries with his kiss and, unable to stand the delicious wet heat of her any longer, he let go.

He held her when it was over while their bodies cooled and their blood settled.

"Tomorrow seems an infinite time, a thousand hours of torment in one torturous day."

"A necessary time, if all will go well. I need to stock the ship with food and water and then try to find enough men to man the ship to France. As 'tis, only the most basic crew is left. My first mate, Jerry, dismissed the lot of them after they dropped the last of their shipment at the Royal Exchange. They sailed up to Southampton's port with naught but ten men." He pressed a kiss on her forehead, where black hair met fair skin. "But do not worry over it. All will be well; you'll see. The *Nuala* is a fine vessel and will bear us to Calais safely."

"I do not fear the voyage. 'Tis the escape I dread."

"I will come for you at midnight, and we will leave as we did the night we married. 'Tis a small matter to have the ship anchored just off the shoreline from where we wed, and a small dory left for us on the beach, a better idea than trying to sneak you through town and off the docks. We will row out to the *Nuala* and be gone hours before dawn. Bring only what we can carry. Remember to bring a warm cloak, for it can get colder than a mother-in-law's kiss at night once we're out to sea."

Camille pictured herself with Patrick, on the deck of a great ship with the wind in their hair and the salty air stinging their eyes. She would slip her arm around his waist and he would draw her close, safe at last and free most of all. He would grin at her, the kind of smile she felt as much as she saw, and she would mirror it back to him, her own smile of restless freedom. "'Tis difficult, this waiting. I want our life together to begin now, this minute, this second."

"In due time you will have all you desire, my love."

Camille sat up with a start, suddenly despondent. "Indue. I shall have to leave her behind."

Patrick ran his hand over the elegant length of her spine, passing over the raised scars with the regret that didn't fade no matter how often he saw, touched, or thought of them. "I am sorry, Camille. There is no way to take her. There will be much left behind, I'm afraid."

She sighed heavily, thinking she would never see her brothers again, or her horse, or her cottage. "Always a price to be paid."

"Will you feel 'twas worth the cost, Camille?"

She turned to him and saw his understanding. He would gain a wife; she would lose her past. But like birth, or rebirth, there was bound to be pain. "If choosing between you and my own life, I would choose you."

She lay down next to him again, settled against his body, and hid a yawn behind her hand. As he smoothed her hair, he felt her body grow warm and relax. "You need to sleep. Tomorrow night will be a long one."

Camille drifted into sleep as he stroked her hair. She never heard him leave.

The day inched forward. Camille jumped at every sound and laughed too brightly at inane banter exchanged with her guests. Bret sought her out at every turn, looking into her eyes meaningfully as he tried to get her attention. He appeared to want to speak privately with her, but Camille avoided him until after dinner, when finally he cornered her in the empty dining room.

"Last night meant more to me than you could possibly know, my lady. Holding you in my arms was a delight I wish to experience again."

Camille felt her face grow hot and bright. She looked down to the floor where the light of late afternoon settled across the Persian rug. She spoke the first lie that came to her mind. "My month has come due, and I should be most humiliated if you sought me out tonight."

"Right. A natural thing, and I will need to understand as your future husband." Bret cleared his throat and looked away. "How long does it take?"

"'Tis a womanly burden I am shamed to discuss. Do not press me for four days, I beg of you."

"Fine, very well." He looked at her for a second, and then back to the tapestry on the wall. "Do you need to lie down, then?"

"I do, actually. My back aches."

Bret's discomfort grew, palpable to the point of nearly making Camille laugh out loud. He took her elbow and led her to the stairs. "I shall make your excuses, my lady. Feel well."

Camille murmured her thanks and ascended the stairs, annoyed with herself she hadn't thought of the lie sooner and spared herself Bret's affections of the night before. Thunder rumbled in the distance, and lightning ripped across the sky. She went into her rooms and lay on the bed, trying to rest for the night to come. She had almost fallen asleep when Amelia entered and stood over her. "You are not well, child? You do not look ill."

"My month's menses, is all."

"You need to learn to endure such affliction. Childbearing is much more a hardship, and you will suffer greatly if you do not push yourself through minor discomforts."

"I am certain I will feel better on the morrow."

Amelia pursed her lips and made a neutral sound deep in her throat, as if she mused upon something she chose not to speak about. She walked about the room slowly, hands clasped beneath her breasts. "So you say." She stopped, faced Camille, and looked at her full in the eyes. Pale and frankly predatory, she stared at her only daughter. "Child, I wonder if you have realized the full extent of how I have attempted to protect you."

"Protect?"

"Yes, though I am not surprised by your lack of insight." Amelia moved closer to Camille, closing the space between them. "I have little to say in the lives of my sons. I accepted this from the moment of their births. They are your father's heirs, dissipating under his incompetent thumb. But you, Camille, are my responsibility. And for all my efforts to guide you, I have been saddled with the most headstrong child, a girl who is so much like her father's mother that no amount of discipline can remove her streak of independent thinking. It seems to me my methods have been thwarted at every turn, and that nothing in the whole of England will make you see reason."

Camille took a deep breath and chose her words with care. "Pleasing you has always seemed unattainable, Mother. Though you may not believe me, I have longed to please you most of my life. Why do you find me so disappointing?"

Amelia tossed her head with frustration, her eyes flashing. Lightning lit up the room, a bright flare of stark brilliance. "Leave it to you to focus on my failing. I have seen to your education, your training, your comportment. I have allowed you to read, cipher, write, and ride. But none of that was enough for you. You took my gifts and insights and still needed more. You have been greedy and grasping from your day of birth, always wanting something more than what I was able to give—more than any woman has a right to want."

Camille sat still and silent, absorbing the meaning behind what her mother had just said. "I never sought to make you feel inadequate," she said gently.

Amelia turned, presenting her narrow back to Camille.

She regained herself and pivoted, her face a mask of cosmetics and emotion in the dim light. "Sleep the night, and we will discuss the nature of your reeducation on the morrow. I pray we will both find solace amidst our regrets."

She left and Camille stared at the closed door, replaying her mother's words and sifting through the uneasiness they had left behind. All her life she had felt as though Amelia knew the rules to some game they played while she withheld any chance of Camille's winning or even fairly competing.

But that no longer mattered. Camille was done with that life and all the misery it had held.

She got up from the bed and gathered from the armoire her cloak, an extra gown, and several sets of undergarments. She rolled and stuffed them in a satchel, adding a bunch of rags for when her menses really did arrive, along with her comb and favorite soap. Inside Shakespeare's *Romeo and Juliet,* she pressed the letter her grandmother had left for her before she died, and then added that to the satchel. She bit her lip against the wave of sadness in realizing she had so little to take from the house where she had spent twenty years.

The air felt heavy, the evening hot. Camille fanned herself and stepped out onto the balcony to watch the lightning that sliced over the trees. Wisps of breezes swayed the hem of her gown and the curls on her shoulders, the scents of a storm swirling around her. In the distance dark clouds gathered, the growling of thunder sounding like an angry watchdog, a prelude to violence.

She sank to the floor of the balcony, tucked her gown around her feet, and looked up to the fierce sky. Visions of the weeks spent with Patrick swept through her head in a succession of images, from the first day she had met him to the night before when he had held her until she slept. Only weeks, but they felt like a lifetime. Camille rested her head against the cool brick of the manor and closed her eyes.

She slept dreamless sleep.

Stinging drops assaulted her face, waking her. The heavens opened, offering a nasty barrage of wind, thunder, lightning, and needles of rain. Camille leaped to her feet, gasping. She rushed into her rooms, lit a candle, and hurried to the mantel where her clock ticked away the seconds. Emotion gathered like the storm and tears fell like the rain as she saw two hours had passed since Patrick should have arrived for her.

Cursing, she flayed herself for sleeping while something might have happened to him. She looked around her room, paced, whirled, and then paced again. Wringing her hands, Camille returned to the balcony, squinting as the storm lashed in her face. It was too dark to see anything, so Camille went back into her room and began stripping off her gown. She pulled her corset from her body and threw it to the floor, ran to her armoire, and pulled out the breeches and shirt she had worn the night she married Patrick. As she dressed she worried that she had misunderstood Patrick's and her plan. What if he had wanted her to meet him on the beach? Or at the cottage? Panicked and distraught, she doubted everything, especially her memory.

She flew out the French doors, awkwardly straddled the rail, and tried to lower herself. Her hands slipped off the wet marble balustrade, and she fell to the sodden ground, twisting her ankle. Camille struggled to her feet, limping toward the woods. The earth shook with every resounding explosion of thunder; jagged flashes of lightning tore across the sky. Rain pelted the leaves, funneling water in rivulets, blinding Camille as she hobbled through the trees. The pain in her ankle shot up to her knee and she tripped and fell. Snarls of bushes scratched her face and Camille felt her warm blood mingle with the cold rain on her skin. Finally she made it to the clearing, scarcely able to make out the form of her cottage, but she could smell the heavy scents of earth and roses carried on gusts of humid wind.

Into the cottage she stumbled, pursued by swirls of wind and rain before she slammed the door. Fumbling around in the pitch dark, she found the flint and lit a candle, causing long waving shadows to roam around the small room. She searched her table but found nothing from Patrick to indicate he'd been there that night. Camille steadied herself with a fortifying gulp of air and tried to settle her nerves as she pushed her saturated hair away from her face and rubbed at the cuts on her nose and cheeks. Staring into the tiny flickering fire of the single candle, she forced herself to recall what Patrick had said, to make sense of his not coming for her. But there was nothing to explain it, unless something had happened to him. Something horrible. And Camille felt her whole body go numb with the thought and the worry.

A new thought dawned, and Camille knew what she needed to do. Sitting at the small table, she scratched out a quick note and then extinguished the candle. She paused just a second in front of the fireplace, where they had spent a night of discovery and passion. And then she moved on, staggering out into the storm.

Grunting with pain and pushing ahead into the inky, tempestuous night, Camille barely noticed the vines that reached down to snag her hair and scratch her face. She limped ahead, single-mindedly, more determined than ever before.

When she reached the beach, she sank down to the wet sand and waited. Exhausted, soaked, in pain and bleeding, Camille listened to the howl of the storm competing with the rage of the churning sea. She sheltered her face with her hands against the fury of nature.

Even after the storm finally abated to soft rain, she continued to wait. Eventually the rain also stopped. Mist rolled in off the water, fog turning the whole earth gray as the sun inched into the sky. Dawn came and Camille peered out to the waters, looking to the ocean for the answer to her question.

The fog dissipated under the heat of the morning sun, burning away. As Camille searched, the sky took on the first shade of blue. Clouds blowing back out to sea turned golden from the mounting sun. Up and down she scanned the coast, and no ship, great or small, fettered the undulating white-tipped sea.

Camille turned in a circle, looking all around the empty coast in the early morning. She was alone but for birds and ocean, crabs and rocky stretches of desolate beach.

"I have nothing," she whispered to herself. She reviewed her few options, looking through her anxiety for a solution to find what had happened to him. Worry clenched her heart like a fist full of razors. The only choice left to her was to return to the hated manor, wake Eric, and plead with him to take her to town and find Patrick.

She tested her weight on her ankle, but could not bear to walk on it. So she limped, dragging it behind her as she made her way back.

The manor seemed to still be slumbering, sparkling from the storm and steaming from the heat of early morning. Camille stumbled up the steps and through the front doors, breathing heavily from her exertions. Scents of chocolate and tea greeted her, accompanied by the rushing footsteps of servants carrying trays up the stairs and into the dining hall. She hurried to the stairs, intent only on waking Eric. With both hands on the handrail, she began pulling herself up the long, winding staircase.

"Gallivanting so early, child?"

Camille froze, sick inside. She turned and saw her mother standing in the doorway to the parlor. Amelia wore a morning gown of pink trimmed in white lace, her face perfect, a cup of chocolate in one hand and the Bible in the other. Fear condensed in Camille like ice over a pond.

"Do you have something you wish to confess?"

Pieces of conversations fell into place. Camille saw that her mother showed shock neither at her appearance nor that she was wet and had been out most of the night. In a heartbeat, suspicion turned into sure knowledge. "What have you done?"

"I have waited since dawn for your return, as would any mother. After the storms woke me and I checked on you, I found your bed empty and your balcony doors wide open to the downpour."

Camille approached her mother, limping, dripping and bleeding, like a ghoul escaped from a crypt. "I asked you what you did. Tell me!"

Amelia held up a warning forefinger. She entered the parlor, holding the door politely as Camille followed her and closing it behind them. She placed herself primly on one of the chairs, taking into her hands the sewing she had left there. "We will discuss your absence and we will discuss the events surrounding it, but you will not shout and spread our family business to all of our guests. I will not have them awakened by your washerwoman's tones. Now sit and tell me what you have done to your face. Do you seek to damage your only asset?"

Camille reached up and touched her face, feeling the raised scratches and the burn of the cuts. "All wounds eventually turn into scars. You of all people should realize that."

"But I, however, have taken great pains to see the beauty of your face be preserved. What would you be without your appearance, child? A willful girl of little grace and a surly disposition who bears a marred appearance is unlikely to win herself a man's affections."

Camille's composure snapped, her blood a boiling race through her body. She was in front of her mother in a second, grabbing her shoulders and shaking her roughly until her wig was knocked askew. "Where is he?"

With a quick swipe Amelia stabbed Camille's left hand with her sewing needle. Camille let go of her mother and pulled back, holding her injured hand to her chest.

"You bitch," she snarled. "I will kill you if you've hurt Patrick."

Amelia sat back, satisfied, and rested her sewing in her lap. "Ah, excellent. You're finally ready to discuss the mariner."

CHAPTER 9

Amelia stood and swept to the looking glass that hung over a mahogany side table. She settled her wig in place, patted it, smoothed her gown, and turned to face her daughter. "The truth always comes out, child."

"Truth is all I have ever wanted. All I want now. Tell me where he is." Words and breath clogged in her throat, a jumble of emotions and needs. She dropped to her knees, willing to plead if that would make her mother tell her. "I will do anything you want."

As she looked down at her daughter, something close to pity flitted across her features for just a second. And then she smiled. Maliciously. "Your mariner has left Southampton."

"Left?"

"It would appear that, like all the Irish, he chased the pot of gold at the end of the rainbow."

"You speak in riddles and time wastes."

"Time, you say." Amelia began to walk about the room, musing aloud. "Time will be the only thing left to you, child. Time to ponder your predicament. Time to meditate on your mistakes. Time to learn the value of obedience." Amelia warmed to her topic; she stopped pacing to watch the effect of her words on Camille's face. She ignored the horrible sadness in her eyes and chose to see only the wickedness of her actions. "But most of all, you will have time to learn, Camille. I will delay your impending marriage until I feel you have learned all that a woman of your station should know. By God, I will see to it that you receive an education in propriety even if I have to see you broken to do so. I will not have a daughter who conducts herself as commoner trash.

"You thought you had me fooled, didn't you, child? You continued to sneak and chase after that seafaring commoner right under my nose. And so, I admit I am pleased at this outcome. 'Twill be a lesson learned that none could teach."

Amelia seated herself again and picked up her chocolate, sipped lightly, and then enunciated every word with great satisfaction and cheer. "Your mariner has left England. He has left you. I offered him enough coin to purchase a small country in exchange for his departure, and he accepted my terms. He sailed at midday, yesterday."

"No," Camille whispered.

"Indeed," Amelia replied calmly. "Really, child, you must know that naiveté ceases to be charming after childhood. You find it difficult to accept that this commoner, this seafarer, would turn away from a fortune of his own in exchange for a girl he scarcely knows? Foolishness," Amelia declared. "Your Irishman possesses the wisdom to know that there will be many females easily seduced by his handsome features and his poetic ways, but that the wealth I offered him was incomparable."

Camille turned her mother's words over, even as she remembered Patrick's. She recalled his vows on the beach and the words spoken in the cottage. Camille could still feel his hands on her body and his promises in her heart. "I can hardly expect you to understand what Patrick and I share, Mother. To feel what we feel requires a soul, and in that you are lacking. I am weary of your mendacity, and I want the truth!"

"How dare you call me mendacious, you little twit! You

lie as you breathe! You sneak in direct violation of my command. Truth! You tryst with the mariner on the beach. Truth! You attempt to sail away with that man with no regard to the shame you would bring on your family. Truth! All truth!"

Camille grew pale and silent, sick with the weight of how much Amelia knew. Finally, she dared a question. "If you knew all of this, why did you allow it to continue?"

"To give you the opportunity for a valuable lesson, of course," Amelia replied. "I approached the mariner privately and made him aware I knew of your trysts. He immediately and correctly surmised that any chance of leaving and taking you with him was no longer an option. What then prevented his taking my offers of fortune?

"I had my man look into your Irishman's situation in London and had word sent from Paris. Your Patrick has nothing outside of his father's wealth. Nothing. Until now, that is."

Camille lifted her chin. "Patrick loves me. Nothing of your lies could make me believe differently. I will not believe. You can beat me, and I will still not believe. Patrick loves me."

"Love?" Amelia tilted her head, considered the word. "Perhaps he did love you, and even now loves you still. But even a commoner, nay, especially a commoner, knows the value and heft of a fortune of one's own. Such a fortune will buy far more than the foolish fancy of the heart. I admit, he did balk at the idea. He even seemed affronted. But in the end, he saw the wisdom of my offer. He realized you were gone to him forever. He relieved me of the coin reluctantly, child, I admit that." Amelia leaned forward and leveled her pale eyes on Camille, narrowing them until they looked like shards of ice. "But he took it, just the same."

Denial and fear pumped through her. Her head spun and her stomach slid in slick knots. She could hear Patrick's words, spoken to her on a starry night in front of the ocean. *You are wrapped up in my hopes and dreams.* She thought of how she knew him, from the rhythm of his breath to the taste of his skin, the truth in his eyes and the gift of his love.

She would not believe. "I want to know what you have done with him. Tell me, or you will not be safe from me. Tell me, Amelia, or you will have to eat and sleep under guard. With my own hands I will burn Beauport and bring shame on this family such as you cannot imagine. God damn you, you will tell me!"

Amelia continued on, unaffected by Camille's threats. "You misdirect your fury, child. Scream rather at the lover who abandoned you." Her eyes went suddenly wide and she inhaled theatrically. "Don't tell me you have been completely duped. Did you fall for his obsequious fawning and excessive flattery? Don't you know that a man tells a woman those things for one thing, and only one? Did you fall right onto your back and spread your thighs? Did you exchange your virtue for words and sentiment?"

Camille looked at the floor, frustrated beyond measure. Amelia did not press for an answer, but rang a silver bell. A servant appeared in seconds, her brows lifted in mute inquiry. "Has my son returned?"

"Yes, Your Grace."

"Send him in. Only him, for now."

The light step of the servant faded. Amelia looked at her daughter from forehead to feet, taking in the mess of wet, snarled hair, dried blood and weeping scratches on her face, to the bedraggled boys' clothing, damp and hanging on her slim frame. A mess of a girl, but still exquisite in an essential way, beautiful in the way nature is when wild and unchecked. But it was not pride that simmered in Amelia's breast.

"I am not taken aback by your lack of trust in what I say, child. There has been no great love between us that you would accept my words when they bring you naught but disappointment. I am not ashamed of my efforts to relieve you of the mariner, but I expect that for a time you will resent me for doing so. One day, perhaps. you will see the reason behind my actions, and you will understand. You will see that you were headed down a path that would leave ruin and shame in its wake. Believe me, I know the outcome when headstrong girls such as yourself are left to their own devices."

Camille did not reply. She heard her mother's words distantly over the repeating of Patrick's in her mind. *A promise is forever, Camille. Have a care with my heart, for I have never loved a woman before you.* A love such as the one they shared could not be lies. Patrick would never be disloyal to her for money, no matter how great the wealth. The man she knew would rather wear rags than to accept a bribe and betray their love.

Eric entered the parlor and closed the door. He shifted, cleared his throat, and looked at the wall rather than face his sister.

"Your sister needs additional information regarding her Irish mariner. Provide it," Amelia instructed.

Camille looked at her brother, seeing his discomfort and the way he swallowed again and again, as if to rid his mouth of an unpleasant taste. "Don't do it, Eric. Don't lie for her."

Eric rubbed his hand over his face, exhaled on a breath. "He is gone. Sailed."

A tear slid down Camille's cheek, burning as it passed over her open cuts. "Don't let her do this to you."

"It is done. For you and Patrick, it is done. He does not want my land, and he left yesterday. I checked his rooms at the Goodrow Inn. He is gone. I am certain." Eric wanted to flinch at the harrowing grief on her face as his words tore at her heart. "I am sorry, Cam. I hate to hurt you like this."

"Patrick loves me."

"Patrick is gone."

"He loves me," she whispered, her voice desperate.

"He sailed."

"Patrick would not lie to me."

Eric lifted his broad shoulders and spread his hands. "I only know he is gone."

Amelia watched the crumble of Camille's resolve play out on her features. She rose and came to stand over her daughter. "Do you believe?"

Camille's head swam with memories and doubts. "I don't know what to believe. He said he would . . ." she couldn't finish. She couldn't give voice to the words he had spoken.

"Words, child. What are words? They are sounds in the air, nothing more."

"His words were everything to me."

Victory shot through Amelia as Camille spoke of him in the past tense. But she showed no triumph. Not yet. "Lies. For all we are aware, he has been honing his skills on girls in all the ports of the world."

Camille lay down on the floor and closed her eyes.

Amelia went to the door and held it open, gesturing for someone to enter as Eric left. Amelia closed the door again and delicately cleared her throat. "Camille, you have a guest."

She sat up and looked at Veronica, seated uncomfortably on a small chair. Veronica's pretty face looked pale, her lips devoid of their usual color. She sat with her hands neatly folded on her lap. "My lady."

"Why are you here?" Camille pushed her damp hair away from her face.

"I have come at your mother's request." She licked her lips, looking down at her hands. "It appears we were both seduced by the same man."

The words sliced into Camille's heart and down through her gut. Everything faded away, leaving only pain. Like the vilest illness, every part of her body ached. A mist of sweat condensed on her skin even as she felt frozen down to her bones. The chamber pot sat only a few steps away behind a screen. Camille stumbled to it just in time to relieve herself of what little was in her belly with a few violent retches.

She sat back on the floor and pulled her hand across her mouth. Veronica went to her side and laid her hands on Camille's trembling shoulders. "Please forgive me, my lady. I did not know him to be involved with you. Had I known, I would have sent word to you immediately."

Camille looked up to Amelia, a seed of doubt sown amidst so much evidence. "How did you manage to orchestrate all of this?"

"I did nothing of the sort. A word with the innkeeper told me your seafarer received a certain feminine guest, and a coin placed in his hand gave me the name of the girl."

And then Camille remembered the day in town, when Veronica had stood before her dressed in a crimson gown. *I seek to dazzle a very handsome man.* A gesture of her tiny hand to the Goodrow Inn. *You will know where to find me, my lady.* Camille felt her gorge rise again. "You were in bed with him?"

Veronica looked to Amelia and then Camille. "I did go to his bed. He said such pretty things, like poetry. He spoke of Shakespeare and stories. I let myself be seduced by him." Veronica looked again to Amelia, who nodded imperceptibly. "He gave me a gift. Told me it had belonged to his father." She held out a small brooch, a whale carved in ivory.

Camille lay back on the floor, letting her hair fall around her face like a shroud. When she spoke it was barely audible. "What will you do to me?"

Amelia finally smiled her victory. "I will take you to London, child, where you belong. Bret will wait for you; I can assure you of that, though he will not be pleased about your bedding the Irishman."

"What of our guests?"

"They can stay at Beauport or leave, as they wish. I have need to leave the country before I am stifled."

Veronica couldn't stop staring at Camille, sympathy on

her face and regret tugging down the corners of her lips. Amelia stood and ushered the girl from the room, pressing a small sack of coins into her hand. When the duchess returned to stand over Camille, she poked her with the tip of her shoe.

"Rise and begin to salvage what remains of your pride. Go to your rooms. Have your hair combed out and your face seen to. Get dressed and wait for me to send for you. I will send the staff to pack your things. We will be leaving this afternoon."

Like a wraith, Camille did as she was told, methodically and without emotion. Nothing mattered. Not London or Bret, Amelia or the freedom she had craved. Patrick had left her. He had betrayed her.

She believed.

Rain had returned and fell steadily. The continuous drumming of the cloudburst could scarcely be heard over the flurry of activity that took place in Camille's bedchamber. Servants completed the final packing that can be done only in the last moments before departure. Free from the watchful gaze of the duchess, they chatted and gossiped. Their voices ranged from hushed revelations of secrets to gasps and giggles as those not present lost pieces of their privacy.

Once in a while, the girls glanced over to the large bed where Camille lay, and then back to the others with eyes full of questions and guesses. None of the young servant girls dared to approach or speak to their mistress with whom age was their only commonality.

Camille stared at the ceiling, far too wracked in her own thoughts to notice the attentions of the staff. Pain pervaded her body. She longed for true illness to come so the trip to London would be delayed. To stay in her bed and keep reality at bay seemed her only viable option for surviving the devastation of Patrick's betrayal and desertion.

A dream bloomed in the dark recesses of her mind, an image of Patrick returning and tossing the coin in Amelia's face, picking Camille up, and carrying her away.

She pushed the picture away, snuffed out the hope like a flame from a candle. He hadn't come for her, and he never would. He had taken the money as he had taken Veronica to his bed. His words had been lies, his actions a ruse. He had seen her weakness and used it.

And she had let him. Invited him. No, she thought wearily. She had begged him.

Flanna stepped into Camille's room uncomfortably, her chapped, coarse hands smoothing her apron with self-conscious strokes. All chatter ceased as the servant girls looked incredulously at the kitchen help who had forgotten her place in the cellar and kitchens.

Flanna cleared her throat, obviously nervous. "May I have a moment alone with Mistress Camille?"

One of the girls stood and held her shoulders back, tilting her nose up. "We're needin' to make a trip with these trunks anyway."

The girls hefted the baggage and left the room. Flanna backed out of their way and ignored the indignant whispers that began before the girls reached the doorway.

Flanna glanced about the elegant rooms, surveying the domain reserved for the upper-level servants. She had worked in Beauport for more than forty years and was seeing the upstairs for the first time.

She walked over to the large bed with light footsteps, approaching Camille, whose blank stare at the ceiling had remained unchanged since Flanna's unprecedented arrival. Camille's usually vivid eyes were dull, and her skin was pale beneath welts and scratches.

"Dearie?"

Camille didn't respond.

Flanna waited a long moment and then gingerly sat on the side of the large bed, careful to not wrinkle the buttery yellow silk coverlet, aware its worth would have paid a year of her salary. Camille showed no response to Flanna's impertinence. Growing even bolder, Flanna took Camille's slack hand in her own.

For a while, Flanna sat and held her hand, not seeming to notice or care that Camille hadn't acknowledged her presence.

Finally, Flanna spoke again. "I overheard a bit of what happened."

Camille didn't move.

Flanna continued on in her soft Irish brogue, as if unaware of Camille's indifference. "I was beautiful, once. Not like you, but I had a comeliness of my own. Long ago, my hair had more red than gray, an' my figure had curves where needed, an' none where not. I could turn a man's head, to be sure. But the only man I ever cared to impress was young Harry Orr. He had the face of an angel an' the devil in his eye. He could talk the sweet out of chocolate an' he charmed the reason out of my head. I followed him all the way from Ireland to England, just on the might that he'd marry me. I left my family an' my senses that day, an' I never could go back since my da an' mam knew I'd given myself to Harry."

Flanna's lilting voice grew softer and her accent thickened as she relived a past that was so long ago, at times it seemed as though it had happened to someone else. "He made such promises; we made plans and we dreamed. He spoke of love, you see, an' I saw my future in his every word. Then he deserted me. He left me, an' I had nothin' an' no one. I found myself alone in a country that hated my people an' had no place for me. But that wasn't the worst of it. The worst was being rejected by the man I loved." Flanna's eyes misted. "Aye. That was the worst of all of it."

Camille said nothing, but her hand tightened around Flanna's.

Flanna smiled gently. "Aye, dearie. I come here to tell you, you'll survive this. Your heart is strong, you see, an' you will survive. It's goin' to be slow goin', sure, but you'll find the days will get easier as they pass. An' pass, they will. An' you will heal. Aye. You will heal."

Camille took a deep, ragged breath, and spoke the first words since her final exchange with Amelia. "I love him, still. 'Tis what hurts the most."

"Aye," Flanna agreed. "A broken heart will cause pain like nothin' else."

"Heart?" Camille asked bitterly. "My heart is gone. It has been torn from me. It sailed with the *Nuala* yesterday at midday."

"I'm sorry," Flanna whispered.

"You're sorry; I'm sorry; Eric's sorry. Everyone is sorry except the one who left and the one who paid him."

Flanna looked away for a moment from Camille's naked pain. She spoke words she knew would sound trite. "The Good Book says 'This too shall pass.' You will be happy again one day."

Camille turned her head to the side, looking out the French doors to the balcony where the rain fell. "There is a saying that happiness is for fools and children, and so, yes, I suppose I should be happy, fool that I am."

"There is no foolishness in loving."

"I trusted, completely. I loved, completely. And now I have learned. Completely."

Flanna tightened her hold of Camille's hand. "No! You learned nothin' of love an' trust. Only harsh truths of self-ishness and greed."

Camille turned her head from side to side, trying to drown out the sounds in her head. "He is gone, Flanna. He left me. How could he do this? His betrayal of our love causes nearly as much pain as it does anger. In truth, I know not what to feel first. I ache and then I rage, all in this inescapable vessel that is my mind and body! Even in his absence, he tortures me. He haunts me. I hear his voice and I feel his touch. He is everywhere because he is inside me!"

Flanna stroked a kind hand along Camille's brow, trying

to comfort her. "You followed your heart. There is no shame in that, dearie. Shame belongs only to the one who abuses such a gift."

"There is nothing left for me. He is as gone as my innocence."

"You are so young. There is a future for you," Flanna insisted gently.

"What does the future hold for me? Loveless marriage and endless childbearing?" Camille looked directly into Flanna's eyes. "I would rather take my own life."

Flanna leaned forward, never breaking the hold of Camille's gaze. "You mustn't say such things. It is a sin against God an' a sin against yourself. You will find the courage to get out of your bed an' stand up to the outcome of your choices."

Camille's eyes filled and became magnified by tears that did not fall. "Can't you see that I found what I was looking for? I tasted paradise. I found my soul's mate." Camille swallowed hard and could speak only in the barest whisper. "Only, it was a figment of my thoughts. He does not belong to me as I do to him."

Flanna sighed heavily. She smoothed Camille's hair with the gentle understanding of a woman for whom life had denied the opportunity to have her own child, but whose kindness and empathy made her instinctually maternal. Camille leaned into the touch, finding comfort in the basic caresses that had been withheld from her since the death of her grandmother.

"So much like Lady Elizabeth," Flanna said softly, as if reading Camille's thoughts.

"I am nothing like her. My grandmother was wise and strong."

"You are more like her than you know," Flanna asserted in a low voice. "I have lived in Beauport longer than many folks live their whole lives, an' though I am old an' tired, my memory is long. I remember your grandmother well."

"How am I like her?"

Flanna closed her eyes in memory. "Wisdom an' strength come from experience. Lady Elizabeth lived her life with feeling. She burned with the life inside her body, just as you do."

"What else do you know, Flanna? Do you know what caused her sadness?"

Flanna coughed lightly and rose from the bed. Her hands again smoothed her apron. "I need to be goin' back to my work. If the duchess finds I've been to see you, I'll be back to toiling in the gardens."

Camille lacked the energy to press for the answer Flanna avoided giving. "This is good-bye, then."

"Aye, dear lass. Godspeed you to London safely, an' may the Lord lift your pain as the days pass."

"Thanks to you, kind Flanna."

The old cook reached out to touch the younger woman's hair once more. "I will miss you, dearie."

Flanna turned and made her way from Camille's rooms slowly, limping from the perpetual ache in her hips.

Camille resumed her study of the ceiling. Shadows borne of a gray and rainy day lit by candles played across the patterned plaster. Molded and carved vines trailed along the length of the room where the ceiling met the wall. But Camille could find no appreciation for the work of the unknown artisan this day. She mused only on the events that had led her to this place of suffering.

No answers could be found. Patrick's betrayal and Amelia's deception made sense to Camille only when she thought about it with her mind. If she felt it with her heart and soul, all reason fell away, leaving only intense anguish. Patrick left. For all the valor of his words and bearing, once he knew their love had been exposed, he had accepted a bribe and left her. He hadn't even said good-bye.

Camille realized that there is a price attached to everything in life. A price to be paid for every pleasure, and a price to be exacted for each mistake. And he had beggared her.

She gave up the struggle for understanding. She could

find no reason to continue to torture herself for what she had no power to control, no ability to change. It was done. Patrick had sailed.

She let out her breath in a long, soft sigh. She pushed herself from her bed and stood before the looking glass, smoothing her traveling gown of fawn-colored muslin. Brigid had laced Camille into her gown and pulled her black hair back from her face in a thick twist, coiling it into a heavy bun at the nape of Camille's neck. The maid had then left her with the remainder of the toilette at Camille's request to be alone, leaving to her mistress the slipping on of stockings and shoes and the placement of her hat.

Camille reached for her stockings and began to pull them on. The gossamer silk tangled on the amber bracelet that hung around her bruised ankle. The gems glowed like a circle of captured sunlight. Warm and mysterious, the amber glowed from within. It lured Camille to stare into its depths of clear yellowish brown, gold, and red as if she could uncover the hidden secrets of its origins.

Better still that I could find the truths of its owner, she thought bitterly.

Camille untwisted her stocking from the bracelet and smoothed it along her calf and thigh. She lightly touched the outline of the jewelry under the silk, unsure of how she felt about wearing it.

In an instant, she was back on the moonlit beach, feeling Patrick's strong fingers fasten the bracelet around her ankle as he promised to love her forever.

A new image replaced it, of Patrick giving Veronica a brooch while he told her a story of his father.

A sob gathered in Camille's throat, choking her and stealing her breath. Through a haze of tears, she set her hat atop her head and stepped into her shoes.

She left the amber bracelet where Patrick had fastened it. There it would remain, serving her as a reminder of the beauty of what they had shared, the perfection of loving him and feeling loved in return, the agony of betrayal, and the exorbitant cost of all of it.

Camille stood in the threshold and glanced back at her rooms a last time. Then she turned and stepped out, pulling the door closed firmly. She walked through the empty halls, knowing it would be a long time before she would return to Beauport.

As she descended the curving staircase, she saw Bret poised at the bottom, leaning against the railing. He sneered up at her, his handsome face holding nothing but loathing. She reached the last step and stood there, using the height of the stair to hold her at eye level with Bret.

"I assume you will accompany my mother and me to London," Camille stated dispassionately.

"I will."

"Does my mother await us?"

"She does."

Camille remained insouciant. She shrugged lightly and brushed past Bret. Bret grabbed her upper arm and turned her abruptly, forcing her to again face him.

"You were not dismissed."

Camille jerked her arm to free it from his hold, but found his grasp too strong. "Let go of me!"

"You played me," Bret snarled. "You are everything Amelia said you were."

Anger sparked in her eyes, emerald fire. "Is there no one who does not know?"

"I have the right to be informed of my future bride."

"You have no rights to me, Bret. Not yet."

"I beg to differ."

"I can't imagine you begging for anything."

"Not from you, no. From you I will never beg. I will simply take what God and king decree as mine."

"Perhaps," Camille agreed with a shrug. She thought of his panting, rough affections in her bed, and her ire rose. "But not before. And so, my betrothed, I tell you again, *take your hands from me.*"

Bret's hand squeezed tighter around her slender upper arm. Camille laughed at his attempt to control her with brutality. "I tell you now, Bret, that approach will not work. Ask Amelia."

Bret's anger only increased at her flippant attitude. "I have tactics I'm sure your mother has not tested, and weapons I know she does not possess." Bret pulled Camille by her captive arm until she pressed against his body. He slid his free hand down her back and held her hips against his so she could feel the full meaning behind his threat.

He brought his face to hers and seethed his words through clenched teeth. "Now that I know your games and your contrived ploys, I will never again be a fool for your sweet words and smiling lips. Know that in the future I will concern myself only with your behavior and to hell with what you feel. Your Irishman is gone. You would do well to resign yourself to your destiny."

Camille held her head back so she could meet his eyes with the fury in her own. "If you are looking for a wife who will fear you, you have chosen poorly. You seek to warn me of future violence and rape in our marriage bed, and you demonstrate your strength as you bruise my arm. You may do the things you threaten, but I shall warn you as well. Know that each one of us sleeps at some time. You would do well to do so with one eye open, for you may find me above you."

"You are trying my patience."

"You are trying my stomach."

Bret's hold tightened even further, wrenching a small cry of pain from her throat as she renewed her struggles.

"Unhand my sister!"

Eric strode into the foyer and clapped a strong hand down on Bret's shoulder.

Bret released her and turned on his heel to confront her intruding brother. "You are interfering where you have no rights."

"She is my blood. What is your claim?"

"She will be my wife."

Eric's hand squeezed Bret's shoulder until his thumb dug in just below his collarbone. "Only a coward abuses a woman. What do you think such a craven would do if he met up with a real man?"

Bret pushed Eric and wrenched himself free. Bret opened his mouth to retort, but Amelia's voice cut him off.

"You call yourself a real man? What are you basing that on?"

Eric paled at his mother's words. His gaze rested on Camille for a second. Eric wanted to tell his sister everything. He wanted to reach out to her and give her some comfort from the suffering he knew he had helped to cause. But if he did, Amelia would ruin him. That he knew most of all.

With a groan of frustration, Eric spun around and strode away. He wanted to be away from the house, his mother, and her victims, hating himself for being counted among them. The door slammed on his way out.

A satisfied smirk spread across Amelia's face. "Are you both prepared to embark on our journey?"

Bret nodded and took Camille's elbow. "We are."

Camille tolerated Bret's touch and allowed him to lead her from the mansion and into the rain-dampened day. She stepped into the carriage and seated herself on the plush bench seat. Amelia and Bret followed suit, and Bret pressed himself next to Camille, his muscular thigh rubbing with familiarity against Camille's. She said nothing; she didn't pull away. She only stared out the small window of the carriage to the fields that stretched away from Beauport, knowing that past the groves of fruit trees, manicured formal gardens, and fountains lay the dense stretch of woods that enveloped a small cottage.

The memory of her cottage and what she had experienced there hit Camille like a blow to the back. She felt with certainty that if given the choice, she would trade her entire future to savor one more day with Patrick and the bliss they had shared; she was more than willing to crawl on her belly through the spines and thorns of the underbrush to reach the cottage and Patrick. If only for one more day.

Camille took in a deep breath and held it. She held it until she wanted breath so badly she could think of nothing else. All faded away in the burning of her lungs, so she could not think of Patrick or their vows, the cottage or the love they had made. And then she held it a moment more, relishing the brief moment where nothing else mattered outside elemental survival and the most basic of human need.

And then she took a breath.

Bret reached up and rapped on the roof of the carriage, and Camille heard the sharp whistle of the driver, signaling to the carriages in front of and behind their own that the duchess had indicated her readiness. The carriage dipped and rocked as the weight of the footmen boarded and took their seats. In a moment they lurched into motion and the entourage began the three-day journey to London. They rode under heavy guard, well prepared for the likelihood of being robbed. Coming under siege while traveling had become so commonplace that it was viewed simply as a nuisance to be anticipated and countered.

The rain picked up again. Its drumming noise drowned the sounds of the wheels grinding through the grit of the long driveway and muffled the canter of the horses. But nothing of nature outside of death could take away her longing or stifle the sounds in her head that screamed for the want of what she had lost. As she stared out the small window, watching the water that fell from the sky run in rivulets over the carriage, Camille thought it to be a baptism, a consecrated departure from her loss of innocence and her ability to believe in anyone but herself.

Camille watched Beauport and the vast lands surrounding it slowly disappear from view. Her plans to leave her home had come to fruition. The irony caused a wry grin to twist Camille's lips.

"You are pleased, child?" Amelia inquired.

"I am quiescent, Mother."

Amelia nodded with satisfaction. "If that is true, nothing could please me more."

Bret cast a sidelong look at Camille. His lips twisted again, as his own thoughts were of the night before, when he had so wanted to woo her with tender words and soft caresses. He had to look away from her. He found it difficult to look at her beauty and hate her still, even as he pictured her clasped in the arms of the Irishman.

Bret stared out the window beside him and watched the countryside roll past. It would be a long trip for all of them.

CHAPTER 10

The Atlantic Ocean

Patrick awoke on the deck of the *Nuala*. His head pounded and his body ached, and a sickening realization clawed at his gut.

Camille would have waited for him.

He groaned with frustration and pain, longing to push his hands against his head where the discomfort seemed the worst. But thick ropes bound his hands behind him and lashed him to the pinrail at the base of the mizzenmast. The sun beat down on him from a cloudless sky, and a light wind brushed over his face. The sea felt calm, the pitch and sway of the ship as familiar to him as his own heartbeat.

They had been waiting for him in his room at the inn. Armed with knives and pistols, they had tried to overtake him at first without violence, using threats in an effort to coerce him to cooperate. But he had fought them despite the odds and his lack of weapons. He had been half crazed, vicious. He killed two men with a fire poker and wounded two others. Still, he had lost the battle and taken a hit on the base of his skull. He hadn't been aware of anything else until he awoke on the *Nuala*.

His worry grew. What would she think? Would she

assume he had abandoned her, or would she agonize with anxiety that he had been injured or laid low with illness? Either way, Amelia would have intervened, Patrick felt certain. He knew without any doubt the duchess stood behind his capture.

He wondered why she had had him taken, and not killed.

And then he speculated upon the lies she must have told Camille. The thoughts cleaved him like a blade, wounding him and churning his stomach like the waters beneath the hull. He could hope against his certainty, but he knew she would eventually believe the worst. Her insecurity would prevent otherwise, and a lifetime of beatings and ridicule would not have prepared her for trust. Not in their love, and not in herself. She had felt too alone in the world for too long.

So immersed in his musings as he was, he didn't notice the black cat approaching him until it began stroking itself against Patrick's boots.

"Sidney, you're still aboard?"

At the sound of the familiar voice and the mention of his name, the cat paused in his actions and looked at Patrick directly, his greenish yellow eyes full of feline wisdom. Sidney held his tail straight up, bent slightly at the tip in the shape of a question mark, as if to solicit from Patrick the reasons strange men stood at the helm of the great ship on which he had been born. Nothing sounded from Patrick except a low grunt of pain. The cat seemed to dismiss the large man and his questions in the same instant, returning to glide around Patrick's boots, weaving in and around with precision, evenly distributing the self-induced petting uniformly around his lithe body. Pure pleasure took the cat to a higher plane. Sidney began to purr, the rumbling, vibrating sound punctuated periodically with a sound resembling the chirping of crickets.

"If only you could tell me how long I've been out and when we set sail," Patrick grumbled.

Sidney ceased his stroking again, now with an expression

of impatience at the second interruption. His patience ran out. The cat padded away, his tail held regally erect, as if his function aboard the ship were one of honored guest rather than for control of the rodent population.

Patrick ignored the pain behind his eyes and began to look about for any clues the ship or sea might offer. He had been deposited aft, and from that vantage he could not see land. The sea felt calm, and the winds were light. But he had remembered a storm blowing in before he had been taken, which meant they had sailed quite a few leagues.

Or rather, he thought, they had drifted. How they had gotten very far, Patrick couldn't guess. The sails hung slack from being improperly cast, slapping against the winds until the tall masts creaked. The lines had been tied down, but the knots were sloppy and Patrick knew they would never hold if put to the test of a good squall. Rigging and ropes crowded the rough deck, and the topsails had been raised, but not secured. These men who had taken him were clearly not experienced seamen. Even still, Patrick mused, why then had his scant crew not been used for their skills, unless his men had been injured?

Heavy footsteps could be heard approaching. Patrick closed his eyes and pretended to still be unconscious.

"Did ye make sure 'is ropes 're trussed tight enough?"

A laugh sounded from another man. "Aye, Birney. Fer a one what swears 'e ain't scared o' the bloke, yer spendin' yer time worryin' after 'is ropes."

The sound of a solid whack of fist meeting gut resounded across the deck of the ship, followed by the sharp intake of breath. "Yer a bloody, ungrateful bloke, 'Errick! I took ye out o' England an' saved yer ass from Newgate. Ye should show yer thanks to yer betters."

"An' ye ought to quit swingin' at me, else ye find yerself another man short on yer crew," Herrick warned with a gasp.

Birney ignored Herrick's warnings and took a few steps closer to Patrick, eyeing his captive cautiously. The ocean winds had knotted and tangled the man's hair and blown the dark auburn mass away from his face, allowing a close inspection of the man they had been generously paid to take hostage. His skin had readily darkened under the glaring rays of the sun, not searing him to a bright red as Birney and Herrick had been burned. Years of squinting into the horizon had carved grooves around the eyes and mouth of the man called Patrick Mullen, but the darkness of his skin and the craggy contours of his face did not diminish his looks. Even Birney could see that the man had a beauty uncommon to a male, combined with the rugged look of an animal, both graceful and dangerous. Birney had felt his strength and seen the way the man fought. Though Birney sought to contain the man, he did so with all the caution commanded by a wild creature of the forest, for the cunning beast would kill if given an opportunity.

The man had everything Birney did not, and just that simple comprehension was enough to make Birney hate him.

A new thought dawned on Birney's slow brain, and he landed a quick kick to Patrick's side. When his hostage didn't move or flinch, Birney began to relax his guard.

"Are ye goin' to move the bloke below deck?" Herrick inquired, keeping well out of the reach of Birney's ham-like fists.

"Nah. Let the bugger bake out 'ere. 'E'll be less likely to give us trouble if 'e's not feelin' to form."

Herrick looked up to the sky, seeing not a single cloud to offer relief from the relentless sun. "If 'e's sick 'e won't bring much of a price at the block."

Birney snorted his disagreement. "A bloke 'is size will bring more coin than ye've ever seen."

Herrick shrugged his annoyance, choosing to voice only his logic. "If 'e's well an' strong, 'e'll bring even more."

"I says we ain't movin' 'im," Birney said flatly.

Herrick shuffled his feet and rubbed at his bristly chin, feeling disgusted with the poor choices being made by the man in charge of their mission. "Yer lookin' to punish the man for 'is fightin' us when we took 'im, but ye would 'ave done the same if 'e 'ad come lookin' to take ye. Ye would 'ave fought just the same as 'im. 'E's a man who was lookin' to protect 'is life, an' in my mind ye can't fault 'im for that."

Herrick rubbed his chin with more vigor as if uncomfortable with his own verbosity, but he forced himself to continue. "This man 'as a long road in front o' 'im. 'Is 'ead is wounded an' the sun is strong. Yer more likely to kill 'im while seekin' yer vengeance for yer battered pride."

"It ain't me pride, ye stupid jackanapes! Did ye forget the bugger killed Big Ed an' Willy?" Birney snarled.

Herrick's reasonable attitude didn't change. "'E thought we were gonna kill 'im an' 'e fought back."

"Nah, I saw the look o' death in 'is eyes. 'E meant to kill them an' 'e was lookin' to send the rest o' us to hell on the end o' 'is sticker. I ain't never seen a man with eyes like that," Birney said with conviction, widening his own watery hazel eyes for emphasis.

Herrick shrugged his heavy shoulders again, already weary of Birney's superstitions. "Are ye goin' to take 'im out o' the sun, or not?"

Birney hesitated for only a split second. "Leave the bastard. Maybe a few days in the sun'll teach 'im some respect."

Herrick nearly sneered at the word 'respect' as it was spit from Birney's mouth. Since Herrick had known Birney, there had always been this demanding of respect, usually garnered by torture, force, or humiliation. Herrick had his own scars gathered in reaching that conclusion. Herrick jerked his head in a sharp nod and walked away to busy himself with checking the binnacle, mindful not to show the disgust he felt.

Birney turned on his heel and moved away from Patrick, heading for the gundeck, where stores of issue rum were lashed out of the way of the small cannons.

Patrick kept his eyes closed and shifted his body, trying to find a moderately comfortable position to seek sleep. The pain in his head had not abated, and a new ache had been added to his side, but Patrick felt only satisfaction. The overheard conversation between his captors had not provided him answers to all his questions, but had given him all he needed to proceed with his escape.

Patrick awoke to the welcome greeting of an evening sky, long after the blistering sun had made its descent. The heavens spread out like midnight blue velvet that glittered with diamonds of stars clustered to form the familiar constellations of summer. The crescent moon hung suspended high above, telling Patrick that the night held many more hours at its disposal.

The pain in his head had eased somewhat, abating to an ache that no longer nauseated. Patrick took a deep breath of the salty air and mentally tallied his resources for escape.

The *Nuala* was a large merchant vessel of remarkable luxury. Conlan, Patrick's father, had named the schooner Nuala, declaring the craft to be just like Patrick's mother: uncommonly beautiful, tall, and proud, but also unassuming in her own way, unafraid to work her share or carry a burden. The schooner possessed amenities for comfort in the captain's cabin, such as a stove for heat and a bed large enough to hold Patrick and a companion comfortably. But more than that, it held some of Patrick's happiest memories. The *Nuala* was the first ship on which Patrick had walked the decks as captain, and the only ship in his father's fleet aboard which Patrick felt at home.

Since the death of his mother when he had just turned eight, Patrick worked to pull his weight. No longer a lad with a mother to watch over him, Patrick was transformed by Nuala's death into a young man with responsibilities in the space of a tragic afternoon. Patrick learned the ways of the sea and the art of commerce. The life of a sea merchant held few comforts, for the ocean was harsh, wild, and unforgiving, with damp, cold, endless months between trading ports. Pirates roamed the seas as far as the West Indies in search of merchant ships to loot. Survival and hardship had become words not worth speaking or thinking, for they were only the way of life. And yet Patrick had remained with his father, working for him in an industry that appealed more to Conlan than it ever had to Patrick.

Conlan had never found peace, and for that Patrick felt regretful for his father. In his desperation to be free of his own father's corrupted way of life, Conlan had headed in the opposite direction. Conlan became as honest a man as Patrick had ever known, so scrupulously fair that his reputation had grown apace with his fortune, earning him the name 'the Merchant King.' But still, his father had not known serenity. Conlan had held Nuala's hand as she died and he watched all their dreams die with her. Wealth, success, and land meant nothing without family. And for that reason, and only that reason, Patrick stayed with Conlan. For that same reason, Conlan had allowed his pirate father, Rogan, back into their lives, finding small solace in a measure of understanding and forgiveness.

Together, three generations of Mullens sailed the far-flung corners of the world, bringing tobacco, molasses, sugar, and dyes from America and the West Indies, silks and spices from the Levant, printed calico and pepper from India, wine and foods from France and the Mediterranean, tea and porcelain from China, and coal from Newcastle, to be bartered, sold, and traded at the Royal Exchange on the Thames.

The waves beneath the keel slapped against the hull and rocked the ship, and the feel of the motion brought a slow grin to Patrick's lips. He was certain the ship drifted aimlessly. The sails flapped and slapped uselessly at the wind. Without a man to adjust the rigging until the wind blew the sails tight and a man at the wheel to guide the vessel, they were simply drifting with the currents of the sea, tossing about like a bottle on the water.

Footsteps came from behind, and this time Patrick

didn't hide his wakefulness. Herrick came and stood over him, his face illuminated in shades of yellow and gold from the tallow lantern he held at chest height. Patrick could see a glint of intelligence in his life-weary face.

"Nature calls," Patrick stated.

"Aye, that's why I be 'ere."

"Will you unbind me?"

Herrick grunted a sound to the negative and grabbed Patrick's elbow, helping him to a standing position.

Patrick stretched as best he could, relieving the muscles that ached from prolonged sitting and a thorough beating.

"If my hands remain bound," Patrick began reasonably, "and my feet are bound as well, how do you recommend I walk to the head, unlace my breeches, and hang it out so I can relieve myself?"

Herrick grunted again. After a second he seemed decided. He whipped out a horse pistol from his waistband and a sharp dagger from his boot. With a quick slash he cut the ropes around Patrick's legs and then his wrists.

"If ye try anythin' I'll put a shot in yer 'ead," Herrick said flatly.

Patrick didn't reply but did make haste to the head to relieve what had been paining him for hours. Relief coursed through his body like wine, a sensation he felt down to his feet. He fastened his breeches and turned around to face Herrick. "There are many things in life that bring a man pleasure. A long-awaited and much-needed piss ranks among the top five."

Herrick grinned. "Aye. Match that with a willin' wench, a roasted leg o' lamb an' a cold mug of ale, an' you got yer own kind o' 'eaven."

Patrick stretched again and groaned slightly. "I ache in places I didn't know I had."

Herrick shuffled his feet and rubbed his bristly chin with his free hand. He squinted at the man in the dim yellow light of the tallow lantern. "I can't leave ye untied."

Patrick shrugged indifferently. "Understood."

"Ye'd try to escape."

"I will."

Herrick's eyes narrowed slightly. "Ol' Birney will kill ye as soon as look at ye."

Patrick didn't suppress his grin. "He will try."

Herrick grunted again as he measured the man who stood in front of him, seeing his strength, intelligence, and confident determination. This was not the sort of man they had been told they were to seize, not the pampered son of a rich merchant, whose ship would supposedly be as easy to take as the man himself. No one had been prepared for a fight that would leave two of their men dead, nor a loyal crew that could not be bribed or forced to serve. Herrick had certainly not expected the mild rolling of the calm seas to sicken Wiley until he spewed every few minutes, rendering him useless as he lay moaning in his bunk. He didn't feel reassured by Birney's paranoid and superstitious nature, and had come to the clear realization that they were as likely to safely reach the Americas to sell Patrick into slave bondage as they were likely to subdue him.

And now, as Herrick stood in front of Patrick, he wondered why he had agreed to Birney's offer at all. Surely Newgate wasn't as bad as being adrift on the ocean, where pirates, bad weather, and rapidly dwindling supplies all lay in wait to kill them one by one. And then he remembered Newgate, with its indescribable filth, sicknesses, stench, and vermin, where his inability to garnish the keeper upon entering the prison had caused him to be stripped of all his possessions and thrown into a stinking cesspit. The memory of roaches and lice crackling underfoot and bouts of typhus made Herrick shudder and reconsider his earlier thought. Nothing was worse than Newgate's hell, and he would have just as soon made a contract with Satan himself to avoid being sentenced there again. Birney's offer to buy out his debt in exchange for his services had done just as well.

"Where is my crew?" Patrick asked.

"Below deck," Herrick replied, his tone telling volumes of the nature of the crew's confinement.

"Injured?"

"Aye."

"Badly?"

Herrick hesitated, and then answered honestly. "Aye."

Patrick mentally ran through the list of men that had been aboard the *Nuala*. Jerry, Marcus, Ned, and Liam, along with Tate, the young orphan from the English parish whom Patrick had rescued two years ago from the hands of a cruel merchant who had obviously wanted the boy for more than an apprentice.

Thinking quickly, Patrick kept his voice neutral. "Before or after you took me?"

"Before. When there were still five o' us."

Herrick suddenly turned and looked around, peering past the dim light of the lantern. Nothing past the ring of light moved, and no sound could be heard above the slapping of waves against the hull and the creaking of the tall masts. From behind a stack of empty crates, a cat emerged from his prowling and stopped to stare at Herrick and Patrick, eyes glowing in the reflected light.

"Nervous?"

Herrick jerked his head in the direction of the cat. "I ain't never seen so many black cats in me life."

Patrick laughed. "They keep the rats and mice to a minimum. I assure you, they are not the devil's playthings, as some would have you believe."

"I ain't a believer in that tripe," Herrick insisted. "But I ain't used to 'em just the same. It's said that only witches keep company with 'em." Herrick dragged his gaze away from the cat and shrugged his shoulders. "Well, if they have powers, then I 'ope they use 'em to know to stay out o' ol' Birney's way. 'E'll kill 'em on sight."

"He has a penchant for killing."

"Killin' is easy for a man like 'im. 'E 'as no God an' no loyalty. Only greed. That 'e 'as plenty o'."

"What about you?" Patrick asked bluntly.

"Me? I ain't no angel, if that's what yer askin'."

"I'm asking if you have God and loyalty."

Herrick paused and ran a hand across his chin, rubbing the rough whiskers that defied a clean shave. "Me mum was a good sort, God fearin' an' kind. 'Er death were a blessin' since she never seen what I become. But no matter what I ever done, I figure I'll pay for it with God, though even 'E knows a life like mine would make any good man turn bad. An' as for loyalty, aye, I 'ave that. I ain't a saint, an' I ain't proud o' the way me life 'as gone, but I ain't never gone back on me word. I 'ope that counts for somethin'."

"Sometimes a man's word is all he has."

Herrick jerked his head in quick agreement and a readiness to be back to the matter at hand. "Turn around so I can wrap ye back up. If Birney knows I'm talkin' with ye, I'm as good as shark bait."

Patrick turned and offered his hands behind his back. He turned his head to offer a final thought over his shoulder. "Herrick, if a squall hits this ship, we'll all be dead. If you want to live, it will be in your interests to free me. I give you my word that if you do, no harm will ever come to you from my hand."

Herrick tied Patrick's hands together behind his back, this time binding him slightly looser so Patrick would be more comfortable. He stooped to lash Patrick's ankles as well, straightening as the task was done. "I'll bring ye up some food."

Herrick turned on his heel and strode away without looking back, pausing a few times to steady himself as the swells beneath the ship rolled the deck. Patrick watched the light from the lantern fade into darkness.

Patrick stretched out on the deck, still hungry and thirsty despite the watered rum and ration of bread and cheese that Herrick had brought up without further word. Herrick had conceded to untie Patrick's hands while he ate, but had leaned on the railing, his arms crossed and pistol in hand, his mood distant and irritable. Once the food and drink had been consumed, Patrick was once again bound and left alone in the darkness but for his thoughts. In those, solitude didn't exist.

She was with him. A whisper of voice in his ears, a touch of silk flitting over his skin. Lavender-scented hair, soft as velvet and black as midnight. Eyes as green as Ireland, a heart as deep as the ocean.

Patrick reclined bound as a prisoner on the deck of his own ship, with his life in shambles and his crew taken hostage. Still, his bondage didn't compare to Camille's, for he had every confidence that he could escape. His frustration mounted as he thought about Camille's mind being filled with lies. Would she believe them? he wondered. Even as the question posed in his mind, he knew she eventually would. It would be more likely for Camille to accept that she had been betrayed than to find reasons within herself for his love. How could a woman who felt deep inside that she was unlovable trust that his love was not only abiding, but that it was real? So real that he had killed two men in his efforts to avoid being taken from her. So achingly real that he would gladly give his life to spare her a moment of the pain in thinking it had all been a cruel deception.

But she didn't know any of that. All Camille knew was that when midnight arrived, Patrick had not been there.

"Please, Camille," Patrick begged in a hoarse whisper as he looked up to the unanswering stars, "please believe in me. Remember my words. Believe."

As the words left his lips, he remembered her words, whispered with disbelief in early morning. *Even after the years pass and I am slowly stripped of my beauty, you will love me still?* An ache settled in Patrick's heart. She would doubt his love for her beyond his ability to assuage her insecurity with his words. And he was not there to speak the words she needed to hear.

Pure frustration seethed through Patrick's bound body. A ragged groan of impotent wrath tore from his throat as his body arched against the bonds that held him.

A quiet rustling behind some nearby crates caught Patrick's attention. Patrick leaned toward the movement, straining his eyes in the darkness, expecting to see a stealthy cat with its dinner caught between gleaming teeth.

But instead of the sleek outline of an emerging cat, the slight form of a gangly boy of twelve appeared.

"Tate!" Patrick whispered, and his tense muscles began to relax. "Are you injured?"

"Nay, sir. The devils don't know I'm aboard," Tate matched his hushed tone to Patrick's, but he could still hear his self-satisfaction.

He felt the familiar stirrings of pride at the sight of Tate. When he had purchased the boy by outbidding for him at the block, Tate had been bone thin, illiterate, and skittish. Patrick had seen the hungry gleam of lust in the eyes of the man who had wanted him for his own. The thought of the life of abuse and sodomy that stretched in front of the boy had been too much to contemplate. He'd placed a bid well out of the range of the other merchant and brought Tate aboard the *Nuala*.

During long days Tate learned the rigorous ways of the sea, just as Patrick had as a child. At night Patrick brought him into his cabin, where lessons of speaking and reading were mixed with ciphering and history. Tate had applied himself and done well, and his body filled out with regular feeding and grew apace with his mind. He no longer flinched at the slightest movement, and the hunted look of desperation had slowly left his expression. Every day spent with Tate had been a pleasure for Patrick, but none so much as this night, when his appearance meant survival and escape for them all.

Short, gusty winds flapped the loose sails. Moonset

approached as if time had sprouted wings, but Patrick forced his voice to remain calm and reassuring. "Tate, see if you can untie me."

Tate scurried behind his captain and began tugging and pulling against the firmly tied knots. Herrick's knots were fastened without skill, but they were tight and strong, and Tate's small, slight fingers could not undo them. Frustration built within the slim boy, and he began tugging and pulling against the ropes with increasing fervor, knowing that he wouldn't be safe until Patrick was free.

"Calm and easy, Tate. No good will come of us losing our patience. See if you can loosen the rope by tightening the knot."

Tate pulled on the thick, rough rope with all that was left of his might, to no avail. Though darkness cloaked the boy, Patrick could hear the tears in his voice. "Sir, I can't help you. What will happen if I can't free you?"

Patrick forced himself to chuckle softly and sound at ease. "We'll be fine, Tate. Now come and sit in front of me. We need to make a plan."

Tate crawled around Patrick and sat on his heels expectantly. The days since the *Nuala* had been taken had been long, hot, and spent in hiding. His captain had been brought aboard, trussed and unconscious, after the crew had been taken below at gunpoint, where all Tate heard were the screams and shouts of the men who were his only family. He hadn't eaten anything in days, and if not for the barrel of rainwater lashed to the starboard side, he would probably be dead. But his captain and hero had awakened, and Tate perched himself obediently in front of him, ready to obey his every word. He would do anything for Patrick, take any risk, and fight to his death if need be. He only wished he possessed the strength of a man.

"You're hungry, Tate?"

Tate shook his head in a quick, affirmative motion. "Aye, sir, but I've been hungrier than this. Don't worry for me."

Patrick smiled at the bravery of the young man before him,

remembering the pointed, gaunt face of the boy he had rescued, how all his bones has stood out in stark relief against his pale, dirty skin. Indeed, the boy had known hardship.

"Still, the hunger is no doubt making you weak. Have you been at all successful in sneaking below deck to grab some food?"

Tate's eyes widened. "I didn't dare, sir. I was too scared one of the blokes would see me."

Patrick's voice grew firmer, commanding. "You will need to go below and get a knife."

A tremor of panic turned Tate's empty belly. "A knife," he repeated, knowing he sounded stupid. But he was so afraid of the armed, dangerous men.

"Aye, son. The ropes are thick, and you are weary."

A swell of happiness bloomed in Tate's heart and replaced his apprehension. Patrick had just spoken Tate's dream, that the man he looked to with respect and love could think of him as his own son. He reached out and touched Patrick's shoulder briefly. "I'll do my best, sir."

"I know you will, Tate. Now, take it slow and stay in the shadows. There is no rush, so take no risks."

Patrick watched as the lad set out for the door to the lower cabin, doing as he had been told and staying cloaked in darkness. He hated more than anything to have to place the burden of their escape on Tate's narrow shoulders, but he could see no other way. The knife that would cut his ropes would also provide him with a needed weapon.

But even as he strained in the gloom to see the form of Tate near the cabin, he felt a dark sense of foreboding. The hair on his neck stood on end, and Patrick knew that he had made a grave mistake.

He called out to the boy, softly at first and then with increasing volume. His urgency to have Tate safely by his side grew unchecked. Panic bloomed and seized hold of his body, rushing through his blood until it felt as though it had seeped into the marrow of his bones.

* * *

Hours had passed since Tate had disappeared below deck. Patrick tortured himself with recrimination, worry, and guilt. He knew that if anything happened to Tate, he would never forgive himself for sending a boy to do a man's job.

Dawn approached and the ascending sun stained the sky in shades of peach, pink, and yellow, turning the sea to liquid, rippling gold. But he was oblivious to the majestic glory of creation. With eyes trained on the door of the cabin, he focused on sending Tate mental messages to stay low and out of sight until nightfall.

The door to the cabin opened. Birney shuffled out, squinting as the light seared his watery eyes, sensitive from a night of heavy drinking and smoking. A leather strap wrapped around his thick fist was held taut. Birney tugged on it, hard. Tate stumbled out onto the deck, attached to the other end of the strap by his neck. Birney laughed crudely and pulled again. "Dance, puppet, dance!"

Tate's wide, frightened eyes met Patrick's briefly before he struggled to his feet. He pulled his lank shoulders back in a show of courage. "I'll be the one laughing after my captain kills you."

Birney snarled and jerked the leash, another snap of his powerful arm. Tate fell to the deck hard and lay still, gasping for breath.

"Let the boy go!" Patrick demanded.

Birney whirled and faced his captive, instantly furious at the sound of authority in his prisoner's voice. "Yer not the capt'n, ye swine. Keep yer 'ole shut, or I'll shut it for ye."

Patrick struggled against his bonds with renewed vigor. The ropes cut into his wrists, but the knots held tight. "Damn you, let the boy go!"

Herrick came out of the cabin and saw that Birney still held the boy by a strap. Pure disgust carved Herrick's features. "I though ye said ye'd let the kid go."

Birney pulled on the leash and cackled. "'Errick, yer a

mollycoddle if'n I ever met one. Ye don't know how to have any fun."

Herrick snorted and scowled. "I'll take a wench over a laddie any day."

Birney gestured to the vastness of ocean that surrounded them. "Aye, but we're one wench short."

The nature of their conversation sickened Patrick's stomach. "For every second you have hurt him, I will make you suffer tenfold before I kill you. I swear it."

Birney and Herrick faced Patrick, Herrick with a look of disbelief at Patrick's effrontery, and Birney's full of rage at being threatened. Then Birney saw Patrick as he was, bound, furious, and completely helpless. He grinned, revealing small, rotten teeth. "Yer not in a way to make threats, Irish. I'll just as soon make ye watch what I'm gonna do to yer boy by way of makin' ye regret forgettin' yer place."

"My place will be as an avenger."

Birney didn't understand the threat fully, but took the meaning. He pulled on the leather leash, another hard tug. Tate gasped, trying to drag breath through his bruised throat. He hauled the boy to his feet and dragged him in front of his large body, throwing an arm around the slim waist and holding him close. With a smirk to taunt Patrick, Birney pressed his face close to Tate's and pressed a wet, odorous kiss against his cheek. His tongue slipped out, licking the soft skin not yet roughened with the bristle of a beard.

A groan of rage from Patrick mingled with a squeal of fear from Tate. Birney laughed, loving the sweet taste of the boy's skin, thrilling with the knowledge that Patrick was helpless to do anything but watch as he took his pleasure. With one hand holding Tate immobile, he used his other to tear the shirt from the thin chest that heaved with panic and exertion. Birney's rough fingers roamed Tate's torso, pinching his nipples, leaving welts in their wake.

Tate's eyes went wild, rolling around in his sockets until the whites showed around his pale blue irises. His mouth opened, a silent scream while his fingers clawed at the leather thong around his neck.

Patrick had never known such a feeling of helplessness. He strained against the ropes until his hands ran with blood. His pounding heart sent a deafening rush in his ears, and he fought with every fraction of his strength to break free. In a split second, Tate's frantic eyes met Patrick's. A low, keening cry of terror bled into Patrick's groan of guilt and frustration.

Birney pulled the boy closer against his chest, jamming his knee between his thighs and rubbing his pelvis against the narrow frame, as the boy's struggles added fuel to his carnal desire. Birney's attention never veered too far away from Patrick's distress. The sight of Patrick's impotent hatred for what he was doing fed the lust that coursed through his veins and heightened his enjoyment. Birney began to turn the boy around, ready to bend him over and complete the act his groin ached for.

"Let him go and I swear I will give you more wealth than you can spend in a lifetime." Patrick fought his bonds, desperate to stop what had begun, tears coursing down his cheeks. "Please. By all that is holy, please."

Birney grinned malevolently, his watery eyes burning brightly. "I got all I need right 'ere."

With a rending tear, he split the back of Tate's breeches. Tate began to cry.

"No!" Patrick yelled, arching and straining against the ropes that would not give way. "Please, no!"

Herrick couldn't take any more. He couldn't tolerate the tears of a child about to lose his innocence, nor could he stand to see the helplessness of the man who plainly loved the boy. Herrick had seen rapes before, too many times to even attempt to fool himself into thinking that the screams and sights would not plague him in his sleep. All fears of Birney and potential repercussions fell away as Herrick heard the kid call Patrick's name in a voice choked with tears.

Herrick pulled his cutlass from its scabbard. "Enough, Birney. Let the kid go."

Birney never stopped unlacing his breeches, unveiling his protruding, swollen member.

Herrick wasted no time. In a swift motion Herrick struck out with the cutlass, whistling the thin blade between Tate and Birney and severing the leather thong that held Tate around the neck. The blade nearly caught the tip of Birney's nose, and a shriek of fury came from the man whose passions ran higher than the masts that swayed overhead. Birney kept a hand on the boy's arm and fumbled for his own blade.

"Ye bastard!" Birney screamed. "I've a mind to split yer skull!"

Herrick shrugged his heavy shoulders and took on a stance to fight. "Ye can try, but first let the kid go."

"'E's mine," Birney said possessively, tightening his hold on Tate's arm until the boy whimpered in pain.

Birney's sexual lust combined with his lust for blood. His still-exposed manhood remained thick and full, as his whole body was charged with an excitement greater than he had ever known. He lunged at Herrick with his blade outstretched, lacking in skill but full of a primal frenzy that turned him especially deadly. Herrick parried and returned the strike, nicking the side of Birney's arm. Birney kept his hold of Tate and thrust out again. Herrick dodged the blade with more grace than his build suggested, whipping his blade around to meet with the flesh of Birney's arm once more. This time, he struck more deeply. A cry of pain and outrage curdled in Birney's throat.

Tate knew only fear. Panic increased his strength. He tore and clawed at Birney's grasp of him, seeing everything in haphazard, magnified dimensions through wild eyes filled with tears and sweat.

"Be still, Tate!" Patrick shouted, seeing how the boy grew too close to the fight in his efforts to release himself.

But Tate could not hear through the pounding in his

head. He whirled himself around, trying to drop to the deck.

Birney lunged out again, aiming for Herrick's gut. But he buried his blade in a much smaller target. Tate sucked in his breath and looked down at the knife in his side. He raised surprised eyes to meet Patrick's.

And Patrick watched in frozen, helpless horror as the light in the boy's eyes went out. He could only watch as the child crumpled to the deck.

Birney let go of Tate's arm and pulled his blade free. "Ye'll pay fer this 'Errick, ye bastard. Ye'll get me a wench as soon as we 'it land, an' ye'll pay fer a fortnight of my use."

Herrick scarcely heard him. He stared at the blood that leaked from the boy and surrounded him in a crimson halo. Though he didn't want to, he raised his eyes to meet Patrick's for an instant, and then turned and strode away. Herrick knew he would die before he would be released from the memory of the agony in the man's eyes.

But Patrick didn't look away. Couldn't. Couldn't bear to take his eyes from the boy he'd sent to his death. Forced himself to watch as Birney shoved Tate's body to the side and pitched it, limp and lifeless, over and into the hungry waters.

A knife. Go below, stay to the shadows.

A child, dead.

Sobs wrenched his body until he scarcely breathed.

CHAPTER 11

London, 1743

Camille smelled the rankness of London long before she saw its outlying buildings. Thick smog choked the horizon and darkened the sky as thousands of domestic and industrial fires belched endless clouds of sulfurous smoke into the air. Piles of human waste and offal lined the road at the outskirts of the great city, deposits made from the night-soil men. Almost in unison Camille, Amelia, and Bret pressed perfumed handkerchiefs to their noses to mask the sickening stench.

Nausea nearly overwhelmed Camille's composure as she swallowed back the bitter bile in her throat. "I detest London," she whispered.

Amelia's painted brow rose triumphantly. "The first words deigned to be spoken since our departure, and a complaint, no less."

"No surprise there, Your Grace," Bret said blandly.

Amelia cackled. "No, dear boy. No surprise at all."

Bret's arm rested along the back of the bench seat, and every so often he would allow his hand to wander, to touch a lock of Camille's hair or smooth the length of her neck with the tips of proprietary fingers. His anger with her seemed to have faded the day after they left Beauport, but his biting contempt had remained intact.

Camille bit her bottom lip and struggled to maintain indifference to Bret, her mother, and the outcome of her life. Three days of travel spent in silent agony, with no relief in sight. As the carriage conveyed her into the venal city, she searched her heart for an inkling of hope. None came to lessen her sorrow. Patrick had left her, and, when he did, he took with him the part of Camille she had valued the most: her trust and her ability to believe. All the beatings, degradation, and humiliations dealt by her parents hadn't accomplished that. But Patrick had done it, and she had let him. It was the bitterest truth of all.

Amelia couldn't have been more pleased. The palpable loss of Camille's pride brought a shine of satisfaction to the duchess's countenance every time she looked at her humbled daughter. She watched Camille, delighting in her suffering. Just the sight of her daughter's eyes, strikingly green and so much like Kenley's, irritated her. But Amelia knew the difference between her husband and daughter. She could never hurt Kenley without hurting herself in the process. However, the power to bring misery to her chit of a daughter was a task to be accomplished with verve. Getting rid of the Irishman had been a stroke of genius and a never-ending source of triumph. It had succeeded in bringing contrition to Camille when nothing else would.

Now, as they entered London, the sight of Camille's distress heightened Amelia's gratification. The city would be set to buzzing with the arrival of the duchess's only daughter. The aristocracy would remember Camille's uncommon beauty. Mothers would be primping their daughters in preparation, trying in vain with dress, wigs, and jewelry to outshine the beauty of the Bradburn girl, whose black hair, flawless white skin, and jeweled emerald eyes made her beyond competition and comparison. Perhaps for once, Amelia would not be disappointed by the daughter who had rarely brought her anything but vexation in the past.

Camille's humiliation left her vulnerable to her disposal.
Amelia knew she could force Camille into nearly anything after her ordeal with the Irishman. With a contentment so great that Amelia nearly wanted to clap her
hands, she had endured the trek from Beauport into
London without caviling.

The road into London widened, and the stench of
human waste abated slightly, mingling with the squalid
smells of the Thames as they entered the main square of
the city. Past Blackfriars and Bishopsgate Without parish
they traveled at a clip-clop pace, causing the denizens to
turn and admire the entourage of sleek, shiny black carriages whose gold-emblazoned ducal crests on the sides
announced to one and all that the Duchess of Eton had
returned to her city. As they traveled, Amelia sat with her
head at a regal angle, to allow anyone who might catch a
glimpse of her an opportunity to appreciate her bearing.

However, Camille didn't see admiration in the gazes of
the city dwellers. Instead, she saw eyes of hunger and
poverty that looked at the flaunted wealth while calculating
that one of the iron-banded wheels of the carriages would
have paid for six months' worth of food for their starving
families. She saw bricked-up windows of buildings that told
tales of families forced to sacrifice daylight in their meager
homes because of window taxes. She saw animals on
leashes held by people whose children darted around
the dangerous streets, speaking volumes of the value of live-
stock to human life. Camille pressed back into the velvet
cushions, unable to continue to look at the dirty faces and
tattered clothing of the people on the streets, whose in-
digence reminded her that one had so little control over
the life one was born to live.

Without needing to be so ordered, the drivers took the
scenic route into Whitechapel before finally heading east
to the urban sprawl where London's wealthiest, most
lordly courtiers set up residence. Years before, Amelia
had commissioned the build of their London home. Of

grand scale and even grander appointment, the house boasted leaded glass windows and a large dome of glass that filled the house with light on all but the gloomiest day. The stone structure rose from the long cobblestone drive with majestic grace, commanding attention to its gabled, mullioned windows and elegant spires.

Amelia looked with satisfaction to the gardens. "You see the Tudor roses?" she asked with a smile. "They are the finest in England."

Camille didn't ask how the roses managed to thrive and bloom in the soot-choked air or to comment that it was likely due to imported fresh air from France. In any event, her sarcasm wouldn't be appreciated by her mother. The roses bore too much resemblance to the ones that surrounded the cottage, and Camille averted her eyes from the delightful blooms.

The carriage came to a stop, and a footman scurried to open the door and help the duchess alight. Leading the way, Amelia swept into her home. As she glided forward, she gestured to her daughter to take notice of the improvements that had been made since Camille had last visited London. Bret followed behind them both, strolled into the parlor, and poured himself a liberal draught of brandy before plopping into an overstuffed velvet chair.

Amelia joined Bret in the front parlor, accepting a glass of sherry from the servant who stood waiting. With a contented sigh, Amelia seated herself across from Bret and looked around the gracious room, pleased. The gold and plum ornate furnishings suited her taste much more than the masculine, country atmosphere in Beauport.

Camille hesitated in the foyer, watching the maidservants and footmen hasten to carry the trunks upstairs and begin unpacking. Never before in Camille's life had she felt so out of place.

"Don't stand mooning about in doorways, child.

Come, sit, and enjoy a drink after a long trip," Amelia said impatiently.

Camille obliged silently, accepted a snifter of brandy, and perched on the edge of a high-backed chair.

Bret looked Camille over warmly from head to heels. "You look as fresh as one of your mother's rosebuds, Camille."

Camille's brittle facade of composure began to crack as Bret's lustful eyes touched her in places he was unwelcome. She forced a polite smile but said nothing. She sipped the scalding amber liquid, welcoming the burn that traced its way through her body. Once, Patrick's words and touch had done just that. With a simple glance, he had brought her a hot awareness of her body and a humbling awareness of her soul. Camille forced herself to stop the recollection that would steal what remained of her poise.

Amelia sighed irritably, breaking into Camille's thoughts. "Why don't you just go to your rooms if you insist on moping?"

Though the journey from Beauport to London had been long, Camille didn't feel tired. Inside her was a restlessness she couldn't quite name. "Actually, Mother, I would enjoy walking a bit and stretching my legs. Would you mind if I went to the stables to look at your horses?"

Amelia frowned her annoyance, but could see no reason to forbid it. She waved her hand in the air, rings glinting, bracelets sliding over her thin forearm. "Go if you must."

Camille stood quickly and left before Amelia could change her mind. As she walked through the house, she noticed that her mother had commissioned several murals depicting Grecian life: columns and vines framing amply proportioned women being ministered to by handsome, nearly naked men. At the far end of the house was the prep kitchen, bustling with activity as servants and cooks worked to prepare the evening meal for their returning mistress and her daughter.

Camille smiled crookedly as she made eye contact with

a woman who stood at a chopping block, thinking of Flanna with her crisp apron and busy hands. The woman returned the smile. "Can I be of service to you, Mistress?"

Camille declined, a negative shake of her head. "No, I am only heading to the stables."

The woman gestured to a door in the corner. "Go through there an' follow the path, past the out-kitchens. The stables are not too far, an' difficult to miss."

Camille nodded her thanks and headed out the door, disappointed with the perpetually dark sky. Down the path she saw the carriages in front of the large stables, as the stable hands unhitched the teams of horses and led them in one by one to be rubbed down and fed. Camille passed them without word.

The stables had been built to mimic the lines of the grand house, on a smaller scale. The large doors yawned open to catch errant summer breezes. Camille walked into the dark shelter, inhaling the much-loved scents of horses and leather. She wandered farther into the cool, musty building, running her fingers along the smooth wooden pens. The snort of a horse from around a corner caught her attention, and she moved in that direction.

A lash cut into flesh. A man moaned while another cursed.

She rushed around the corner, not wanting to see, unable to keep from looking. A man's arm rose and then lowered, quick and brutal; she heard the sound of leather slicing through skin. Dizzy, sick, her knees turned to sand while her back burned with memory.

How many times had she held on to her bedpost while her own skin was ripped apart? she asked herself. Too many times.

The man with the lash raised his arm again. Her breath caught in her throat, silencing her scream. She didn't think, couldn't form a thought. But her hands clawed at the wall, where a braided whip hung coiled on the wall amidst saddles and reins. Blindly Camille held to the base and struck out. The whip sliced through the air with a sonorous whistle, hitting the man with the crop squarely on his back. It ripped through his shirt and laid into his corpulent flesh. The man howled and whirled, pain, surprise, and rage shaping his features into a hideous mask. He pulled his riding crop back, ready to lash out at his attacker.

But the assailant the man turned to face was a young woman with black hair tumbling around her shoulders in disarray, framing a face lovelier than his dreams with eyes that glowed as green as a feral cat's. The witch shook out the whip and snarled a sound in her throat, a wild animal hungry for blood. The man dropped his riding crop and took a step back, almost tripping over the young man crouched on the floor in bloodstained straw. Before the fat man could scream in protest, the whip landed on him again, biting into his abundant flesh and leaving a trail of blood along the raised welt. Camille took a step closer, her eyes flashing and her heart pounding. She shook out the whip again and pulled it back for another strike.

The man dropped to his knees, pleading. "Mistress, please, stop! I beg you!"

But she didn't stop. Couldn't stop. She whipped him again, this time wrapping the coil around his arm, tangling and pulling as she tried to pull back once more. He begged, screamed, and begged again.

His voice penetrated her mind. Blubbering and invoking the Lord's name, he held onto the whip so she could not free it. She looked down at her hand and saw the pommel of the whip there. And then her knees began to shake. Struggling for clarity, she whispered, "Who are you?"

The fat man scrambled away a little farther, still on his knees, still holding the end of the whip. "I am Clive, milady, the head groom. I have the charge of the stables and the hands in it."

Camille looked down on him, at the sweat coursing

down his bloated, pasty cheeks. She smelled the reek of his sweat, and knew it for the scent of fear.

A spurt of power shot from her loins to her chest, and she felt her nipples tighten. She tried with all her might not to enjoy the sensation.

"Why do you lash this man?" she demanded, gesturing to the young man who had scuttled to a corner. Even in the dim light she could see the wary look in his eyes.

"The duchess has given me a free hand with the servants in my command, and I assure you this man is an insubordinate. The whipping is the least he deserves, and by all rights he should be dismissed." His voice shook, but he struggled to hold his ground in front of the woman who still held the whip. It was all he could do to look into her eyes, glowing uncannily green in the muted light, and not cross himself.

Camille took a step closer. "I asked the cause of the whipping, not your justification."

"Milady, this man pretends to be mute, but I know he can speak," Clive blurted, eyeing the small, feminine hand holding the whip. Her knuckles were white on the grip, but her hand was steady.

"How are you certain?"

"He speaks to the horses! I heard him!" He ran a chubby hand through his pale hair, spiking it with sweat and blood.

"What did he say?"

The unexpected question shook him further. His back and arm stung worse than the most vicious slap and blood seeped into his shirt and made it stick to his skin. The witch of a girl still held the whip, and each time he answered her questions, she stepped nearer to him, silently daring him to back away again. No one, not the magistrate or even the king himself, would stop a mistress from beating her servant, even if the beating led to his death. He knelt before her as vulnerable as a man could be, hoping that his reasons would provide him with a reprieve from her anger and punishment. "I don't know exactly what he said, but I heard him saying something."

Without realizing it, she dropped her voice, soft and dangerous. Just like Amelia's. "Something?"

"Aye, milady. He whispers to the horses and they respond. When I question him about it, he faces me and says nothing. I swear to you, he pretends to be mute!" Clive's face began to redden as he saw the anger flare brighter in those eerie green eyes.

"He says nothing and you call him insubordinate? You whip a man for not being able to speak? What is your penalty for blindness? Death?" She laughed, a mirthless, ruthless sound that made his skin crawl.

"I say he can speak."

Camille tightened her grip on the whip until her hand ached. "Perhaps I will whip you for abusing my family's staff. What do you think the appropriate measure should be for one who deals so harshly with another?"

Clive flinched. "Milady, I beg your understanding. I discipline in the way the duchess approves. She has instructed me to use a firm hand and not allow the staff leniency."

"And yet you ask for that from me," Camille said distinctly.

Clive's shoulders slumped and he spread his hands, showing his lack of defense. Tiny drops of blood dripped from his elbow and rained noiselessly onto the straw at his feet. "As you wish, milady."

She could whip him, if she chose. She felt a rush of moisture between her legs, and her cheeks flamed with a combination of excitement and shame.

Her hand holding the whip twitched. Just a few days before, she had held up a hand mirror and looked at her back in the looking glass, and saw the web of thin silver scars that stretched across her skin. How many times? she asked herself again.

Her hand twitched again.

"Get out," she said through gritted teeth. "Get out, and do not let me see you whipping man or animal, or it will be the last time your hands are capable of holding a whip or anything else, I swear it. And know this"—she leaned forward and emphasized every word—"I will find leniency in my heart only once."

Clive hurried to his feet and bowed slightly before rushing from the stables to tend to his wounds and his pride in the tavern.

Camille heard the door of the stable slam shut and she moved closer to the young man who remained in the corner where he regarded her with soul-deep brown eyes. She took in his high, proud cheekbones and dark hair curling loosely around his handsome face. He wore the rough clothes of a stable hand, but he met her eyes as evenly and with all the nobility of any lord. Long, thick lashes swept down for a moment, breaking the intensity of his gaze. She held her breath and waited. He said nothing, but he raised his eyes to meet hers again. His eyes were so dark and penetrating, she thought for a moment he would see into her and know her secrets before she could hide them.

Camille released her breath, but she was not released from the power of his stare. Without noticing, she dropped the whip. Slowly, she sank to the floor of the stables in front of him, unconscious of the straw that clung to her skirts or the shaking that made her jaw clench. Still, she felt caught by the unwavering concentration of his eyes. Without knowing why and with fingers that trembled, Camille reached out to touch his hand.

He caught her slender fingers and held on to them, weaving hers within his own. Her breath broke at the warmth of his skin. Slowly, he reached out his other hand and brushed a lock of black hair away from her face, smoothing the wild tangle of hair that had come unbound in tandem with her emotions. She sat breathless under his touch, allowing it and welcoming it. Somehow, needing it. He soothed her with his touch, gentling her with warmth and tenderness, in much the same manner as he tended the horses. He held her hand and stroked her hair and then her face, and she felt much of her restlessness easing. She wanted to stay locked in that moment, suspended forever in the welcomed kindness of another who knew what it was to be beaten for being different.

"I am Camille," she whispered.

He nodded and continued to touch her, sweeping over her, warm and gentle. In the thrall of his compassion, feelings began to surface, and tears began to choke her. Silent and still, his hand held hers while the other continued to brush away her tears as they fell. The responsiveness and quiet of him brought out more of Camille's emotions, quiet sobs and shuddering breaths.

She wept for her own beatings, for his, and for what it had felt like to cut into another man's skin. She cried because Patrick had betrayed and left her, and because her own family had taken part in causing her shame. Memories of Patrick came to the surface and she cried harsh and bitter tears of rejection and regret. She wept because she felt truly alone in the world, with not one person to love her. Camille allowed herself to shed tears for the loss of her innocence and the death of her hopes, until her tears ran dry and she could weep no more.

She raised red eyes and a tearstained face, looking up to him, becoming locked once again under his soulful dark eyes. She accepted a handkerchief from him, wiped her eyes, and hiccuped. But strangely, she felt no embarrassment. "You are the one who was beaten. Why is it I am the one who sobs like a child?"

"Perhaps they are tears left over from a child who would not weep," he replied in a whisper, nothing more than a slice of voice carried on breath.

Camille's eyes widened. "You *can* speak."

"Among other secrets. I have just entrusted you with the one that can cost me my life."

Camille got to her feet, quickly searched the stables, and saw they were still alone. She went back to him, sinking back down to the floor. "Thank you."

"I thank you. You spared me a thrashing that would have continued until I lost consciousness."

A tremor passed through Camille as his words called to mind beatings with a similar crop that had done just that to her.

"Why did you interfere?" he asked softly.

Camille let out a small sigh that broke into tiny breaths. "I cannot bear it."

"To see one beaten or to be beaten yourself?"

"Both," she whispered.

He nodded and said nothing. She looked at the man with awkward curiosity. "Will you tell me your name?"

His chin raised a notch, nearly imperceptibly, but Camille noticed it. "Jonah."

Camille started to say something, then held back. She thought for a moment before asking, "Why are you trusting me?"

"Are you not worthy of my trust?"

She dropped her eyes to the floor and twisted the handkerchief into a ball. "I do not know."

"Perhaps it is my necessity, no?"

She lifted her eyes back to his, suddenly suspicious. "What do you want?"

He didn't answer, but shifted his body until he sat cross-legged on the dusty floor, wincing at the pain in his back.

Camille twisted the cloth tighter and sighed. "It makes no difference. I have nothing for you to take." She started to rise to leave. "Good day to you then."

"I am a Jew." His fingers drifted to his naked chin, recently shorn of his thick beard, and then to his bare sideburns, where his forelocks had once curled nearly to his shoulders. "I am in hiding, and I have disgraced my people."

He watched her face for revulsion, fear, or bigotry. Camille's face registered only curiosity. She sat back down.

"What is worse, I am wanted for murder."

She raised a brow and swallowed heavily, thinking of the

bloodlust that had made her whip a man and make him bleed. "Are the charges founded?"

"Do you see a murderer behind my eyes?"

In an instant Camille was back at her cottage in Beauport; she could hear Patrick's deep, quiet voice. *What do you see when you look at me?* She shivered and rubbed the gooseflesh on her arms. "How can I know what is in your heart merely by looking at you? Only a fool would presume to know."

He heard the asperity in her voice and he sighed heavily. "Indeed."

She spread Jonah's handkerchief flat on her lap and began pleating it. "You do not speak because you are wanted for murder?"

Jonah gestured to himself with the sweep of his finely boned hand. "I can wear the clothing of a pauper and perform the menial tasks of a stable hand, but I would be hard pressed to mimic the rough speech expected of a man of my station. I am educated well beyond what is average, and was afraid it would give away my ruse. I plan to work here only until I have enough coin saved to flee England. Unfortunately, it is taking longer to save than I had hoped." Jonah picked up the hem of his ruined shirt and smiled ruefully. "My silence is costing me a small fortune in shirts."

Camille drew in her breath and looked at Jonah, guilt stricken. "I have let you comfort me and I have not seen to your wounds. Are you badly hurt?"

He shrugged. "When compared to the noose at Tyburn or a stint in Newgate, my wounds amount to nothing."

"Still, they should be attended to." She thought quickly, remembering the kind eyes of the woman in the kitchen. "Hold here. I will return."

Marion looked up from the pot of soup on the stove and found herself face-to-face with the young woman who had breezed through the kitchen earlier in the afternoon.

Straw clung to her rumpled gown and tangled in her disheveled hair. Her green eyes looked enormous in her pale face, puffy and red. With a cry of alarm, Marion's forgotten spoon clattered to the floor as she reached out to Camille. "Mistress, what happened to you? Are you injured?"

"I am well, but there is a man in need."

She spoke quietly and quickly, explaining the happenings in the stables. Marion nodded a few times and listened to every word. When Camille finished, she agreed to help with an inclination of her head and a few brief instructions to the other women in the kitchen. In a moment they were heading back to the stables, armed with a pot of salve, a bowl of clean water, and linen strips.

Jonah stood waiting for them by the pen that held the large stallion called Smoke, rubbing between the eyes of the magnificent horse. Smoke lifted his large head at the sight of the two women and snorted. Jonah turned to see Camille, Marion, and the ointments in the basket, and he let out a snort almost identical to the stallion's.

Camille laughed at his dubious expression, knowing he could smell the stink of the ointment, but that he couldn't complain in front of Marion without revealing himself. Marion spoke crisply. "Rendered fat and herbs recommended by the apothecary. You'll not die, or else the salve can be returned for a full refund."

Jonah narrowed his eyes into slits and glared mutinously, backing against the stall.

Marion set down her things and faced Jonah. She set her hands on her hips and fixed a look that brooked no argument. "Turn 'round and take off your shirt."

Jonah looked at both the women, saw he would receive no quarter, and grudgingly turned to present his back, shrugging out of his shirt. Marion ministered to his wounds without comment, except to make low clucking sounds of disapproval. When she had finished tying the last of the bandages, she reached into her basket and pulled out a heel of cheese and a small loaf of bread. "You'll need your strength."

Jonah accepted the fare gratefully, nodding his head in thanks. Marion gathered up her things and turned to leave, tossing a comment over her shoulder as she turned the corner. "I'll leave you two to your conversation."

Camille waited until the footsteps faded and gestured wordlessly for Jonah to follow her as he slipped back into his ruined shirt. She led the way to a ladder and climbed to the loft. Jonah followed until they were alone between bales of hay and bags of feed. "Is this enough privacy for you to tell me why you are accused of murder?"

"Will you tell me about your tears?"

"Do you always answer questions with a question?"

"Does that bother you?"

Camille laughed. "You first."

Jonah grew serious. "I am an only child. My father died many years ago, when I was still a boy. My mother never recovered from his death, and as the years passed, she must have grown very lonely." He sighed with the weight of his guilt, knowing that nothing would ever take it. "If I had been paying more attention to my mother and less to my precious books, perhaps I would have noticed how vulnerable she had become.

"After a time she seemed better. I noticed the light in her eyes again, and I would hear her humming while she did the baking. I did not ever think it was because she had found a man. But she had. He had set his sights on my mother, pursuing her with gifts, praising her dark beauty. She took him to her bed, and eventually found herself carrying his child. But this man turned out to be a lord, married with children of his own. Needless to say, he was unable to accept the bastard child of a Jewess, and unwilling to help her with the burden."

Jonah's tone dropped and his eyes went far away as he remembered the shame in his mother's face when she confessed her circumstance to her only son. "I was not pleased by this man's lack of respect for his responsibility. I went to see him, and we had an ugly confrontation. He called her a filthy Jew and dirty whore. He taunted me with the things she had done to him in their bed. He said she had left her stink on him for days after.

"I attacked him. I have never been a violent man, nor have I ever put my fists on another. But I went after him." His hands clenched in his lap as he remembered the feel of the man's neck giving way as he bore down, his every thought to squeeze the life from him. "I tried to kill him, and would have if the noise hadn't called the attention of his servants. They came running to the room and pulled me from him. I left the house at a dead run. I kept running until I had reached the river, and then finally I collapsed. I think I must have slept then, because it was morning before I made my way home to face my mother."

Jonah paused as grief and regrets gripped his heart. "The next day the man was found dead, stabbed to death in his bed. Whether this man knew of what was to come or not, I shall never know, but the man had already arranged to have my mother killed. She died in an alley, alone and afraid, strangled to death with a thick rope. And so my mother is dead, along with the child in her belly. I am in hiding from the constables who believe me to be the killer of my mother's lover. I am also being hunted by a paid assassin, hired by the brother of the lord, who fears I will escape justice and seeks to have me killed in retribution."

Camille listened intently to the whole story. "How do you know who hunts you?"

The slow grin slid across his face again. "Your mind is quick, Camille. There is a union of men who work for hire. As a child I was friends with one of them. He sent word to me in warning before I went into hiding."

She imagined what it must be like, to run for your life and be unable to mourn the loss of a beloved mother and the child she carried. Her heart went out to Jonah, who had given so much of himself to her when his own pain must be so great. She brought her eyes up to his and saw the expectation in his mesmerizing brown eyes.

"I believe you," she said simply, and then reached out to touch his hand. "I am sorry for your loss."

Jonah accepted her sentiment with a gracious nod of his head. "Your turn, Camille."

She turned away and went to the tiny window, looking out over the tended lawn. "I loved a man, and he loved me." She laughed, but it was a small, bitter sound. "It is an old story, no?"

"It is your story," Jonah said softly.

She heard Patrick's voice again. *It would be a tale of great love.* "It was all a lie," she said flatly. "He left because my mother bribed him. And there was another woman, a girl in town. He told her the things he told me." Camille drifted off, lost in memories that were like cinders on a hearth, still full of molten heat. "I keep telling myself the pain will fade. That the need for him will die if I can only keep reminding myself it was all a lie."

"But your heart will not oblige you?" Jonah prodded.

"No. It will not." A single raven flew by the window and Camille tried to remember the omen that signified. "I don't think it is within my power to stop loving him."

"Then stop trying."

"Stop trying?" She turned around and saw Jonah in the dusky light, his hip propped against a bale of straw.

"Yes, it is a logical choice. You will undermine any effort to stop loving this . . . ?"

"Patrick," Camille supplied.

"You cannot force yourself not to think a thought, so do not fight it. When Patrick comes to mind, stop and indulge your memory. In time, the memories will come with less frequency."

Jonah sounded so certain that Camille felt a glimmer of optimism. Perhaps she would be able to put the memory of Patrick, their love, and the vows they had exchanged behind her. With that hope came the need to talk about all of it. Slowly, haltingly, the words came and she unburdened herself without embarrassment for her foolishness. He listened with unwavering intensity. And when she finished, he knew about the marriage, the secrets, bribes and deceit, and the ultimate betrayal that had cost her everything.

His dark eyes never left her face. Jonah studied the vibrant color of her eyes, the soft curves of her mouth, and he noticed the gentle way about her that was not mincing or coquettish, but direct and without pretense. "The man was a fool, Camille. You are wonderful, and there is not a sum of money that could tear a man from your side if he had any sense."

She shrugged away his compliments. "It did."

"But you are not alone with this anymore."

Camille felt suddenly shy, but she couldn't deny the curling of hope that flickered inside her, like a tiny flame that struggled to burn. "Neither are you alone, my friend."

She turned and made her way out of the stables, hoping Amelia had been too caught up in her own homecoming to take notice of how long she'd been gone. As she walked through the stable doors and caught a faint breath of fresh air mingled with smoke, cooking smells, and the fecund scents of horses, Camille remembered what the single raven signified.

An omen of change.

CHAPTER 12

Late summer brought wind. The trees bent and groaned, dropping leaves and seeds. Londoners conducted their daily lives as usual, but they covered their hair with shawls, clapped hands upon hat brims, and rushed to get indoors.

Camille lay in her bed, tossed to her side, and slid a hand under the pillow, trying to get comfortable. Trying to sleep. It wouldn't come. She listened to the dirge of the gusts as they deadmarched over the house. Branches slapped the roof and rattled against the windows.

But it wasn't the wind that robbed her rest.

Dressmakers had been visited, fabrics selected. Under Amelia's discerning eye, gowns and all the necessary accoutrements had been ordered for autumn's season. London society welcomed Camille into its circle, and on Bret's arm she found herself escorted to gatherings of the finest families. Long carriage rides in the park occupied many of her afternoons, and prolonged dinners filled the evenings, where Camille's beauty and quiet manner immediately established her as a sought-after guest with whom to grace one's table.

She tried to forget. She pushed herself through the

routines of her days and withstood Bret's affections in bed at night. And then she would try to sleep.

But her dreams would not accommodate her.

They were long and vivid, filled with understanding and devotion, passion and promises. In her dreams, she trusted, gave, and felt the love and happiness again. But then there was laughter. Mocking and accusing voices laughed at her, echoing through her mind, gawking at her gullibility, shaming her stupidity.

Sleep and the rest of my life, she thought, and none of it within my control. A burden weighed on her. An unsolvable problem that could not be hidden too much longer.

Camille rolled over and lit a candle. A groan of frustration escaped her as the timepiece disclosed hours until morning. She sat up and ran her hands through her hair, staring at the shadows shifting across her walls and ceiling. She pushed her covers down and held the candle over her ankle, staring at the glowing amber against her skin.

"You won't leave me," she whispered. She touched the gems hesitantly, as if she expected them to burn her fingertips. "Or is it that I won't let you go?"

She sighed and set the candle down, knowing the restlessness inside her couldn't be wished away. But more than that, the ache in her heart wouldn't heal. Loneliness threatened to swallow her. She clutched her arms around her as if she could replace the feel of his. A long, quiet moan slipped from her throat, a sound of desolation. She wanted him back. She didn't care about Veronica or bribes or even his lies. She just wanted him back.

And the devil returned, whispering for her to leave her mother's house and find him. It said to sell her belongings, hire a man to track him, sail the ocean, and find him. And then beg at his feet to take her back.

She beat the voice back with reason. Told herself all the things meant to stifle the love she felt for him, about how he had used her, manipulated her. How he had given to Veronica what had meant so much, how to him it had been only words. Just another one of his stories, whispered in the ear of a listening woman. She told herself the pain wouldn't kill her. She reassured herself she would survive.

She reminded herself she was not completely alone. She had a friend, and he understood.

But simply surviving didn't seem like enough, when she pictured it. Marriage to Bret, deference to Amelia, and every last bit of what she had been, and what she had now, taken from her. Amelia would strip it all like a vulture at a carcass, picking her bones clean of every last fraction of what she had shared with Patrick.

But he was inside her, tangible and alive. Growing. And the problem had no resolution she could think of.

She slipped out of bed, wrapped her heavy velvet robe around her, and belted it tightly around her narrow waist. She extinguished the flame, left her rooms in darkness, and took to the long hallways of her mother's home, treading silently to the servants' quarters and down the back stairwell. Camille stealthily left the house and walked to the stables, not pausing to notice the stars that valiantly shone despite the polluted skies. The wind stung her eyes and slapped her face; she rushed with her head bent.

The heavy door of the shelter gave way under her hard pull, sliding out enough that she could slip between the rough wood and enter into the forbidding blackness. The wind smacked the structure as if it beat on it with fists, demanding entrance. Horses snorted and stamped their feet at her intrusion into their haven. Camille clucked her tongue in reassurance as she passed, hushing the horses as she felt her way to the ladder and up to the loft.

A lantern burned low, pushing back the darkness and guiding her way. Camille ventured to where Jonah lay sleeping on a pallet of straw, covered with blankets she had pilfered from the main house. His face looked like a boy's while he slept, as innocent as an angel. Soft and methodical, the sigh of his breath lured her closer. She sat and tucked her legs under her, wrapping her robe tighter around herself to ward off the chill of midnight. And some of the ache went away.

It calmed her, the sounds of Jonah's regular breathing. It soothed her as nothing else had. She closed her eyes and tried to match her breathing to his, inhaling and exhaling slowly until the peace of his slumber hypnotized her.

Her stolen calm lasted until she heard the subtle change in his breathing and opened her eyes to see the lantern's light reflected in his.

"I'll go. I didn't mean to disturb you," Camille whispered.

"You woke me; you didn't disturb me."

Jonah rolled onto his side and watched her in the dim light, noting her pale face and drawn features.

"You still aren't sleeping nights?"

Camille let out her breath in a long sigh. "I don't know what's wrong with me."

"You aren't eating, either. You've lost flesh you can't afford to lose," Jonah observed bluntly.

"Nothing tastes good."

Jonah said nothing and stared at Camille, his dark eyes inscrutable in the long shadows cast by the single lantern. As always, his silence prompted Camille. "You already know."

Jonah inclined his head. "I am familiar with the signs. How long has it been?"

"Since June."

"So late winter, then?"

"Yes," Camille whispered.

Jonah leaned back into his down pillow, another gift from Camille. "My mother vomited every morning when she was with child. Are you feeling well?"

Camille played with a piece of straw, twisting and tying it into knots. "I'm fine, I suppose. A little queasy, but it passes. It is fatigue that troubles me, yet I can't seem to sleep."

"Patrick?"

"Yes. The dreams end with his laughter, while I hold my

belly and plead with him to love our child and me. I beg him not to leave, until his form vanishes into mist."

Jonah nodded in understanding. Thoughtful silence fell over them, each contemplating what future lay in wait. Below them the sound of a horse moving about in his pen mingled with the rustling of a barn cat on the prowl.

"You will come with me when I flee England," Jonah said.

Camille shook her head. "No. I would only slow you down."

"Quite the contrary. No one will be looking for a man traveling with a woman in the delicate condition."

Camille winced at his casual use of the phrase and unconsciously placed a protective hand on her abdomen. "I don't know, Jonah. I dare not burden you with what is my concern."

"You have not said you do not wish to leave with me."

Camille stared into the blackness behind Jonah and said nothing. Jonah reached out and tugged at the fabric of her robe. "You trusted a man with your future once. Have you the courage to try again?"

Emotion tightened Camille's throat, making her lips shake. "If I stay, my mother will have the child taken from me. Only if I leave England will I have any hope of keeping my baby."

"So, you will leave with me?"

Camille battled her apprehension as if it were a living thing, stifling its life by stealing its breath and replacing it with her words. "Yes, Jonah. I will go with you."

"Good," Jonah said, contented. "Your child will need a man in its life."

Memories of her own childhood haunted her: a distant father, a dissatisfied mother. "I don't ever want my child to feel unwanted."

"Do you want the child?"

A tender smile shaped Camille's lips. "Yes. Like nothing else."

"That is all a child needs, Camille."

She placed her hand over Jonah's, gratitude sweeping through her like summer wind, warm and welcomed. "What would I do without you, my friend?"

Jonah's slow grin appeared. "You shall never have to find that out."

She touched her belly once again. "We will need a plan, Jonah. I cannot hide my condition for too much longer. Already, my stays are growing more uncomfortable."

"I was thinking about heading north to Scotland. Does that thought appeal to you?"

"Scotland," Camille repeated, liking the feel of the word on her tongue. A land with a rich past, where her baby could have a future. "Yes, it appeals."

Jonah yawned and stretched. "It will take me another two fortnights of pay, but I think I will have enough coin saved at that time to make the trip."

"Four weeks," she said bleakly, thinking of the effort it would take to continue her charade of contented acceptance of her new life in London, the snug fit of her new gowns. And of Bret's visits in the evenings, his unwanted kisses and the sickly scent of his spilled seed on her nightclothes.

"I'm sorry, Camille, but I see no way around it. I have already sold everything I own that held value. I wish I were a rich man to see us both out of this trap."

"Honor and courage are your riches, Jonah. You don't need to remind me it is my presence on the journey that will bring double the expense." Camille paused thoughtfully. "I have many pieces of jewelry my mother would not likely miss. They could be sold if you would handle the transaction."

"You will not be sorely distraught to sell your jewels?" Jonah knew that women in general put a value higher than monetary on such things.

Camille laughed bitterly. "I'm certain. They are naught but the finest of shackles."

"Fine, then. But be wary of what you sell, for they will

never be recouped. Your life with me will be simple; of that
I can assure you."

"You will not lie to me, manipulate me, or whip me?"

"Never."

"You will love my child?"

"I already do."

"Then my life will be satisfying."

Jonah grew quiet as he worked out details in his head,
mindful of the many extra precautions that would have to
be taken with Camille accompanying him.

But Camille's mind wandered on another path. She hesitated to approach it with Jonah, but knew it needed to be
discussed. "Jonah, will you expect things of me?"

"Things?"

Camille felt awkward and shy, and she welcomed the dim
light that hid her blush. "Will you make me say it directly?
I know you are more perceptive than that."

"Are you asking me if I will expect you to take on a wifely
role?"

"Yes."

"Do you love me, Camille? Could you love me the way
you loved him?"

"I will never love another like that."

Jonah leaned forward and looked at her directly. "Do
you think you could love me like a husband?"

Camille thought of Jonah's kindness and how important
he had become to her. Soon, they would leave England
together, and if Jonah were true to his word, they would
become a family, of sorts. Her child would need a father
and a home filled with love and security. All of this Camille
knew with her head.

But her heart knew other things. Her heart knew a love
that stretched past deception and made her love Patrick
despite what he had done to her. She knew a love that had
made her want to pull Patrick inside herself and let him
touch all her secret places. Camille knew what it was to want
to die rather than live without him. She remembered well

what it was to stand in front of a man and vow to God that she would never love another until death took her, and mean every word she spoke.

And she didn't feel that way for Jonah, much as he mattered to her. Regardless of the fact that Patrick had broken her heart and their vows, Camille still loved him and still wanted him. Their child grew in her belly, and soon she would have a son or daughter who would bear a resemblance to the father who deserted her, and Camille hoped for the baby to have its father's eyes, that she might see them again.

Jonah watched Camille in his patient manner, waiting for her to answer his question.

"I would never deceive you, Jonah. I don't think I could feel that way about you."

Jonah nodded his acceptance of her answer. "Perhaps one day you will feel differently."

"I cannot imagine it," Camille replied honestly.

Jonah laid his head back on the pillow and smiled. "I am irresistible to women. Your mind will change."

Camille gasped and began to giggle, leaning over to swat him on the shoulder. "Rake."

"Yes, that would be a new image for me and could assist us on our journey out of England," Jonah said with mock solemnity. "I will assume the persona of London's most notorious rake, and you will appear to be one of many women I have impregnated in my lust for sensual pleasures."

Camille laughed. "You're impossible."

Jonah grinned and reached out to playfully tug on a stray curl that hung in disarray down to her waist. "I believe it could work, Camille. You said yourself we needed a plan."

He let out another yawn and pulled the covers around his long frame. Camille's smile faded. She felt bad for waking Jonah and keeping him awake when he worked such long, arduous hours during the day. Yet, she couldn't seem to bring herself to leave.

She thought Jonah looked very comfortable on his pallet of blankets and straw. She remembered the cold bed in her room, and the sleepless hours spent in its miserable clutches. Impulsively, she moved closer to him and lifted the corner of the blankets in silent question. He moved over and she climbed next to him, settling in on a soft blanket already warmed with his body. Jonah draped his arm over her waist and pulled her close to him, his head against her hair.

Warmth and peace stole over Camille. With her future settled and Jonah's arm around her, Camille finally found rest without dreaming.

Dawn broke as Jonah shook Camille's shoulders. She smiled sleepily and snuggled a bit closer to him, not wanting to lose her hold on restful slumber.

He clenched his teeth at the feel of her warm, soft body pressed against his. He pulled away his hips to ensure that Camille wouldn't feel the involuntary response in his body, making it difficult to hold her without pressing full against her curves and begging her to let him love her.

But he would never do that. Even as the urges hammered through his belly, he thought of the life that bloomed in hers. A life that he had had no part in creating.

He rolled away and sat up. The pale blush of daybreak filtered through the tiny leaded windows of the loft, sending diffused light across Camille's features and illuminating the shadowed tilt of her closed eyes, the enigmatic sensuality of her lips. His eyes lingered on the pulse that throbbed in her neck, then traveled up the slim column to the hollow of her cheek, and then he touched the smooth contour of her forehead. Jonah finally suppressed a groan and doubled over a bit more. The intimacy of watching her sleep was doing nothing for cooling the heat in his loins or smothering the warmth in his heart.

He reached out and shook her, gently bringing her into consciousness. Camille opened her eyes and saw Jonah's face, his strong features serious, his deep eyes searching hers.

"Is something wrong?"

"Nothing. It is morning, and you must hie yourself inside lest you are discovered."

She stretched and sat up. "I'll go now. Thank you for sharing your pallet."

A tremor ran through Jonah. "It was my pleasure, my lady."

She touched his face, pressing her hand to the stubbled cheek of her only friend. "I'll try to meet you tonight, to bring you some of the jewelry."

She stood and shook the straw out of the folds in her robe and picked a few stray pieces from her hair. Without another word, she made her way from the loft and out of the barn as silently as possible. The kitchen fires had been lit, and a pot of water set on the stove to boil, but the staff was elsewhere, and Camille ascended the servants' stairwell without being seen.

As Camille walked the long hallway to her room, she pressed her hand against her belly. For the first time since she had realized that her encounters with Patrick had led to the creation of a life, she allowed herself to look to the future with anticipation. Patrick had given her a child, and Jonah had given her hope.

Amelia ascended the front staircase and watched as Camille entered her room. Her only daughter's face glowed with serenity, and bits of straw clung to the back of her robe and in the blackness of her unbound hair. Amelia narrowed her eyes until they glittered. Silently, Amelia followed in Camille's path and entered behind her.

"Can't keep your legs together?" Amelia slammed the door.

Camille gasped and jumped, whirling around to face the fury of her mother. Her mind whirled for an explanation. She settled on one closest to truth. "I woke before daybreak. I visited the horses."

"The horses," Amelia scoffed. "What stud did you really visit, you tart? Must you always sink beyond the depth of my lowest expectation?"

Camille braced herself with the knowledge that her days in her mother's house were limited. She didn't permit any luxury of rebellion, for a turn with Edward's lash would endanger her child. With an even, respectful tone, Camille tried to save herself from a beating. "I am no different than yesterday, Mother. I have not lain with a man or compromised my chastity in any way. Disturbing dreams ruined my sleep, and what began as a visit to the kitchen for food ended with my taking an apple to the stallion, Smoke."

Amelia looked Camille over from head to heels and pursed her lips, uncertain as to the truth behind the clear green eyes that looked at her so seemingly without guile. "You are facile, child. I admit I can't decide whether to believe you or beat you."

Camille spread her hands beseechingly. "Have I given you any indication that I am resistant to my life here in London? I have complied with all of your wishes for me, and striven to please you to the best of my ability."

Amelia walked slowly around Camille's room, seeing the bed that had obviously been lain in. Other than the rumpled bed, Camille's possessions were in perfect order, just as Amelia expected. Camille had indeed conformed to London life, and not shown an inkling of the patterns of her life in Beauport. Just the other day, Amelia had seen Camille press a willing kiss upon Bret's lips. She could find no indication to doubt her daughter, and yet, she couldn't quite believe her. Something was amiss; Amelia could feel it. It combined with her other suspicions. And with that Amelia decided to go forward with her plans. The child needed discipline. The child needed humbling. Then and only then would the truth reveal itself. She already knew nothing of heaven or earth could make Camille reveal what she chose to keep secret.

"I will choose to accept your explanation, child. Dress yourself and come to the breakfast table. Bret will be joining us, and I'm certain your new crimson gown will please him."

Camille nodded her obedience and rang for her maid as Amelia swept from her rooms.

An hour and a half later, Camille entered the dining room as she had been instructed, wearing the red gown of her mother's choosing. The burdened table stood laden with crystal from Ireland and silver from Italy, chocolate and tea, croissants, creamed fruit, and sweetmeats from distant corners of the Empire. Amelia and Bret sat across from each other at the center of the table, and the sinking feeling Camille felt had nothing to do with the plushness of the Persian carpet beneath her feet.

Bret stood as she entered, waving aside the servant's aid in pulling out Camille's chair. His long, sinewy form looked resplendent garbed in gold silk and cream velvet, and he didn't appear to notice or mind that his breeches clung indecently to his manhood. His shoulder-length blond hair hung in waves and framed a face so innocent, one nearly forgot that appearances were not an indication of character. He pressed his face in her hair as he slid her chair in, and breathed the barest of whispers in her ear.

"You are riches beyond measure. Ruby gown, ivory skin, ebony hair, and emerald eyes." Bret trailed his fingers along the length of her neck and touched the delicate lines of her collarbones. "And all of it silk."

Camille swallowed hard and tilted her head back in a silent invitation for a kiss. Bret needed no further prompting. He dipped his head and sampled from her moist lips, pressing his tongue into the velvety warmth of her mouth. He sucked lightly on her bottom lip before he pulled away, leaving Camille flushed with revulsion at her own submission.

He laughed softly and rubbed his knuckles against her

cheek. "No need to blush, petal. Your mother more than approves of our union, and knows what passes between a man and a woman."

"So does our Camille," Amelia reminded scathingly.

Camille's color deepened, and Bret chuckled. "Don't forget, Your Grace, 'twas an Irishman who initiated her to the art of love. Dare I say Camille is practically a virgin in my eyes?"

Amelia cackled with glee. "Indeed, dear boy. Indeed."

Camille's hand stirred involuntarily in her lap, and she had to consciously keep from touching her abdomen. Bret seated himself next to Camille and poured her a cup of chocolate, allowing his arm to brush against the side of her breast as he leaned across. He turned his attention to Amelia.

"What are your wishes for the wedding, Your Grace?"

Amelia sipped lightly from her steaming cup of tea and tapped the rim thoughtfully. "I want all of London-town to seethe with envy. I shall be the sun, and Camille my rainbow. When the ceremony and festivities have concluded, I want to know that no one will be able to call to memory a finer day, a more lavish gown, a more sumptuous meal, or a more beautiful bride. The king himself should be put to shame. Why, if it is done properly, the king shall feel need to produce a daughter that he too could host such an event!"

"Ah, envy. 'Tis the motivation of every woman's actions, to inspire pure lust in others for what they have."

Camille tilted her head to look up at Bret. "Is your opinion of women so low?"

"Perhaps so accurate."

"I think not."

Bret's brilliant blue eyes took on a glint of curiosity. "What motivates you, Camille?"

Camille met his gaze evenly. "Hope it isn't revenge."

Bret paused a moment to digest her words and then threw his head back and shouted with laughter. When he recovered, he grew serious. "Do you think life with me will be so distasteful?"

"Would you wish your choice to be taken from you? Would you wish to be forced into a marriage with one you do not love, or even know?"

Bret shrugged his broad shoulders, making the silk of his jacket whisper against the silk of the upholstered dining chair. "That is the fate of nearly every woman in your situation, Camille. And, in truth, your situation is not so different from my own. As you know, my father ails and will not live much longer, and my mother is pressing me for marriage as well." Bret glanced to Amelia, and his eyes burned brighter. "My freedoms and choices are restricted for many, many reasons."

"If given the choice, would you have chosen me?" Camille asked bluntly.

Bret reached out to tuck an errant curl behind Camille's ear. "I think yes, Camille. I would have wanted you as my own no matter what the circumstance."

Camille arched an eyebrow. "Then our situations are very different."

Amelia interrupted with a lifting of her hand. "The Duke and Duchess of Somerset have given Bret over to me for you, Camille, and you may or may not realize that he is one of the most sought-after bachelors in all of England. No one in London knows of your escapades with the Irishman, and I will not have you shame our family in the eyes of my peers and friends alike with your open dismay over your impending betrothal. Should I have to remind you again of what by now should be plain, my next reminder will come through your skin, not your ears."

Camille cast her eyes downward and looked at her clasped hands. Though she knew Amelia wanted her contrition, Camille found it nearly impossible to keep from spitting in her mother's face with the knowledge that she would soon be fleeing London, Bret, and Amelia. Unable to bring forth anything resembling compunction, she said nothing.

Silence reigned, and Camille forced herself to eat something for the sake of her child. Once the meal was concluded, Amelia stood and shook out her skirts.

"I am expected in town. I leave you to each other's company."

Before Amelia left, she cast an arched brow to Bret. "I will trust you will see to your duties, and provide my daughter with all she needs."

He looked away, then back to the duchess. He nodded briefly, standing as she left the room.

Bret turned to Camille after Amelia had exited the room. He grinned wolfishly. "You're all mine for the afternoon, petal."

"I'm no more yours this afternoon than I shall ever be."

Bret slammed his fist on the table, rattling the porcelain and making Camille jump in her seat. "Damn you, Camille, you confound me at every turn!"

A quick vision of the night before congealed in her mind, of Bret rubbing himself against her pelvis, hurting her while he relieved his lust. Something inside her snapped. "I don't care for you."

"That is not how you kiss me."

"My kisses are to appease my mother. Nothing more."

"You are far too confident of yourself."

"Does that intimidate you, my lord?"

Bret clenched his teeth in frustration and pushed his hair away from his face. "Hardly, wench. I'd never be cowed by a woman."

Camille leaned forward and smiled smugly. "Oh? Are you calling my mother a man?"

Bret grabbed her by the shoulders and pulled her out of her chair. He held her to his long form and kissed her, silencing her protests. His tongue invaded her mouth, pushing her lips against her teeth until they hurt. She squirmed, pushed, and tried to break free, but he continued ruthlessly. His hands squeezed her arms, holding her still, bruising her. As he held her tight, he ground his pelvis hard against her stays, pressing them into her belly. She felt his arousal hard and hot through her clothing, a tumescent weapon.

Finally, he relented and released her. Camille's hand struck out and made contact with his cheek with a loud crack. Just as quickly he slapped her back, spinning her around and dropping her to the floor.

"You will be my wife and a duchess in your own right!" Bret snarled. "Comport yourself!"

Camille pushed herself up and shook back the hair that had fallen loose from her gold combs. "And what of you?"

Bret towered over her like a splendid Greek god with powerful muscles draped in gold and fair, shining hair that cascaded around a chiseled, handsome face. His eyes glowed, burning as he glared down at her. "I will give you what you need, wench: a firm hand, a sound beating, and a come-uppance that is long overdue. Your mother was more than right about what will be needed to get you in check."

Camille scoffed, "Keep taking orders from the old witch. You'll never be your own man!"

Bret leaned down and slapped Camille again, this time drawing blood from her bottom lip. "You don't have any idea of what makes a man."

Camille laughed out loud, as the pain fueled her desire to make Bret hurt in the only way she could. "Neither do you. You are nothing more than Amelia's pathetic whipping boy, doing her bidding as she directs it. Why don't you go and run behind her skirts? You're long overdue for your next assignment. Go, my lord. Go on. You haven't received orders in at least fifteen minutes. Don't you need to ask if you can piss in the pot?"

"You are a foul-mouthed shrew."

"Good for you, my lord. 'Tis the first thing I've heard you say that actually sounds as if it were of your own opinion."

Camille stood up and wiped the blood from her mouth

with a white linen napkin, and then threw the cloth in his face. "The last of my blood you'll shed."

A muscle twitched in his jaw; his mouth drew into a firm line. He wanted to strike her again, make her stop. But even now, after he had hit her twice, she mocked him. Amelia was right, he thought again. Camille would never be mastered if he couldn't rise to the task.

Yet what the duchess proposed turned his stomach. *Amelia's pathetic whipping boy.* The words infuriated him with their accuracy. He clenched his fists and looked at Camille standing her ground, silently daring him. Amelia's words came back to him, reminding him of all her suspicions. Conjecture that made his skin crawl. And he decided he would not be controlled by two women. Not when one could be dealt with.

Bret turned on his heel and strode from the room.

Camille collapsed onto a chair, shaking. She had wanted to be cool, to lead Bret down the path of thinking all was well, that her manner had grown more docile. Only when she had fled London would Amelia and Bret know that she would not be dominated any longer.

But she hadn't done that. All Bret's touching and kissing had finally worn away at Camille's reserve. And now she worried that her pride might have undermined her own plans.

Camille chewed lightly on a long, tended fingernail and reflected on what her next move should be. Clearly, the sooner Jonah could sell her jewelry and add it to his meager savings, the sooner the two of them could be free.

Freedom. Again, Camille faced it, and still she craved it. This time, she could not afford to lose it. For the sake of her child, she would not risk her pride again.

Camille rose and hurried to her rooms, anxious to have the deed done and be away from England, forever. She gathered her jewelry and wrapped each piece in a soft cloth before placing them in a velvet traveling bag, saving only a brooch and a ring that had belonged to Elizabeth and the amber bracelet that circled her ankle.

Some things were too precious to sell.

A glimpse of herself in the looking glass showed a pale young woman with bloodstains on her cheek, chest, and gown, hair disheveled, and a look of purpose in her green eyes. She thought of Jonah's reaction if he saw her as she was.

Thirty minutes later, Camille stood clad in a new gown of pale gray silk. Stiff black lace stood from her collar and framed her face. Softer lace frothed from her sleeves and fell over her slender hands in stark contrast to the white of her skin. The gown was her loosest, giving her the freedom to relieve some of the pressure of her stays. Hair in place and emotions in check, she left her rooms to head to the stables in search of Jonah.

New steps being taken, she realized, toward leaving England once again. Just as she had thought she'd be doing with Patrick, weeks ago. A new plan, a new friend, a new life, and a baby coming.

But the old ache still remained.

She needed to move on, she knew. She needed to leave the past where it was, move to the future. Her child needed a mother who could cope, a mother who could love him enough for the father he wouldn't have.

As she thought of the baby in her belly, her face softened and her eyes shone. A baby that would take too long to come. She wanted him now, to hold him to her breast and nurse him. To nuzzle the soft fuzz on his head and whisper quiet lullabies in tiny ears. Little hands wrapped tightly on her fingers, chubby feet kicking at his bunting. She could almost smell him, the crown of his head as she pressed a kiss against it; she could see the toothless smile and hear his infant's cries for her. The needs he had that only she could meet. And her arms felt empty. She pictured the child a bit older, taking steps away from her but then running back to the safety of her embrace.

And she knew she'd be a good mother. She would

protect her baby, love him unconditionally, pour into the baby all the love in her heart. The love his father hadn't wanted. She saw a little face in her mind, a vision of soft cheeks, stormy eyes, and red glints in his silky hair. She hoped the baby would look like Patrick, a piece of him that would never leave her.

CHAPTER 13

The Atlantic Ocean

Patrick didn't know what day it was. For that matter, he wasn't sure what month it was. The night sky displayed the constellations of late summer, but Patrick didn't spend too much time worrying about the date. Instead, he spent nearly every waking moment thinking about and waiting for the right moment to escape.

Captivity didn't come easily to a man like Patrick. He had been the son of the captain his whole life, until he became captain of his own ship. Never had he been treated with anything less than honor. Now, he spent his days tied like an animal on the deck of his own vessel.

Tate's death had taken something from Patrick, and in the place of what was gone grew a fury unlike anything Patrick had ever felt. It transcended the ropes that held him, making Birney's eyes dart with fear whenever he came near. Birney no longer trusted Herrick with Patrick's bondage. When Herrick had taken measures to attempt to release Tate, Birney saw a weakness in the man that he couldn't respect. And so it was each day that Birney brought a ration of food to Patrick, and held a pistol to his head as he allowed his captive time to relieve himself, before tying him back up.

Beneath Patrick the sea swelled and churned. He smelled the scent of a storm in the winds. Though the skies remained blue and only lightly dotted with clouds, Patrick knew a gale brewed as well as he knew Tate was dead. When the squall hit the ship, with its sloppy rigging and loose, flapping sails, his own death would greet Patrick in the form of drowning while lashed to the base of the mizzenmast on the port side.

The *Nuala* had continued to sail in a southwesterly direction, Patrick judged by the constellations. If the squall didn't sink the ship or change its direction, they would eventually wind up somewhere in the Caribbean. Patrick figured that his captors could sell him and his crew into bondage there even more easily than in the Americas. The sugar cane and tobacco market flourished there, as well as lumber, and merchants thrived on slave labor.

What Birney didn't count on was Patrick's motivation for retribution. The boy Birney had tormented and killed had been like a son to Patrick, and with a father's love Patrick sought a father's revenge.

There was also the matter of his crew. His men had followed Patrick's orders and brought the *Nuala* to take Patrick and Camille to their future. They had fought to save the ship from being taken; a few of the cowardly had fled ashore, and several had been killed at the time of the attack. One by one, the others whose injuries had led to their deaths were thrown into the ocean while Patrick watched. Of his entire crew, only two now lived.

Patrick looked on as Herrick attempted to trim the sails, trying to catch the strong winds. Though he possessed adequate strength for the task, he lacked the proper skills. The sails whipped around without snaring the currents. The heavy rigging came free and swung around to hit Herrick in the gut, knocking him flat on his backside.

Herrick sucked in breath and cursed simultaneously, an impressive feat in Patrick's estimation.

"It's like Solomon said: 'Everything is vanity and a striving after the wind.'"

Herrick glared at Patrick briefly and got to his feet. He grasped the rope again and started over.

"You're wasting your time. A storm is coming. The sails should be dropped."

Herrick glanced up to the blue sky and went back to adjusting the rigging. Patrick looked on at the burly, coarse man, noticing that though his clothes were rough, they were fairly clean and carefully mended. Wiry bristles that defied a clean shave shadowed most of his face and neck, and bushy eyebrows dominated his squinting eyes. Patrick recalled the first conversation he had had with Herrick, and the glint of shrewdness his uncultured speech hadn't concealed.

"You don't believe me?"

"I'm as good as puttin' Birney's sword in me own gut if I'm caught talkin' to ye."

"Perhaps, if you're caught. But you'll be dead for certain if you don't heed my warning."

Herrick dropped the ropes and threw his hand to the sky in frustration. "The skies be clearer today than yesterday."

"Haven't you ever heard of a 'sea change'? Storms at sea don't gather like they do on land. They blow over you and swallow you up if you don't know what to do when they hit."

Herrick shrugged heavy, tired shoulders. "Then it'll be over."

Patrick ached from being tied, and he had grown weary of being a prisoner. He had watched a boy he loved die, and he faced never seeing Camille again. What remained of the crew who counted on him for orders and looked to him for survival met only disappointment as they lay lashed and injured in the hold of the ship. Days of hunger, discomfort, and grief bled into each other and forced Patrick to question his most basic, primal elements. Like

Herrick, Patrick knew about craving the relief that death would surely bring.

But Patrick had also known freedom and known it well. To consider dying in bondage was unacceptable, and to give up on survival simply inconceivable.

"Over for you and me like it is for Tate?" Patrick asked, his voice rough.

Herrick looked up at him and didn't hide the regret in his craggy features. "I didn't want that to 'appen to yer boy."

A long moment passed as the two men looked at each other directly.

"I never thanked you for trying to save him." Patrick swallowed hard over the lump in his throat. "You have my gratitude."

Herrick waved away Patrick's words. "Yer boy's gone. Yer thanks aren't needed."

Patrick looked down to the ropes at his ankles. "I couldn't save him, couldn't protect him."

"'E ain't the first kid Birney 'urt. 'E ain't the first person 'e killed, neither. If you 'ad broken loose, Birney would 'ave killed ye, too."

"It could have gone that way. Or perhaps I would have killed Birney, and we would all be free."

Herrick raised a thick brow in doubt.

Patrick decided to get to the point before Birney came on deck and Herrick resumed his silence. "A storm is coming, and when it hits you can leave me bound and die, or free me and live."

Herrick shuffled his feet and peered at Patrick. "I figure either way, I'm dead. Birney'll kill me for lettin' ye go if the storm doesn't kill us all."

"Only if he lives," Patrick said succinctly.

Just then the door from the main cabin flew open. Herrick turned his back to Patrick and began to wind the lines into a more manageable coil. Birney stumbled over to Patrick, drunk and stinking of rum. He tried to land a kick in Patrick's side, but missed and hit the thick base of the mast. Too inebriated to feel real pain, Birney grunted his irritation and staggered to the rail to relieve himself. When finished, he loosely fastened his ragged breeches, rubbed his bleary eyes, and headed back to the captain's cabins.

"If Birney is drunk when the storm drowns him, it will deny me the pleasure of killing him with my own hands," Patrick said gruffly.

Silence fell over the men as Herrick threw the coil of rope to the deck in disgust and headed aft to the binnacle to check the course. Frustration and uncertainty shaped his features as he struggled with Patrick's warnings and his own inadequacy to manage the vessel.

"What's left of yer crew is close to death," Herrick confessed, as he gave up and came to stand in front of Patrick.

"What happened to my men who died?"

Herrick rubbed his whiskered chin and grunted. "The first went from a gut wound gone putrid. The last went after Birney gave 'im the same treatment 'e were lookin' to give yer boy. The bugger fought back, an' ol' Birney finished 'im when 'e were done. The other ones jest died, an' I'm damned if'n I know why."

Herrick squinted into the horizon off the stern and spoke as if to himself. "I ain't the sort o' man what likes pointless killin'."

"What about pointless dying?"

Herrick grunted again. "Ye don't give up, do ye?"

Patrick followed Herrick's line of vision and looked out over the white-tipped, rolling waters. "No."

Herrick shuffled his feet, running a rough hand across rougher whiskers. He looked from the sea and sky to the flapping sails, from the prow to the stern, and then back to Patrick. "Don't make me regret it."

Quickly, as if to act before he decided against his own judgment, Herrick took a dagger from his boot and severed the ropes that bound Patrick's ankles and wrists and handed the blade hilt first to Patrick. He reached for his cutlass and his pistol and put them at Patrick's feet.

"If 'e kills ye, I won't bear the guilt of it. If ye kill 'im, I 'ope ye'll mete out yer word."

Patrick slipped the dagger into his boot and stood, strapped the cutlass to his waist, and checked the pistol's priming. Patrick caught Herrick's eyes and grinned in a way that sent shivers down Herrick's back.

Herrick saw the change in the man before him, a transformation from hostage to warrior that took the space of only a second. The Irishman stretched his broad shoulders and strong arms, standing on powerful legs.

"Get to the capstan and lower the sails," Patrick ordered. Herrick immediately obeyed.

Patrick turned and strode away in the direction of the lower decks, captain once more and ready for battle and revenge. As he neared the captain's cabin, he measured his steps, silent and stealthy. A loud belch from the cabin made him unwillingly recall the image of Birney's slobbering mouth on Tate's cheek. The image brought the grief of Tate's senseless death to fresh and aching recall. Patrick paused and tightened his grip on the pistol. Pain and suffering feed fury, he reminded himself, but sadness and mourning have no place in battle. He would grieve for Tate later.

Patrick opened the door, grateful the well-oiled hinges made no sound. He slipped inside and closed the door. Birney sat at the thick desk that dominated the room; he appeared to be studying some charts that were spread out in front of him. As Patrick drew closer, he saw Birney was passed out, his head propped in his large hands. A stream of thick drool oozed from his slack lips, dripping to form a puddle of saliva and ink on the charts, stinking as much from lack of hygiene as from rum. The grizzled would-be pirate shifted his weight and half snored, half belched before slouching down in his chair, never opening his eyes.

Patrick shook his head, disgusted. This man who had

taken him hostage and killed Tate was nothing more than an ignorant, greedy, depraved man. Not a monster, but a useless product of a culture that didn't educate, care for, or even acknowledge their indigent. But even though Patrick recognized that, he couldn't pity it. And he'd be damned if he wouldn't rid the world of it.

Patrick surveyed his cabin and saw that few of his belongings had been disturbed. The drawers had been riffled through in search of monies or valuables, the locks on the chests busted open and the contents explored. But for the most part, it didn't appear too much was missing. A large trencher of cured meats and cheeses sat on the corner of the desk next to a bottle of rum and an unopened bottle of wine. The food looked untouched. Patrick sat across from Birney and began to eat, taking his fill of the food intended for him and Camille. A quick swallow of the rum to rinse out his mouth was plenty, for the uncut issue rum was black as sin, potent as hell.

After his hunger had been adequately sated, Patrick dropped to his knees and looked under his bunk. Relief, incredulity, and more relief swept through him, dizzyingly. He reached under and dragged out a long, rectangular sea chest from beneath the high bed. The chest had either been unnoticed or ignored, another of the countless mistakes made by his inept captors. He threw open the top and out wafted the smells of another lifetime.

Rogan's weapons lay in a cocoon of disintegrating velvet, forged, polished metals untouched by time. Some things never changed, and for Patrick one of those things came in the form of those implements of war, Rogan's tools for destruction and protection. He still looked at them with awe, but not as he had as a young man. He no longer saw romance and adventure in the gleaming blades. Realities of death and rape stained Patrick's fantasies of the romance and adventure of his grandfather's notorious past, as blood had stained the weapons. A saber and a cutlass nestled up to a large axe, and various throwing knives lay beside distinctly foreign-looking stars and blades, the uses for which Patrick had been schooled. Rogan had seen to it that his grandson had become as much warrior as merchant. A piece of both of them.

Patrick discarded Herrick's cutlass for Rogan's, preferring the excellence of its balance and weight. The saber he slung over his shoulder and back, fastening the belt across his chest so the scabbard hung between his shoulder blades. A second dagger slipped into his right boot, and two tiny metal stars in leather pouches were carefully tucked into his belt. Patrick pulled his hair back away from his face and fastened it with a leather thong, closed the case, and slid it back under the bed. Patrick Rogan Mullen stood, armed for battle.

But war would wait, because the sea would not. Patrick felt the urgency in the sea beneath his keel, and knew that if he would have retribution from Birney, he would have to survive to have it. With thick rope he bound Birney's hands together and then wound the rope around Birney's thick waist and tied it tight. Quickly, he patted Birney down, removing his weapons one by one and tossing them into a pile. Birney's eyes fluttered, and he groaned in protest when he couldn't move his arms, but his inebriated state didn't allow for him to come fully to consciousness. Patrick unceremoniously dragged the burly man from the chair and out of the cabin, not caring that Birney's head thumped against the floor.

He pulled the limp weight across the rough planks of the deck and out to the pinrail of the mainmast, where he bound him with enough ropes that Birney wouldn't be able to so much as flinch when the waves hit him.

Herrick looked up from the sails he was tying down, his expression impassive. "I feel the sea changin'."

Patrick nodded briefly and looked out to the churning waters. "Aye, 'tis a big storm that brews."

"'Ow likely is it we'll live?"

"'Tis a foolish man who doesn't go into every storm

thinking he'll die," Patrick said. "And a dead man who fears it."

Patrick gestured to the fore-and-aft sails. "Tie them down, making sure the yard is lashed. Do it quickly, and then secure the contents of my cabin. I need to see to my men."

Below, on the gundeck but out of the way of the small cannons, his two remaining men lay bound and ill. Patrick knelt, slashed their bonds, and pulled the gags from their mouths. Liam and Jerry pulled themselves to sitting positions and faced their captain. A wave of dizziness overtook Liam, and he lay back down with a thud.

"It took long enough, sir," Jerry said hoarsely.

"Aye."

Liam shuddered against the pain of his infected wounds and the sickness running rampant in his body. "A squall?"

Patrick touched Liam's brow and frowned at the dry heat. "Aye, Liam."

Patrick turned to Jerry. "Can you walk?"

Jerry got to his feet unsteadily, his success at getting upright his only answer. Patrick nodded and picked up Liam, carrying him to his cabin where Herrick was already at work stowing away Patrick's belongings and foodstuffs. Patrick laid Liam in his bed and gave him water until he could drink no more. Jerry took a mug and dipped it into the barrel of water, quenching his thirst as well, before eating as much as his belly could hold. Patrick took the rum and held a rag under Liam's wounds, pouring the alcohol into the oozing holes in his chest and belly, ignoring his moans of pain. With the symmetry of those who have worked together for years, Jerry handed Patrick a length of rope without being asked. Patrick put a few quilts over Liam and then bound him to the bed.

With Liam seen to, Patrick shifted his attention to survival, as the wind began to increase and rock the ship. "Herrick, get to the quarterdeck and lash yourself to the rail, leaving enough length to move about. Jerry, are you well enough to check the binnacle?"

"Aye, sir."

"Fine. Chart our present position."

Jerry nodded and obeyed. Herrick followed Jerry out the door of the cabin, but stopped short at Patrick's voice. "Your other man. Where is he?"

"Forecastle deck. 'E's been ill since we set sail, pukin' with every swell."

"Seasickness generally abates after a few days," Patrick said.

Herrick grunted in agreement. "Wiley 'as a weak belly."

Patrick sighed with resignation. "Fine. Strap him to his bunk so the waves don't throw him to the deck."

Herrick left the cabin, and Patrick glanced back at Liam, already sleeping. Patrick felt completely alone despite the men aboard the *Nuala*. The wind began to whistle and howl. Through the thick windows of the cabin, Patrick saw the sky grow dark.

"I hate being right," Patrick mumbled to himself.

He left the cabin and bolted the door against the winds. As he headed aft against the gale, rain began to pelt his face. Patrick held to the rail and made his way to the helm, grabbing the chest-high wheel and turning it until he felt the strong pull of water against the rudder. Waves rolled and churned around the ship, tossing it high and then dropping it with a crash into the next trough. Water seemed to come from every direction, spinning the well-built vessel about like a top. Patrick held to the wheel and spun it, trying to guide the ship with the storm.

With his feet spread wide apart, he steered away from the wind, riding each wave like the foam that it threw, knowing that the sea was not something that could be fought or controlled, but could only be ridden out. Lightning ripped across the sky and reflected on the waters, illuminating everything in a glare of bright white clarity. Thunder clapped and rumbled, one bolt following the next without a pause, as lightning continued to light up the ship with staccato flashes. Herrick yelled something to Patrick, but his voice was drowned out in gusts of wind.

Patrick lashed the wheel in place and struggled across the deck to check on Jerry, nearly tripping over Birney's legs. Ahead he saw Jerry, secured to the rail on the forecastle deck. Satisfied, Patrick headed aft to retake the wheel, noticing that Birney had not awakened from his drunken stupor. Patrick grabbed the wheel and held firmly, the well-worn wood familiar under his hands. This wasn't the first squall to hit the *Nuala*, and God willing, it wouldn't be the last. Patrick rode the high, angry waves with patience. Waves crested and dumped on the deck of the ship, washing away anything not lashed down. Again and again lightning sizzled around him, hitting the water with loud cracks and sending water twenty feet and more into the air. The howl of the wind competed with the deep rumblings of thunder, making even Patrick's thoughts difficult to hear.

What felt like several hours of exertion probably took half that, but Patrick couldn't tell and didn't care. Only survival mattered. When the sea began to ease, the shift was nearly imperceptible, but he felt it. The winds gradually slowed, until the howling ceased and only the creaking of the ship could be heard between fading rumbles of thunder. Waves stopped washing over the rail, and instead only buffeted the sides of the hull. Rain continued to fall, then slowed until it finally stopped. The worst of the storm spent, Patrick turned to Herrick, still lashed to the rail on the quarterdeck with his clothing and hair plastered to him, his face pale.

"I'm going to get some rest," Patrick said.

Patrick headed to the cabin, soaked, exhausted, alive, and free. Free most of all. Free to exact vengeance, and free to return to England and find Camille. Again, he would know what it was to hold her in his arms, to whisper in her ears the words that overflowed his heart. Deep inside he ached for her, missed her, longed for her. Like an amputee who knows his leg is gone but still feels the itch of his foot, Patrick could feel Camille inside him as much as he knew she was so far away.

Patrick entered his cabin, glad to see Liam still sleeping. He untied the ropes that had held Liam on the bed before he stripped off his sodden clothing and dressed in dry garments from his sea chest. Then, without the energy to do anything else, Patrick collapsed into the hammock in the corner and fell asleep.

When he woke, faint glimmers of dawn streaked the horizon. Patrick rose and felt Liam's forehead, dismayed his fever hadn't gone down. He shook Liam to semi-consciousness and pressed water on him again, forcing him to drink more than Liam wanted. Patrick pulled away Liam's shirt and saw his wounds were full of smelly pus, tinged green around the openings. Even if they were back on land within the month, Liam wouldn't live that long.

Patrick soaked a few strips of linen in rum and then took his dagger from his boot. With the tip of his blade Patrick lanced the wounds, releasing the pus and relieving the pressure. Patrick squeezed as much of the infectious fluid out as he could and then poured more rum into the wounds before applying the soaked bandages and wrapping the whole of it up with clean fabric. Liam thrashed from the pain and burning until deep sleep overtook him and he settled, muttering occasionally in Gaelic, calling for his mother.

Patrick stood and headed to the main deck. He found Jerry already at the binnacle, eyeing Herrick cautiously. Patrick caught the exchange and couldn't suppress a grin, realizing that an alliance with a man who tried to kill you didn't come easily.

Patrick studied Jerry and saw his skin looked good, his eyes clear. "You look better."

"All I needed was some food, sir."

"How far were we thrown?" Patrick asked.

Jerry grimaced. "I scarcely know where we are, sir."

Patrick stood at the rail on the stern, his legs wide apart, his hands clasped behind his back. The ocean stretched around him in every direction, and their provisions were less than adequate.

Birney stirred with a series of grunts, flatulence, and curses. Patrick moved to stand over him, wanting the first moments of the man's captivity to begin with fear. Patrick pulled his pistol from his waistband and put it against Birney's nostrils. Through the haze of his hangover, Birney felt the cold metal pressing upward against his nose and opened bleary, watery eyes to see gunmetal and the Irishman, captive no longer and smiling a promise of death. He tried to pull his hands up in an instinctual need to protect his face, then screamed as he found his hands bound to his waist.

"Do you think Tate felt as afraid as you do now?" Patrick asked with quiet menace. Patrick cocked the pistol. "What about now?"

"I didn't mean to kill yer boy!" Birney protested, his eyes wild and bulging from his head.

"Don't bore me with your intentions. The lad suffered and died at your hands."

"It were 'Errick an' 'is interferin'!"

Patrick shoved the pistol further up Birney's nose. "You would have raped the boy."

"I was only funnin'! I wouldna 'urt 'im!"

Patrick pulled the pistol from Birney's nose, clasped his hands behind his back, and began to pace the deck slowly, thinking out loud as he walked. "So the child's death was an accident, and the attempted rape only a prank. Most of my men are dead, but I assume you don't care to bear the brunt of that blame, either."

"Ye killed two of my men!" Birney interrupted.

Patrick stopped, silencing him with a glare colder and

more dangerous than the waters surrounding them. "Don't speak again."

Patrick resumed his pacing. "For your crimes, I could see you hung from the yardarm, or impaled on the bowsprit. Perhaps I shall simply see you gutted and fed to the fish."

Patrick stopped and stared at Birney, savoring the panic in the man's eyes. He let the moment linger for a long while. "But I think not."

Birney sagged with relief.

"Instead, I shall afford you the treatment you allotted to me," Patrick said, and then his voice grew as sharp as a blade, and just as cold. "For a while, at least. Then, I'll give you the treatment you gave Tate."

Patrick turned and headed to the binnacle, forgetting Birney and putting his mind to the matter of his ship and their predicament.

Birney caught Herrick's gaze and began to yell. "'Errick, ye bastard! I saved ye from Newgate, an' this is 'ow ye see to yer debt? Ye lyin', cheatin' whoreson, I'll see ye rottin' in 'ell! I'll kill ye wit me own 'ands!"

Patrick's voice, deep, loud, and booming with authority, cut Birney off. "Jerry, gag the insolent bastard. I have no ear for his garbled tongue!"

Jerry rushed to the mainmast, more than content to shove a rag in Birney's mouth. Herrick left the quarterdeck and stood by Patrick's side. "Ye kept yer word, an' I do see out me debts."

Patrick looked into Herrick's lined and weathered face. "Have no fear. I, too, see out mine."

Herrick nodded his understanding with a brief jerk of his head and returned to cleaning up the mess of rigging strewn about by the storm.

Alone at the helm, Patrick studied the notes Jerry had made prior to and after the squall. The *Nuala* had been blown about a league westerly, and Patrick had been fairly certain of their location before the storm had hit. With a series of short commands, Patrick called for the two men to raise the mainsail, the mizzen sails, and the foresheets. Patrick squinted to the topmasts, knowing that not raising them would slow their progress, but that it would be more than his sparse crew could handle. Together, Jerry and Herrick followed Patrick's orders, and when the sails were up, Patrick lashed the wheel in place and grabbed hold of the rigging. Loud claps resounded as the sails one by one caught the wind currents, and the schooner began to pick up pace. The slip-slap sounds of the waves against the hull were replaced by the hush of water being sucked beneath the prow and curling around the ship. Patrick headed aft, undid the line holding the wheel, and trimmed the ship on a southwestern course.

He would sail the ship to the Caribbean. They didn't have enough rations or men to make the journey back to England safely. Once in the islands, they could stock the ship with food and provisions, take on an adequate crew, and repair the *Nuala*. And then sail back.

Only then did he relax. The sky stretched clear to the horizon. Patrick stood at the wheel with his feet spread wide and his hands behind his back, as the wind whipped his hair away from his face. He squinted into the sunlight and concentrated, hoping Camille could hear his thoughts if he focused hard enough, if he repeated them often enough.

I'm coming back.

CHAPTER 14

London

Camille paused on her way into the stables. A prickling along the nape of her neck sent a shiver down her spine. For an instant, she felt she was not alone.

She looked around, seeing no one. Nothing disturbed her solitude or the silence, yet her feeling of being watched haunted her. Camille entered the shady stables. But she was still alone. Only horses stood in their stalls, placid in the late afternoon. Cats roamed in search of rodents, as silent as shadows amidst the musty scents of straw, dung, and saddles.

A vague emptiness stayed with her, as if she had lost a thing of irreplaceable value or forgotten something vitally important. The awareness had been so familiar, like her own voice.

She shrugged away the feeling. "How odd," she murmured under her breath.

Shafts of afternoon sunlight filtered in through the small windows, settling on the rough planks of the floor. She closed the stable door to keep the interior cool. Hay clung to her gown. She bent, brushed it from her hem, and picked up her skirts. No need for Amelia to question her venture into the barn. She slipped farther into the stables and climbed the ladder to the loft where Jonah had taken to sleeping, and where she had lain with him, more comfortable than she had been in her big, lonely bed. His pallet remained as it had been the night before, blankets pushed aside from when they had awoken. She bent and smoothed the thick woven cotton, her heart full and warm as she thought of Jonah's generosity and caring.

Camille saw a vision of rugged Scotland's shores, windy and overcast. The ocean threw bits of foam in the air as it hit jagged rocks, and her son ran on the dark, pebbly sand, chased by waves and his Uncle Jonah.

She leaned against a rough-hewn post and let her fingers wander her belly. "Funny how I always think of you as a boy."

How round would her stomach get? she wondered. How much did she need to eat and rest? When did you know if the baby was hungry, and what if her breasts didn't make enough milk? She had no one to ask.

But it wasn't the first time Camille had had to take care of herself. She laid aside her worries. After all, she reasoned, women had babies every day, women far less smart and resourceful than she.

On the main floor of the stables, Smoke reared, bucking in his stall, displeasure rumbling in his massive chest. Camille's heart started to pound. A horse never made that sound unless in danger. She hurried to climb down the ladder to find the groom or a hand, but the stables were still devoid of human life. Again Smoke bucked against the stall, voicing his displeasure. The whole stable seemed full of the noise of the great stallion's aggravation. Other horses took his cue and began to whinny and snort, stamping their feet.

Camille grabbed a quirt and rushed around the corner to Smoke's stall. His large eyes rolled in his huge head, exposing the whites. He reared again when he saw her, hitting the stall hard enough to splinter the thick wood.

"Whoa," Camille said gently. "Easy, Smoke. Easy."

She moved a bit closer, her mind whirling for an explanation to the stallion's extreme upset. Smoke tossed his head high and pulled back foaming lips to reveal yellowed teeth. For an instant, his eyes looked down and met Camille's. She saw pure fear.

"Smoke?" Camille whispered.

Powerful hands grabbed Camille from behind. Camille's scream was drowned out by Smoke's.

Camille found herself thrown to the crude floor planks. Her face hit hard, and the quirt bounced from her hand. She opened her mouth to scream again, this time for help. Her attacker gagged her mouth and pinned her shoulders to the floor. Camille struggled to flip over, needing leverage to fight back. He grabbed her hands and bound them with reins, picked her up by the shoulders, and pushed her over a bale of hay, pinned to her belly.

He thrust his knees between her thighs and spread her legs, preventing her from moving. Camille realized his intent as he pulled up the back of her skirts.

Only one thought tore through her mind, the way a bullet ricochets. *Don't hurt my baby!*

But Camille couldn't beg him to stop. She couldn't plead for the life of her child. She could do nothing but scream in her mind as her body was raped. She felt his blunt probing, felt him tear into her, ripping, hurting, stealing. Stealing what was only Camille's to give. Blood ran down her legs, warm and sticky. Camille struggled until her strength ran out, until pain outweighed her shame.

Nothing outmeasured her fear for her child.

Oh my God, he's killing him. He's killing both of us.

Smoke barreled against the stall, kicking with his powerful forelegs. As if the stallion knew Camille had been gagged, he screamed his outrage for her.

The rapist thrust into her again and again. The pain turned into agony. Tears slid from beneath tightly squeezed lids, and she choked back vomit. He shuddered

over her, withdrew. Camille turned her head, wanting to
see his face as much as she loathed to. A black cloak
swirled as he released her from his hold and stood, his face
hooded in an expressionless mask of black leather. Tiny
slits for his eyes glittered as he loomed above her. He
watched her for a prolonged moment. Camille felt para-
lyzed. She could do nothing more than stare with mute
horror into his grotesque mask.

Hands garbed in leather reached down to pull Camille's
skirts over her exposed legs, covering her. His cloaked
flared as he whirled around and left the stables in silence.
Smoke settled at the man's departure, bumping the stall
and nickering to Camille for reassurance.

Camille slid to the floor, lying without strength to rise.
Blood left her in pulses. Her torn and bloody gown spread
out in waves around her. The gag in her mouth prevented her from calling out for help, her arms bound
behind her back. And she was alone, anyway. No one to
call for, no one to help her. She wondered if she would
die there in the stables, or worse, if she would live.

She closed her eyes and thought of the God of her
youth. The God she had been told was merciful and just.
The God who loved her without conditions.

She squeezed her eyes tightly and prayed to die.

Jonah lifted Camille from the floor, cradling her to his
chest. He ran to the main house as lightly as he could,
trying to avoid jostling her. When he reached the kitchen
door, Jonah kicked it open and rushed inside, startling the
cooks. Marion looked up with a gasp.

"Dear Lord! Call the mistress!" Marion commanded her
daughter Jane as she ran to Jonah's side. She ran a hand
over Camille's brow and looked into the anxious face of
Jonah, whose tears streamed down his cheeks. The blood
soaking the bottom half of her gown dripped onto the

immaculate floor; the bruises and cuts on Camille's cheeks and mouth told everything.

"Rape?"

Jonah nodded, spoke, and revealed himself once and for all. "I believe so."

Marion turned and grabbed her basket of ointments and clean linen. Her hands flew as she filled a basin with clean water and threw smelling salts into the basket. "Follow me."

The cook led the way to Camille's chambers, holding her breath as she prayed for the life of the beautiful young woman in Jonah's arms. She opened the door to Camille's rooms and Jonah rushed to lay her on the bed. Jonah wondered how so much blood could come from one woman, and he silently worried for the life of Camille's child. Marion pulled blankets on top of Camille, straightening up just as Amelia came through the door, followed closely by Jane.

"Your girl says Camille has been raped?" Amelia demanded of the cook.

"Aye, Your Grace. Jonah found her." Marion turned to Jonah. "In the stables?"

Jonah nodded, never taking his eyes away from Camille's unconscious countenance.

"Did you see anyone else in the stables?" Amelia asked Jonah.

"He is mute, Your Grace," Marion quickly interjected, glancing at Jonah with a look of warning.

Amelia sniffed her annoyance. She walked over to her daughter's bed, picked up a corner of the blanket, and saw the blood. "Perhaps when Camille awakens, she can offer insight as to what happened."

"I can send Clive for a physician, Your Grace," Marion offered rapidly.

Amelia didn't reply. She dropped the blanket back in place and stared at Camille. Finally she spoke. "No. I won't have all of London buzzing. Send for Niles. His studies in medicine will finally have found a usefulness."

Marion sucked in her breath and forgot her place. "Oxford is a day away at a hard ride for the best of horsemen. Master Niles's legs are weak. There is no way he can get here quickly enough!"

Amelia arched a brow and leveled her frigid gaze on Marion's plain face. "You will tend to her while we await his arrival."

Marion opened her mouth to reply, but Amelia cut her off before she could speak. "Mind yourself, cook. I do not make a habit of arguing with servants."

Marion nodded briefly and backed away with her head bowed. "Yes, Your Grace."

"See to any and all of Camille's needs. I'll post a girl at the door who can run into town to obtain anything you require." Amelia turned and left the room.

Jane used the hem of her apron to wipe her tears. "I'll send Clive to fetch Master Niles." She stumbled from the room at a near run.

Marion and Jonah stood alone in the room. They looked at each other desperately. Then Jonah closed the door and threw the bolt. "No one else touches her until her brother arrives."

"Fine. Get me the basin and a cloth." Marion began stripping the torn, bloody gown from Camille's battered body. The kind hands of the cook eased the laces of Camille's corset and pulled it away, leaving Camille in her gauzy shift. Marion looked at the small, rounded bulge that protruded from an otherwise completely flat belly, between hips so slim the bones were evident. She looked at Jonah, her brows raised in silent question, afraid to voice her concern lest the girl be betrayed yet again.

Jonah met Marion's gaze evenly. "Yes. It is what you think."

"Yours?"

"No. Not mine."

Marion began washing the blood from Camille's legs. "I'll make no mention of it."

"I appreciate your discretion, but there is more."

Marion never paused in her work, wringing out a cloth and turning the water scarlet. "You don't have to tell me."

"I love her."

Tears glided down Jonah's cheeks. He smoothed Camille's hair and dabbed at the cuts on her soft mouth with a clean rag. "I wanted to protect her. If you have eyes, you see her hopeless state here. I told her I would help her."

"This is not your fault."

"She was coming to meet me. I was late returning."

Camille moaned in her unconscious state and tried to pull her legs up. She shifted and stirred in obvious discomfort. Marion continued to clean Camille's slender, bruised legs, putting fresh rags between them to stanch the flow of blood that wouldn't stop.

"She is losin' the child, I think," Marion said quietly.

"No. She mustn't lose it. It is all she has to live for."

Marion saw dark red clots and pieces of tissue in the blood that left Camille, and she slowly shook her head. "She will have to find somethin' else."

Camille opened her eyes to the darkness of her room. Her body ached worse than from any beating she had ever taken. From deep inside her belly and between her legs intense pain throbbed. Her head hurt and her mouth and throat were parched. She wondered what illness had laid her so low.

And then the memory came back. It flooded her mind with its reality, and Camille began to scream.

Marion and Jonah bolted upright from the floor where they had taken to resting, caring for her in a constant vigil. They were beside her in an instant, soothing her the best they could until Camille stopped crying out. Camille's hand clutched at her abdomen, feeling through the covers for the tight bulge that had become familiar. She searched Jonah's face for a denial of her worst fear.

But the look in his eyes tore her heart open and shoved icy spears of panic into her gut.

"No." Her hands gripped her belly tighter, her eyes wild and desperate. "Please, Jonah, tell me no."

"I cannot."

"You must," she insisted. "If he is gone, I will die, too."

Jonah wasn't sure if Camille spoke about Patrick, their baby, or both. He was certain only of the tight grip of her hands on his, her pale, shaking lips, and the agony that tensed her whole body. Jonah ran his thumbs over her fingers, and his voice came as a choked whisper and a paltry sentiment. "Your strength is not a choice you can make."

He watched while the light in her eyes turned dusky and then went out.

"I didn't choose any of this."

Jonah bowed his head, understanding her meaning. "I'm sorry."

Camille let go of his hands and touched her belly. She rolled to her side facing away from Jonah, with her legs pulled up and her arms crossed over her chest. Pictures and snippets of her memories of Patrick ran through her mind unbidden, and Camille remembered the night they had lain together, consummated their love, and created the life now dead. The roses around the cottage had filled the night with their heady, sultry fragrance, whispering around them with caresses of moonlight. Patrick held her close to him, and though Camille now knew his words to be lies, they had been everything she'd ever wanted to hear and more. Still, she remembered his voice, the stormy intensity of his eyes, the warmth and strength of his body pressed against her own. The wounds on her back had long ago turned into scars, but she could still feel the press of his lips against them, taking her pain until her knees felt weak.

The child that had grown inside her had been the only thing left of her love for him. The one tangible thing in the world she could love without restraint, with an assurance to be loved in return.

My baby, she thought. My baby is dead.

A sob formed in Camille's chest, large and heavy until she felt there was not enough air in the room. Camille pulled in deep breaths that expired in broken sighs. She clasped her arms tighter to her, trying to replace the feel of Patrick's on her, yet conscious of the void of the baby who would never fill them.

She tried to dream it away. Labored to divine what was to come. Something to cling to, something to hope for. But it was all gone. Like her child. As forsaken as the promises Patrick had made, as lost as her heart, as lifeless as her baby.

There were no dreams to make it better. Nothing would ever make it better.

She was alone as she had always been. Love and children and friendship, just an illusion to sharpen suffering when the fantasy fades.

Sympathy and guilt ripped Jonah's heart as he stared at Camille's narrow back and the slump of her shoulders. He longed to climb beside her in the big, deep bed and hold her against him as he had before. He listened to the stifled sobs of the young woman who wanted to weep but couldn't, until he felt consumed with anger for the undeserved agony in which she suffered. The rapist was out there, somewhere. Faceless and nameless, like the man who had killed his mother. Jonah shook with rage. He trembled with the desire to hurt, to wound, to watch the man die. He wanted to make him bleed, to watch the life run out of him in a red river as it had from between Camille's legs.

What had been done to Camille had been done to his mother. A wound in his heart ripped wide open again, hemorrhaging. The man needed to die, Jonah thought

viciously. The man needed to die screaming. But first he
would need to find him. He would need to be calm. To
be strong. To be all the things for Camille he hadn't been
for his mother. It was too late to avenge his mother's
murder. Jonah had hidden, saved himself, and let her killer
go free. But not now, he vowed. Not this time.

Jonah inclined his head to Marion, a gesture for the
cook to take her leave. Marion's eyes glistened with tears
of understanding and sympathy. She left the room and
closed the door without a sound. Jonah leaned over
Camille to pull another blanket over her, and as his body
heat touched hers, Camille shuddered against the memories of the rape.

The tremor of rage shook him, disgusted him. Only the
night before, she had let him hold her, and she had
trusted the feel of his body. But no more. Rape had stolen
the innocence of such a moment.

With a small chair pulled up to the side of the bed,
Jonah sat, forced calm into his tone. He began to question
Camille. "Who did this?"

She shuddered again, from present pain and remembered agony. "I don't know."

"You did not see him?"

"He was masked . . . and cloaked."

Jonah flattened his lips at the mental image, thinking
what terror Camille must have suffered. His thoughts
raced. He recalled when his mother had returned from
trysts with her nobleman, and the cologne that had clung
to her clothing. "A scent, Camille?"

She forced herself to go back to the stables in her
mind, searching for a clue to identify the man who had
violated her and killed her child. Scents. She remembered the odor of horses, dung, and straw as she was
flung to the floor, and of wood and leather. The sickening smell of her blood mixed with his spilled seed, and the
heavy scent of a wool cloak too warm for the weather
mingled with his sweat. She felt nauseated. The pain be-

tween her legs throbbed. She kept her head turned away from Jonah, not wanting him to see her shame. "Nothing. Please leave me, Jonah."

"I will not leave you. I want to help you."

"My child is dead. There is no helping me."

Jonah struggled with his frustration. He saw the wounds on her face; he had seen the blood leave her body in pulsing waves. Still, Jonah knew that youth and health would see to it that all visible signs of the rape healed away. It was the mental and spiritual wounds Jonah worried for. Those were likely to scar deeply. Camille's voice broke his heart as she spoke into the silence.

"I never heard him come in," she said softly, keeping her face averted. "He grabbed me from behind. My strength was no match for his." Her voice trailed off into the barest of whispers. "I wanted to scream. I wanted to fight. I would have begged for the life of my baby. I would have offered him the jewelry. Anything. I would have given him anything."

At the mention of her jewelry, she lifted a hand and gestured to her gown, still crumpled in a heap on the floor. "The jewels are fastened in a pouch under the skirts. Take it all and buy your freedom, Jonah. It is my gift to you. Thank you for your kindness."

Jonah drew back as if he had been struck. "I will not! You will leave with me when you are well."

Camille shook her head, still averting her face from his. "No. I will remain in London. Scotland holds no promise of freedom, and the future holds no promise of happiness. My child was my purpose. He is gone, and I am finished."

"Finished living?"

Camille sighed, long and deep. "Go, Jonah. Leave me with this."

"No. I would help."

Camille couldn't look at him, but she could feel his eyes on her, seeing her. Seeing more than she wanted anyone to see. "Please go, Jonah. When you refuse me, you take more of my choice."

Emotions seethed through Jonah. Anger for Camille's violation, fury for the senseless death of a child so wanted and already loved, and rage at the unknown man who had taken from Camille what could never be regained. The power of those feelings collided wildly with the depth of his compassion and sorrow. He exploded. "That monster raped your body! He did not rape your soul!"

Camille had been assaulted and degraded, raped and left to bleed. She had been forced to hold in her screams of outrage and pain while a masked stranger panted and grunted, shoving himself deep inside her while he ripped her baby from her womb. She would not be told how to feel. She finally looked at Jonah directly, her feelings unleashed. "I don't want your help, Jonah. I want the pain. I want the suffering. I want to lie in my bed and mourn the child I will never hold and never know. I want to lie in my own blood and recall the attack. I want to wallow in my own self-hate and self-pity, and do you know why?"

Camille's voice shook as she answered her own bitter question. "Because it is all I can feel. Most of all I want to hide from all who will look at me and know. They will know because I wear it, Jonah. I wear my shame like a leper wears his disease. It is inside me. It is on me. It is everywhere I look."

"What happened to you was savage and brutal," Jonah countered resolutely. "It will take enormous strength to heal from it. But healing is not for the weak. You will have to confront it, see it, and not allow it to define you. You will have to gather your strength together and wrap it about you. Your courage will be your armor, your will to survive your shield."

Disgust for herself and for Jonah's platitudes crept into Camille's tone, and for the first time she sneered at her only friend. "I don't want your opinions of how I should behave. It was not your child killed, or your body defiled.

I'm through with hearing you tell me about bravery. You have been living in fear and hiding since we met."

Jonah's shoulders sank. He saw the mixture of grief and fury through the cuts and bruises on her face. Jonah possessed enough wisdom to realize there were no words to ease her suffering, and no promise of the pain ever leaving he could offer. He was as helpless to help her as he was to avenge her, and his own weakness sickened him. "As you wish," Jonah said quietly.

He left the darkened room and closed the door. Marion stood waiting in the corridor with her back against the far wall. "How is she?"

"Angry. Bitter. More alone than ever before."

Marion wrung her chapped hands together, still feeling like blood stained her skin, though she had washed again and again. "Poor child."

"Yes," Jonah said, remembering the fear and self-loathing on Camille's face. "There is nothing to be done for her."

Marion's expression grew far away. "Not even time will take her suffering."

CHAPTER 15

Off the coast of England

The seas grew more restless and choppy as the *Nuala* neared England.

Patrick had been able to gather only a crew of twenty men who sought passage to England. He had been forced to wait a month's time for just that paltry crew and to have repairs made to his ship. But he'd wanted to leave, been anxious to get back to England, and so he had settled for the smallest number of men he thought would see them through. Barely enough men to man the ship on shifts. But they were skilled enough, he thought. They had made it across the Atlantic with little difficulty, and the weather had cooperated. The rations were plentiful, with enough fruit to keep the men happy. And enough rum, too.

What a sorry lot they had been when they had limped into the bay at Bermuda, unable to make it to the Caribbean. Torn sails, three hungry men, a man so ill he couldn't move, and another whose wounds made him so weak he couldn't stand. The prisoner had remained gagged and tied, at Patrick's orders. No jail would suffice. He had his own plans for the man who had killed Tate.

They left Wiley behind, so weak with dehydration from

his seasickness his body looked like a dried autumn leaf. But they took Liam home with them. Patrick hadn't known if he'd make the voyage alive, but he did know Liam would want to be buried in Ireland, either way. And Liam's mother would never have forgiven Patrick if he had allowed her son to die under the care of strangers. So they hired a doctor to accompany them, even though the man's price had made even Patrick cringe. The good doctor was with Liam even now though, Patrick noted, and so true to his word and worth the coin. It looked as though Liam would live, and the *Nuala*'s captain would not have to face the wrath of an Irish widow who loved her son like she loved her country.

He checked the binnacle and then scanned the sails, calling out for Jerry, who hung in the rigging, to trim the topsail. England lay ahead, a dark cluster of clouds barely visible on the horizon. It was the most beautiful thing Patrick had seen since the last time he had seen his wife, sleeping in her bed while he watched.

He could see her now, as if she were in front of him. Black lashes resting on soft white cheeks, pink lips barely parted with breath, and hair the color of midnight spread out across her pillow. And he could smell her, too, sweet with lavender and the delicate, indefinable scent of a beautiful woman.

But he was not the only one on board the *Nuala* who was lost in thoughts, memories, and regrets.

Birney heard the captain's shouted order, and sneered at the sound of the voice. But he did so without real heat, too tired and weak to muster up anything sincere. The past weeks, while tied like an animal, he had learned a few things. One was that fear was something he couldn't get used to. Another was that other times in his life he had been only hungry, and until recently he hadn't known what it was to truly starve. The captain allowed him only enough to eat so he didn't die, and only enough to drink to keep him alive. And he had learned most of all that the Irishman was not a man to be toyed with.

Birney grew more sullen with each passing day. With myopic, watery eyes he watched the activities of the ship's scant crew while he wondered which day the captain would see fit to execute him. Superstition and religion combined to turn each of his days into long, lugubrious passages of time wherein the teachings of hellfire danced in his head and ate him alive with greedy flames. He had thought of begging Patrick to end it now and quickly, but his pride wouldn't allow that. Birney toyed with the thoughts of taunting the Irishman into a fit of rage, hoping that Patrick would pull the pistol from his waistband and put a shot between Birney's eyes, but his fears of the unknown wouldn't allow that. So Birney awaited his inexorable fate, knowing that there would be no escaping the Irish captain.

But Patrick had not concerned himself with Birney of late. He had given orders as to how he was to be dealt with, and all but forgotten him. The only focus he allowed himself came in the form of returning to England, that he could find Camille. Birney was nothing more to him than an extraneous detail that needed completing before arriving at their destination. Patrick had never lived in a country long enough to have an inclination to abide by its laws. The laws that governed him were of nature, survival, and the immutable principles of men who lived at sea. They held their own brand of justice and retribution.

Jerry headed aft and met Patrick at the wheel, interrupting Patrick's thoughts with worries of his own. "We're only a few hours out, sir."

"Aye."

"What're we going to do, sir?"

Patrick trimmed the ship and lashed the wheel in place. He stood with his feet planted wide apart, and his hands clasped behind his back as he looked out over the waters and scanned the sails with keen eyes. "You're going to take the *Nuala* to Ireland and deposit Liam with his family."

"And you, sir?"

"I'm going to find my wife."

Respect and position prevented Jerry from asking Patrick about the sudden marriage and the reasons their ship had been taken, though he had formed much in the way of his own explanation from fragments of overheard conversation. "Will you be returning to the ship, sir?"

"I don't know what the future holds."

"Where shall I lay down the *Nuala*?"

Patrick ran a hand through his wind-knotted hair with a quick swipe. It wasn't the first time he felt burdened by his responsibility. He had longed for years to find a place to settle where he could leave the rigors and hardships of the ocean behind, where he could enjoy the wealth he had accumulated and the pursuit of his own dreams. But all of that would have to be put on hold once again. "Stay in Ireland with Liam until I send for you."

"Aye, sir," Jerry said automatically, but decided in an instant to risk another question. "One more thing, sir?"

"Of course."

"Do you know where to find her?"

Patrick turned quickly to Jerry, hot words of irritation on his lips. But his brusque mood dissipated as he looked into the eyes of a man whose heritage was like his own, and who had no other family but himself and Conlan. A man who had very nearly died on his own ship. He answered him truthfully. "No, Jerry. She's likely been taken to London with her mother, but I don't know where in the city the house is located. I'm not even sure if she'll want to see me."

"Why is that, sir?" Jerry dared, his curiosity taking over his sense of rank.

Patrick shrugged broad shoulders with a heavy motion. "I only know what we had. I can't be certain of what all of that will mean to her now."

"But she is your wife."

Patrick suddenly remembered the starry night in front of the ocean, when he had held his warm bride on the cold sand and vowed to love her until death. He could still hear her voice, quiet but not timid, softly pledging the same.

Impatient and curt once again, he jerked his head toward the binnacle with orders for Jerry to mind the course. If he continued to think about Camille and that night, or muse upon what lies she may or may not have been told, or what she might or might not believe or still feel, Patrick felt certain he would go mad.

They would be dropping their anchor by the shores of England by nightfall. Patrick turned his attention to Birney. He strode across the deck to where Birney sat lashed to the mainmast. "It's time."

Patrick took his cutlass and severed the ropes that held Birney, grabbed his upper arm, and dragged him to his feet. He looked the man over, searching the grizzled face for the expected dread and seeing only resignation. Patrick searched his own feelings for resentment, but found only empty sadness. When Tate had been killed, Patrick had wanted Birney's blood spilled, flowing freely. He had wanted the man to die crying like an infant, terrified, and begging.

But tying this man to the mast and flogging his skin from him in strips would not bring Tate back, nor would it place Patrick back in the inn the day he was taken. Making the thug before him suffer with a thousand tiny cuts from his dagger before throwing him into the salted waters to die in a foaming sea of agony would not make anything different, except serve to make Patrick have one more unpleasant memory stuck in his mind. These feelings within Patrick surprised even himself, and Patrick acknowledged that a year ago, even six months ago, he would have wanted to watch Birney pay dearly for his actions with agony worthy of a Turkish prison. But his time at sea had been long, hard, and exhausting, and the only emotion

Patrick could now summon was a sense of obligation and duty to rid the world of a known rapist and killer.

"I didn't mean ter hurt yer boy," Birney swore, trying one last effort to save himself. "If'n ye'll let me live, I'll serve ye the rest o' me life."

"You have no more life." Patrick dragged Birney over to the rail, pulled out his pistol, and fired one shot to Birney's head. He shoved the dead man over the rail into the sea, not bothering to watch as the corpse bobbed up and down and turned the white-tipped blue waters scarlet. Birney would spend eternity in a watery grave just like Tate, along with Marcus and Ned and several other of his men to whose parents Patrick would have to explain their deaths. Justice had been satisfied. He turned away from the rail, gestured for Herrick to clean up the mess on the rail, and vowed never to think of Birney again.

England was nothing more than a dark shape hugging the dusky horizon as they approached. Patrick readied the dory with his weapons, clothing, rations of food and water, and a small brassbound chest full of important documents, pouches of English currency, and gold, the currency of the world.

A half a league out from England's shores, the *Nuala*'s heavy iron anchor was dropped and the tiny dory was lowered into the waters. Herrick slowly shimmied down a rope and clumsily set foot into the rocking dory, almost tipping the whole of it over before seating himself gingerly on a plank seat and hanging on to the sides. Patrick turned to Jerry and shook his hand.

"Godspeed, Jerry."

"Don't give Liam and me another thought, sir. We'll make it to Ireland."

"I have no doubt."

Patrick hauled himself over the rail and grabbed the rope to begin his descent. Jerry's voice gave him brief pause. "Sir, whoever paid for our being taken will not be pleased to see you return. Be wary."

Patrick looked up at Jerry and grinned, that wild smile that never failed to make Jerry think of pirates and old legends of Patrick's notorious grandfather. "Don't you know love makes a man reckless?"

Jerry couldn't suppress a smile in return for his captain, and watched as Patrick dropped effortlessly into the dory, picked up the oars, and began to row to shore. It was with no small amount of concern for Patrick that Jerry remembered all the things that had been done to his captain in the name of that love. All they had lost, all they had suffered. Jerry waited by the rail until they reached the bank. "Good luck, Captain."

Patrick and Herrick pulled the dory to shore. They picked up their burdens and bundles without a word spoken. Patrick faced inland and began to walk in long strides, leaving Herrick to stumble through the sand in his wake. The way for Patrick was familiar, the path unchanged with the exception of the season. The course for Herrick was not new, either, and soon the two men stood in front of the cottage.

Moonlight bathed the humble stone structure in pale, silvery light. Long, dark shadows surrounded the glen, but enough light filtered through the trees to illuminate the now-bare rosebushes. Snarls of brambly branches stood out in stark relief in the dimness, the magical roses that had graced them in wanton droves now but a memory whose tales were told in withered petals lying on the ground.

Patrick pushed open the door to the cottage and set his things down on the oaken floor. He lit a lantern and began his search of the place, as if he knew precisely for what he was looking.

It didn't take him long to find the paper on which Camille had written. The parchment looked wrinkled and the handwriting hurried.

> *Patrick,*
> *I waited the entirety of the night, and have gone to look*
> *for you. If you return, please find me on the beach. You know*
> *our place. I hope your delay was nothing serious, though*
> *I worry for you.*
> *Please hurry and find me, my love.*
> *Always, Camille*

He clasped the paper to his face, inhaling deeply as if
the scents of ocean and lavender could possibly cling for
all that time, sweet and soft. But she had touched the
paper, written those words, left the quill to bleed, and gone
to find him. Patrick's chest tightened at the thought of her
needing him, aching for him, wanting him, worrying. As
he did for her now, always, but from so far away. After a
long while, he folded the note carefully and tucked it into
his shirt. Her written words called to him in his mind as
if he could hear her soft voice, husky with need. "Please
hurry and find me, my love."

Resigned to waiting another night, Patrick frowned
darkly and began to remove his boots, his manner again
curt. "Get comfortable, Herrick. We'll stay the night here
and begin in the morning."

Herrick sat on a rough, rickety chair and likewise removed his boots. He grabbed his satchel of meager clothing to use as a pillow, lay on the hard floor without
complaint, and tried to get some sleep. From the looks of
Patrick, he dared not ask any questions.

The night was cool, the hour late. Patrick lay on the
small pallet with his hands behind his head, staring up at
the shadowed ceiling. He passed the night in silent contemplation, lost in memory.

When Herrick opened his eyes to the early morning
light, he saw Patrick sitting on the pallet with papers
spread all around him. Patrick looked up, his eyes dark

with what could have been fury or frustration, maybe both. Herrick grunted, jerking his head in the direction of the papers, questioning Patrick in the way only men understood.

Patrick held them in tight fists. "She had something here. Something important."

Herrick wisely said nothing. Patrick's eyes burned, stinging from lack of sleep and tears he didn't wish to shed in the presence of another man. He gathered the papers into a pile and stuffed them into one of his packs.

The peculiar pair left the cottage and Herrick fell into step behind Patrick once again, this time keeping up better as they traversed the trail, glad to be back on land and rested. Patrick took to the trail silently, methodically, stepping over roots and decaying branches, passing by nut brown lichen and spongy moss, treading on leafy ferns and scrubby underbrush. He pushed dangling limbs out of his way, letting them go to slap at Herrick as if he had forgotten the man followed him. He stopped short at the end of the line of trees that defined the woods.

The clearing opened, widened, and spilled into lush, tended lawns and gardens. The beginning of the properties at Beauport. Behind him, Herrick sucked in his breath, seeing the brick house in the distance sprawling with majestic white columns and impressively large, mullioned windows glinting in the morning light like the dew that sparkled on the grass.

"Ye says she lived 'ere?"

"Aye."

"An' ye meant ter take 'er away?"

Patrick didn't hesitate. "Forever."

"Gor," Herrick said under his breath. "Ye'd 'ave ter drag me away, kickin'."

"'Tis not as you think, not as you see it."

But to Herrick, who had known only poverty, Beauport looked like heaven must, with abundance of everything in life that brought pleasure.

Patrick dismissed Herrick and his fascination with wealth that made the grown man's jaw hang slack. He kept to the line of trees, skirting the property to reach the back of the house and passing the west side where Camille's balcony extended over the slumbering rose gardens. Finally he could see the back doors, the doors used by the servants. Chimneys chugging smoke and scents of baking breads in the early morning told Patrick where the kitchen was located in the great house. He crouched down and got comfortable, relying on the patience that comes from spending a lifetime at sea.

Flanna emerged sometime later, stooping down with the stiffness of an old woman to pick up a small bundle of firewood. Patrick motioned for Herrick to remain in the shade and approached Flanna. The cook saw the figure of a man out of the corner of her eye, coming from the woods. She turned toward him with curiosity, cocking her head to one side as she awaited his advance without fear.

When Patrick stood about twenty paces from her, he stopped. "I'm Patrick Mullen," he said simply.

"You're back for Camille," Flanna surmised.

"Aye."

Flanna's perceptive eyes measured the man, taking in the rugged build, the dark auburn hair streaked with sun and pulled back from a face out of an Irish fable, with a voice like mellow brandy. Eyes the color of the ocean met hers evenly under magnificent brows and over a stubbled, firm jaw. He didn't smile, nor did he scowl. He just watched her in a way that made her want to smooth her gray hair and lick her lips. So this was the man for whom Camille had risked everything, Flanna thought. Suddenly, it all made perfect sense.

"She's gone months now."

"To London," Patrick stated.

"That's right," Flanna replied, surprised.

"Camille told me about you. Told me you were kind to her."

"'Twas no burden. I love Camille."

"So do I," Patrick said softly.

"Why, then? Why did you leave her like that? I never saw one suffer the way she did."

The words sliced through Patrick's heart. "I was taken from her. It would be a long story in the telling, best summed up with the duchess."

Flanna's brows knitted. She spoke with the bluntness of a woman grown old. "They say the duchess paid you to leave."

"She paid to have me taken, by force."

His words rang true with Flanna, for she knew better than most the lengths the Bradburns would go to see to it their family was not shamed. "But you came back for her," Flanna said, more to herself than to Patrick. She was hard pressed to keep a sigh from passing her lips, the sigh of the romantic girl in her heart who never grew up. The one who wanted to believe in fairy tales and happy endings, despite the realities life had taught her.

"Aye, I came back. I won't stop until I find her, but 'twill be easier if you'll tell me where she is."

This time the sigh slipped out, and Flanna moved closer to Patrick. With a woman's heart and a soul as idyllic as King Arthur's, Flanna rested her hand on Patrick's arm in what she hoped seemed like a motherly gesture, though the warmth and strength of him pleased her. "I've never been to the city house, myself, but I'll go an' get one who has who'll tell you. Find Camille, lad, an' take her from this life. She's never belonged to it since the day she was born."

Patrick grinned down at the old cook, took her hand from his arm, and pressed a kiss to it. "I can see why Camille liked you so well, kind Flanna."

Kind Flanna, she repeated in her mind. Exactly what Camille had called her the day she left Beauport. Flanna's throat tightened and she smiled back at Patrick through a mist of tears. "I'll go an' fetch Molly."

After Flanna had hurried Molly out to the back and the

directions had been given, the young servant girl from London was sent back into the great mansion, and Patrick said his thanks and good-byes to Flanna. The old cook watched as the man who loved Camille more than life walked back to the woods and jerked his thumb to a menacing, unkempt man who obediently fell into step behind him. The odd pair set off, and Flanna stood by the door with her shoulder pressed to the frame, waiting until they had disappeared from view. Flanna imagined the tearful reunion, and Patrick whisking Camille away from England and into his strong arms. So wonderful, and meant to be. The sigh slid out again, wistful and full of hope. "An' if you're of a mind," Flanna whispered longingly, "take me, too."

The journey to London took too long for Patrick's liking; the hired livery stopped at every town and village along the way. Tired and travel weary, they arrived in the city five days later. Patrick unloaded his belongings from the conveyance and headed to the nearest inn for a pint, a piss, and a bowl of soup. Herrick followed him again, shuffling along in the wake of the tall, handsome man like a beggar who wants a coin.

The day proved to be typical of English weather in autumn: wet, cold, and blustery. Patrick had pulled on a thick knitted sweater and handed one of the same to Herrick, tired of seeing the man pretend to be unaffected by the damp chill while wearing threadbare clothing. Herrick had pulled on the finely crafted garment, the nicest article of clothing he'd ever had on his body, and thought to himself that if he had been born better or had known better, he would have wanted to speak like Patrick and walk like Patrick. Maybe even be respected by Patrick.

Passing by a few raucous pubs spilling bawdy laughter, Patrick finally stopped in a quiet inn that advertised HOT SOUP on a hanging board out front. The mellow scents of good food and ale combined with the warmth of the fire relaxed Patrick, and he stretched out his long legs, leaning back in the sturdy wood chair to savor a pint of dark, pungent brew. He cocked an eyebrow at Herrick, hiding a grin behind his mug as his traveling companion swilled ale as though a treasure lay in the bottom of the tankard.

"Ah, that's good," Herrick declared with satisfaction, slamming the empty flagon down on the table. He pulled his wrist to his face, ready to wipe his lips with his sleeve, and then noticed the fine, clean sweater and paused, confused.

Patrick threw his head back and laughed before tossing him a napkin. "If you didn't drink it so fast, you'd not have a mustache of foam to wipe away."

"If I didn't drink it that fast, I'd not now be havin' meself another."

"Fair enough," Patrick chuckled, and flipped another coin onto the scarred table.

A matronly barmaid brought Herrick another drink, and Patrick waved away her offers for a refill for himself. He had another journey in front of him.

When the soup bowls were empty and their hunger sated, Patrick looked at his timepiece and stood.

"Time?"

"Aye."

Herrick stood and rubbed a hand across his chin. "Ye need some backin' up?"

"I don't think there's a need."

"The witch were pretty set on seein' ye gone fer good."

"I'm sure she'll be disappointed to see that I'm not that easy to be rid of."

"Or maybe she'll see to it ye can't ever come back again. Birney offered ter kill ye first off, but she wanted ye not just gone, but punished. Said she liked the picture of ye losin' it all an' laborin' yer life away, knowin' ye touched fer what ye 'ad no rights."

Patrick looked away from Herrick and into the flickering flames of the fire. The papers he had taken from the cottage were tucked in his bag, a tangible memory of his time spent with Camille, what they had shared. "I had every right."

Herrick shuffled his feet and followed Patrick's gaze into the fire. "Ye did or didn't, don't matter ter the duchess."

"It matters to me, and God willing, it will still matter to Camille." Patrick produced a small purse and handed it to Herrick. "Thank you again for setting me free."

Herrick's eyes widened at the heft of the coin. He had never held so much wealth in his hand, let alone to call such fortune his own. He saw a vision of himself in tailored clothes, with clean fingernails and neat hair. The mental picture didn't fit, and he replaced it with one of himself in a pub, the man of the hour with enough coin to buy every bloke a pint and plenty left over for a week of gaming and wenching. Yet, the means for the gain didn't feel right, and the heavy pouch weighed on his conscience. "It were me savin' me own arse an' hatin' Birney what made me cut ye free. Ye don't 'ave ter pay me fer it."

Patrick shrugged carelessly and picked up his bags. "It makes no difference why. I pay all my debts." He set his things on the table and gestured for the barmaid. While he awaited her approach, he cocked a brow at Herrick. "Now stay out of trouble."

Herrick stuffed the pouch in his breeches, relieved. "Can't make that promise, me friend. It finds me no matter where I go."

"With that mindset, you'll be in debtor's prison before the year's out."

"Nah, me luck's changin'." Herrick grabbed his own bag and slung it over his shoulder. He headed out of the inn, stopping to glance over his shoulder and hold a hand up to Patrick, who returned the short wave. He turned and left, letting the sounds of music and laughter spilling from taverns lead his way.

Patrick shook his head as the man left, knowing full well the small fortune would be gone in less than a month's time. He arranged with the barmaid for a room. Her words and body language indicated in a less than subtle way that she was his for the asking, but Patrick's focus was fixed upon the image of another woman in London. He ordered a hot bath, savoring his first good soak in too long, he decided. He shaved and dressed, taking care with his appearance, regretting he wouldn't have time to have his hair trimmed. When he stood fully dressed, he regarded himself in the looking glass with a critical eye, wondering if Camille would like what she saw. The clothes were fine, camel breeches nicely tailored with a waistcoat of navy velvet. His skin had darkened from his hours on the decks of the *Nuala*, and stood out in contrast to the wintry white of his shirt. Patrick raked a hand through his damp hair and let out his breath in a rush.

The time to seek out his love had arrived. Finally.

CHAPTER 16

London

Camille drank deeply, emptying her glass. With a sigh she pulled the bottle of brandy out from under her bed. She stared at the bottle for a long time with eyes blurry from drink and inconsolable depression.

She put the bottle down and walked unsteadily to the window overlooking one of London's finest properties. Even in the clutches of wind and rain, which darkened the bare trees and littered the ground with limbs and dead leaves, the tree-lined, sculptured property retained its refined elegance.

But elegance was not what Camille saw. She saw a world full of danger and violence. Somewhere out in the streets of London prowled the man who had assaulted her body and killed her child. A man in a black leather mask whose grotesque, expressionless face loomed over her as he raped her every night in her nightmares.

The horrible dreams varied slightly from night to night, but always ended the same. She awoke from them screaming and sweating, gasping for breath as though she were coming to the surface after being underwater for too long.

The brandy helped. It was her liquid solace, her amber friend that soothed the pain and dulled reality.

Camille turned away from the window and tightened her dressing gown around her thin waist. The full-length looking glass in the corner showed her reflection, and in her almost lucid state, Camille was dully surprised at her own haggard appearance.

Her hair hung to her hips, unbound and disheveled. Combing it took an effort Camille couldn't muster, and the touch of another on her body had become intolerable. Her bloodshot eyes looked enormous in her gaunt face, her skin pale like the clouds that overcast the sky and dropped rain on the city. And like the rain that fell, she was cold. Dark circles told tale of sleepless nights spent avoiding the nightmares that plagued her. Marion sent trays of all Camille's favorites several times a day to try to tempt her to eat, but food was tasteless and her appetite nonexistent, so her figure had grown frail and bony.

She knew she looked terrible. She knew she was drinking too much and not eating enough. But she didn't care.

Her hand rested for a moment on her concave belly. Her child had been torn from her womb with cruelty and pain. Did it suffer? Was it agonizing? Day and night she wondered with aching sadness about the fate of her unborn babe. Lad or lass, did it scream unheard as it struggled to hold on to its too-brief life?

The way she clung to hers, precariously.

Betrayed. Violated. Devastated.

Repulsed, she turned away from her ragged appearance to the bottle of brandy on her side table. It asked no questions. It required nothing from her. And yet it eased her pain and warmed her body.

It had been there for her the night her brother Niles had arrived from Oxford, three days after they had expected him, his journey lengthened because his legs had been weakened from a childhood bout of polio. When he hobbled into her room, she had been only half alert, drunk on brandy and shame. She had endured his long fingers probing her most private flesh, torn and bruised. He had confirmed in his quiet voice that her child had indeed left her body, though the emptiness in Camille's heart had told her days before. He told her the bleeding would last weeks more, and he had tried to act as though he felt no embarrassment.

Camille asked for Eric, and Niles shook his head. Camille asked if her father had come to see her, and again, Niles answered in the negative. Then he had left her, speaking to Amelia in the corridor in tones meant to be hushed, though Camille could hear them. She heard Niles tell her mother there had been a child, and the shriek of fury that followed. Amelia had not come to see her since, leaving Camille to lie in her darkened room, alone and afraid of what punishment would surely come.

But then she grew weary of waiting, worrying, and mourning. She was sick of the pain in her heart and in her groin and tired of the burdens of her guilt and fears. So she drank more, and they went away for a while. And when they returned, strengthened by her hangover and her fatigue, she drank again.

A knock at her door sounded, startling her. Camille rushed to clumsily grab the bottle and her glass and stash them under her bed. She seated herself in her chaise and pulled a throw about her legs.

"Enter," she called, distantly aware that her own voice sounded rough and strange.

Amelia stepped in and closed the door behind her. Her pale eyes assessed her daughter, indifferent and detached. "You look frightful," she said bluntly.

"Why, Mother, what brings you to my rooms this morning? Is the dressmaker ailing? The jeweler on holiday?"

Amelia permitted a tight smile in response. "Nay, daughter of mine. Mind your sharp tongue in my presence, or I shall give you a few slaps to bring some color to your cheeks." She moved to stand by the unmade bed, a wrinkle forming between her brows. "I have come to see you in regard to your future. I believe you have spent enough time in your rooms and 'tis time for you to rejoin life."

"I wasn't aware you cared how I spent my time, so long as I am not disgracing you in any way."

Amelia walked about the room, looking at the mess and dust that had accumulated over the course of weeks since the rape. The torn gown Camille had worn when attacked remained in the corner balled up, though the dried bloodstains were visible. Apparently, Camille was not permitting the staff to care for this portion of her home. She had not been informed of this. Amelia's pale blue eyes glittered with anger. She would tend to that matter later.

"Child, is it my lack of visits to you that makes you say such things?" Amelia asked.

"You have not come to see me since . . ." Camille's voice trailed off. She was unable to say the words though she thought them every waking moment. And the sleeping ones, too.

"I have had matters that required my attention."

"Two months of constant business? You must be exhausted."

"Apparently, my attention has been needed here," Amelia continued, as if Camille had not spoken. "Your rooms are filthy and you are unkempt. Why is it your soiled gown has not even been removed?"

"Soiled? 'Tis not soiled. 'Tis ripped and bloody. It serves to remind me of all the reasons why I should not leave my rooms. It stays where it is."

"And the filth? Your state of undress? What purpose do they serve?" Amelia challenged with a raised brow.

"I do not wish to be touched."

Amelia sighed and seated herself gingerly on the side of the bed, repelled by its unmade state and her daughter's sullen, surly demeanor. "All of this nonsense will end today. I have allowed you more than sufficient time to recover from your ordeal. Today you will bathe and dress yourself appropriately. You will be receiving a guest, and I will not have you looking as you do."

"I do not wish to see anyone."

"Your wishes are of no consequence. You will see who I say, when I say."

Camille laughed suddenly, a bitter sound that held no happiness. "Ah, yes, the duchess has spoken, and so it shall be."

"I should hate to call for Edward under such circumstances, but I will not allow you to mock me, child," Amelia warned calmly.

"Of course I should not do that. 'Twould be most inappropriate."

"You have hardly ever concerned yourself with what is appropriate," Amelia said, her tone vitriolic. "That has been the source of most of your problems."

"Are you going to tell me of my problems, Mother? You think you know the inner workings of my mind so well? Please, enlighten me." Camille sat back and tilted her head curiously. "I await your observation."

"You are far too thin-skinned for such truths, daughter. You cannot even bring yourself out of your rooms since the attack. Should I speak to you of the weakness of your character with candor, I fear you would not be able to come out from beneath your bed." Amelia smiled coldly. "Of course, you will have company under there, won't you? Perhaps I should send word to Kenley about the rapidly dwindling supply of brandy. I'm certain he would send more."

"You are hardly the one to speak of the evils of alcohol consumption," Camille snapped. "And you could not have the slightest inkling of what happened to me in the stables. Nor do you care."

"My sentiments exactly. Look at yourself, Camille. You are disheveled, unclean, and your words are as rough as your appearance. You hide in your rooms day and night, letting no one see you, not even the mute, from what I am told." She spoke the words with derision as she looked at

Camille. "Why? Because you were raped." Amelia ignored her daughter's flinch at the word. "You lost a child that you were better off not having. The child of that seafaring, fortune-hunting commoner you took to your bed without any understanding of what you were doing."

Amelia rose from the bed and began to pace, warming to her topic. "And then you turn on me, your own mother, and accuse me of a lack of sympathy and understanding. Understanding of what? Of the fact that you have defied me at every turn. I have told you countless times of the impropriety of your actions. Ladies do not gallivant about unescorted! And when you do so anyway and receive your just desserts, 'tis I you so readily turn on." She pointed a finger accusingly at Camille. "'Twas your own fault, Camille. Every warning I made has come true, because you were too headstrong and disrespectful to heed me."

"I did not deserve to be attacked, Mother." Camille gritted out.

"Oh no? Were you not told never to leave home unescorted?" Amelia demanded.

"Yes, but . . ."

"Indeed," Amelia continued, speaking over Camille. "And as for the child you carried, did you approach me and inform me of my impending grandchild? Nay! You sought to hide it from me! Why?"

"Why do you think?" Camille retorted, aghast that her mother even would ask. "You would have ripped my child from my breast!"

"And rightly so! You are not the daughter of some fishmonger to bear children out of wedlock in the street. You are a Bradburn, and by all that is holy, you will begin to act like one!"

Camille held herself silent and still, letting her mother's words rain on her like the cold, uncaring drops that fell outside. Her exhaustion felt too great to bear, her strength to fight ebbing. Camille glanced to the bed where her bottle lay hidden, waiting, ready.

Amelia stood in front of Camille and looked down on her daughter.

"Have you learned nothing? Your man betrayed you and left for a bribe. This after you gave him your virtue and conceived his child. You came to London, but you remained as always, unwilling to follow the structure for a lady of your bearing. You were raped due to your own disobedience, a violation which resulted in the death of the child you claim to have loved." Amelia's expression was as incredulous as her tone. "Had you been mindful of the standards to which you are held, the rape would never have occurred. You are beset at every turn due to your own foolishness and headstrong defiance. When will it be enough? When will you realize that your way of doing things does not work?"

Camille sat in shock. The truth of her mother's words echoed in her ears. Suddenly everything was clear. All the pain, all the sadness and loss had been her own doing. All because she had chosen to love. Love was pain, and her mother had known that all along. Amelia did not suffer because Amelia did not love.

And the rape? Amelia was right about that, too. Camille knew that if she had not been trying to leave, always fighting against who she was born to be, then it would never have happened. A daughter of her stature would never leave the house unescorted, and she knew that. Camille closed her eyes for a moment as the realization dawned on her, the weight settling onto her shoulders and yoking her forever to the brutal truth.

The rape had been her fault.

She had only herself to blame and she would forever carry the blood guilt of her innocent unborn babe on her hands.

Everything. All. Her fault.

The moments ticked by, marked by the timepiece on the mantel. With each click of the seconds gone by, it seemed Camille could feel the weight of her own guilt settle into her body. She knew it would never leave her, like the past that foretold the future. The revelation came to her like a thunderclap on a cloudless summer day. Her only possible redemption lay in rebirth.

With that acceptance came another realization. Camille was shocked by the fact that she had not seen what was now so plain. For the first time in months, Camille's life had a purpose. She would become the lady she was born to be. She would become just like Amelia. And by doing so, she would never hurt again. And even as the thought came to her and the decision was made, Camille felt better, some of her strength flowing back into her.

"You are right, Mother," Camille whispered in wonder. "I am sorry. I will do as you say."

Amelia's lips curved into a smile of conquest. "Excellent," she said with satisfaction. "You have finally chosen wisely." Slowly, carefully, Amelia let the tips of her fingers touch the top of Camille's head.

For the first time in Camille's life she felt a sense of parental approval. It reached inside her and spoke to the child inside who had hungered for that very thing since her first young awareness that it did not exist. And that was so long ago.

"Will you help me?"

Amelia's smile expanded. "Help you? Child, I will do more than help you."

Amelia swept to the door and opened it, gesturing entrance to the one waiting in the hallway. A woman entered with the rustle of voluminous silk skirts.

Hair as red as a robin's breast was coiled and piled atop her head, moored there with the aid of intricately carved golden combs. A gown of rich amethyst velvet cut in the latest of London fashion clung to her lush figure before falling in a full skirt to the floor. Light green eyes stared out from a face that was not beautiful, but sensual in its own stunning way. Her small, perfectly formed lips were set in a polite smile, and she extended a perfectly manicured hand in greeting. Camille detected the scent of roses seeping from the folds of her gown.

Camille took the woman's hand and dropped it as quickly as she could. She pulled her throw closer about her body, suddenly extremely aware of and uncomfortable at her bedraggled state.

She felt as dirty and ugly as the deed that had been done to her in the stables.

"Camille, this is Miss Estella. She has agreed to spend a few hours each day with you, tutoring you so you can unlearn your dreadful habits and begin your life anew," Amelia announced before turning to Estella. "What do you think of her? Is there aught you can do?"

Estella walked slowly around Camille, touching her hair lightly and examining each feature closely. "I believe I can work with her. She certainly has beauty, although she is much too thin. With some grooming, the proper clothes, a bit of weight, and my counsel, we will have her ready in no time at all."

Camille turned questioning eyes to her mother, who stood watching the exchange with open satisfaction on her coldly beautiful, heavily painted face.

"Have me ready for what?"

"A small gathering to celebrate your betrothal," Amelia said softly. "Won't that be wonderful?"

Camille knew she was being tested. The two women stood over her, both watching her face for any signs of rebellion. But there was none.

"Yes, lovely," Camille agreed.

Amelia and Estella both relaxed a bit and glanced at one another. They exchanged smiles, both pleased by Camille's cooperative attitude.

"We will begin with a bath." Estella's voice took on a businesslike tone. "Then we shall dine."

The thought of leaving her rooms sent a violent tremor of fear through her body. Every fiber of her being screamed *danger.*

"I'm feeling fatigued. I'll take a tray in my rooms."

Miss Estella's citrine eyes narrowed. "I know about the rape," she said bluntly. "Bear in mind that while I have sympathy for your ordeal, I will not be permitting you to cloister yourself like a nun."

Because her tentative touch on her daughter's head had not been rebuffed, Amelia risked patting Camille's hand reassuringly. "Child, we all know that you would not have been raped if you hadn't been disobedient. 'Twas your foolishness that led to your humiliation, but we will see that you are never so careless again." Her tone was soft and soothing as she touched Camille in a gentle and tender way that she had never done before. "I can attest to the fact that there are no masked attackers lurking in any of the corners of our home. You will come to see that the rules in place are there for your own protection. So long as you obey them, I can assure you that you will remain unharmed."

Her mother's words sparked a recognition, an awareness, a fear too ugly to be confronted. She forced her voice to speak. "I never told you of a mask."

Amelia's painted forehead creased and she pressed her heavily rouged lips into a small bow before answering. "It must have been the cook, Marion."

Camille licked her lips, finding them as dry as her throat. She felt like paranoia tugged at her, wanting her to succumb to its coil of suspicion and accusation. It all made sense, even as she didn't understand any of it. Camille felt confused and ashamed of her confusion, and she wanted to pretend it all away. From under her bed her bottle of brandy called to her, reminding her that much of the agony of her guilt could be assuaged and that nearly all of her humiliation could be numbed away.

Later.

But for now, she would have to bend and mold herself into a version of what was expected of her. A version of Amelia.

"A bath sounds inviting. Thank you."

While Estella called for a bath to be drawn, Amelia came and sat next to Camille. "Camille, I want you to know that I am proud of you, child. You have found the strength to rise above your ordeal, and for that you will be rewarded. I shall speak to the jeweler, for you will be needing an array of gems to stagger the wits of even a princess." She touched Camille's cheek gently. "Perhaps emeralds to match your eyes? Would you like that, dear?"

A voice deep inside Camille screamed so it could be heard, a primitive sound that cried that she had risen above nothing! Camille ignored it.

"I should like that very much, Mother."

"Of course," Amelia said, lightly touching Camille's raven hair. "You are a Bradburn, my dear, and so long as you act like one, you shall be treated as one."

The large brass soaking tub in her small bathing alcove was filled nearly to the brim with steaming water carried in buckets by several of the servants. Estella drizzled scented oils into the water and laid out large towels and scented soaps.

Amelia smiled her approval. "I will leave you in the capable hands of Miss Estella. After you are finished and have joined me downstairs, I will see to it that your rooms are thoroughly cleaned. Enjoy your bath."

Amelia swept out of her room and closed the door with a gentle thud.

Camille stood awkwardly in front of the tub, knowing that Miss Estella waited for her to disrobe. The length of her dressing gown hid the amber bracelet that now hung loosely around her bony ankle. She was as reluctant to allow it to be seen as she was to remove it, her only link to past happiness, however brief it had been.

"Would you please look through my wardrobe and find a suitable gown?" she asked neutrally as she began to loosen the tie of her dressing gown.

Estella looked Camille over carefully first before nodding and leaving the small alcove. Relieved, Camille slipped out of the robe that had grown dingy from too frequent wearing. She slid into the steaming, scented water and let out a small sigh of appreciation. She slid under the water, wet her hair, came up, and reached for her favorite soap. Estella stood there, waiting.

"No." Estella handed her a new lump of soap. "You will use this."

Camille sniffed it, inhaling the scents of lemon and vanilla. Amelia's fragrance. The aroma sent a chill down her spine.

"'Tis pleasant, but I prefer lavender."

Estella handed it back firmly.

Camille took the soap and looked at the red-haired woman with annoyance. "I cannot make the simplest choices for myself?"

"Your choices have carried you from one disaster to the next. Your mother does not wish for you to make any decisions for the time being, and I echo her wisdom." Estella pressed a cloth into her hands, her tone still cold but the look in her eyes relenting, warning. "Only you can manage your fate, my lady. You alone."

Camille took a deep breath and began to lather her hair and body, breathing in the scent of her mother all around her as it seeped into her skin until it was all she could smell. The hot water was an unction, the soap a cleansing of more than her surface. The fragrance that had always exuded from her mother now saturated her, too. It became the scent of her failures. Her submission. And more than anything, her rebirth.

Camille descended the stairs and swept into the parlor, followed closely by Miss Estella. Amelia looked up from her sherry, her expression pleased, her demeanor genial.

"Lovely, Camille, truly lovely. You are a vision. Come, let me see you."

Camille obeyed silently and approached her mother,

spinning once so Amelia could admire both Estella's fine handiwork on her hair as well as the gown of green velvet that complemented the color of her eyes. Estella had swept her hair up, piling it high atop her head in a mass of shiny black curls still damp from her bath. Strands of gold beads were discreetly entwined with emerald-and-diamond-tipped pins. The gown, cut low across the swell of her breasts, was as tightly laced as possible, and though it hung loosely, it complimented the shape of her body. Stiff ecru lace stood up around the collar, framing her oval face, pale and gaunt, a study in neutral shadows.

Camille felt uncomfortable to the point of nausea.

"Would you care for a drink? Perhaps some brandy?" Amelia offered.

"Yes," Camille replied too quickly. She saw the look of warning on Estella's face and quickly corrected herself. "I mean, that sounds appealing. Thank you."

Amelia waved away the aid of a servant and filled a snifter herself, pressing it into Camille's outstretched hand.

Camille drank deeply, quenching the thirst satisfied only by the warm amber liquid she had come to depend on. That she had come to need.

"I have some good news for you," Amelia said, smiling. "Bret is here."

"Good news," Camille repeated.

"Why, yes, dear. He has been quite distressed that you have been unable to see him these months past. Dare I say he has worried over you?"

"Worried?" Camille whispered in horror. "Does he . . . know?"

"About the rape? Why goodness, of course he knows," Amelia said calmly. "He knows of the rape and the child. And the miracle of it is, he is willing to marry you anyway."

Camille's face flushed and her heart pounded in her chest. "You told him."

"Well, you refused to see anyone for weeks and weeks.

I had to tell him something; it might as well have been the truth. As your future husband, he had the right to know."

Camille looked to the floor, intently studying the intricate pattern of the Persian rug. She willed herself to feel nothing, to go cold. The humiliation might finally push her to the brink of hysteria if she allowed herself to feel it. No love, no feelings, no pain. Her old nature fought inside her like a demon for its survival. She took another deep swallow, concentrating only on the heat that stole through her otherwise numbed body.

When she looked up, her face was a facade of apathetic calm. She set her mouth in a tight curve of a smile and sipped from the brandy, her fingers curled tightly around the base of the snifter, holding it in place of hope.

The knock at the door caused the women to look at the doors of the parlor in expectation. Bret came into the room unescorted and approached Camille without hesitation. He lifted her hand and pressed a kiss to her skin, his lips dry and pale.

"My lady, I have been desolate since hearing of your tribulation."

Camille nodded her head slightly, the movement being all she could muster. Nausea gripped her belly and her blood turned cold, like the droplets of rain that clung to Bret's hair and dripped onto her gown as he leaned over her.

"How I've missed you," he breathed. "It pains me to recall our last encounter. I beg your forgiveness."

He dropped to one knee in front of her and pressed her limp hand to his chest. "You needn't say a word, Camille. I promise to you now, I will make you forget the past. We have a future together. Nothing else matters."

Camille felt his touch, inhaled his scent, and heard his words. But she did so with only the barest of comprehension. She felt as though she were floating around her own mind, hovering just outside of reality, where Amelia and Bret were not much more than players in a traveling show, speaking words they didn't mean and pledging vows they wouldn't keep. From the corner of her eye she saw Estella seated on a small, high-backed chair, her hands folded in her lap and her citrine eyes watching in rapt attention. Camille could feel Amelia's gaze on her, too, measuring and evaluating, always scrutinizing.

Drifting through her own mind, away from her pain and her truest self, Camille found some peace. The peace of deciding not to choose. The peace of surrendering when a fight cannot be won.

But Camille did not see Patrick, standing outside the parlor windows in the steady rain, shrouded by the shade of an evergreen and the dusk that was rapidly turning to dark.

CHAPTER 17

Patrick stood in the shadows and watched Camille. He saw nothing else. Her head tilted up as she accepted a snifter of brandy from Amelia, and the faintest glimmer of a smile curved her lips. She drank deeply.

He had seen the man arrive in his carriage, alight and rush into the house, covering his hair like a woman to protect it from the rain. That man now held her hand, kneeling before her as Patrick longed to do. Jealousy gripped him, taunted him, luring him to make a mistake. But Patrick knew better. Her eyes soothed his envy, resting on the blond man with disinterest. And something more, though he could not define it.

She had lost weight. Her collarbones outlined her bare shoulders with delicate definition, under a neck too slim and a face turned lean. Patrick saw her glance about the room, her eyes desperate, her skin pale. He could feel her need even through the windows, as if it were carried to him on gusts of wind and drops of rain. It seeped into him, her need mingling with his. And he ached.

He consumed her with his eyes, fed on her. If he had known it would be like this, seeing her, feeling her, he doubted he could have withstood the waiting. He felt a yearning for her undiminished by time, untouched by distance or hardships. Everything he had done and endured to get to this moment seemed a trivial detail in his journey back to her, back to them. So he waited.

With an effort, he dragged his gaze from her and looked about the property again. The street entrance welcomed with lights and grand appointments. He dismissed it. He scanned the front of the home, taking note of which rooms were lighted or dark. Patrick surveyed the perimeter of the property, thankful for the rain that no dogs scented his arrival. Skirting to the side of the home, he looked down the long drive where the carriage bearing a ducal crest had headed and saw a huge stable flanked by a carriage house and several small outbuildings. He returned to the safety of the shadows under the evergreen and resumed his study of Camille.

It wouldn't be safe to try to get to her yet. He would have to wait. Wait and watch. He would see when she ascended the stairs, watch through the many windows to see where the glow of her candle led him. See the light from her rooms to tell him where she could be found, alone. And then he would go to her.

Camille pushed the food around her plate, seeing and smelling the fare and finding it repugnant. She sipped her brandy and managed a tiny sample of the flaky pastry that topped the meat. It turned into a floury lump on her tongue, needing brandy to wash it past her throat. Finding that method worked fairly well, Camille continued to drink with each bite, until the food became less and less disgusting. Even Amelia and Bret became more tolerable, as the alcohol turned them into almost interesting dinner companions. Camille laughed, flirted with Bret, and made pleasant conversation with Amelia and Estella. A sense of warm well-being filled her and all at once she didn't feel it would be so difficult to allow the life Amelia had designed for her to grasp her, define her, devour and digest her.

She could do it. Now she knew for certain.

The rain had stopped, but Patrick took no heed. Surrounded by weighty scents of wet earth and pine, he watched her simper and chatter with Kimball, basking in his attention like a rose in the summer sunshine.

But there was more. Something wrong, something missing. She was obviously drunk, her eyes too bright and her face too flushed. He mentally paired her taut, desolate expression in the parlor with the laughing woman he saw now, who drank to eat.

Patrick felt the stirrings of fear. Something had happened, and Camille had suffered. He saw it in the way she held her glass and the way she swallowed her food as if she fought a retch at every mouthful. He grew impatient, his foot tapping the sodden ground. The wind breathed around him and echoed the whispers in his head, feeding his apprehension and nourishing it into panic.

She felt dizzy, sick, unhinged. Her hands clutched the sides of the dining room chair, but she could not steady herself. From far away her mother's voice filtered to her, the words taking time to fit together in her mind that she could decipher their meaning.

"I said, do you want more brandy?"

And strangely, Camille did want more. Through her self-induced drunken illness and the numbing effects of the brandy, Camille could still feel the pain. It had not left her. And so, it seemed, it would never leave her. Camille nodded her assent, dully aware that she would soon be purging the excess. She wondered if the heaving spasms would block out her thoughts, or if even then the rape would be with her.

Bret put his hand over Camille's snifter, blocking any more alcohol from being poured. "She's well beyond her limit, Your Grace."

"Nonsense, my boy. The girl can answer for herself."

Bret raised a brow. "Since when, you say?"

Amelia looked at Camille, whose unfocused eyes stared at the table, her face pale, her lips trembling. A small seed of pity took root, and Amelia put the brandy down. "She has had enough. Take her to her room, Estella, and put her in bed."

Estella rose obediently and took Camille by the shoulders, steering her up the stairs and steadying her when she nearly fell. Bret's eyes followed her ascent; his lips twisted, and his eyes became distant. Amelia looked him over, as pity left her and annoyance returned.

"After it all, you remain soft? What will regret leave with you, except your own demise?"

Bret sighed heavily. "I have done your bidding, like a good little boy. But your schemes were never mine, and it is not a failing in my character that they weigh heavily."

"Everything with you is a failing of character. Were it not so, you would not be here today."

Bret sighed and looked down to his plate, his food now as unappealing as his companion. "Yes," he whispered. "I have made many mistakes. But none has caused me such suffering as have the past few weeks. Obeying you was a disaster I'm only sorry I'll live to regret."

"Your work in the stables was a necessary evil."

"She is destroyed."

"She will survive. People of her mettle always do."

"She will not be the same. How can she ever overcome what I have done? How will I ever move past what I have done?" Bret buried his face in his hands and a tear escaped from the corner of his eye.

"Sit up! Stop your bawling. I'll not have you fall apart now and ruin everything. Had you not done what you did in the stables, Camille would have borne a bastard and disgraced us all. The silly chit thought she had hidden it from me, as if I had not borne four children of my own! She was a fool to fall for the mariner, and a bigger fool to take him to her bed. What was done in the stables was done for her own good and for the good of the family, and was a repercussion of her own sins. What did it matter, after all, since she was no longer a virgin. So you took her! You will be her husband, and soon it shall be your right."

"I am not certain I can wed her."

"Nonsense. You will do as I say, or I will bring your world crashing around you. You think you suffer now?" Amelia set down her sherry and leaned forward, enunciating every word. "My daughter will marry you, and be a duchess in her own right."

"And if she does, she will still not right your wrongs. Forcing Camille to live your life and follow your path will not undo your mistakes. Your vicarious journey through your daughter is bound for disaster. She is nothing like you."

Amelia sat back in her chair and narrowed her eyes until they glittered. "She is not clever like me; that is true."

Bret could only stare at Amelia, transfixed by the mask of cosmetics and the insane light in her eyes. "Black-mailing me into a loveless marriage is clever? Having a man sold into bondage as a slave and orchestrating your own child's betrayal and rape is clever? Dear God, how could I ever have listened to you?"

"Because I own you," Amelia replied smugly. "Your choices were over the day I bought and paid for you, dear boy. No one forced you to gamble away an entire family's fortune, and no one pressured you to murder a man to prevent his telling your father. You came to me for help. *You* came to *me*. And don't lose sight, Bret. No one, not even myself, could have made your body obey me in the stables."

"I hated what I did, and you know it."

"I know it, do I? I saw the mess you left between her legs. It looked like you enjoyed your task well enough."

"It made me sick to do that."

"Yet you spilled your seed, just the same."

"I hated it."

"Not enough to stop."

"I should tell Camille everything. Start with the mariner and finish with the stables."

"You do, and I'll ruin you. I'll force your father to repay me and send him and your mother to debtor's prison, where they can rot while their son's neck is stretched at the Triple Tree. Don't have an attack of conscience at this late date, Bret. You'll bring ruin not only to yourself, but to your entire family."

Bret stood and paced the room for a few turns before whisking up his glass of brandy and going to stand in front of the dying fire. He sipped his drink and watched as the flames feasted on what remained of the wood, crackling and hissing as it disintegrated what was once alive and whole.

Patrick slipped in through the servants' entrance. He closed the door without a sound and stole noiselessly to the back stairs, winding his way to the upper level. He crept through hallways, peeking into rooms and crouching in darkened doorways. From somewhere in the house, a door was opened and closed with a thud. Patrick followed the sound, chancing the duchess and her companion would not likely be through with their conversation any time soon, based on the intensity of their expressions. But his time would be limited. He moved quickly.

He saw the flick of skirts go around the corner, and caught a glimpse of red hair highlighted by the single candle she carried. Her maid had left her. A grin caught Patrick's lips. He stole to the door the woman had just closed, opened it, and slid inside.

The room was dark, but for the light cast by the fire. Patrick wasted no time getting to her side.

Camille lay sleeping, but not restfully. Each breath caught in her throat before softly escaping her lips. Her hand twitched, as if pushing something away. Or someone, Patrick thought. He sat on the side of her bed and touched her hair, soft and silky from her maid's brush. His hand moved to caress her face, starting at her creased brow, gentling her and smoothing away her frown. He touched her lips, tracing the outline of the mouth he had kissed when he sealed a wedding vow he still held sacred. Her breathing grew more peaceful and her breath bore a small sigh of contentment. He replaced his fingers with his lips, touching hers lightly and breathing in the warmth of her breath scented with brandy. Patrick rubbed her cheek with his own, reveling in the satiny touch of her skin on his.

Camille turned to him in her sleep, her hand shifting to rest on his thigh. Patrick sucked in his breath and held it, remembering well the sweet sensuality her innocent touch had brought to him, unskilled, unselfish, and full of curiosity. He brushed another kiss against her cheek, loving her beyond all judgment, wanting her beyond life. His lips moved to her ear, pressing tiny kisses along the delicate curves until she shivered, moving closer to him.

She murmured in her drunken sleep, turning her head back and forth as though she struggled to regain consciousness and join in the loving that cascaded warmth through her body.

Patrick stroked her neck with his fingertips and breathed her essence into him, like a starving man who finally feasted.

"Camille," he whispered. "I'm here for you."

Camille turned in the direction of his voice, responding to him despite her intoxicated repose.

"Patrick," she breathed.

That single word ran through him like nothing else.

Patrick forced himself from the bed and went to her armoire, gathering a gown and a cloak. He went back to her and ran a hand over the curve of her waist before wrapping her in the quilt and the cloak. He slid his hands under her to scoop her into his arms, and as he did, her hands reached to him, touching his chest.

"Patrick," she whispered. "Please don't leave me."

Her eyes were still closed and her words were slurred, but the aching in her voice was there, stabbing at his heart. Patrick knew she was too drunk to understand. He knew she thought she was dreaming. But something had hurt her more than his leaving, and he knew that, too.

"Never, my love. I would never leave you."

"He is gone."

"I am here."

Camille turned her head to the side, and her hands turned to fists, clutching at the fabric of his shirt. "No, he is gone forever."

"I will always find my way back to you, Camille," he said softly, wanting to ease her sadness.

"I never saw him."

"Never saw who, Camille?"

But Camille had slipped back into her tortured slumber, her hands relaxing as if she had surrendered. Patrick swore violently under his breath and held her closer.

The door swung open and Amelia entered, for once showing surprise as life dealt an unexpected turn, confounding her plans.

"You," Amelia gasped accusingly.

Patrick held Camille closer, backing away one step. Camille turned her head, burying her face against Patrick, still unconscious and seeking the warm refuge of his body. Patrick tightened his hold of her, determined.

"Let her go, Duchess."

"Never."

It was then that Amelia began screaming, calling the staff, not by names but with a shriek that rattled the windows.

One by one they thundered up the stairs, racing to the aid of their mistress and her daughter. Bret stumbled across the threshold, facing Patrick for the first time and knowing without a doubt who he was and what he had returned for. Bret reached for his sword, a heavily encrusted, finely wrought piece that served as a gentlemanly adornment, but bladed just the same.

Amelia leaned heavily against the door frame, pointing a long, carefully tended finger at Patrick. "I caught this man trying to ravage Camille."

Bret swung a glance at Amelia, his eyes narrowed and his breathing labored. "Are you certain, Your Grace?"

"Of course," Amelia snapped.

Patrick found himself surrounded by a staff of women and men, all brandishing crude weapons of some sort, the cooks with knives and the maids with heavy candlesticks. An ancient man wearing the dignified garb of a butler held a pistol with both hands, aiming the weapon at Patrick with such concentration his whole body shook. None of the staff looked as though any explanations would be listened to, let alone believed. Patrick slowly lowered Camille to her bed, pulling his arms away from her reluctantly, as his hands slipped away from her warmth.

Camille stirred in her drunken sleep, trying to regain her senses as the room spun. The dream felt so real. As real as her sickness, as real as the rape, as real as Patrick had once been to her. Camille turned to her side, falling further into her senseless state, and it all drifted away like smoke from a flame.

Patrick held up his hands, displaying his lack of resistance. "I am not here to hurt Camille."

"Nonsense, and hold your tongue!" Amelia snarled. "Everyone out of my daughter's chambers. We will handle this matter downstairs."

Marion slipped from the room without notice, frowning in deep thought.

Patrick found himself escorted by the tip of Bret's blade

and the muzzle of the butler's pistol, taken down to the front parlor, and relieved of his weapons. He faced Amelia.

"There were deaths aboard the *Nuala*," Patrick told Amelia.

"Pity one wasn't yours."

Patrick gestured to the pistol. "Will you be attending to that matter now?"

Amelia began to pace the parlor, her composure rattled and her mind racing. Her thoughts whirled in an eddy of ideas, conjuring and dismissing ways to rid herself of the mariner once again. This time permanently. Finally, she stopped and faced Patrick, struck once again as a woman by his appearance and by the haunting mental image of him entwined with her daughter, naked and full of lust.

The effect of his eyes on her gave Amelia pause, and for just a second she felt a flickering of her own desires. Desires that wouldn't be repressed forever. The desires of a woman who had once felt passions not driven by hate.

The desires of the flesh.

Amelia pushed the thoughts aside, her fury mounting at herself for her feelings and at the Irishman for inspiring them. "Sit down and have a drink. The matter will wait while I decide my recourse."

Patrick accepted a snifter of fine brandy from an attendant who had as recently as five minutes ago held a menacing fireplace poker aimed at him. Patrick grinned, an ironic smile for the strangeness of life in general.

The Irishman's untamed smile sent a tremor though Amelia she felt to her toes, warm and maddening. "Do we amuse you? You enter our home without invitation, attempt to kidnap our only daughter, and then you sit in our parlor and simper like an idiot? I fear for your mind, Mister Mullen."

"My mind is intact, Duchess. What of yours?"

Amelia let out a short laugh and poured herself a sherry. "So tell me: were my men easily overcome? They came at a high price, and with good recommendation. I admit I am taken aback by your return."

"I am here, am I not?"

"Indeed," Amelia replied quietly, and her eyes ran the length of him.

Patrick saw her longing gaze. He shifted his body and stretched his legs out in front of him, crossing them comfortably at the ankles. "Tell me, Duchess, why I am so repugnant to you. Tell me why the thought of Camille with me drives you to have me ruined and possibly killed."

"It is not personal, Mister Mullen. My daughter chose you for who you are not, and I had to remove you from the equation for the same reason."

"Were I a man of title, I would be suitable then?"

Amelia thought of Bret, who could be coerced and cajoled, and then Patrick, who knew no master. "No. You would never suit me."

Patrick lifted a brow and let his eyes slide down Amelia's curvaceous form and then travel back up, pausing at all the interesting places. "I thought we were discussing my suitability for your daughter, Duchess."

Amelia sneered despite the tingling in her thighs. "Actually, we are not discussing anything. I am saying you will never see Camille again, and so you will not."

"I love her."

"Love," Amelia spat. "A typical sentiment from an Irishman."

"Poor Duchess. Does no one love you?"

Amelia drew back, eyes wide, breath held. Then her face flooded with color under the stark white of her powders. In the light of the candles and fire her eyes shimmered. "I do not care for such intimacy."

"Perhaps it has not been given to you properly."

Amelia glanced around the room and saw all eyes on her, seeing her moment of weakness. She felt certain they could perceive the heat and moisture gathering in her body and hear the thumping of her heart. Bret stared at her hard, his lips flattened and his hands curled into fists.

"Wait," Amelia whispered. "Wait here. See he doesn't move."

Amelia rose from her chair and fled the room, heading to her writing desk where she sat and penned a quick note. She folded it, sealed it with her crest, and penned a second note. For a long while she sat and stared at her own handwriting as if it had been written by another, seeing each slant of each word and wondering if she would regret what she was about to arrange. Moments turned to minutes, ticking away in the silence of the house that had never known the briefest time of real happiness. Amelia's fingers shook as she folded the second paper, and she glanced at her signet ring, gems in gold. A symbol of her status and her burden combined.

Then she imagined a life without all the animosity and resentment, as she wondered what the present would be like had the past been different. But to remember the past was to recall all the lies and secrets. If Amelia didn't protect the family, she knew no one would. Then, mind set, Amelia returned to the parlor and handed both letters to Bret. "Take this and read the other. Follow my instructions exactly. I will tolerate no errors."

Bret took the papers, his jaw held tight. "This will be the last of your bidding I do."

Amelia grabbed his arm and clenched it so her fingernails dug into his skin like talons. "Don't gamble on that, my boy."

Bret whirled on his heel, stalking from the room. His shoes clicked on the floors as he left, echoing through the house until he slammed the door behind him.

Patrick looked to Amelia, seeing that the nick in her armor had been covered over and that her composure had returned. "What will you do with me?"

"I'll give you better than you deserve."

"Will I have to be surprised?"

"Do not be obtuse. If you get anything short of your own death, count yourself fortunate."

"Rather, I am abstruse."

"Do you want to war words with me, boy?"

"Do you think yourself a worthy adversary?"

Amelia let out a little giggle that revealed her enjoyment. "You want to establish my worthiness for you? Ah, that is laughable."

Patrick met her eyes evenly and readjusted his weight in a feminine chair too small for his frame. "Why don't you tell me what happened to your daughter?"

Amelia looked away from him quickly, a motion that Patrick knew to be avoidance and also to be a break in her rhythm. He saw her hands twist in her lap.

"What did you do, Duchess?"

"Do?" Amelia repeated. "I didn't 'do' anything to Camille except protect her from herself. Everything I have ever done for that child has been from a desire for her own good."

Patrick let her words hang there in the silence of the parlor, knowing her servants stood at the ready to try to kill him if he attempted to leave, but also that the servants stood there listening. Amelia shifted nervously in her chair, squirming under the obscure scrutiny of Patrick's stare.

Amelia's heart began to thump again, and perspiration gathered on her palms and under her arms. She looked to the timepiece and saw only minutes had passed since Bret had left to do her bidding. It would take time, too much time for him to make the arrangements and return. She couldn't spend another minute with the Irishman, letting his burning eyes bore into her. His face was too disconcerting, his smile too slow and easy, his body too confident and tempting, his voice too deep and resonant. Amelia stood suddenly, almost tipping her chair over.

"Watch he doesn't move. Advise me as soon as Lord Kimball returns."

Amelia walked quickly from the room without a backward glance, her skirts swirling at her feet until they flared.

Camille turned and shifted in her spinning bed, trying to reclaim the moments when her dreams of Patrick had been so real she could smell the damp cotton of his shirt and the scent that was his alone, like the woods after a cleansing rain. The alcohol remained heavy in her blood, a numbed buzzing in her mind. She thought she heard his voice from far away speaking her name.

"Patrick," she whispered, her skin covered with a fine mist of sweat. "Come back. I'm so sorry. Oh God, I'm so sorry."

It became her prayer, her mantra, pleading with God to forgive her and with Patrick to still want her. But no reply came. Just the quiet sounds of the rush of fire over wood and the indifferent, methodical ticking of her mantel clock.

Bret returned with the magistrate and several armed guards. Patrick stood and faced them, as the click of heels on marble heralded Amelia's return. The magistrate had the rumpled look of sleep about him, a hastily pulled-on wig and puffy eyes, though his suit was perfectly pressed. He looked about him, glaring at all he saw.

Amelia stopped and stood poised in the doorway to the parlor, her face set in stony lines and her eyes reddened. With a flick of her hand, she dismissed her servants and waited until the doors were closed. "I trust you understand my terms?"

The magistrate swung around to face her. "I do, Your Grace, though I cannot see the wisdom of your course."

"I will not have the stigma of scandal attached to such a court trial, nor to my daughter."

The magistrate thought of his own twin daughters, who had only as recently as a year ago been married off.

Had they been scandalized by the same sort of disgrace, he knew neither their comely faces nor generous dowries would have been enough to convince a man of quality to marry either of them. What sort of man would want a girl who had been so badly used? Still, he thought, justice had its way in a civilized society, and the man deserved a trial.

"I understand, Your Grace. But if the man is innocent of the crime for which he is accused . . ."

"He is not innocent," Amelia interrupted harshly. "He stole my daughter's virtue."

"Rape is a serious accusation, Your Grace."

"Rape?" Patrick exploded. "Is this what you mean to do, Duchess?"

Amelia looked directly at Patrick. "It is done."

The magistrate faced Patrick. "You will have to come with me."

"This will not hold up in trial, Duchess. You know I have never harmed Camille."

"There will be no trial," Amelia said flatly. Amelia moved a step away from Patrick, not meeting his eyes. "I will not have my family's name abused. You will be imprisoned for your crime, and the magistrate will accept my word of what transpired, along with a significant donation to the parish, and of course, his family."

"I have committed no crime," Patrick gritted.

"Newgate is full of 'innocent' men," the magistrate said neutrally.

"I *am* innocent, sir. If you will only wait until the morrow when Lady Camille is feeling well, she will confirm I am not guilty of such a heinous act."

Amelia positioned herself between Patrick and the magistrate, pressing her hand upon her chest as if pained.

"My daughter has been greatly tormented by her ordeal. She is understandably humiliated, and I will not allow such a questioning. Any of my servants can confirm this man was found in her rooms, holding her against her will. I understand your need for justice, and I pursue the same.

I caught this man in the act of defiling my child, stealing her future and her innocence in his lust. You question his guilt, yes, but at the same turn you question my integrity. To have this man standing in my own parlor after what he has done is perverse. My daughter lies in her bed recovering from this man's abuse, and yet here he stands! If you do not take him now, I swear I will go to the king himself!"

The magistrate hesitated for a second, thinking in that instance what the king would do to him should the duchess state her case in his audience. Besides, he reasoned, the outcome of the trial would already be determined. No court in England would side with a commoner who had broken into the home of a duchess, with witnesses to confirm he had been in the room of her daughter. Decision made, he signaled and the armed men surrounded Patrick, their guns drawn. They shackled his wrists and ankles while Patrick stared at Amelia, aghast.

"You cannot do this! I have done no wrong!"

"Get him out of my sight," Amelia said, her voice growing shrill. "The thought of what he has done to my daughter makes me ill."

As the men led Patrick from the house in chains and iron cuffs, he turned to look at Amelia. "I will return for her, Duchess."

"You will never again see the light of day."

"You can't chain me from her. She is mine, and I am hers. I will return for her."

Amelia raised her hand to Patrick in a sweeping gesture. "Do you see? Even now he threatens her, while he insists it is love that drives him. He is wicked and contumacious."

The magistrate stood out of the way as Patrick was pulled from the house in chains. He faced Amelia, twisting his hands. "God forgive me if the man is innocent. Newgate is a hell you could never fathom, Duchess. A strong, strapping man like that will wither and die in a few long, grueling years, if sickness doesn't kill him almost immediately."

"See he is kept separate from the others. He is a resource-ful and shrewd man who should not be underestimated."

"Duchess, please listen to one last plea. If the man were tried and found guilty, he would be sentenced to hang forthwith. Why not follow the legal recourse and see him pay for his sin?"

"The delicacy of my daughter's reputation is at stake. Not to mention, the delicacy of her mental state. The man has taken too much from her already."

Amelia drew a sheaf of papers and a sack of coins from a small drawer and handed them to the magistrate. "Please see the children in the parish are fed and clothed this winter, and also that your family is kept comfortable. I will not soon forget this act of understanding and kindness, or your discretion."

Then Amelia turned from him, obviously troubled. She paced a few turns, picked up her sherry and sipped lightly, then set it down with disinterest. The fire had burned low and the room took on the chill of the damp night. Amelia hugged her arms and rubbed, feeling cold to her bones. Bret sat in the wing chair, watching her in silence. The magistrate shifted his weight, waiting to be dismissed and suppressing a yawn. He still had the prisoner to take to Newgate, a task that promised to be unpleasant. All eyes rested on Amelia, who held herself against the chill and bit her bottom lip.

She turned to the magistrate, her voice low and her eyes averted. "See he has food daily, adequate blankets, and fresh water."

Amelia turned and hastened from the room.

CHAPTER 18

Jonah sat and listened to Marion's tale, saying nothing until she finished.

"You are certain the man was Patrick?"

"The way he held her was beautiful."

"He came back for her? Perhaps the duchess was not truthful about the terms of their separation."

Marion sighed, wistful. "He did not look like a man who ever wanted to be apart from her."

"Camille did not respond to him, though?"

"She was sleepin'."

"Sleeping?"

"Aye."

"Drunk again?"

"I think so. Jane says that Mary says she drinks brandy all day long. All night long, too."

Jonah let his breath out in a frustrated sigh. If he exposed his ruse, he'd be sent to prison and would be of no help to Camille. But she was drowning in her pain and he wanted to assist her. He grasped Marion's hands in his own, holding tight.

"What did the duchess do with him?"

"I have no way of knowin' for sure. Andrew says the doors were closed after Lord Kimball returned."

"Then what?"

"That's all I know. I asked everyone. No one knows what she did with him. The only matter being discussed is the Irishman's effect on the duchess. Mary said that Rachel said the duchess wept."

"I have to see Camille."

"Will she see you this time?"

"She won't want to, but I must."

Marion thought about Patrick, and the way he had held Camille, his body tall and strong as he cradled her in his arms. "Aye, you must."

"But first, I need to find out what happened. Quite a task for a mute, eh?"

"I will help any way I can."

Jonah squeezed Marion's coarse hands tighter. "She will need both of us. We will begin tonight."

Bret arrived while Camille, seated at the dining table next to Estella, picked at her lunch. With eyes red from lack of sleep and too much gin, he still approached her, a bag in his hand.

"Miss Estella, if you'll excuse us, please," Bret murmured.

Estella left the room without a word, closing the French doors behind her, leaving them alone.

Bret sat next to Camille and opened the bag. First, he pulled out a bit of cheesecloth wrapped in a bundle. He handed it to Camille.

"A peace offering."

Camille accepted it and unwrapped the cloth, revealing a generous square of chocolate. She looked up to him, her own eyes reddened and puffy, in tacit question.

"'Twill make you feel better."

"Vomiting made me feel better."

"I promise the chocolate will be better than vomiting."

Camille laughed and took a nibble of the candy, tasting the sweet melt on her tongue, pleasing all her senses. She took a second bite, and closed her eyes at the simple delight of the flavor and creamy texture. "'Tis good," she sighed.

"I am not finished spoiling you."

Bret took another bundle from the bag, this one wrapped in purple velvet. He slid the fabric from a crystal bottle filled with amber liquid. "Brandy. Of the finest made."

Camille paled at the sight of the liquor, still queasy from the night before. "No, thank you. I shall never imbibe again."

Bret shrugged, the velvet of his jacket brushing against the silk of the chair. "Either way, keep it. 'Tis difficult to come by, and you may want to serve it to guests."

Camille nodded slightly, uneasy with his kindness, and Bret set the decanter on the table. "Are you ready for your next gift?"

"Why are you doing this?"

Bret hesitated, but only for a second. "Of all the people in the world you know, do you think there is anyone who understands you better than I do?"

Patrick had held her in her dreams and been so real. He had comforted her and touched her, beyond skin and into her heart, loving her until she ached. But only in her dreams. When she awoke to a thumping head and a sick stomach, he was as gone as he had been for months, absent from her life in every way that mattered. Camille looked at Bret, with his handsome features and elegant clothes, seated next to her bearing gifts and claiming understanding. And on some level, she guessed he did understand. He knew about Amelia and her control, the rape, her lost child, and her desire to drink away her pain. He seemed to accept all of it, and still extended his offer of marriage and title. Camille took another bite of her chocolate, and as the decadent flavor spread across her tongue, she let her mind slide over Bret's question, turning it in her mind, looking at it from every angle.

He understood her situation. But he did not understand

her. He didn't know who she once had been, a girl who dreamed of writing and running, riding horses as untamed as her spirit across an ocean shore as wild as her illusions. Bret didn't know about her poetry or her reading, her cottage or her most private thoughts.

And Bret didn't care. But even as Camille acknowledged that, she knew that the girl who had held all of those things close in her soul, who had risked and schemed and lied to have even a taste of it, had died. The girl had gotten ill with Patrick's deceptions. She had weakened from lack of nurturing, as the writing stopped and her inner voice began to silence. And then the rape and miscarriage made the girl sick inside, weak, like a parasite that saps energy from within. But it was the guilt that finally killed her. Guilt that seeped into every organ, poisoning, tainting, until death is inevitable, unavoidable, welcomed.

Whispers of warning filtered through Camille's mind, even as she spoke. Warnings unheeded. "I do not know too many people, I suppose."

Bret laughed softly. "Is that what you're doing in your pretty head? Cataloguing your acquaintances?" He reached out and brushed a curl from her shoulder, so gently she scarcely felt his touch. "Such a mind you have, so literal and without the foolish nonsense of most women."

An ironic smile curved Camille's lips. "Are you saying my longings are of a masculine bent?"

"I should hope not, or my gifts are likely to be wasted." Bret reached inside the bag and carefully withdrew a long-stemmed pink rose, its bud tightly furled and its thorns removed. "It comes from my mother's greenhouse. I thought you would enjoy a preview of next summer, with a promise of a happier season than the last."

Camille accepted the flower and inhaled the delicate scent, bringing back visions of the cottage and the magical roses that had surrounded it. "'Tis beautiful. Thank you."

Bret didn't say that the petals were as pink as Camille's lips, and just as soft. He didn't comment that he found her scent infinitely more delightful. And he forced his mind not to travel the path that led him to the afternoon in the stables, when he had found her just as vulnerable as the rose, easily plucked and left to wither and die. If he thought about that day, the remorse would overwhelm him. Instead he reached into the bag once again and pulled out his final gift. He handed her a small velvet pouch tied with ivory ribbon.

"'Tis the last of my gifts this afternoon, and I hope the most appreciated."

Camille eyed the sack warily. "Your ploy is transparent, and disappointingly predictable."

"Directly to the point. 'Tis without a doubt my favorite of your qualities."

"You overestimate the persuasion of candy and flowers."

"What of the brandy? Perhaps a drink will help you to relax and enjoy the moment."

Camille's belly lurched and gurgled, but she longed for the comforting warmth, the numbing tingle a glass of brandy promised. She nodded her head in affirmation, and Bret poured her a generous aperitif. She sipped deeply. And then again.

"How do you find it?"

"Excellent."

"I'm pleased. I swear I will keep our home stocked."

Camille said nothing.

"Will you open your gift? I await your reaction as anxiously as a lad anticipates his first kiss."

Had it been only a day since Amelia stood over her and hammered her with the truths of her actions? Would this be the price of her surrender? Camille wondered only briefly, before squashing the thoughts as they arose, wanting only the paltry peace that capitulation could offer. Her narrow fingers shook as she plucked open the ribbons and reached into the pouch, pulling out a ring of gold set with a diamond nearly the size of her thumbnail, surrounded by smaller diamonds that glittered in the afternoon light.

Bret looked at the ring without passion. "This was my mother's ring, but the center stone has been in my family for many generations. It has been intended for my bride before I was even born."

Then he looked at her directly, and his face took on an earnest expression. "I want you to be my wife, Camille."

How can I wed you when I am married to another?

Camille closed her eyes. A thousand denials rushed to her lips, but she voiced none of them. If she opened her mouth, she feared the words that would spill forth. She steadied herself for a long time, until she could open her eyes and not weep, until she could speak and not scream.

"I will," she whispered.

Bret lifted her left hand and pressed it to his lips, before taking the ring and slipping it onto her third finger. He held her hand up, like champagne at a toast. "To our future."

Patrick sat on the filthy cot in his tiny cell and stared at the door of rusty iron and scarred oak. When they had brought him in, he had been taken beyond the common rooms that housed most of the prisoners, where the overwhelming odors of rancid food and unwashed bodies turned his stomach. According to the duchess's orders, Patrick found himself thrown into a stone room barely large enough to contain the cot, the barrel of rum-laced water, and the chipped chamber pot that occupied it.

And in this cell he was expected to rot and die without benefit of trial. There was to be no justice, for no crime had been committed. Not a soul knew of his whereabouts, but the ones who had sent him there. So, with a piece of flint, Patrick lit a single tallow candle and surveyed his situation.

Because Amelia had commissioned it to be so, Patrick had been left alone and not stripped of his clothing, assuring the magistrate he had been relieved of his weapons. He still wore his fine garments, though the

weather and the foul cart in which he had been transported
had sorely abused them. And this meant he had not been
thoroughly searched. And so they had not found his purse,
filled with gold and English currency. He hadn't bothered
to bribe the guards, not yet anyway, knowing the money
Amelia had paid would outweigh the amount he had on
his person. But there would be time for that, he knew.

Patrick reached into his boot and pulled out a dagger,
its jagged blade glinting in the candlelight. He felt in his
other boot, where another sheathed dagger was hidden.
In his belt were the Chinese throwing stars, and in the back
of his waistband, another knife.

Patrick had not attempted to use them for his escape
in the Bradburns' London home, knowing that even the
most precise skill with a blade paled to the speed of a
bullet. The ancient butler had patted him down, and
only his sword and his cutlass had been taken. But more
had been given.

He had seen the look in Amelia's eyes, found her weakness, and touched her fragile need. Unloving and unlovable, the duchess had created her greatest fear.

Jonah waited until nightfall to sneak from the property. He crept to the shadow of a tree where a horse stood
tethered to the trunk, chewing patiently on the last few
shoots of green grass. Jonah nickered to the gelding,
untied the reins, and hoisted himself into the saddle. His
heart hammered wildly in his chest as he calculated the risk
involved in heading into the city, where anyone could recognize him.

Jonah thumped the gelding's ribs and set off, encouraging the beast into a pace that drowned his pounding
fears. For Camille he would risk it. For his mother he would
prove he could do it. And for himself, he would not run.
Never again.

London sported more taverns, inns, coffeehouses, and

brothels than could be searched by one man. But Jonah had motivation. He stumbled into the loudest first, swaying on his feet and slurring his words. He spilled ale down his shirt and laughed, then leered at the round curves of bawdy women and chortled. He slammed his fists on his table and cursed the bloke who had taken him for his monies in a fair game of poker, and called out for anyone who knew the man to tell him his whereabouts.

"His name is Patrick, I tell you! An Irishman with a face from heaven and a way with cards from hell! He made a pauper of me, and I want a chance to win it all back. My luck's a-changing, I swear it is!"

And when the tavern came up short of information, he staggered into a brothel. Then he interrupted a political debate in a coffeehouse, and was pushed out the door and onto his backside into the street. Again and again he tried the same routine, down by the docks where information spread the fastest and was always for sale. But no sailor knew of this Patrick, nor did any of the whores or madams whose dimpled shoulders lifted with shrugs of indifference and invitation.

Exhausted and spent, Jonah turned back toward the house as the first lights of dawn began to turn the sky pink. He sagged in the saddle, repulsed by the stale smells of ale, smoke, and musky women clinging to his clothing and hair. He arrived back in time to rub down the gelding and was just finishing watering him when Clive entered the stables. Jonah immediately grabbed a pitchfork and began to clean the stalls, attending to his morning duties while Clive ran down a list of needs.

And Jonah listened with half an ear while he planned for the night to come.

Marion waited in shadows while Jonah received his orders. After Clive lumbered away, she slipped to Jonah's side and tugged on his sleeve, leading the way into the darker, quieter recesses of the stables.

"You look tired."

"Exhausted, more like." Jonah ran a hand through his hair, his fingers getting snarled in wavy tangles. "I want a bath. Even the horses' trough looks appealing."

"You got no information, then?"

"Nothing. No one has heard of him."

"Jane says the magistrate was here last night."

"The magistrate?" Jonah turned this information around in his mind.

"Aye."

Marion touched Jonah's hand lightly, her expression so earnest and open that her plain face turned beautiful. "Gossip around the kitchens leads the mind to thinkin' the duchess brought charges on the lady's love."

"Newgate," Jonah said bleakly. "I would need to search there."

And his own fears took him within himself, a journey of predestined court trials, filth and wretched illness, nooses and a disgraced family name. Children he would never father, books he would never read, freedom he would never enjoy.

Jonah's shoulders slumped and he leaned his back against the rough wall of the stables. But his legs grew weak and he slid down with a thump, stirring up dust. "I cannot."

Marion toyed with the hem of her apron, twisting it and pulling it through her chapped fingers. She looked from Jonah to the window, where she could see the shadow of the great house. "If not you, then who?"

Bret turned away from Camille, who lay sleeping in her bed. She had drunk from the brandy until she felt tired again, and he had helped her to her room and covered her with a blanket. Her face was so pretty, he thought. So delicate and pretty, but somehow alluring. A sensual promise beneath the facade of her innocence. He cast a glance over his shoulder and looked at her again. Sunlight reflected off the diamond on her finger as her hand lay on her pillow and her hair framed her face as midnight frames the moon. He couldn't help thinking that she was the picture of what every man craved when he longed for a wife in his bed.

He couldn't bring himself to touch her. The idea of bundling with her now made his skin mist with cold sweat, and a strange tingle ran down his spine. Every time he closed his eyes he saw her in the stables as he had left her, a dirty rag sticking out of her mouth and blood running from between her legs. And then the horror in her eyes.

He felt exhausted. Gin couldn't take the memory or bring the sleep. Nor could playing cards relieve his tension anymore.

Nothing was like it used to be, he thought. Amelia had changed everything. Or had he done it to himself? Wasn't it his own fault, when he had lost his fortune and then fired a shot in the back of the man who had held the winning hand? No, he told himself as he ran a hand over his face. No. It had been Amelia. She had scented his weakness as a dog smells fear. She had convinced him she could take his troubles away. She had lured him with promises of wealth, marriage, and safety.

Until she owned him, body and soul. He had sold himself for a king's ransom, with a virgin bride thrown into the bargain for good measure. And he had counted himself lucky. Until the terms of the agreement had weighed more than the fortune and the bride was no more a virgin than he. A pregnant bride, no less. He snorted in disgust.

But Amelia had had a plan for that, too. Rape her, she had said. Rape her and one of two things will happen. Either she'll lose the child and be humbled and grateful you'd have her at all, or she'll carry the bastard anyway, and be humbled and grateful you'd have her despite it. We'll winter her in France and get rid of the bastard. By that time, the chit will be so broken she'll do whatever we tell her.

And to his own disgust, he had done it.

Camille began to stir, restless and uneasy in her sleep. She turned and shoved her hand over her face, as if she blocked something, and then she covered her abdomen with her slender hands, her face contorted in grief. She sobbed a little, tiny hitches in her breath. And then she rolled to her side again, and a tear slid from the corner of her closed eyes.

Bret sank to his knees in front of her bed. He rested his forehead on the bed before her, and his shoulders shook with silent sobs. Dry, heaving sobs until his throat ached. And then he collapsed on the floor and closed his eyes.

Something moved and Bret looked up, catching only a glimpse of a shadow. But Bret knew who it was. He had been seeing them for days. He curled up into a ball, shaking with fear. "Forgive me," he whispered. "Forgive me my trespasses."

But the shadows closed around him and he could hear the smothered sounds of a crying baby; he could hear the gunshot and the thud of a dead man, followed by the splash of his watery grave in the Thames. "I am only human. I was weak."

The shadows shifted and grew darker, more ominous. Bret crawled to the door, clutching at the handle with quaking hands, clawing for his release from the horror of his slain victims. "No," he begged. "No."

The door finally came open. Bret fell out into the hall and rose on trembling legs to run down the stairs and out of the house.

When Camille awoke, the sky had turned dark. She sat up and reached to the nightstand, lit a candle, and got out of bed. The brandy still had her in its dizzying clutch, and she shook her head as if to clear her thoughts. Her rooms reeked of lemon oils, beeswax, and lye soap from the cleaning Amelia had ordered. Every surface gleamed, lustrous and elegant. The fire had burned low, and orange embers glowed in the hearth. She knelt and fed dried twigs to the cinders, blowing on them until they sparked and began to burn. She waited patiently, placing thin logs on the fire and watching as the flames licked over them like feasting tongues.

She sat back and enjoyed the simple pleasure of the warmth.

What a turn life had taken, she thought. Absently, her fingers stole to her ankle to touch the amber bracelet. And then she sighed deeply. A sigh full of aching, but also of resignation. Her fingers dropped away from the golden gems. She stood and walked around her room.

Her eyes fell to the stack of books she had brought from Beauport. Books of prose and poetry whose messages and images had no place in her new life, she thought. She picked up the stack and walked to her armoire, balancing them in her left arm while she yanked the doors open. The books on top slid and slipped, dropping to the floor with their pages exposed. She stacked the books in her arms on the bottom shelf one by one, lingering over the worn leather. And then she bent and picked up the others, consciously trying to avoid seeing the words inside, lest she be drawn into worlds where she no longer belonged.

As she picked up *Romeo and Juliet*, paper fluttered to the floor. She sat on the floor and picked it up, placing it in her lap as she looked at the familiar scrawl of her grandmother's handwriting. She reread the letter, though she could have recited it by heart.

Dearest Camille,

My time has come, I can feel it. I lie in this bed and I wonder what words to leave to you. I struggle to find wisdom to impart, but I have none. I have only my own truths. In each of us there lies our truth, hidden in parts of us we show to no one else. 'Tis our secret heart. My hope is for you to find someone whose heart is like yours, who can see into you and share your truths. 'Tis rare to find such a true love, but possible. And such a joy it can bring you, darling. Joy that can carry you through a lifetime.

Protect your heart, Camille. I was young once, like you. I made mistakes and I used poor judgment. I hurt people, even those I loved deeply. I have regrets, like a sickness. I also have memories so wonderful, so pure and real, they are the balm and the cure. Protect your heart, and know when to give it. This is the only truth I know.

Her throat ached with a painful welling of regrets and grief. Why hadn't her grandmother trusted her enough to tell her what she meant?

"You can't bury secrets forever, Grandmother," she said softly. She slipped the letter back into the book and set it on the shelf. She closed the doors.

But isn't that what I'm trying to do? she thought. Smother it all away where I don't ever have to look at it?

"'Tis too much. It just hurts too much," she said. Her hands touched her belly and her heart constricted. "No more. I will not do this to myself again. I made my decisions. 'Tis decided. 'Tis done."

She rose and went to the looking glass, fixed her hair, and smoothed her gown. She cast a glance back to the armoire. They tugged at her, the words from a woman loved and long dead. And then she turned back and saw her own hollowed cheeks and pale skin, the green eyes as familiar as they were foreign. Her gaze dropped to her finger where her diamond flashed, cold and hard. She looked back to her reflection.

Her restlessness returned, a stirring of emotion in her breast, a need to be on the move, to get away from her own past, her own reality. She tapped her foot and breathed deeply, turned around, and spied the decanter of brandy Bret had brought to her room.

And in an instant, she crossed the room, poured a glass, and drank it down until she gagged.

CHAPTER 19

Camille woke in the night, tangled in sweaty sheets and the clutches of a nightmare. Her heart raced; her mouth felt dry. Panic churned in her body like the cold, stormy ocean.

She would do anything to stop it, this feeling as if she were dying. It was not the quick death of illness or gunshot, but a lingering, agonizing death that would take years. Death brought on by the shot glass, the held opinion, the silent resignation, until finally the body succumbed to what the heart could not avoid.

"A half life disappears," she murmured, pushing her damp hair away from her face. "And who will notice I am gone?"

A voice inside her welled up, trying to be heard, insisting she had not completely gone.

Camille jumped from her bed and ran to the window, her nightgown a misty cloud of cotton around her frail body. She threw the window open wide and the air rushed in like a slap from a resentful woman, cold and cruel. It carried the scents of coal fires and rain, and nothing had ever made Camille long more intensely for Beauport, where the salty smell of the sea mingled with the scents of pine and earth in every breath one took.

She drew in the smoky, thick air and forced herself to inhale and exhale until the beating of her heart slowed to a more regular pace and clearer thought dominated.

Shivering, she closed the window and grabbed her robe, wrapped it around her, and huddled in front of the fire, stoking it until the flames burned high and bright. She lit every candle in her room, placing them around her in a circle of light that chased the shadows into corners and held them there.

And she sat in the center of her room, afraid of sleep and scared to be awake. Alone with her thoughts, as always, and more sober than she'd been in weeks.

Her fingers absently toyed with her diamond ring, turning it around her finger again and again as she stared into the fire. She tried to slip away in her mind to a different place, a better place. But the organ of her imagination had withered. Her dreams had died. So she just sat there, watching as the wood hissed and popped, cracked in half and sent a shower of glowing sparks into the air. Heat pumped from the blaze, warming her face until her skin felt tight and her eyes felt dry.

It sparked a memory of when she had been small, maybe seven or eight, and Amelia had brought her to London. She had been afraid of the big house, then newly built, had felt uneasy in all its rooms, terrified to be alone in her bedroom. But Amelia had been no comfort. She had forbidden Camille to leave the room. She told her that fears would never fade if one didn't confront them.

The memory made her smile as she recalled how every sound became magnified in her mind. Every creak had been a ghoul, every tap on the window a demon.

She had been a child then.

Alone in the nights, tutored and supervised in the days. Amelia had been a nearly constant presence, involved only when Camille disappointed or disobeyed. Camille had read in seclusion, dreamed in secret, and yearned in solitude.

Her thoughts and desires had been seditious and evil, and though she had kept them, she'd hidden them like her sins.

Nothing had changed much, she admitted to herself. Amelia still made the rules and set the pace. Camille was still taking orders and swallowing the rebellion that coated her throat like bile.

She looked down at her hands twisted in her lap, long narrow fingers and white skin. The hands of a woman destined to have work done for her by servants. The hands of a woman who was seen by others as incompetent and useless. She untangled her fingers and stretched them out in front of her. It was not how she saw herself. She saw hands capable of much more.

"Perception," she said aloud. "If I believe I am capable, does it make me so?"

And then an answer came to her, so clear and sudden she held her breath.

She needed to know the family secrets if perception and truth would be one.

Branches brushing the windows were not demons from hell coming to fetch her, nor was a squeaky floorboard the restless undead. Nothing was as frightening once you knew what it was.

Amelia had power because Amelia had knowledge. If Camille knew what Amelia knew, that power would shift. She had promised herself she would become like her mother. She would be cold and distant and loveless. But in her heart, she knew it was not what she wanted. What she desired above all else was power. Just the simple power of having a measure of control over her own life.

If she exposed the secret, it would lose its strength. And thereby, so would Amelia.

Maybe then, Camille thought, she could be free. Not free of her life or free of her sins or even of herself, but of her mother's control. She wanted part of that power, to replace things she now despaired of ever having. Power was certainty when everything else could be questioned.

It was permanent in a world where everything else could be taken away.

"Yes," she said aloud, as she blew out candles and banked the fire. "Yes. I will think as she thinks. I will know what she knows. In due time, I will have what she has."

Camille settled into her bed and pulled the blankets over her shoulders. Rain spattered the windows and drummed on the roof, wind moaned and creaked the trees, and the fire crackled and hissed. The bed was warm and soft, and she was not afraid. She had a plan.

For the first time since the rape, Camille slept without dreaming.

When Camille awoke, she rose and dressed with purpose. She took her time with her toilette and with her appearance. She rubbed a scrap of cloth across her diamond to remove any fingerprints and show it at its best. Her belly rumbled and gurgled, hunger pangs that she hadn't felt in months. With a pleasing start she realized she had no hangover and the beginnings of an appetite.

Stronger, she thought. I'm getting stronger. More like Amelia every day.

She strode to the door, with purpose now. A scrap of paper lay on the dark wood of her threshold like a single snowflake on frozen earth. She bent and picked it up, then saw Jonah's handwriting once again begging her to come see him. This time, a note of urgency and demand in his wording.

The stables. She couldn't go there. Never again. Her heart galloped and her stomach seized; any appetite she might have had felt gone. Pure fear replaced it, a gnawing, churning panic that slicked her skin with sweat and made her mouth go suddenly dry. She could smell it, the dusty straw mingled with manure and her blood, his seed. Worse, she could feel it, the pounding and thrusting that had taken everything. Nausea reared and her strength ebbed. Pale and shaking, she went to her bed, sat on the side, and drank from the decanter of brandy on her table, not bothering with a glass. She waited for the trembling to stop as the familiar heat ran in her veins, and a buzz gathered in her ears. She drank again, then set the decanter back down.

And she struggled for control.

No more. I can't be a victim any more, she said to herself silently. I must be able to walk out of my room and stand tall. I must be able to function if I will have any answers. Any power.

Like a woman who survives on instinct, she knew what she needed. And as a woman who had never relied on anyone else, she listened.

Camille stood and left her rooms, ignoring the stabs of panic with resolution borne of brandy and determination. She left Jonah's note on her bed, crumpled and forgotten.

The servants' quarters were deserted as the staff attended to their duties in various parts of the house. There were only a handful of live-in staff, most coming to work in the morning and departing after the evening meal. But there were rooms for personal attendants, the butler, and a few of the cooks. Camille peeked into their rooms and saw the sparse and tidy chambers as the employees had left them. Disorderly rooms were not permitted in any area of the duchess's house. Not even in the rooms she never entered.

Camille saw what she was looking for: an indication of which room belonged to the old butler. She figured him the most likely to have what she was looking for. The necessary accoutrements for shaving sitting out on the washstand were enough evidence as to which room belonged to him. She looked over her shoulder, saw no one in the corridor, and entered. Methodically, thoroughly, she searched his belongings. His drawers were nearly empty, and they stank of castor oil. She slid her hands in the backs of the drawers, frowning once as she pulled out a tattered but lacy woman's stocking. She slipped the lingerie back where she had found it and continued her search. A scarred and chipped armoire stood against the back wall, next to his narrow cot. She pulled open the doors and looked on the bottom shelf, finding only a pair of sad-looking shoes and a deck of cards. The pockets of the hanging garments held nothing but lint and disappointment. Camille stood on tiptoe and felt around the top shelf. Her lips curved in a smile as her fingers rested on something smooth and cold and hard.

She pulled down a dagger, the pommel black, the blade silver, sharp, and serious. It had a leather sheath and absolutely no adornment. That's fine, Camille thought with satisfaction. I don't want pretty. Just protection. She hid the knife in the folds of her skirts and rushed back to her room.

She locked her door and pulled up her gown until her thin legs were completely exposed, even the creamy stretch of skin just above her garters. With a length of her sturdiest ribbon and scraps of velvet to protect her flesh, she bound the dagger to her thigh.

With her skirts dropped once again and brushing the tips of her slippers, Camille stood tall and unafraid. A new determination shaped her face, hardened her features, and cooled her eyes. If any man tried to rape her again, she'd kill him. If she failed at taking his life, she'd kill herself.

Either way, she would be a victim no longer.

Her heels clicked on the floorboards, purposeful and rhythmic as she descended the stairs. Scents of chocolate and tea drifted from the dining room, but sounds of conversation came from the parlor. As she entered, Bret and Amelia looked up. Both smiled and Bret stood. Camille entered, went to Bret's side, and pressed a kiss to his cheek, dry and dutiful. "You are looking well, milord."

"I feel well. You, my lady, are a vision. There is a blush on your cheeks I haven't seen in far too long." He didn't mention the scent of brandy on her breath.

"I rested well."

"Tea or chocolate?"

"Tea, please."

He brought her a cup and placed it in her hands. He smiled down at her as she murmured her thanks. Camille tried to mimic the expression but succeeded only in baring her teeth.

Amelia let out her breath in a huff of annoyance as she got out of her chair and went to the window. The rain sluiced down the glass in rivulets, and the duchess seemed lost in thought as she looked out to the sodden morning. But when she turned, she rested her full attention on Camille with a look that could have halted a charging cavalry brigade.

Camille matched the gaze with the dead seriousness of her own. "Is there something you wish?"

"Something, child, though I know not what," Amelia said, her voice as brittle as her eyes.

"I cannot help you, then."

"Or yourself, or this family. Quite frankly, you have been of no help to anyone."

"Then leave me be." And the poignancy in her own voice sent a flash of pain across her face, as if she had just heard her heart speak.

Amelia saw the look and for a second felt compassion. Until she looked longer and saw only beauty. Pure, youthful beauty that had not faded with suffering, alcohol, misery, or even violent abuse. Such a face to render men useless. To make them want to sin with her. To make them want to slave for her. Even Bret, whose guilt now made him unusable, weak, and groveling. He was as pathetic as the rest of them, unable to see past her daughter's pretty face. Even Bret doesn't appreciate all I have done for him, Amelia thought nastily. And Amelia felt her heart grow colder still, felt it clench with envy. She turned her back to them, her fury humming in her breast.

Bret had seen Camille's look, too, but it only made him feel worse. "My lady, I have something for you."

Camille glanced at him with polite interest. "'Tis unnecessary."

"Your pleasure is my reward. Cover your eyes."

She sighed and set aside her tea, obliging him by putting her hands over her face. Something rustled, made a noise, and then was placed in her lap. Warm and soft and totally sweet, the puppy nuzzled her neck and whimpered.

Camille put her hands in its dappled fur, so silky. She looked at its clear amber eyes, its long ears, and the tiny pink tongue that darted out to lick her chin. The puppy wriggled and turned, got comfortable in her lap, and rested its head on her arm.

Her breath hitched in her throat. This puppy would need her. It would want to be fed and walked and stroked by the fire. It would want to be wild and would need discipline, a firm but gentle hand. It would follow her for affection and do tricks for treats. It would need her. It would certainly love her.

"Do you care for her?" Bret asked anxiously. "She is a spaniel breed, usually for hawking but will do very well as a pet. Your mother says you may keep her, so long as we understand she will accompany us to our new home after we are married."

Camille didn't answer; she couldn't speak. She just curled the pup to her, letting her fingers glide over the tiny muzzle, between the eyes, and then around the soft, floppy ears. Its eyelids had light brown lashes, spiky and short, dropping with exhaustion over eyes the same color as the gems that circled her ankle. She rubbed under its jaw, scratched its throat, and then again behind the ears. The puppy let out a breath and lifted its head up to look at her again, tiny markings above the eyes as expressive as eyebrows.

"Take her away. I don't want her." Camille spoke so quietly Bret could barely hear her, but he saw the sheen of mist gather in her eyes and the drop of the corners of her lips. "Take her back, please."

"She does not please you?"

"No. I do not wish a pet." Camille closed her eyes as Bret lifted the puppy away. She heard him give the dog to a servant to take to the kitchens for a bowl of water. And she felt her heart twist.

But better now than later, she reminded herself. Better to give the dog back than risk loving again.

Amelia couldn't take any more. No one, the duchess sneered inwardly, had ever brought her *anything* to make her happy. No one had even so much as *cared* what would make her smile. She couldn't stand to watch the girl be so unappreciative, not for one more second. In a flurry of skirts and scents, she whirled from the room and slammed the doors.

Bret scarcely noticed. He dropped to his knees in front of Camille and took her hands in his. "My lady, you seemed to find the pup appealing. I thought she would please you, given your fondness for animals. I assure you the dog is as gently bred as you or I, perhaps even more so."

"I do not wish a pet," she repeated.

"As you desire, my lady. I want only your happiness." Bret's skin looked pale, but his expression seemed sincere. Even earnest.

Camille sensed her opening and seized it. "Truly?"

"Of course. If a puppy will not make you smile, I will bring you jewels. If they do not please you, I will build you a castle. If still you are not happy, I will—"

Camille cut him off, her tone quiet, but as hard as steel. "Why don't you ask me?"

"Ask you?"

"Ask me what I wish."

"Anything. I swear I will do anything."

If Camille felt any guilt about using Bret toward her own end, she quickly squelched it. "Flanna. The old cook at Beauport. I want you to bring her to me."

Bret pressed a kiss to her fingers and stood. "'Tis done, my lady."

Before he could leave, her voice stopped him again.

"One more thing. No one will know she is here, especially my mother. Only I will speak with her, and then you will return her to Beauport. You will tell my father and my brothers nothing. You will deliver a note by messenger that a Harry Orr has passed away, and that his widow has a letter from Harry for Flanna. The note will also say that transportation has been paid for, and an escort provided. You will be that escort. You will meet her in town and bring her to London. You will ensconce her in a very comfortable inn and you will spare no expense. And I want you to purchase her three new sets of clothes and a warm cloak. When it is done, you will notify me. This is to be our secret alone. Just you and me."

Bret glowed at the notion. Then his smile vanished. "If she will not come? What then?"

Camille looked at him, her face as hard as Amelia's, her eyes just as cold. "Be inventive and resourceful. I want to see her. Can you be inventive and resourceful?"

"Yes, of course." He nodded, turned to go.

Her voice halted him one last time. "And take the dog. I don't want to see it again."

But Bret was taking orders willingly, and he wouldn't have argued no matter what she had asked for. He strode from the room with purpose, relieved to be on a mission of atonement.

Camille sat back and listened to the rain, the whistle of Bret's driver, and the rumble of the carriage. She turned the diamond ring around and around on her finger, all the while staring unseeing at the wall.

Herrick spent his day drinking, running up a tab he couldn't pay. But it didn't matter, because he wouldn't be around when collection time came due. It was just a matter of time until they found him, and the only reason he hid in the tavern was to delay that moment for as long as possible.

Even in his drunken haze he berated himself. How could he have let this happen again? Wasn't it less than a year ago Birney had bailed him out of the same situation? He had sworn it would be different this time. Vowed he'd learn to read and promised himself he'd get a decent job for a decent wage, maybe find a nice woman and make a home. Hadn't he heard about the factory by the river, where they made crates and needed strong men for hard work?

But no, he'd gotten in over his head after all that money Patrick had given him. Started drinking and gambling again, and ran up debts in too many taverns to number. Gor, but he was a generous bloke when he'd been drinking, he thought regretfully as he took a deep pull from his glass. Buying every last chap a pint, and even a pint for their whores.

It'd been fun, though, he admitted to himself. A really good time down to the last day.

And now he'd pay.

Herrick considered himself a fair man. Not necessarily honest or ethical, but he abided to a sense of principle in that a man paid for his indiscretions one way or another. And he wasn't resentful in the least about paying the piper for the festivities. He just wanted to delay the unbearable hell of Newgate for as long as possible.

"Ah, Newgate," he sighed into his cup. "Ye nearly killed me the last time."

A shudder took him as memories poured through him like ale from a cask. Such filth and disease. Fleas and rancid water and excrement. Herrick could never, would never, understand why animals were allowed in the prison, and why people were subjected to living like their beasts, pissing and defecating where they ate. The prostitution made him sick, too. Women in rags alive with vermin, covered in sores and stinking of rotted teeth and decaying flesh parading around, trading sex for everything from food to money to a sip of cleaner water. Not that they didn't get anything in return. Pregnant women didn't get executed in Newgate.

Two constables sauntered into the pub, spied Herrick, and approached him. Herrick raised his glass in mock toast, regretful only that he didn't feel quite drunk enough to face what lay ahead of him. "To me future 'ome."

Jonah huddled in the rear of the stables, staring into the gloom. He sat so still the animals didn't register his presence, and mice rustled in feed bags as if he weren't there. Cats slithered in corners, stealthy and silent, hidden in shadows, biding their time until a foolish mouse lost its guard.

She wouldn't come to see him, he knew. He'd tried, given notes to Marion to slip beneath her door. But she hadn't come no matter how urgent his message, and now he feared he could never tell her what he knew.

He buried his face in his hands. He had failed his mother, his unborn brother or sister, and now he was failing Camille.

A whoosh and a thud in the corner had Jonah looking up. A cat emerged with a mouse still wriggling in its teeth.

And Jonah had an idea. He stood in a rush and ran to grab his stash of papers. He sat, stripped a quill, and dredged it in ink. He wrote another note, this time with words that would be unavoidable. He stuffed it in his clothing to keep it dry and ran out into the rain to find Marion in the kitchens.

Camille returned to her rooms, motivated by only one need. She crossed to her nightstand and grabbed the bottle of brandy, washing down her feelings and uncertainty with a few burning gulps.

She sat on the bed and didn't bother with lighting a candle. A fire had been lit by the staff, distributing warmth and light in equal measure. The day had been long, and Amelia even surlier than usual. It puzzled Camille, for she had given Amelia everything she had said she wanted. Burying her head in her hands, she rubbed her forehead where an ache gathered. How did one wish for a way out of their own skin?

She slid from the bed and began to undress, relieved to remove her shoes, stockings, and the weight of her gown. She left the dagger in place, however, as she pulled a nightgown over her head. As she carried her pile of clothing to her chair, a tiny scrap of paper caught her eye.

Knowing it to be the latest in Jonah's efforts to see her, she picked it up and set it on her nightstand without reading it.

Her bed welcomed her, soft cool sheets and fluffy blankets. A sigh of appreciation slipped from her lips. She reached to her bottle and took a few more tugs of brandy, set it back, and looked at the note once more.

A memory of Jonah's face flashed in her mind, so serious and sad after the rape. He cared for her, she knew. He wanted to help her. He wanted to be her friend.

But she rested on her pillow and ignored the note and her own thoughts, pulled the cocoon of covers over her shoulders, and closed her eyes.

CHAPTER 20

London looked more civilized since Flanna had visited it last, but it didn't frighten her any less. The sky glowed ominously, thick with smoke as the sun dropped below the horizon in the gloaming. Factories and churches lined the busy streets; carriages drawn by horses rumbled and rang on the cobblestones.

Everywhere Flanna looked, she saw danger.

Still, she had come to hear Harry's last words. The blond stranger who had brought her was distant and almost silent, but he dressed expensively and had dropped her in front of a row of shops and told her to outfit herself. She wondered if he was Harry's son? Or perhaps his barrister? No matter. Whatever had become of Harry, he must have done well for himself.

And he had not forgotten her, after all.

Now she sat in a room filled with chintz and flowers, with a bed large enough for four people. She could have food or drink anytime she asked for it. She ran her hands over her new gown, a serviceable wool with a smart cut and a flattering color of dusky rose. No apron circled her waist; no meal pressed her for completion. In all her life, Flanna couldn't recall any time ever spent with new clothing and a schedule with nothing on it.

At her age, one didn't question such windfalls. If a gentleman told you to shop, you shopped and you didn't inquire as to why. If he ensconced you in a comfortable inn, you thanked him and lay on the soft bed to rest.

She took a sip of her tea and rested her head back against the cushioned chair. Outside she could hear the shouts and whistles of a city alive with activity. She had been told to await her visitor, and so she had ordered a pot, fixed her hair, put on one of her new dresses, and settled to wait.

When the expected knock on the door sounded, Flanna rose from her seat slowly, moving to the door with a hand on her hip. Camille stood in the doorway, the blond stranger behind her. Flanna's hand tightened on the door, and she stepped back to allow Camille to enter.

Camille swept into the room and turned to Bret. "Leave us. Wait for me in the carriage."

"Take your time, my lady." Bret nodded to Flanna and left, closing the door behind him.

"Dearie, you're like to kill an old woman with surprises." Flanna moved to her chair and sat with difficulty.

"Forgive me, Flanna. 'Twas the only ruse I could design to see you without my parents' knowledge."

"So there is no message from Harry. An' you are different, I see." Flanna measured Camille, the gaunt face, hollow collarbones, cold eyes. "It has not gone well for you, lass."

Camille touched her neck self-consciously, swallowed hard, and wished for a drink. But she needed her wits. Needed her answers. "I will not lie to you."

"Aye, an' why should you, when I have wanted nothin' but your good. Come an' sit by me, dearie. The tea is still warm, an' you look in need of a cup."

"I would appreciate it. 'Tis a cold day." Camille sat and accepted a cup, sipped deeply, and enjoyed the simple pleasure of hot tea.

Flanna lifted her own cup and drank also, then lowered it and watched Camille patiently. Camille sipped again and ran a finger around the rim, tapped the porcelain with her fingernail, and then held the cup in her lap, as if readying herself.

"I have always been fond of you, Flanna."

"Aye, an' I you." Flanna reached out and ran a coarse hand over Camille's. "Take your time then. I know 'tis important, what with all the trouble you went to in gettin' me here."

Camille contemplated her prepared speech, mentally running over all the things she could say that she knew would influence Flanna to give her answers. But she couldn't say any of them. She couldn't verbalize her reasons for needing the information. She couldn't look at the kind face of the old cook and say any of it. Instead, she just blurted the truth. "I want to know my past. My family past. I want to know the secrets."

Camille felt Flanna's hand tremble before she removed it. "'Tis not my place."

"I know you know all of it."

Flanna got out of her chair and rubbed her hip, went to the window, and looked out to the street. "Aye, I do."

"I need you to tell me."

"You have the right, dearie. 'Tis your past, not my own. But your mother would have me killed if she knew 'twas I who told you."

"She will never know 'twas you, Flanna. I swear it. If you're of a mind, I'll arrange for you never to have to return to Beauport. I can see to it you stay in this inn indefinitely, if you so wish."

"I would never accept such a bribe. As I told you, 'tis your past and you've a right to it." Flanna turned and faced Camille, her face set in determined lines. "I don't know what happened to you in these months since you left, but I see you are not the better for it."

"'Tis better you not hear. A private matter."

"Of course 'tis, as is anythin' that makes a woman turn cold. I saw the same look in your grandmother's eyes. It pains me to see it in yours now."

Emotion tried to well up in her chest, her throat, behind her eyes. But Camille pushed it down and turned it off with all the force of her determination. "What pained her, Flanna?"

Flanna limped back to the chair and sat, resting her head back and closing her eyes in memory. "The same thin' that did it to you, dearie. The love of a man she couldn't have."

"Tell me the story."

Because Camille asked so plainly, and because her voice sounded so thick with suppressed sadness, and because Flanna knew she had the right to know, Flanna let her mind return to the Beauport of more than fifty years before.

"I came to Beauport shortly after Harry left me. I was but a child, only ten and five, an' I worked cookin' for your family, choppin' an' scrubbin' an' takin' orders from the head cook. I remember when your grandfather brought Lady Elizabeth home. She was small and bright, quick and so alive. Only maybe a year older than me, you see. An' aye, she exuded life. 'Twas a thought I remembered havin', you see, that Elizabeth seemed to have more life in her than most, seemed more vibrant with it, as if the Lord had given her an extra share. She was like you, dearie, in that. An' your old grandfather seemed the opposite, like a sort of vampire who wanted to feed on her, who needed to drain her of it if he would be whole. He'd only married her in hopes of an heir, after his first wife had died childless, an' truth be told, I think he hated Elizabeth, because she didn't even seem to notice him.

"An' so they lived their lives, together but apart. He tryin' to take what she had, an' she tryin' to hold onto it. Then there came a man to Beauport. A man with a song on his lips and a gleam in his eye, as Irish as me an' twice as full o' stories. He came as a horse trainer, but saw your grandmother one day an' the two of them were never the same. Ah, but 'twas beautiful to see, him an' her together. They'd sneak off into the woods together, though they thought none knew. I knew, you see, for the path they took left them outside the view of the kitchens. I never said a word of it, except to ask forgiveness in prayer. Not for them, but for me, for seein' them made me full of envy."

Flanna sipped her tea and looked at Camille, who sat still and silent, absorbing every word. "'Twas lovely, like a fable. She so fair an' he so dark, hands clasped together an' always lookin' at the other, like some secret language was passin' through their eyes. She loved him, an' he her, one could tell by lookin'. I think your grandfather had suspicions. But when Lady Elizabeth grew heavy with child, the manor seemed to come to life as never before, everyone waiting for the first babe to be born in Beauport.

"An' then your grandfather, he died of apoplexy. Only about two months before the babe was to be born, you see." Flanna cocked her head, remembering the whisperings of the servants. "They said he had found them together in bed, with the Irishman havin' at her from behind, and her big pregnant belly hangin' . . ."

Flanna paused and coughed, set her teacup down, smoothed her skirt, and then began again, her cheeks now a lovely shade of rose to match her gown. "Well, they say he dropped over dead as stone, right in the room, his eyes bugged out an' horror frozen on his face. An' your great-uncle did come to Beauport for the buryin', an' he had questions for your grandmother. Aye," Flanna said softly, "that he did.

"The whole house went still, an' we all waited for the babe. An' everyone knew by now, of course, though none spoke aloud of it," she said, her voice melting into the steam of the tea as she took another sip. "Least of all, Lady Elizabeth.

"When the child was born with a thatch of black curls and eyes greener than the hills of Ireland, your great-uncle knew somethin' must be done, lest the Irishman lay claim to the babe or try an' take Elizabeth to wife. He sent for the Irishman an' your grandmother both. He had them brought to the stables an' had the Irishman gelded while he forced your grandmother to watch on. Then he had him lashed. Finally, he had his throat cut, though they say that was needless, since the man had died from bleedin'."

Camille sat very still. She closed her eyes as the image played out in her mind. And after the image came the realizations. "My father is a bastard," she said in a whisper. "Under English law, because my grandfather died before the baby was born, the title would not have passed to a child who was a known bastard."

"Aye. He bears no more title than me." Flanna set her teacup to the side.

"If the king knew, he'd strip him of all of it, the lands, titles, everything."

"Aye."

"And yet you said nothing, did nothing. You could have brought my father and my mother to their knees."

"Then where would I have worked?" Flanna folded her gnarled hands in her lap. "Dearie, I came to England with nothin' an' I'll leave it with nothin'. My station in life wouldn't have changed, an' I wouldn't have wanted it to. I left Ireland with Harry an' I spent my life payin' the price. But I kept my position at Beauport by the grace of God an' because I held my tongue an' pretended to know nothin'."

"My mother knows," Camille stated.

"Aye. Your da told her one night after too much gin an' a loud fight. They fought in the dining hall, an' I admit I heard every word. Your da wanted to take your mother down a bit, I think. Told her she hadn't been married off very well after all, an' that she could no more ruin him without ruining herself."

"And Grandmother. She had to live with it. She had to live with her guilt."

"Dearie, she had to live without her greatest love. I think that was the worst of all of it."

Camille got out of her chair and wandered the room,

stopping to touch the fabric of a new cloak hanging from a hook by the door. "You are comfortable here, Flanna?"

"Truth be told, I have never enjoyed such riches in all my life. I have but to call for it, an' someone cooks for me."

Camille laughed lightly and turned to face the kind woman she had so often wished she had been born to. "Stay for a while, and rest. I will see to it you have coin enough to see the city and purchase anything you want. Please do this for me. It would truly please me to see to your comforts."

"Your family would be wantin' to know why I was gone an' when I'd be returnin'."

"I'll have word sent that you're staying with a friend who isn't well." Camille made a mental note to have Bret take care of it. "I'll see to it your position is held at the manor. You have my word."

"I'd be grateful." Flanna leaned forward and caught Camille's eyes, holding her gaze while her creased face softened with sympathy. "Now will you be tellin' me what has hurt you so? Did you send your man away and break your own heart a second time?"

"Bret? I didn't send him away . . . he's waiting for me in the carriage." Camille's fingers drifted to her diamond ring and she turned it around her finger. "I'm supposed to be riding in the park."

"Not the blond one. The other. The handsome one. Patrick." Flanna searched her memory and recalled the details. "Patrick Mullen."

Camille's throat got tight, so tight it ached. How much pain could her heart take and still keep pounding? "He left me, Flanna. Surely you have not forgotten."

"Aye, an' he came back for you."

Camille leaned against the wall; the blood drained from her face, her legs turned to water, and her belly flipped over and over again. "Came back?"

* * *

Herrick heard the clock above the Old Bailey strike the noon hour and he got off his cot and headed to the gaol keeper for instructions. Fortune had been with him for once in his life: the gaol keeper had remembered him from his last stint in Newgate. The one known as Thick had seen him brought in and had bellowed out a hearty hello. Not only had he welcomed him, but he had slapped him on the back and offered him an empty cell for his use, with the only stipulation that Herrick do his meal deliveries for him.

Done and done, Herrick had exclaimed.

Now Herrick rushed past the common cells and tried not to hear and see the depravity. He hated seeing the children, most of all. Tiny little things, all skin and bones, with the look of lost hope in their eyes. He hadn't ever had the chance to become a father, but he always thought it seemed the biggest shame of all to see little innocents turned into something twisted and sick, just because their parents wouldn't protect them. If he'd had a child, he'd have protected it. Herrick knew that for certain.

Thick saw him coming down the stone corridor and got out from behind his battered table holding a ring of big iron keys. "Each key 'as a number ter match the cell, an' ye take each prisoner a meal twice a day, an' a jug er water once a day. Do ye ken?"

"Aye." Herrick took the keys and headed to the kitchen where an old man stirred huge vats of soup and ladled them into crocks. As he already knew from before, the prisoners held in the private cells were the prisoners with money to protect them. Serving them food was perhaps the easiest job in Newgate, and if it kept Herrick out of the common areas and kept him fed, doing his stretch this time was going to be as easy as a drunken whore.

Herrick whistled as he delivered the food, mentally deciding he'd take them each the water in the morning, so they'd have it for the day. He'd also see if any of his prisoners wanted things to be purchased for them, for a price, of course, and Herrick figured he could earn some money and pay off his debts in no time.

They were all glad to see him, the only face they saw all day. Herrick chatted with each for a few minutes, careful not to spend too long lest the rest of them get cold soup and decide the new messenger wasn't a reliable sort.

The corridor was long, housing twelve cells on each side. They were windowless and solid stone, each with a rough-hewn oak door set with an iron opening with three slits to let in air and meager light. Very few people received a solitary cell, and the cook had given only seven crocks to be distributed. Herrick wheeled his creaky cart down the uneven floor and stopped as he got to the last cell.

He set the key in the lock, turned it with a screech of rusty iron, and pulled open the door. Patrick looked up at Herrick as Herrick looked at Patrick. Both men grinned and then Herrick began to chortle.

"Yer a mess! Look at yer clothes an' yer hair!" He doubled over, roaring with laughter. "Ye stink, too!"

"I can't possibly smell worse than that soup. What's the flavor today, creamed offal?"

"What did ye do ter land yerself in 'ere?"

"I could ask the same of you. Didn't I give you enough coin to last a year?"

"Ye did, but it weren't enough fer all the wenchin' and bettin'."

"You are a shameless, wasteful scoundrel, and I've never been happier to see anyone." Patrick leaped from his cot and grabbed Herrick in a hug, thumping him on the back. "You're my way out, my friend."

Herrick took a step back. "I'm not 'elpin' ye escape, if'n that's what yer thinkin'. I got meself a good thing 'ere an' I'm stayin' out o' trouble."

"How much are you in for, Herrick? How much debt?"

"Two 'undred an' forty pounds."

Patrick produced his purse and tossed it to Herrick. "You'll have enough to pay your debts and help me get out."

Herrick shook his head. "Yer sittin' in Newgate with a fortune in yer pocket? I figured ye fer a smart man."

"The duchess put me here for more money than I had on my person, I'm sure. I didn't even bother to try to bribe my way out, knowing I'd be relieved of my coin and I'd still sit and cool my heels in this cell." Patrick leaned back against the cold stone and grinned wryly. "I've been watching for any information I could gather, trying to figure out who is in charge and when the guards change and how in God's name I could escape. This prison is as disorganized as it is disgusting. But now that you're here, I won't even have to kill anyone to get out."

Herrick caught Patrick's infectious grin. "An' so I'll pay me debts an' go get yer father?"

"You are even more perceptive than I gave you credit for. But no. You'll be paying your debt and then you'll find my wife."

"Ye mean the daughter o' the woman who put ye 'ere?" Herrick raised a thick brow dubiously. "I said, I figured ye fer a smart man."

Patrick shrugged. "I need to put my fate in her hands. 'Tis as simple as that."

"An' if she won't come fer ye?"

"Then you may find my father." Patrick ran a hand through his grimy beard and hoped he had measured the situation accurately. "But not until she decides. You must find her and leave it to her."

The carriage ride back to the house gave Camille time to think. She wanted to plan and she wanted to feel a sense of control, the very power she had gone looking for when she sent for Flanna. She now knew the secrets. She held the keys to everything she had ever wanted. She could run her own life, at last. Amelia could be broken.

But for the moment all she could do was sit and sway in the carriage, the lap robe a forgotten puddle at her feet, her eyes closed, remembering. He had come back, and he had told Flanna it had been Amelia who had arranged it. He had been taken against his will.

He had not left her, after all.

No betrayal, no bribes, no broken vows.

Camille rubbed her eyes wearily, wishing she could weep if only for a moment. Just enough tears to relieve the pressure in her chest that felt like her heart would explode. Tears wouldn't come, though, for her sadness knew that a leak would cause a burst, and that no control would be regained after it had been unleashed.

She had betrayed him. There was no forgiveness for such a thing. No atonement for believing Amelia over their love, and no redemption for killing their child before it could even draw its first breaths. The weight on her shoulders held her riveted to the seat in the carriage as it stopped. She barely heard Bret offer his hand to help her down. Oblivious to him, she made her way into the house, slumped and numb.

Estella sat in the parlor waiting. She looked up from her needlepoint. As she saw Camille, her face settled into a disapproving frown. "My lady, you are late. Mind your posture and come sit by my side. We will begin today with a review of yesterday's work on the subtle needs of entertaining houseguests in the morning."

Anger slithered through Camille's sadness like a reptile, cold and venomous. She began to seethe. So much taken, so much lost. None of it would have happened if not for Amelia.

Camille raised her eyes to look at Estella, a glacial, penetrating stare that sent a wash of fear over the tutor's spine. "You are dismissed. Where is my mother?"

"She said she was not well and took to her bed. Is there a problem, my lady?"

"Nothing of your concern. As I said, you are dismissed. Leave now, and do not come back. I will have your wages sent to you."

"The duchess retained me for my services. I cannot be relieved of my position except by her." Estella tried to force her voice to sound firm, but it cracked anyway. She avoided Camille's eyes as she picked up her needlepoint.

Camille gestured to Bret and raised a brow. "Get her out of this house and pay her what she is owed."

Bret nodded and did her bidding, making certain to leave as Estella did, lest he be alone again with the moaning, shifting shadows.

Camille left the parlor with a flick of her skirts. She ascended the staircase, taking each step methodically, her hand on the rail. She went down the hall, turned the knob, and entered her mother's room without knocking. Amelia sat up in the bed and shrieked her annoyance. "Get out, you chit! I am ill and you are intruding!"

Camille slammed the door behind her and went to stand by her mother's bed, looking down on her. Amelia had removed her wig, and her shaven head looked unearthly pale in the dim light. With her cosmetics washed away she looked especially tired and worn, and the nightdress she wore hung from her shoulders in limp folds.

"You took him," Camille hissed, and her hand struck out in a flash to slap Amelia's face.

Amelia gathered herself in a rush. She leaped from the tangle of covers to lash back. But Camille was faster and far angrier. She caught Amelia's hand in the air and held it by the wrist, her grip hard and unyielding. "You will never strike me again; do you hear me?"

Amelia pulled back her other hand but Camille grabbed that one, too. "You will never strike me again."

Amelia struggled for a few seconds and then realized she would not break her daughter's hold. "Let go of me now, or I will send for Edward and order the worst lashing of your lifetime. I'll have him flay the skin from your back in strips; I swear it!"

Camille shoved Amelia back onto the bed. "Shut your mouth and listen, hag. Do not speak again unless I bid it.

I know about my grandmother, and I know I am the daughter of a bastard. Touch me again or get in my way, and I'll ruin you."

Amelia's jaw dropped and she sagged back against her pillows. Her world crumbled and her carefully crafted plans fell away in front of her eyes. Some treacherous soul knew too much and spoke too much. "Who told you?"

"Put it out of your mind, Amelia, for I will never tell you. I come here only to inform you that you are no longer my mother and that your reign over my life is over. Do you understand me? You are dead to me. I know you took Patrick from me."

Camille shook with it, the killing rage that made her want to grab a chair and beat Amelia with it until she screamed in agony, and then keep beating her until the screaming stopped. Her hands curled until her fingernails bit into her skin and made bloody crescents on her palms. She wanted to shout the words, but she could manage only a strangled whisper. "You stole my life."

"Do you not understand even now? You brought it all on yourself, child. I sought only to take the rebellion out of you. 'Tis the same rebellion your grandmother had. The rebellion that made your father a bastard and shamed an entire family."

"No. That would never have been enough. Nothing I did was ever enough. You fed on control, Amelia. And now it ends because you will never control me again."

"There are things you do not know, child. Do not fool yourself."

Camille's smile was cruel, fierce, and beautiful. "Test me, Amelia. Test me and see if I will not ruin you."

"You wouldn't dare. 'Tis the same situation your father put me in, so long ago. By ruining me, you will ruin your father, your brothers, and yourself."

"Unlike you, I do not care."

"You would care when you were impoverished. You would care when your beautiful clothes and jewels would have to be sold for food. When you would have to work like a scullery maid for your keep, or a governess to some horrible child, or marry yourself to a lowborn count and spend your life raising his lowborn brats. What you take from me, you take from yourself. Do not make the mistake of thinking revenge on me would satisfy you forever."

"I do not care."

Amelia shook her head. "Such a lack of foresight. Just like Elizabeth, you are. She had no concept of what she did when she took that commoner to bed, just as you did not. Consequences, child, are what should always be considered prior to making a decision. Will you need to be a beggar before you realize that love fades but land and titles endure?"

Camille waved her hand, impatient with Amelia's lecture. "What did you do with Patrick?"

"I had him sent away."

"He came back for me. What did you do to him then?"

Amelia narrowed her eyes, certain Camille could not possibly recall the night the mariner had come to the house to fetch her, when he had cradled Camille to his chest in a way that made Amelia fume. "He came back, child? To London? Are you certain your sources are correct?"

Camille faltered for a second, not wanting to show her mother what she didn't know. "If you will not tell me, I will find him, and I will do as I see fit. Stay out of my way, or you will find out about the consequences of your own actions, Amelia. I tell you this as a warning, a promise." Camille leaned forward and pushed her mother back into her pillows. "I need money. Give it to me."

"Take your hands from me. How undignified, that you would resort to thieving. Undignified and incredibly predictable. What next? Will you hold a knife to my throat and extort jewels?"

Camille thought of the dagger strapped to her thigh and momentarily enjoyed the image of pressing it to Amelia's pale neck. But she let the thought go, not wanting to resort to murder. There were things worse than death, and she wanted Amelia alive enough to experience all of it.

"Give me money. Plenty of it." Camille stood upright and stepped out of Amelia's way as she got out of her bed.

Amelia went to her desk and withdrew a sack of coins. She threw it at Camille and it landed at her feet. "Why should I care how you waste your life? If you will not wrest a lesson from all that you have experienced, I cannot imagine I can teach you anything any longer. Go do as you wish and watch your world crumble. I will not torture myself to stand beside you as it happens. Get out of my house and do not come back."

Camille picked up the sack and turned to leave. She spied her mother's signet ring lying on a tabletop. Gleaming gold and inset with onyx and rubies, it spoke of heritage and tradition, of lands as ancient as the wars that had been fought to claim them. Impulsively, she grabbed the ring on her way out, closing the door behind her without a sound. She paused in the hallway, tumultuous feelings brewing while her mind raced to her options. Pressing on, ignoring the tide of emotions, she hurried to her rooms to gather her things before Amelia changed her mind and decided to take a new tack.

Throwing open the doors to her armoire, she pulled out her gowns and cloaks, her books, and her jewelry. She rolled them and stuffed them into her largest trunk, piling her boots and her shoes on top. She yanked her door open and called for staff to help carry down her things, and then she went to her bedside table to get her bottle of brandy.

Jonah's note fluttered to the floor. Camille picked it up and unfolded it. Her breath left her in a rush when she saw his scrawled words.

Patrick came back for you. He held you while you slept.
I believe I know where he is.

CHAPTER 21

The stables sketched a bulky outline under a darkening sky. Camille stood under a tree, leaning against its trunk as she struggled for breaths through her constricted throat. There wasn't enough brandy in the world to dull the pain. The rapist was behind her, on top of her, plunging into her.

She rested her hand on her thigh and felt the reassuring lump of her stolen dagger under her skirts. No longer a victim, she reminded herself. She was a thief, a sinner, a betrayer, and if someone tried to get in her way or rape her again, she'd be a murderer. But never again a victim.

The thought steadied her and calmed her galloping heart. She forced air into her lungs, steeling her body. She pushed her feet to move, to take steps, to carry her to the stables. The iron handle was bitingly cold under her hands, and she pulled it hard to slide the door open.

The musty scents of horses, manure, hay, and feed smelled like blood and violation. Pure panic twisted in her gut and filmed her skin with sweat. How much strength did she think she had?

Camille leaned on the rough wood of a pen. The mare called Meadow approached her quietly, slowly, as if sensing her mood. She swung her large head over the rails and nuzzled Camille's shoulder, her hot breath warm against Camille's upper arm. Standing up straight, Camille made herself ignore the gentle touch of the horse. She went farther into the stables, averting her eyes from the place where she had been raped.

"Jonah!" she called, hoping her tone didn't sound as desperate as she felt.

Her friend emerged from the gloom. She noticed his face looked haggard, his clothes mussed, and his hair uncombed. He leaned his pitchfork against the wall, gesturing to the loft, and she followed him up to where his pallet lay stretched out as it had the night they had lain together.

"You read my note," Jonah stated.

"He came back."

"Yes."

"You saw him?"

"Marion did. She says he held you."

"I thought it a dream." Camille felt her legs begin to buckle and her vision to blur. "How could I have been so wrong about everything?"

"You were not wrong about him loving you." He said the words for her, even though his heart ripped. She looked so cold, so sad, and so alone. And her eyes—they were huge in her gaunt face, and desolate.

She rubbed her hands together and turned away. Darkness had finally engulfed daylight, and Jonah lit a lantern and sat on his pallet. He ran a hand through his knotted hair and swallowed hard. It wouldn't be easy to tell her any of it, he knew.

"I need a ride into town, Jonah. 'Tis why I come here."

"Where will you go?"

"I've yet to decide. For tonight I will impose on an old friend who is staying in an inn. My trunks should be in the carriage by now. Will you drive me?"

"Do you not want to find Patrick?"

"No," she said quietly.

"But he came back for you."

"It matters not."

"It should mean everything. I do not understand. He did not leave you, Camille. He found his way back to you, so he must love you still."

How could she explain that if Patrick did love her, he loved the girl he had met in a stable at Beauport? A girl who laughed and connected, a girl who read Shakespeare and dreamed. She had taken risks and invited him into her life, her heart, her soul, and her bed. That girl had been free inside, where it matters, and the constraints of her family had not thwarted her desire for life. There had been beauty in her, a generosity of spirit she hadn't valued until it had been taken. Patrick had seen it all, somehow. He had looked into her and understood who she was. He had exchanged vows of marriage; he had given to her until she was full.

But she was not that girl anymore. She couldn't ask or expect him to love the woman she was now, damaged and broken. She wouldn't think it even possible, if he knew all her truths. If he knew she had killed their child when she disobeyed simple rules. That another man had entered her, shamed her, and made her dirty. And that when Amelia had told her the most implausible lies about him, told her terrible, horrible things about him, she had believed it. If she were a woman worth loving and being loved, nothing of earth or heaven or death would have made her accept those lies.

But she had believed. And by believing, she had betrayed.

"I cannot concern myself with what he feels. He will be better without me." She plucked a piece of hay from a bale and twisted it around her index finger. "He will find another woman one day. A woman who will make him happy, give him a family. In due time, he will forget me."

She turned and looked at Jonah. The dried grass fell from her fingers, forgotten. "Will you drive me, or shall I call for Clive?"

Jonah hesitated as selfish thoughts invaded his mind: to take Camille where she wished to go and not tell her the truth of Patrick, and that in time perhaps she would love him, Jonah. He didn't care about the rape; it didn't change how he saw her. With the child gone and Patrick gone, what stopped her from learning to love him? He would be good to her. He would worship her.

His weakness made him sick, and he pushed the thoughts away. He had already failed her once. He couldn't do it again. "I believe Patrick is imprisoned in Newgate, Camille."

Herrick stood on the outskirts of the property. The livery had dropped him at the gates and left him. Herrick patted the lump of money secured in his breeches to assure himself it was still there, and he hadn't let Patrick down.

He started down the long cobblestone drive. Wind sighed in the naked trees, swirled in the dried leaves on dying grass, and tickled Herrick's neck. He lifted his head and sniffed the dampness in the wind, hinting of a storm. He turned up his collar and slowed his pace, taking his time and not wanting to be caught. It would be tricky, finding the girl and not alerting the mother. He planned on bribing the staff, but he knew that to be risky, for you never knew where loyalties lay.

The house was large and dark. Outbuildings were shadows behind it, and Herrick skirted around to the back. The stables were also dark, but the door yawned open. Rain mixed with snow began to fall, wetting his hair and his cloak. Herrick picked up his pace and slipped inside the stables.

Horses rustled in their pens. He breathed in the heavy scents, happy to be out of the weather. He stood for a moment and let his eyes adjust to the dark, waiting until he could see his way through the labyrinth and find a secluded spot to wait until morning. He passed a ladder leading to a loft and saw the yellow glow of a lantern above. Muffled voices, female and male, drifted down to him, but he couldn't make out what was being said. He moved on, hoping for a pen with some warm straw and maybe a horse blanket.

He made no sound; so silent was his passing that even the horses seemed not to notice him. A smile of achievement spread between his rough whiskers. He was going to make Patrick proud of having befriended him.

He didn't see the pitchfork leaning against the wall. His foot caught it and knocked it over. The horse in the pen nearest him reared and bucked against the stall, which made the other horses go crazy. They whinnied and snorted, banging their huge bodies into the wood and making such a racket, Herrick yelped and flattened himself against the wall, bracing for a stampede.

Jonah raced down the ladder. He followed the noise and Herrick threw his hands up, not wanting to get shot for intruding.

"I'm unarmed. Don't shoot, I beg o' ye."

Jonah stopped and squinted in the dim light. "What do you want?"

Herrick held his hands out in front of himself. "I'll go an' I'll not cause any trouble. I'm 'ere fer a mate o' mine, an' doin' 'im a favor by way o' findin' 'is wife. Do ye know the lady o' the 'ouse?"

"The duchess?"

"Aye, an' 'er daughter."

"I am her daughter." Camille held up the lantern to look at the man, grateful for her skirts that no one could see her knees knocking. The sounds from the horses had sent panic clawing at her throat, but she had beaten the feeling back. *Not a victim.* She wouldn't hide up in the loft and hope a man didn't grab her from behind. She had grabbed the lantern and unsheathed her knife. She'd go down there and face him, this time. She'd stick her dagger in his neck, this time.

In the ambient glow Herrick saw Camille, and knew her to be Patrick's lady. Her eyes were the color Patrick had said, her face as lovely, her hair as black. But there was something else. A prickle grabbed at his skin, and he hoped it was only a trick of the flickering light that made her eyes look so ravaged and glitter so hard. His eyes dropped and he saw the sly, silver wink of a blade in her hand. "Patrick Mullen sends me, me lady. 'E's in Newgate, an' 'e sent me ter find ye."

Camille's grip on the hilt slackened, and she lowered the lantern. "You were right, Jonah."

Jonah glanced around the stables and then took Herrick by the arm and led him to the ladder, indicating for him to precede them up to the loft. "Tell us what you know."

He told them everything Patrick had told him. Jonah handed Herrick a drink of water, which he accepted gratefully. Herrick drank deeply and then turned to Camille. "'E loves ye, me lady. I never seen such love before."

Camille leaned back against a bale of hay and turned Herrick's words over in her mind. She saw Patrick on board a great ship bound for slavery, how he lost his boy Tate, and how he killed a man called Birney and reclaimed his ship. She saw him on an island called Bermuda, gathering a crew and sailing back to England to find her. Then the story matched what Flanna had told her, of how Patrick had come to see her outside the kitchens and had found out where the house in London was located. And then he had come and slipped inside, held her, and tried to take her with him.

Until Amelia had had him jailed on false charges of rape. So far beyond mere protestations of love, Patrick had come for her. Camille squeezed her hands around the pommel of her dagger until they hurt.

Camille tallied Patrick's losses. A boy he loved, his freedom, his child she had carried, months spent in horrible circumstances, money, risks taken with his life, and now he'd had his freedom taken again. All because he had loved her, she realized sadly. It was all her fault, all her doing.

Herrick broke into her thoughts. "'E says 'e wants to put 'is fate in yer 'ands. Says it's as simple as that."

"My hands," she murmured. She looked down at her lap where her fingers were wrapped around a shining weapon of murder. "Such trust he has in me."

Jonah wanted to reach out and comfort her, but he hadn't dared touch her since the rape. "What will you do?"

"I will get him out of prison. I owe him at least that."

"What then?"

"I will take him to his father or to his ship, whichever he chooses."

Jonah couldn't keep from asking what he feared the most. "Will you leave with him, Camille?"

She looked up and saw anxiety in his deep brown eyes, but mistook it for concern for a different reason. "No." She stood and dusted her skirt, looking to Herrick and then to Jonah. "I need to get out of here, Jonah. Will you drive me to the inn?"

"Of course."

"Herrick, will you accompany us? We will go to an inn and settle there. I'll provide a room for you, of course. I need to collect my thoughts. I need to plan."

"Aye." Herrick followed them down the ladder and out to the carriage house, standing next to Camille without speaking while Jonah hitched the horses. He had never stood so close to such a beautiful woman, and he spent time just inhaling her scent. He felt so awkward, even more with her than he did with Patrick, for she was a woman and an aristocrat. But she didn't seem to trade on her looks or on her bearing. She spoke to him directly, and didn't appear to care about his rough speech and dirty clothes. Still, he couldn't help wondering what kind of man he'd have been if given a different background and an education. Maybe he'd have found a pretty woman who would have been his wife, had some babies, and made a life for them all.

He shuffled his feet and rubbed his chin, wishing he'd stopped to clean up and maybe shave. He thought about asking her what she thought of the weather, but dismissed it. He rocked on the balls of his feet and considered telling her about Newgate, but decided it wasn't pretty talk for such a pretty lady, and he didn't want to disgust her more than he probably had already. So he said nothing.

It didn't seem to matter, because Camille just stood there silently, wrapped in her cloak and watching as Jonah finished with the reins. Herrick helped load and strap the trunk to the rear of the carriage, and then he opted to ride on top with Jonah rather than inside with Camille. There was only so much torture a dog could take.

No one stopped them from leaving. Camille looked out the window of the carriage and stared at the bulk of the dark house as they passed it. Amelia was in there in her rooms, probably in her bed and still feeling ill from whatever plagued her.

Camille hoped she felt horrible. She hoped her mother suffered with some wretched illness that sapped her strength and made every joint ache, and that she vomited until she couldn't walk and coughed until she couldn't breathe. She hoped it lasted for a long, long time.

Amelia would pay, she vowed. She'd pay for what she did to Patrick. Camille would see to it.

The pain had been difficult enough to bear when it had been mine alone, she thought, but I had deserved most of it. Amelia had gone too far when she hurt Patrick.

"Consequences, Mother," she whispered. The carriage left the property and rumbled down the road that led into the clog of London's streets. "'Tis time for me to thresh what you have sown."

* * *

Flanna welcomed Camille, fussed around the room, and called for a pot of tea and some biscuits. She straightened the rumpled bed and rummaged through Camille's trunks for her lovely gowns, hanging each one with care in the armoire. As she placed the last one on the rack, she let her knotted hands linger for a moment on silk softer than a breath, trailing a finger over lace that bloomed like a flower.

She turned back to Camille, who sat staring at the flames in the hearth. "You were right in comin' to me. 'Tis pleased I am to have you here."

Camille glanced up to Flanna, standing across the room in a long nightgown of flannel. "'Tis kind of you, considering I woke you. I apologize again, but I have only so much coin and I had to provide a room for Jonah and Herrick."

"I would never question your motive, dearie. You've been nothin' but kind to me." Flanna took a seat in the chair opposite Camille and pulled a blanket to her lap. "Now will you be tellin' me, or 'tis it not a thin' you wish to be talkin' about?"

"The latter, Flanna. I am sorry."

"Aye, 'tis as I suspected it would be. Take your time and work it out, love. An' if you feel a need, I have a listenin' ear for you."

Camille nodded, grateful for the quiet place to sit and think, where Amelia did not walk the halls and fear did not lurk in every shadow. The bed looked soft and welcoming, and she longed to lie down and close her eyes, but she knew peace would not be found in sleep. There would be no peace until she got Patrick out of prison and repaid her debts to him. She wished only that she could accomplish it without seeing him.

He would read her eyes.

It held her back, knowing he would look into her and see everything. He would know her shame. She had never been able to hide anything from him. She put her face in her hands and sighed. And then she stood up, crossed to her clothing, and began to unlace her gown. She would see to it the gaol keeper would not doubt a word she said. She would see to it that Patrick would get his freedom back.

And then she would return to the inn with Flanna, crawl beneath the covers of the soft bed, and rest. When she no longer felt tired, she'd see to Amelia. First to her torture, then to her ruin.

She chose the burgundy velvet gown for its décolletage and the way it clung to her curves. She brushed her hair until it gleamed, dark and lustrous in the candlelight. She twisted it, wove in strands of gold beads, piled it atop her head, and fastened it with carved combs of gold. She rubbed lotion into her skin, and the scents of lemon and vanilla filled the room. She pulled on stockings of silk and slipped into burgundy slippers of the same velvet.

Camille looked at her reflection, saw the ghost of what she had been only months before, and wondered what Patrick would think of her after all this time.

Jonah and Herrick waited for her in the front room of the inn, both clothed in black. They each had pistols and knives strapped around their waists, and though their appearance couldn't be more different, the looks of grim resolve were the same.

"Are you ready? Do you both understand what we will do?"

Both men nodded and pulled their cloaks around their shoulders in swirls of black cloth. They set out of the inn as the hour approached midnight. Camille settled herself on the seat and pulled the tapestry robe across her lap. The warming pan threw off feeble heat, and her breath was a frosty cloud in the light of the lantern. She set her bundle beside her and nestled her bottle of brandy on the seat. She reached up and rapped on the roof, settling back just in time as the carriage lurched into motion.

Somewhere ahead, the Old Bailey loomed in the darkness. Inside the carriage, Camille drew in several breaths, as deeply as her tightly laced stays would allow. She rested one slender hand on the bundle next to her and the other on her right thigh, reassured by the familiar feel of her concealed weapon. Though Herrick and Jonah had assured her protection, nothing eased her anxiety like the steel of her dagger, sheathed and strapped under her skirts.

Tonight she would set Patrick free, and she would not allow her fears to control her. Tonight she freed herself as surely as she would him. Like an actor on the stage, Camille had dressed for the part she played. Her elegant clothing became her costume, the curves of her body, her props. Her hard-won knowledge of manipulation would be her inspiration, lending her the wiles to achieve her goal. But she would need more than clever strategy if her purpose would be met. She would need to put aside her fears long enough to confront her past. And if she could do that, maybe she could even win back a future.

Hope.

It had awakened to plague her again, restless, frightening. If only Camille could rid herself of that affliction and be resigned to her fate, she would have peace. But like a sickness that knows no cure, hope had surfaced once again, curling through her blood and infecting her mind. That she longed for what she could never have had been the source of all her suffering, and yet, she couldn't resist her own hope, once again. Against all she had been told and all she believed, came this tiny spiraling of optimism that she could set things aright.

Cold rain began to pelt the carriage, blown into staccato tattoos by stronger gusts of wind, announcing the start of a storm. Camille rechecked her carefully packed bundle and assured herself all was in readiness. Her preparation had been thorough; the necessary arrangements had been made. She would see Patrick out of prison before the night was gone.

Jonah had slowed the pace of the carriage, no doubt due to the weather. The gentler bouncing and swaying felt soothing. Camille readjusted herself on the seat and propped a pillow behind her head, at once feeling incredibly tired, powerless to stop the wandering of her mind. In a breath she was young and innocent once again, living in Beauport by the sea. Memories of Patrick surfaced. Camille knew she lay vulnerable to the force of emotions and hopes too long denied, so long suppressed.

But for once, she let them come.

CHAPTER 22

The Old Bailey jutted into the night sky with impunity.
Here justice got served, and if not justice, then an example
to all frightening enough to cause deference to the laws.

Camille could hear Jonah outside the carriage, clucking to the horses as he tethered them. She heard him ask
Herrick if he was ready, and listened to the grunt of a reply.
She breathed, in and out, forcing regularity. With trembling fingers, she reached out and touched her bottle,
needing another draught to sustain her. Jonah opened the
door and she dropped her hand to the bundle instead,
gathered her wits, and accepted Jonah's hand to alight
from the carriage. Wind slapped her face and flung
droplets of icy rain into her eyes. She pulled her cloak
tighter around her body.

They entered Newgate through the main door. The
stench assaulted them immediately. Unmistakable odors
of unwashed bodies, offal, and illness, combined with
dank water and spoiling food. Camille pressed a perfumed
handkerchief to her face and followed Herrick down a long
stone corridor. Tallow candles stuck in waxy iron rings led
the way. Somewhere in the shadows something once
human moaned, its suffering heard in every syllable.

The one called Thick sat behind his desk, a slab of

scarred oak on sturdy legs. His head lolled back, his mouth hanging open as rumbling snores echoed off the stone walls.

Camille looked to Jonah, then Herrick, and they nodded their readiness. She lowered her handkerchief and inclined her head in response. Herrick cleared his throat.

"Thick. Wake up, mate."

No response. Herrick tried again, louder. "Wake up, bloke! A lady be 'ere to see ye!"

Thick grunted and straightened his head, rubbing his bleary eyes with blunt fingers. "What're ye doin' back, 'Errick, ye bastard? Ye paid yer debts and yer free, or was our 'ospitality so gentle ye came back?"

Herrick took a step forward and leaned on Thick's desk. "I come again on business. A lady be needin' yer ear fer a space."

He moved aside and Camille stepped into the ring of light from a lantern. She reached up and pulled back the cowl of her cloak, revealing her face and hair. She allowed him a moment to gawk, and then she unfastened the frogs at her neck, slipped the cloak from her shoulders, and handed it to Jonah. Thick's eyes traveled from her face to her breasts to her waist, back to her face, and then skimmed her hair and fell again to stare at her breasts. She took another step forward and curved her lips in a smile. She removed her mother's signet ring from her finger and set it on the tabletop, where it gleamed with wealth and importance in the candlelight. "I am Amelia Bradburn, Duchess of Eton. I am here for my prisoner. I feel he has learned his lesson."

Thick's eyes didn't move from the delicious swell of creamy skin above the velvet gown. "What ye say?"

"I say I am here for my prisoner, Patrick Mullen. I arranged for his imprisonment and had him sent here by the magistrate. I want him back. He has served his time."

"If'n the magistrate put 'im 'ere, it be the magistrate who

gets 'im out." Thick looked up briefly as he spoke and then let his eyes drop back down. He licked his lips and sighed.

Camille leaned forward and dropped a sack of coins on the desk. It landed with a solid *clunk* beside the ring, and Thick's eyes widened. "Of course, I understand your plight, my good man. Allow me to compensate you for your trouble."

Greed and lust competed for his attention, and in the end, lust won out. He stared at the elegant line of her neck, the flutter of her pulse, the curve of her smile. He smiled back to her, and hoped she didn't notice the rot on his teeth or the shabbiness of his clothes. "Mullen, eh?"

"Yes, Patrick Mullen. I had him sent here after he displeased me. I am afraid I have a temper, you see." Camille trailed a finger over the swell of her breast and shrugged. "I am accustomed to my way of doing things, and this Patrick angered me. 'Twas a trivial matter; I see that now. I acted quickly, in my haste to see him punished, and called the magistrate forthwith. But I have found leniency in my heart for this commoner, and I have come to set the matter right."

"'E is innocent, ye say?"

"Indeed. Please release him."

Thick scrubbed his hands over his face, confused. What was the penalty for disobeying a duchess? he wondered. Would she see to it that he lost his position if he questioned her authority? Would the magistrate come looking for the prisoner and find out he had let him go? "What if someone comes lookin' fer 'im?"

Camille smiled once again, a brilliant flash that blinded Thick's mind. "You are a smart man to consider every outcome. 'Tis only the magistrate and myself who know the man is here. I will leave my ring with you. If anyone questions you, show it as proof that I alone arranged his release." She withdrew another sack of coins and placed it on the desk next to the first. "I will compensate you for the inconvenience, of course."

Thick looked at the riches on the desk and then back to the beauty of the woman who had come under the shroud of midnight. "Ye really want the bloke out, eh?"

"I do. I must set a wrong aright." Sadness gripped her with the words she spoke, thickening her voice and making her lips shake. "Please help me. The man is innocent, and his being here is my doing. I will not rest until I know I have paid my debt to him."

Thick stood, picked up the two sacks of coins, and fastened them in his breeches. "Follow me."

Jonah stepped forward. "Hold, my lady. 'Tis not a sight for a woman. Allow Herrick to fetch your man, and I will escort you to the carriage."

Camille hesitated, looking to Herrick in silent question.

"'E's right, me lady. Yer not needin' ter see 'ow 'e's been livin'. I'll get 'im an' bring 'im out ter ye."

Jonah took Camille's elbow and then turned back to Herrick. "See to it he is given clean water and soap so he may wash. Give the man a bit of dignity."

Camille watched as Herrick and Thick disappeared into the bowels of the prison, and she let Jonah tug on her elbow and lead her back outside and into the carriage.

Alone once again, she pulled her cloak around her body and covered herself with the lap robe. But she couldn't stop shaking.

Patrick stepped out of Newgate and filled his lungs with the sweetest air he'd ever inhaled. He indulged in a few more deep breaths before approaching the carriage. He paused as Herrick moved to take his seat beside Jonah. "Thank you, Herrick. 'Tis a debt I will repay in any way you wish."

Herrick stopped and shuffled his feet, running his hand across his chin. "I want a life, me friend. I want what ye can't give a bloke like me."

Patrick shook his hand and pulled him into a hard hug, slapping him on the back. "Thank you."

Herrick returned the slap and tugged on the rough blankets Patrick wore like a Grecian toga. "Ye look purty in a dress."

"These are like heaven after those dirty clothes. I couldn't bear to put them back on after I washed."

Herrick jerked his thumb toward the carriage. "Jonah says she is bad off."

An image flashed in Patrick's mind, of the way Camille had taken a swallow of brandy for every morsel of food. "I will see to her."

Herrick nodded and climbed up next to Jonah. Patrick stood for a moment and then opened the door.

Her eyes met his. Each held their breath, and she looked away. He climbed in, closed the door, and sat on the seat across from her.

She looked scared and small. And as beautiful as his memory. "You came for me," he said softly.

She stared at the flame in the lantern, watching it burn. "You put your trust in me. I had to come."

"You could have sent someone else," he pointed out, his voice gentle. He couldn't help noticing how the light from the lantern turned her skin to golden cream, and how her long lashes framed her impossible eyes.

"You could have trusted someone else," she said, and her lips parted and trembled.

"Look at me."

"I do not wish to." She reached up and rapped on the roof, and the carriage began to move away from Newgate.

"You have changed."

She sighed, and her breath hitched. "Everything has changed."

Patrick's hands twisted in the rough fabric that covered his body. He struggled for the control to keep from grabbing her and holding her against him. It was only the desolation in her eyes that stopped him. "Not my love for you, Camille. That has not changed."

"'Twas a long time ago." She stared at the shifting light thrown on the floor by the lantern.

"Not so long."

"You are wrong. 'Twas a lifetime."

"Aye, perhaps you are right. A lifetime before I met you, and a lifetime since I was taken from you." He stopped, held his breath for a moment, and watched her face. He saw something change, a softness, a glimmer in her eyes. "But when I was with you, my love, that was life itself."

She said nothing, aware only that his voice was completely the same. It ran through her like a river of warmth, and she closed her eyes at the sensation.

"Do you remember when you told me that I reminded you of life? We stood in your cottage, with only a few spaces between us and a thousand reasons why we could never love each other." Patrick's voice shook, like his heart, like his hands. "And you said I was like life itself."

"I remember," she whispered.

"Freedom, vitality, honesty. This is what you told me you saw in me."

"Yes."

"You kept me sane when I thought I had lost everything. I had only to remember what you saw in me, and I could see it in myself. I saw myself through your eyes."

Her breaths came shallow and fast. It was as she had feared—his pull was too strong, his love too honest. And there she sat, damaged and disgusting in her own eyes. She had ruined everything they'd had, and yet he reached to her again. "If it had not been for me, you would never have lost everything."

"If it had not been for you, I never would have loved," he said. "You were my magic rose, Camille. I found you blooming in an impossible place, oblivious to those who tried to change you." He searched for words, frustrated beyond all measure to finally be able to speak to her, only to find her so remote and mere language so completely inadequate. "But it was only magic because I understood it. I understood *you*."

Images of afternoon sunlight shafting through the wavy glass windows of her cottage flashed in her memory, and of Patrick as he touched her precious things and read her foolish words of poetry, and of all the things he had questioned her about. He hadn't just treated her like a lady— he'd treated her like a woman. Like a human, complete with feelings and needs. He'd been her magic, too. She felt a burning behind her eyes and in her throat. She pushed it away reflexively. "Great love followed by great loss. 'Tis as I feared it would be."

"Our story is not over."

She lifted her eyes and looked at him. Looked *into* him. And for a brief moment, let him see just what festered inside her. "This is the end. I came to finish it, Patrick, not to prolong it."

Fear sliced through his heart and stabbed in his gut. Not at her words, but at the pain in her eyes. It was the same look she had had the night he came for her, and he watched her drink herself numb. "What happened to you?"

She averted her gaze, suddenly afraid. Terrified he had seen into her soul as he used to do. "Please ride in silence."

"So you can suffer in secrecy? What good will come of that?"

"No good. And no good will come of speaking, either. 'Tis best for us both to go our separate ways."

He couldn't understand what was happening. Hadn't she come for him? "What are you saying? That you will deposit me where you wish and leave me? Am I not a man to decide for myself?"

"For tonight I will take you to the inn. Tomorrow I will take you to your father, or to your ship. You can move on with your life. I came for you, didn't I?" Camille spoke tonelessly now, as exhaustion threatened to engulf her. "I repaid my debt to you. 'Tis done and I am free of it."

"This is why you came for me? To repay a debt?"

"Correct. And 'tis done."

Patrick felt the stirrings of anger. "No."

Camille arched a brow. "What do you mean, no?"

"I am saying, no, 'tis not good enough. I require more payment than that, you see."

"What?"

"I want more."

She sat forward a bit, unaware she struck a challenging pose. "What? What could you possibly want beyond your freedom?"

"Herrick is getting a room at an inn. I want that, too, but for more than a few hours until dawn. I'm tired and I haven't had a peaceful rest in months. I want a hot bath and a soft bed. And I want you to send for my clothes. Of course, I will need to be reimbursed for all my costs. I know you cannot give me back the months of my life, but you can provide for me comfortably for the next few months, and I will consider that equable payment."

Camille stared at him, aghast. "This is not a negotiation."

"You are wrong."

"You will hold my debt over my head and extort what you want?"

He folded his arms across his chest. "Correct."

"You cannot do that."

"Why can't I?" Patrick cocked his head and waited for her answer. Watched as her eyes flashed with indignation.

"I did not order you taken, and I did not order you put in prison. I came and got you out! How dare you demand more!"

"What are you saying, Camille? Is it your debt or not?"

She spluttered to silence and seethed, his plan now so transparent she was more annoyed with herself for not having seen through it than with him for using it. "You are being difficult."

"Tell me."

And she didn't need him to elaborate; she understood him now, as she always had. "I will not."

"Tell me."

She felt a boiling inside her, temper and shame swirling together like a tempest. "I will not!"

"Admit to me the things you can't admit to yourself. *Tell me.*"

"Stop it, I warn you!"

Patrick moved in front of her, knelt on the floor, and took her hands in his. He felt her jerk, as if to pull away, and then she stopped and let him hold her.

It is the same, she thought. The same connected feeling when he touched her. And it didn't matter that he was wrapped in woolen blankets and that he stank of lye soap and brackish water. It mattered not one bit that his hair was greasy and lank. It was the same, and his touch coursed through her whole body, like his voice.

I am not the same girl, she reminded herself bitterly. This cannot work. "Say what you will; it makes no difference."

"Tell me," he whispered. "You need to."

Only words, Amelia had said once. What are words? Sounds on the air, nothing more. But Camille no longer believed that. Words were power. They could devastate, and in some cases, one could hunger for words more than breath. Words were everything. If she tried to tell him of the night in the stables, would her words bring a look of revulsion to those eyes? Would her words make him ill as she told him his baby had died from her recklessness? Once spoken, words could never be retrieved.

If she told him, perhaps he would stop loving her. It was what she knew she should do. But the hurt in his eyes would break her, and she knew that, too.

Camille turned her head and closed her eyes.

"Whatever it is, you can trust me to understand."

"Trust is a dream, Patrick. Understanding is a lie."

He lowered his head to her lap and spoke only four

words that demanded nothing, but asked for everything. "Please stay with me."

He was so close, so open. He filtered into her like sunlight, warm and wanted. She felt so weary fighting it, fighting everything. She longed to touch him, to feel the warmth of his skin on her fingers. She curled her fingers under and pushed the thoughts away. "I cannot."

"I would shoulder it for you," he said. "I am a big lad, and strong. I'll take it for you, Camille, for a while, at least. Let me help you." He ran his hands over hers. "I know I can, if you'll let me."

"My burdens are my own; they are for no one else to share." The image of her little boy running on a sandy beach came into her mind, followed by the memory of the rape and her bleeding womb. She shuddered convulsively. How could she ever tell him about any of that?

"I will protect you," he said, and he sounded definite. "I will never allow anything to hurt you again."

"Impossible," she whispered. "I will take the pain no matter where I go."

"It does not have to be so."

Her lips trembled. "And yet, it is so."

He held her hands tighter in his, words of denial on his lips. Her ring pressed into his palm and he pulled back, lifting it closer to the lantern. Prisms shot through the stones, yellow light glinting on the gold. "Who?"

She swallowed hard. "Bret Kimball."

"Do you love him?"

"No."

"Will you marry him?"

Confusion shadowed her face. "I do not know."

Fury and jealousy made him hold her hand too hard. "You are my wife."

She pulled her hand away from his. "No clergy heard those vows. No one would recognize such a union."

Patrick let out a short laugh of disbelief. He reached down to her foot and pulled it into his hand. With his other hand he yanked down her stocking, tearing the silk. He ignored her gasps of protest.

The amber bracelet glowed in a circle of sunlight around her ankle.

"You wear it still." He looked into her eyes, his own brow raised, satisfied and challenging.

She struggled to pull her leg free of his grasp, as his touch on her bare skin sent too many feelings swimming in her blood. "It does not mean what you think."

"It means in your heart you are still my wife."

"No, that can never be so."

He grinned as he looked into her, and his hand tightened on her naked calf. "And yet, it is so."

Heat shot through her leg and into her belly. A smile tugged at her lips, a glimmer of the girl who had once smiled so easily at him. "You are impossible."

Camille reached out a trembling finger to touch his face, tracing over his cheek just above the unkempt snarl of his beard. He had known her with his mouth and his hands; he had seen inside her with those wonderful eyes. He had given without taking. He had made her so happy.

What was she doing? She dropped her hand back to her lap and let out a broken sigh. "This will not work."

"I love you," he said simply.

"You love who you think I am."

"No. *You*."

"Who I was, then."

Patrick picked up her hand and pressed a kiss on the inside of her wrist, just where the pulse throbbed beneath the surface. "Who you are inside, Camille."

She didn't pull back. She couldn't. But she was certain of one thing. "You don't know who that is anymore. You couldn't possibly."

"The woman who came to Newgate to get me. The woman who risks more than she thinks she can afford to lose."

Camille knew he meant what he said. She knew his love to be real and true. But she had been damaged and broken inside, so much so that she feared she could never be whole again, and she knew that, too. Patrick deserved more than what she could give, and it broke her heart. "I have changed."

"Tell me how."

The carriage lurched to a stop and then bounced as Jonah and Herrick climbed down. Camille pulled her hand away and rested it on the door. She turned back to Patrick once more. "You can rest here. I have arranged a room for you." She paused and then forced herself to speak again, to answer his demand. "We can finish this conversation in the morning."

He nodded and alighted from the carriage, turning to give her a hand down. A groggy stable boy stumbled out and took the reins, yawning as the odd group of patrons headed inside. The inn was dark but for a fire that burned low in the hearth. Camille lit a candle and handed Patrick the key to his room, and he followed her. Jonah and Herrick stopped in front of their room and whispered their good nights. But Jonah waited until Camille was out of sight with the mariner close behind her. He waited until the light from her candle had completely disappeared around a corner. He let himself into his cold room and closed and locked his door.

Camille held the candle as Patrick fumbled with the lock. "You're trembling. You are cold?"

"Aye."

"There was no time for me to purchase you clothing. I am sorry."

"I have endured worse. Dismiss it from your mind."

He pushed open the door, took the candle from Camille, and used it to light several others. Then he gestured for her to take a seat by the cold fireplace as he knelt to make a fire. Camille shivered in her cloak and watched him work, as he arranged kindling over dried grass and lit it. The grass took the spark immediately in a flash of light and heat, and Patrick patiently fed slivers of wood into the flame until the fire took hold. He arranged thin logs over the new embers and sat back, content.

"'Tis been too long since I sat in front of a fire," he said with a sigh.

"A simple pleasure."

"Aye."

She put her hands on the arms of the chair, trying to summon the will and the energy to push herself to her feet. "I will return to my room now and let you rest."

He didn't stop looking into the fire, afraid she would see the depth of his need. "Please stay with me. I was alone in a cell for a long while." He looked directly at her, then. "I have longed for you, Camille."

She took a deep breath and let it out slowly. "I don't want to hurt you more than I have."

"Hurt me by being with me?" He cocked his head to the side. "Camille, I have been beaten and held prisoner. I've committed murder and caused it, too." He paused briefly, thinking of Tate. He swallowed heavily. "I was charged with rape and imprisoned without a trial. I'm not complaining, you see, but only pointing out that it was all for the want of being with you. If you're thinking to spare me by leaving me, it's only then that it was all for naught."

She hesitated, and her eyes fell to the bed and then back to him, looking at his profile as firelight danced across his skin and turned it golden. Words of fables and legends whispered in her mind, fanciful snippets of dreams long forgotten and ignored. "I couldn't possibly. Flanna is like to get worried."

"Flanna is like to get woken. Stay with me, Camille. I promise I will not touch you if you do not wish it." He shrugged lightly, and his accent thickened as his embarrassment grew. He stared at the fire. "I'll not be blaming you if the look of me repulses you, or the smell of me, for that matter. I will hold myself away from you, or I'll sleep on the floor. I only wish to have you near me."

Such a simple request, she thought. Spoken plainly,

honestly, and without motive. Her damaged heart had no defense to his unguarded need. "I have no nightclothes."

Patrick lifted a corner of the blankets he wore and grinned. "Neither do I. But I'll swaddle myself with a sheet like a babe if it means you'll stay."

And in that instant, Camille realized she felt completely safe. She noticed that her hand had not once drifted to her thigh to check her weapon, and that she had not once longed for the numbing relief of brandy. She felt more relaxed in the room with Patrick as they sat by the fire than she had felt since he had been taken.

As much as she knew she had no right to it, she didn't want it to end. Just one night, she reasoned. Just one night so we can both rest, warm and safe. "Only for tonight, then."

He inclined his head in agreement and met her eyes. "I'd like to ask you something, Camille."

She hesitated, then nodded. How could she deny him after all the pain she'd caused?

"What you said, in the carriage . . . You said no clergy had heard our vows. That no one would recognize our union." He paused and cleared his throat, then continued. "I have kept my vows to you, Camille, every one. I have honored you in the only way I know how to—with my body and my soul. I gave myself over to it, to my love for you, and I never once regretted any of the things I've had to do in order to get back to you.

"You are mine, Camille, whether you want me or not, whether you'll deny me or have me. You are my wife, by God; I swear it now as I swore it that night by the ocean. And so I'll ask you, now, do you mean to forswear the vows you made to me?"

Camille sat stock-still, feeling the pounding of her heart, the rush of her blood through her body, and the dense emotion as it clenched and churned inside her, wanting release. "I meant everything I said that night."

His voice grew harder, more insistent. "Do you mean it now?"

"I don't know," she whispered.

"Damn you, Camille, you will answer me. Do you mean it now?"

"I want to, Patrick, but I cannot." She turned her head and closed her eyes to avoid his gaze, unable to bear the weight of his stare and the way he could strip her to her soul, without defenses.

He saw the fluttering of her pulse in her neck and felt his anger relent. "You want to," he sighed, "and that's supposed to be good enough for me? I once held you to my body. I once spoke to you with my heart, Camille, as I do now. There was only trust and love between us."

His voice dropped until it was so low and soft it was like the rush of flame over wood. "If you'll ask me to walk away from you, to rip out my heart and live without it, I tell you this now, I will not go easily. You are mine. My wife. I've fought for you all this time, and whatever the demon is, Camille, I'll battle it beside you."

Camille pushed herself from the chair, swaying with pent-up emotions and pure exhaustion. "Patrick," she whispered, "will you take me to bed and hold me? Will you ease me for now, and not ask questions?"

He got to his feet, clutching the ends of his blankets to keep them from slipping to the floor. Her request had reached out and squeezed his heart. "I will, my love."

She went to him and presented her back. He unlaced her gown and couldn't help watching as she stepped out of the folds of velvet. Her gossamer shift hid nothing, and he feasted his eyes on the slender curves of her body, traveling down to the stretch of creamy thigh above her stocking.

The dagger stood out as black as death against the white of her skin, bound to her with a length of ribbon.

"No questions," he said softly.

Camille sighed as she unfastened the sheath and set the

dagger aside. She had never felt so tired. "We will talk in the morning."

"Aye. Get in bed, Camille."

She hid a yawn behind her hand and climbed into the bed, pulling the cold sheets around her body. Patrick dropped the blankets and went to the washstand, lathered a rag with soap, and gave himself another brisk wash before toweling off and going to the bed. He climbed in beside her. She hesitated a minute, but reminded herself, just one night. She moved close to his body and he pulled her close to him, wrapping his arms around her. And she thought it was like coming home.

Like springtime after winter's siege.

He buried his face in her hair and breathed deeply. "I missed you so."

"'Tis like a dream," she whispered, her eyes closed and her lips parted on a broken breath. He loved her. She could feel it in his arms, like the heat that radiated from his body. He loved her, and she was probably hurting him further by letting him hold her. But it felt so good, and she didn't have the strength to pull away.

"No, Camille. Nothing could be more real than this. 'Tis as it is meant to be," he said.

He cuddled her close to his body. Camille pressed her cheek to his chest and listened to the steady beating of his heart. Meant to be, he said. She knew she could never be with him the way he wanted. More than anything, she wished things had been different. She wished she could be the girl he wanted her to be. Her eyes burned with tears that wouldn't be suppressed. Nothing felt worse than knowing she was letting him down once again. So much lost, she thought. A sob choked her until it escaped.

Patrick stroked her hair and held her even closer. "Sure and you'll let it out, love. You'll let it out, and you'll feel better for it."

The tears were slow at first, then hot and fast. She wept until she was raw. She cried until she was dry. He held her all the while, whispering soothing, meaningless sounds until she could weep no more.

When it was over he got out of the bed and poured her water from the pitcher. She drank it down like a healing elixir, cold, refreshing, and clean. When it was gone, he poured her more. She handed back the empty glass and settled back into the pillows, lifting the blankets when he approached so he could slide back next to her.

Patrick pulled her close once again and brushed damp strands of hair away from her face. The fire burned low.

"Did you make love to Veronica?"

The question came unexpectedly, but he only raised a brow. "The girl from your town."

"Yes," she whispered.

"I took her to my bed once, before I met you."

Camille yawned again, until her jaw cracked. His warmth seeped into her, and she thought how it was not like the warmth of brandy or of wool or fire. It was the heat of life and blood and flesh, visceral and real. "She said you quoted poetry to her. She said you gave her a brooch that had belonged to your father."

"I never gave her anything. I never gave her my heart, Camille. It was a moment of lust after a long voyage." He shrugged slightly. "I am only a man."

"She said . . ." her voice drifted off, and she pressed her cheek against his chest again. "Never mind it. It does not matter, anyway."

"It does matter if it hurt you."

"When she told me, and it sounded so much like what you'd said to me . . ." her voice died off, then grew stronger. "I wanted to have faith."

"I know."

"I am sorry," she said quietly. "There is so much to be sorry for."

He held her closer, burying his face in her hair while he thought about all she said, and all the things she didn't say. "Your believing the lies did not stop me from coming back for you, did it?"

"No. Jonah says you came into my room. He says you held me."

"I did." And he remembered how she'd been so drunk she'd not been able to wake, and he wondered without asking why she had done that. Reflexively, he pulled her closer to his body now, holding his hips away from her so she wouldn't feel his arousal.

"I thought it a dream."

"I know. You spoke to me."

"I did?"

"Aye, and you said 'he is gone.' Then you said 'I never saw him.' I won't be asking who didn't you see, Camille. Not tonight. But I will ask you tomorrow."

She shivered and huddled against him. *Just one night.* In his arms the rape seemed so far away. "The fire is burning out."

"Forget the fire."

"Yes. Let's forget everything for now. Let's pretend it all away. Tell me a story, Patrick."

The sound of her voice was thick and tired, and he knew she had had enough for one night. So he held her and stroked her back and her hair as he told her the story of a peasant boy who could fight like a warrior, and how he made himself a king by the strength of his sword arm. When her breathing grew soft and regular, he stopped talking and tried to join her in sleep.

It wouldn't come. Unable to rest, he fitted the facts like a puzzle, turning them over and moving them about. In his mind he kept seeing her in the firelight, a black dagger strapped to white skin. He matched that to her eyes, so ravaged and sad, and the way she had looked at him in the carriage, as if she were frightened he'd know a secret she dared not tell him. There were also the tears that racked her body as if they were torn directly from her soul.

It all pointed to a likelihood he hated to contemplate.

CHAPTER 23

Patrick woke early, built a new fire, and kept the drapes closed to the sunlight. He glanced around the pretty, comfortable room and then back to Camille, who still slept in the big bed, covers pulled over her shoulders, her hair tumbled across the pillow. In sleep she looked so innocent and vulnerable that his heart ached.

He pulled a blanket around his waist, stood over her, and touched her hair. Then he slipped from the room, taking the key so he could lock it behind him. He went in search of Jonah.

The knock on the door sounded extra loud in the quiet hallway. Herrick opened the door, clutching his breeches in front of him. "Yer up early, mate."

"Aye. Do you have any coin left from the money I gave you?"

"Aye. Quite a bit o' what ye gave."

"Excellent. Would you be willing to fetch me a new set of clothes? There is a ready-made store near the docks. By the time you dress and take a livery there, they should be opening their shop."

Herrick nodded and pulled on his breeches and his tattered shirt. While he completed dressing, Patrick went to the small writing desk furnished by the inn and wrote a list of his needs. "I appreciate it, friend."

Herrick grunted and took the list and the purse, waving once on his way out the door.

Patrick sat on Herrick's rumpled bed and looked at Jonah, who had awoken and now sat in his bed watching Patrick with a measured gaze.

"She sleeps. Do you mind if I wait in your room while I call for a bath?"

"Not at all. I have a razor if you care to make use of it," Jonah offered.

"You don't like the beard?"

Jonah looked at him appraisingly. "Perhaps if I were a mouse looking for a nest."

Patrick laughed and left the room to make arrangements for the use of the bathing chamber. When he returned, Jonah had already dressed and had wet and combed his hair. Patrick noticed the razor and a mug, brush, and comb had been set out on the washstand. "My thanks."

Jonah nodded and set to tidying the bed while Patrick laid wet towels over his beard to soften it.

"You care about her," Patrick stated.

"Deeply." Jonah put the pillow back in place and looked around for something else to occupy him.

"I am at a disadvantage, Jonah. You see, I cannot hope to help her if I do not know all the facts."

Jonah smoothed the sheets though they were not wrinkled. "It is not for me to betray her confidence. Speak to Camille."

"You would see it as a betrayal?"

Jonah gave up and sat on the bed, watching as Patrick stropped the razor. "Camille would see it as such, and so I do."

Patrick lathered his face and began to scrape the blade along his skin, whisking away the beard that had itched until he thought he'd lose his mind. When he was done, he pressed a clean wet towel to his face and sighed his pleasure. He wiped away the last of the lather and rinsed the razor before turning back to Jonah. He deliberately didn't respond to what Jonah had said. "Thank you again. My bath should be ready now."

Patrick wrapped his blanket tighter around his waist and headed down the hall to the bathing chamber. A huge copper tub dominated the room. A table stood to the side of it, holding folded cloths for drying next to soaps and oils. Patrick sniffed the soaps, selected a bar, and stepped into the steaming water, then sat down and leaned back, his eyes closed in appreciation.

The water had cooled by the time he opened his eyes again, and he scrubbed his skin and hair until he felt clean. After toweling, he left the blankets and wrapped in the damp cloths; he went back to Jonah and Herrick's room to wait. Jonah sat in the same place where Patrick had left him, except his head was now buried in his hands.

His voice sounded muffled. "I do not know the right thing to do."

"I will not ask you to be disloyal to her, Jonah."

"Is it disloyal if it helps her?"

"I don't know," Patrick replied fairly. "Even the purest of intentions can lead to disaster."

Jonah looked up and met his eyes. "I love her."

"I guessed as much."

"You will resent me for that?" Jonah half asked, half stated.

Patrick shrugged. "You don't know me, nor I you. But I know Camille, and I can't do so without loving her. I wouldn't expect different from you."

"I thought about hiding the truth from her," Jonah admitted. "I thought I would convince her to leave with me, and that in time . . ."

Patrick watched Jonah curiously, wondering why he made this confession. "Why didn't you?"

Jonah's shoulders slumped and he hated himself for his

weaknesses. He'd been too afraid to help her, too afraid to protect her, and in the end, too afraid to try to steal her away. "She would never love me the way she loves you."

Patrick sat on the bed across from Jonah, relief in his voice, his body, and down to his bones. "Loves. Not loved."

"Indeed. It is not lack of love that keeps her from you, Patrick."

"What, then?"

Jonah looked up to the ceiling. "God forgive me if I am wrong." He thought that perhaps for once he would do the right thing, and let the consequences be damned. And then he looked back to Patrick and told him about the day he had met Camille, when she had saved him from a brutal whipping. He told him about their fast friendship and the plan to leave England together. He told him about the day in the stables when a man in a mask had raped Camille. Then he told him about the child she had been carrying, and how it had left her in a hemorrhage of blood, and how Camille had been drinking herself numb ever since.

"Our child," Patrick said on a breath. He let the idea wash over him, of a baby he'd never known he had created, secreted away in Camille's body and then ripped from its safe cocoon by force. He wondered if it had been a boy or a girl, and he said a silent prayer for it, that it hadn't suffered too much, and that it was safe in the Lord's memory.

"She blames herself."

"It is not her fault," Patrick said quietly, more to himself than to Jonah. "Jesus." He sat back and stared at nothing. Rape. He imagined all too vividly Camille being pushed down, her legs shoved apart, and then brutally entered. He thought of the tearing of flesh and the blood.

And then the picture of a black dagger against white flesh, and green eyes gone cold and ravaged, like a fierce, frightened animal.

"Who?"

Jonah didn't need an explanation. "We do not know. Camille said he wore a mask."

"Jesus," Patrick said again. "And her mother . . ."

"The duchess did not care to expose the family to scandal. The magistrate was not called until you arrived for Camille."

"I could have assumed as much." Patrick cursed foully under his breath. "And Camille . . ." his voice died out, and all he could do was sit helpless. Nothing could give Camille back her child, or take away the memory of being violated. He could love her, but that wasn't enough, and he was man enough to realize it.

The door opened and Herrick entered, bearing wrapped parcels of all shapes and sizes. He dumped the lot of it onto his bed, pulled the smallest from the bunch, and tossed it to Patrick. The aroma of fresh scones wafted into the room as Patrick tore the wrapping. After weeks of near starvation, his belly lurched and grumbled at the sight of food. "Herrick, you are a god among mere mortal men."

Patrick, biting into a scone as he unwrapped the other packages, saw that every item purchased by Herrick was some shade of brown. There were tan breeches, a tan shirt, a brown jacket, brown stockings, and brown leather boots that looked like they'd be a little too small.

Herrick looked up from the scones as Patrick dressed. He grimaced theatrically. "I 'ope yer fancy clothes fit. If'n I never go back ter that shop it'll be too soon."

"After I get back to my accounts and I have access to my money again, you're up next for new clothes, Herrick." Patrick adjusted the breeches, ignoring that they were too short, and tucked in the shirt that actually fit properly. He pulled on the boots, which were tight but wearable.

Herrick scowled and took another ample bite, chewing forcefully. "Wit'out me, mate. Ye can do it wit'out me."

Patrick pulled on his ill-fitting jacket and ran a comb through his hair, then grabbed a few scones and the key

to his room. "My thanks." He glanced at Jonah meaningfully. "For everything."

Jonah only watched him silently as Patrick left the
room. He prayed he hadn't made things worse.

Camille had awakened and found Patrick gone. She
tried the door and felt the lock. The key had gone with
Patrick.

Still, she had not been afraid, and this puzzled her.
Being afraid had become like breathing, involuntary and
necessary for survival.

She washed and dressed, then combed out her hair with
her fingers and pinned it back so it was out of her face,
cascading down her back. She stirred up the fire, added
wood, and sat in front of it, staring into the flames. Hunger
growled and made her feel almost whole, as if a part of her
body had awakened to a need outside alcohol and denial.
She craved food as she craved life. She wanted to live. The
dawning had come with the light of morning, when she
had opened her eyes and realized things she had tried so
hard to deny.

She wanted to live. Not just to exist, but to live.

In the face of that realization, the fear of the unknown
melted away like wax from a candle's flame. She looked
at the diamond glittering on her finger and then lifted her
ankle to her lap and studied the amber bracelet.

It glowed, secretive and seductive, wrought in gold,
like snared sunlight. Hidden flecks and bubbles were
locked inside the gems like ancient secrets, whose tales
were told but whose truths would never be known. She ran
her fingers over the stones, and knew the bracelet had
graced the arm of a vicious pirate who had still found
enough love inside him to leave a legacy to his grandson.

She wondered how much love was left inside her.

The memory of the night past poured through her the
way a river races to the ocean, fast and relentless. It had

been the same. So much had changed, and they were both different. But it was still the same, when she laid her head on his chest and felt his heart beat against her cheek.

The key turned in the lock and he pushed open the door, stood there, and watched her. She lifted her eyes to his, looking him over, from his shaven face to his new clothes to his damp hair curling at his shoulders. He smiled, that same reckless grin that somehow held a promise.

"You look rested," he said as he came closer.

"You shaved."

He rubbed a hand across his chin and his smile deepened. "I brought you scones, and I ordered a pot of tea."

"Will you join me?"

"Of course." Patrick sat in the chair opposite her and watched as she bit into the scone as though she hadn't eaten in weeks. He waited until she had finished. "We will talk now."

She sighed, long and deep, a sound of resolve. "'Tis inevitable."

"'Tis necessary."

"I do not know where to begin," she said softly.

"Start with the day I was taken."

"I waited for you, and you did not come." She let the memory take her back to that day. "I went to our cottage, and still you did not come. When I ran to the ocean, your ship was not there. Then I went back to the manor. I had hoped to find Eric, and to ask for his help to go to town and find you. But my mother was waiting." Camille drifted off into memory and began relating the story of how she had been hammered with lies until she had believed. She looked at the floor as she told him how Veronica had come to the house and what she had said. "It was then that I believed, when she said you quoted poetry to her, and you gave her a brooch carved in ivory, a brooch that had belonged to your grandfather."

Camille stood, walked to the window, and looked down on the busy London street. "It made me ill."

"It was not true. I never touched Veronica again after I met you that day in the stables."

"Never?"

"I swear it."

Camille's shoulders lifted in a shrug. "'Twas then that we came to London."

"Tell me everything, Camille. You can trust me with it."

Pressure gathered in her chest again, and her mouth went dry. "I betrayed you, Patrick."

"How? I do not blame you that you believed. I do not blame you for any of it."

"That is not all."

"Tell me, Camille. Like all of it, tell me because you need to."

It gathered in her, a tempest of emotion. It demanded release. It would be held in no longer. "There was a child."

"A baby."

"Yes," she whispered. "I carried your baby."

He watched as she leaned her face against the cold panes of the window, and as tears as clear as glass slid down her face. He ached for her enough to want to tell her to stop.

He loved her enough to let her finish.

"I went to the stables. I was going to escape it all, you see. Run away. And there was a man. I was alone, and he grabbed me."

"He raped you." Patrick wanted so badly to make it go away, or at the very least, he wanted to do and say the right things. He floundered for wisdom.

She nodded, swallowing hard against the constriction of her throat. "And the babe . . ."

"Is gone," he finished.

She nodded again and sagged against the wall, covering her face with her hands, suddenly sapped of strength. "I am ashamed."

"You are very brave," he said, a catch in his voice. "You have been bearing this all alone."

"I am weak. The babe is gone because I disobeyed.

You were hurt because I disobeyed. I was violated because I disobeyed. It is all mine; can you not see? I created the whole mess."

"No, love. You endured it. You didn't cause it." He searched for words. "What did you want, Camille, when you did what you did?"

"I wanted you, Patrick. All along, the only thing I wanted was you," she confessed softly. "And when I thought you didn't want me, I found out I was going to have your child. All I wanted in this world was to hold that baby and have it look up at me with your eyes, so I could see them again." Her voice broke and tears slid down her cheeks, but for the first time since Patrick had been taken, Camille didn't push her feelings away. She gave herself over to them, and spoke the secrets of her heart. "I would have ransomed myself to Satan for another day with you. Any punishment I would have received for that would have paled to the hell of losing you."

She shook her head, as if to clear the apostate thoughts from her mind. "So I had Jonah for a friend, and a chance to escape, this time with my child. I had to risk it. I had to try again. If not for myself, then for my child. So I went to Jonah with my jewels, now a thief and proud of it, because I stole to protect my baby and give him a future."

Her whole body shook now, but she continued. "I never heard him, didn't even see him until it was over. I had to just wait for him to finish, because I couldn't fight him at all." Her breath came in gasps. "But it didn't end when he finished. It never ends. I close my eyes and he's there. He hides in the shadows and stalks me. And our child . . . he is gone forever."

"You didn't cause it, Camille."

"I did!" she said, nearly frantic. She felt as if she would come out of her skin. "I disobeyed. I believed. I disobeyed."

"You were protecting our child."

"I was careless!"

"You were protecting our child," he said again.

"Patrick, don't you see? I would not listen. I would not obey. And because of all of that, you suffered, I suffered, and our baby is dead!"

"Aye, my love, I do see." He caught her eyes, and in an instant it was as it had been that day in the cottage so long ago, when mere words couldn't match the soundless communication of their eyes. When he spoke, his voice was gentle. "I see a woman with the soul of a poet, who would rather risk a beating than turn aside from something she knew to be magical. I see a woman with the mind of a scholar, who can spend nights staring out at the stars and who dares to question her place on this earth. I see a woman with the face of an angel, whose beauty is so deep it transcends mortal imagining." A tear ran down his cheek and he pressed on. "I see a woman with the heart of a lioness, who dared to risk everything she had and everything she knew and everything she was for the sake of her child, that he might have a future that held more than control and hatred."

Camille thought her heart might break, but then wondered if it wasn't just the walls around it crumbling. "Patrick," she breathed. It was all she could say.

Patrick stood, ready to go to her, to hold her, soothe her, kiss it away.

But the door was flung open and Amelia stood in the threshold, flanked by Bret and the magistrate. Gone were any signs of illness as the duchess stood arrayed in a gown of gold velvet and ivory lace, her wig dressed high with diamond-tipped pins. Amelia looked from Patrick to Camille and then back to Patrick. Her painted lips pulled back in a sneer.

"As I thought it would be," Amelia snarled. "You whoring little chit."

Camille stood up straight, rage flooding her body, smothering her sadness. "I warned you."

"You are an imbecile. Did you think I would slink away at your pathetic threats? It seems the thug who guards

Newgate was caught trying to sell my ring. You cannot even rescue your man without my finding out. You will never learn, will you, child?"

"I thought you wise enough to know when you are bested. I will ruin you."

"You have no proof of anything. Nothing but gossip and conjecture. I will deny your claims as will your father, and you will stand alone and foolish in front of a feckless king." Amelia tossed her head back and looked at her daughter with eyes narrowed into glittering slits.

"I will stand by as I watch you stripped of everything you hold valuable," Camille said with her jaw clenched, her hands fisted into hot little balls at her sides.

"Nonsense," Amelia declared with the wave of her hand. She swept into the room and looked Patrick up and down. "You did not care for my accommodations?"

"As I remember, I refused your offer to accommodate me in Southampton."

Her face turned red under her cosmetics. "Knave," she hissed.

Patrick bowed slowly, with an exaggerated flourish. "At your daughter's service, Your Grace."

The magistrate watched the exchange with a worried frown. He looked at the girl, who did not look like the ravished victim, but who looked like an angry daughter found in the arms of her lover. As immoral as that might be, he thought, it was hardly cause to send a man to the gaol. Without a word, he turned on his heel and walked out of the inn. He wouldn't falsely imprison a man a second time. Not for all the king's gold.

Amelia saw him leave and her lips flattened. "Coward. Leave it to a man to skulk away in the face of unpleasant duty."

Bret hesitated in the doorway, unable to take his eyes from Camille. She was different, he thought. Her face was no longer pale, and her eyes as vital as life and fire. Seeing her hair streaming around her waist and her cheeks blooming with color, Bret comprehended. *She loved Patrick as she loved life.*

The demons in Bret's mind had demanded penance since the afternoon in the stables, when he had torn into her and stolen her ability to trust along with her child. He had spilled her blood. He had broken her heart. And it would stop. He wouldn't hurt her again.

He turned to leave, and Amelia's deadly cold voice stopped him in midstep. "I will tell her everything."

Bret paused and wondered how Amelia knew just where a person's weakness lay, like a predator that could sniff out the most vulnerable in a pack. Threats of ruination and Newgate, the Triple Tree at Tyburn, and sending elderly parents who already despised him to debtors' prison no longer held weight.

It was the thought of Camille's knowing what he had done to her that made him weak in the knees, as if his joints had turned to sand. It was the threat of the horror in her eyes. He turned to Amelia slowly. "To expose me is to expose yourself."

"I can live up to my actions."

Amelia stood tall and called his bluff, staring into him with eyes as cold as diamonds, and just as unfeeling. Bret hesitated and then faced Camille, who stood watching the exchange with a mixture of confusion and dread plain on her face. He cleared his throat and forced himself to watch her as he spoke, his guilt demanding the repentance for his sins. "'Twas me in the stables."

Amelia gasped and took a step backwards. Patrick took two steps forward, murderous.

Camille reached out and grabbed Patrick's arm and he stopped, still as stone. He clenched his teeth and his fists, reminding himself it was Camille who had suffered. He pulled his breath in and pushed it out in determined bursts, willing his body to submission. It should be she who finished it.

And when she was through, he'd have his turn. It had been his baby, too.

She went and stood before Bret, her legs shaking, her belly tensed. "You?"

He dropped to his knees before her. "Yes," he whispered. "I raped you."

Camille looked past the tears that rushed over his face and she saw into his eyes. Saw the sorrow and the remorse. Her throat convulsed a few times and sweat trickled down her back. For a reason unknown to her, she remembered when her attacker in the stables had reached down and covered her with her skirts after he'd finished. "Why?"

"There is no excuse for what I did to you or your child. No excuses, no forgiveness."

"Why?" she demanded, this time harshly.

Bret glanced around wildly. No escape. Ever. Not from the room, not from her hurt, not from his actions. "To break you."

"Break me?" She looked to Amelia, realization dawning, and then back to Bret, whose face had gone stark white. "Break me of what?"

"Your spirit," Bret said, and he closed his eyes, unable to look at her any longer. "Your mother suspected you were breeding. The rape was to rid you of the child or provide you with enough humiliation so as to allow the child to be taken."

Camille sank to the floor, unable to muster the strength to stand. The memories flooded her mind, first of the rape in the stables and then afterward, when Bret had brought her gifts and treated her with gentleness. "You hurt me."

"I did." Tears ran down his face and his neck, soaking his lacy cravat. But he didn't blubber, as he wanted to. He held that in and let her have her say.

"You ripped my babe from my womb. *You killed my child.* You stole my heart, Bret."

"I will not beg your forgiveness. There is none for what

I have done." He bowed his head and tears dropped to the floor, tiny splashes staining the hardwood.

"No. There is not." Camille looked up at her mother, who stood motionless and expressionless. "You did this."

Amelia lifted her hands and held her palms face up. "I could not have forced his body to obey. 'Twas my idea, but ultimately, 'twas Bret's doing."

"You are depraved," Camille said, aghast. "You are sick and hateful and demonic."

Amelia pulled her shoulders further back, unwilling to let her daughter twist the facts. "I only protected you from your own actions. The decisions you made would have led to disaster, and I simply preempted a debacle with decisive action of my own." She warmed to her subject, self-righteous. "I prevented the very thing that ruined a family when your grandmother failed to keep her thighs together. Bastard children and Irish commoners. Hah! The irony is almost more than I can bear."

But Amelia's perverted version of the facts wouldn't work this time. Camille wouldn't allow it. No, she thought resolutely, I cannot allow myself to do this anymore. I must decide to be done with Amelia's manipulation of my mind, or else be sacrificed to her sickness. The rape was in the past, the baby gone forever. But she was still breathing, still alive, and sins and mistakes aside, she still deserved a future.

Camille looked away from her mother and Bret—to Patrick. He stood there watching her, his eyes full of rage and restraint. She knew he controlled himself for her sake, and saw what it cost him: his tight lips were rimmed with a band of white, and the muscles in his jaw leaped and twitched, his eyes intent and focused.

But she saw more than just that. She saw everything in Patrick: honesty and courage and love. Love most of all. She saw a love that wouldn't be broken or violated. She saw strength that couldn't be crushed with lies or betrayal.

She saw her future.

She rose to it and to him. She stood and reached out her hand, feeling the warmth of him surround her, and his strength as he took her hand, holding it as hard as a promise; he would never let her go again. "Take me home, Patrick."

Fury blinded Amelia until she turned purple with rage. Bret had turned on her; Patrick had never wanted her. Everyone chose Camille, and no one saw the depth of her struggle for perfection. Everything she had planned, worked for, cared about, all she had done, and the chit was going to walk out on it. No one walked out on Amelia. She reached into her reticule and pulled out the pistol that the ancient butler had trained on Patrick the night she had him sent to Newgate. She held it outstretched in both hands, shaking not with nerves but with pure wrath. "I will see you dead before I allow you to ruin everything."

Camille backed away a step, tightening her hold of Patrick's hand. "Think about what you are doing. Murder is punished with a noose, Mother."

Patrick pulled Camille behind his body. "You have one shot in that pistol, Duchess."

"I would get nearly as much satisfaction spilling your blood as hers."

Bret got to his feet and took a step closer to Amelia. "Give it to me."

Amelia was beyond reach. A new thought pierced her brain. "Camille, go to the carriage. Return with me now or I will kill the mariner."

"No!" Camille wrenched away from behind Patrick and ran to the door. "I will come with you, but do not hurt him."

Amelia threw her head back and laughed out loud. "You are a fool! I kill him and you are mine forever."

She pulled the trigger and a shot roared in the room like thunder and lightning combined. Bret leaped forward as Patrick moved, and when dead silence filled the room, it was Bret who lay on the floor, bleeding from the neck.

Camille fell to his side. With strange clarity she noticed

the jagged hole torn through his skin, blackened from the powder at the edges. His blood poured out in pulses, his body heaving, his mouth working as if he tried to scream but couldn't. She felt the blood seep through her gown where she knelt, warm and sickening, but she gently lay her fingers over his wound. "Go in peace, Bret."

He nodded once and opened his mouth as if to speak, but only a froth of blood bubbled forth before the light in Bret's eyes went out. The last thing he saw was Camille's face as she leaned over him.

The magistrate listened without speaking, then took the duchess into custody, ignoring her screams of indignation.

"I will send word to your father," Patrick said.

Camille didn't respond. She was still staring at the floor, wet with a mopping after Bret had been carried out and the blood had been wiped away.

Just like that, she thought, *and he is gone forever. So fragile life is.*

Patrick poured her a cup of tea and pressed it into her hand. Flanna had come, as had Jonah and Herrick, running to the room at the sound of gunfire. Herrick had been sent to fetch the magistrate. Jonah had been sent away lest he be seen. Flanna had looked at Patrick and then Camille, and given word that if she were needed, she'd be in her room.

They were finally alone. Camille sipped the tea as if it held healing properties and then set the cup down with a small sigh, distracted and restless. "He didn't hate me."

Patrick didn't need to ask whom Camille spoke about, and he kept his own feelings to himself. "No."

"That helps, for some reason."

He didn't respond, for what could he say? That he was glad the bastard was dead, and that his only regret was that it wasn't his hand that had dealt justice? But no, he thought, better to keep silent, for only Camille had to bear the burden of the memory, and while revenge had its place in healing, so did forgiveness.

Camille couldn't stop staring at the floor where Bret's blood had stained the wood. "She will die for killing him. My father—he will not care, but for the disgrace. And my brothers will shed no tears. My father will keep his title; my brother Eric will keep his heritage. And she will be forgotten. No one loved her, Patrick. Not even me."

"'Twas her choice. You loved her as a child, no?"

"Yes, as a small girl." Camille remembered a time when she had ached for her mother's touch. A gentle word, or a smile of praise. Something. Anything.

"You have your future, Camille. A world of choices to make that are all your own." He ran a hand through her hair and felt the familiar surge of pleasure that touching her brought. He wanted to keep her with him always, but it had to be her choice. "Tell me. What will you do?"

Her need for revenge had died, she thought. Gone with Bret and the promise that her mother would no longer have any control over her. The scandal Amelia's trial and hanging would cause would mean Camille's disappearance would hardly be noticed.

She was finally free.

Images came back to her, of a sandy beach with turquoise waters chasing a small boy, and laughter gilding the salty air. Of her hand in Patrick's while they stood on warm sand, watching birds glide on a breeze. She could see it all, like a memory of a day gone by.

She let herself want it again. She let herself hope.

EPILOGUE

Barbados, 1745

Patrick found Camille on the beach, digging for oysters with her toes, up to her ankles in water bluer than the sky. A small pail stood near her, crusty on the bottom with white sand. He grinned, loving the way her hair swung at her shoulders, cropped, unfussy, wavy, and as black as midnight. She turned as he approached her, a smile of greeting on her face, her tanned nose lightly freckled.

"Flanna says she has never seen oysters this size."

"You would think after a year on this island, she would be accustomed to the differences."

"She says one doesn't grow accustomed to miracles."

Patrick laughed and picked up the pail. "I won't argue with that. Come with me, Camille. I have a surprise for you."

She dusted the sand from her hands on her skirt and followed him, grabbing his hand as she picked up her pace to match his. "Why the hurry?"

"'Tis something I've been working on for a while. You will see."

He led the way to their house, past the structure of soft white wood and stone they had had built when they arrived. It sprawled out, with wide windows to face the ocean. But it had been built for safety, too, with sturdy shutters to close out the strong winds when storms raged. It was then they would stay indoors, where good food was always cooking and a game of chess was always in play. Patrick pulled her along through the gardens that surrounded the house, pushing leafy ferns and vines of fragrant jasmine out of their way as they rushed past. Behind the main house Patrick had had a small cottage constructed, where he could work uninterrupted as he kept detailed ledgers of the trade that went through the island.

The cottage had been built to his specifications, nearly an exact replica of the one in England. He ordered Camille to close her eyes as they approached, then took her shoulders and positioned her. "Go ahead and look."

Roses, pink as the inside of a seashell, bloomed around the cottage. They had been planted closely together, so that as they climbed, they would run wild over the stone.

"Tudor roses," he said softly, watching as her green eyes turned soft and her lips parted in surprise. "I bought them from a trader."

"They are reborn in a new land," she said.

"Aye, like you. They are thriving."

"Magic."

"Of the best kind. 'Tis the kind you make yourself."

Camille wrapped her arms around his narrow waist. "I have a surprise of my own. A sort of magic I am working on."

Patrick grinned and pulled her closer, knowing that only six weeks ago she had said she felt ready to conceive a child. "Are you certain?"

Camille shook her head, then bit her lip and nodded. Then she shrugged. "Fairly certain. I am late, but I do not feel any different. But I think so."

He kissed her, long and deep, and the kiss turned from celebration to hunger. The cottage door was only a few steps away.

Herrick looked up from the ledgers as his employers

stumbled in, locked in an embrace. He rolled his eyes and cleared his throat loudly. "Shall I leave you two in peace?"

Patrick and Camille broke apart, laughing.

"Are you looking over the shipment of coffee?" Patrick asked, adjusting his clothes.

"Aye. Your da says we were expecting eleven cartons, and I show only ten. I wanted to double check."

Camille wandered back outdoors as the men discussed business, still unaccustomed to hearing Herrick speak, his rough voice saying cultured words. Patrick had worked with him every day, until Herrick almost never made mistakes. She swore she'd never get used to seeing Herrick with his wife, either, a plump, cheerful woman who had been widowed with five children. She could bring Herrick to his knees with just one of her exotic island smiles, and often did.

Camille's smile faded and her expression turned melancholy as she thought of Jonah, who remained unmarried and lived alone in Scotland. It hurt her to picture him isolated in such a fierce land. Word came slowly to the islands, but they heard talk of the young Pretender with eyes for the throne, and another Rising seemed inevitable. She hadn't had a letter from Jonah in a month, and she hoped him to be well; he was not a man suited to war. So stubborn, he was, when he refused to accompany them. Stubborn, but probably right, she conceded. After all, didn't people have to decide their own futures?

She bent and sniffed a rose, inhaling the familiar scent, sweet and heavy.

Patrick joined her outdoors, and she smiled as she looked up to him. Would she ever grow tired of seeing him?

"Thank you for my surprise," she said.

"There is more."

"More?"

"Aye. A very special gift that arrived only this morning. Go around back, Camille. By the stream."

Camille did as she was told, wondering why her belly

churned with nervousness, as if her heart already knew what her eyes would soon see.

Indue stood under the shade of a leafy palm tree, her nose to the ground as she sniffed the strange soil. Patrick stood beside Camille, took her hand, and pressed his lips to the inside of her wrist.

"Eric sent her." Patrick didn't say he had sent the request and made the arrangements.

She looked up to him briefly, eyes full of gratitude. Then she ran to Indue, wrapped her arms around her thick neck, and pressed kisses on the short, coarse hair, so familiar and so missed. She ran her hands down her mane, and then around the wide, expressive eyes. Indue nickered softly and nudged her, and Camille felt happiness bloom in her heart, that her brother had thought to be so kind to her. That her brother had even thought of her at all. Camille turned back to Patrick.

"I am at a loss."

"Do you like your surprises?"

"More than calm seas and clear skies."

"More than biscuits and gravy?"

She wrinkled her nose. "Your favorite, not mine. Definitely more than biscuits and gravy."

"More than my kisses?"

She smiled as he pulled her close. She tilted her head up and looked into his eyes, the color of the ocean before a storm. "No. I like nothing better than your kisses."

"And my babies? You will like having my babies?"

"It is time." Camille rested her hand on her abdomen and closed her eyes. I am blessed, she thought. "It is our time."

More Historical Romance From
Jo Ann Ferguson

__A Christmas Bride   0-8217-6760-7   **$4.99US/$6.99CAN**

__His Lady Midnight   0-8217-6863-8   **$4.99US/$6.99CAN**

__A Guardian's Angel   0-8217-7174-4   **$4.99US/$6.99CAN**

__His Unexpected Bride   0-8217-7175-2   **$4.99US/$6.99CAN**

__A Rather Necessary End   0-8217-7176-0   **$4.99US/$6.99CAN**

__Grave Intentions   0-8217-7520-0   **$4.99US/$6.99CAN**

__Faire Game   0-8217-7521-9   **$4.99US/$6.99CAN**

__A Sister's Quest   0-8217-6788-7   **$5.50US/$7.50CAN**

__Moonlight on Water   0-8217-7310-0   **$5.99US/$7.99CAN**

Available Wherever Books Are Sold!

Visit our website at **www.kensingtonbooks.com**.